The National Review

TREASURY
OF
CLASSIC
BEDTIME
STORIES

Written by Thornton Burgess

Illustrated by Harrison Cady

ISI Books
Wilmington, DE
2006

The National Review Treasury of
Classic Bedtime Stories, Volume Two
© 2006 by National Review, Inc.

Library of Congress Cataloging-in-Publication Data:
The National Review treasury of classic bedtime stories / written by Thornton
Burgess ; illustrated by Harrison Cady. -- 1st ed. -- Wilmington, DE : ISI Books,
2003, 2006.

v. ; cm.

ISBN: 0-9627841-8-4 (v. 1)

ISBN: 1-933859-10-5 (v. 2)

1. Children's stories--Collections. 2. Children's literature--Collections. I.
Burgess, Thornton. II. Cady, Harrison. III. National Review Research Library
(New York, N.Y.)

PZ5 .377 2003   2003113214
808.8/99282—dc22   0311

Jacket Design by Luba Myts

PRINTED IN THE UNITED STATES OF AMERICA

CONTENTS

Buster Bear, Old Mr. Toad, Prickly Porky, Old Man Coyote, Paddy the Beaver, Poor Mrs. Quack, Bobby Coon, Jimmy Skunk, Bob White, Ol' Mistah Buzzard,

About Thornton Burgess

BEFORE ANSWERING THE "who" as to Thornton Waldo Burgess, the man whose stories appear in this book, we will briefly address the "why," as in—"Why a book of *his* stories?"

While putting together *The National Review Treasury of Classic Children's Literature* (published in 2002) we were impressed (mightily so) by "Tommy and the Wishing Stone"—Mr. Burgess's 12-part story, serialized in *St. Nicholas Magazine* in 1914 and 1915. Accompanied by the wonderful drawings of the great Harrison Cady, these stories of Tommy—a boy exhibiting all the moods and ups and downs and day-dreamings of youth—and the delightful menagerie of forest creatures he befriends are beautifully written, entertaining, and instructive.

The Burgess-Cady combination in "Tommy an the Wishing Stone" was very unique and very special. So you can imagine our delight when we (the "we" being not-so-elderly *National Review* folk who simply didn't know that Mr. Burgess's stories existed) by chance stumbled over a copy of another Burgess book—"The Adventures of Reddy Fox" (also a product of his partnership with Mr. Cady). We then discovered that this "Adventure" was but one of a 20-book "Bedtime Stories" series, and that above and beyond this series the two had collaborated on *many* other fantastic children's books. Oh happy day!

At *National Review*, we have taken a liking to the idea of republishing wonderful old children's literature. And we particularly wanted to publish a book with content that a beginning reader could handle, or that parents and grandparents and baby-sitters could happily read to wee ones before being tucked in for the night. Of course, there exists no formula to dictate whose stories best match this criteria, and which most deserve being republished. The heart alone dictates. And the collective heart here said to republish the first half of Mr. Burgess's magical Bedtime Stories, which we did in 2003. This second volume of *The National Review Treasury of Classic Bedtime Stories* publishes the remaining 10 adventure stories. So that is the why. Now, as to the "who."

As should be obvious, Thornton Burgess was a prolific author wrote more than 170 books. He entertained wo generations of American children with his Bedtime stories, as well as his "Old Mother West Wind," "Green Forest," and "Green Meadow" series.

Millions of American children followed and learned from the exploits of his wonderful menagerie of woodland denizens, including Reddy Fox, Johnny Chuck, Peter Cottontail, Unc' Billy Possum, Mistah Mocker, Jerry Muskrat, Danny Meadow Mouse, Grandfather Frog, Chatterer the Red Squirrel, Sammy Jay, Prickly Porky, Buster BearBlacky the Crow, Lightfoot the Deer, Ol' Mistah Buzzard, Paddy the Beaver, and countless other creatures who inhabited the Green Meadows, cavorted with the Merry Little Breezes, and hijinxed in the Briar Patch.

In addition to his books, Mr. Burgess wrote a daily newspaper column (featuring his beloved critters) for the old *New York Herald Tribune*. According to the Thornton Burgess Society (its website is www.thorntonburgess.org) he had written some 15,000 stories for newspapers by the time he laid down his pen!

Born in 1874 in Sandwich, Massachusetts, (he died in Hampden, Massachusetts, 91 years later in 1965) Thornton Burgess is a truly unique figure in American literature. One will be hard pressed to find him in compendiums of and encyclopedias on that subject, but most who are included in such do not come close to having his impact. Who else but Dr. Seuss and a handful of others can claim to have thoroughly entertained two generations of American youth?

Looking back now, nearly a century after he wrote his first book, one finds Thornton Burgess's writings to be refreshingly old-fashioned: His tales are clean, wholesome, fun, innocent, and instructive. His are horizon-opening stories that one will look back upon, as an adult, with fond and cherished memories. He deserves—more than ever—to be known by a new generation of young readers.

About Harrison Cady

THERE IS THAT special "something" about the artwork of Walter Harrison Cady that strikes a rich and deep chord in the heart. Simply put, he captures with ink and pen the wholesomeness and joy that Thornton Burgess captured with the written word. The two men formed the perfect partnership.

Our first publication, *The National Review Treasury of Classic Children's Literature,* includes numerous Cady's illustrations. *St. Nicholas Magazine* regularly used his drawings to accompany stories by great writers such as Frances Hodgson Burnett, L. Frank Baum, and Carolyn Wells—and, of course, Thornton Burgess.

Harrison Cady did not have any formal art training. Instead he relied on a keen eye for nature, an unrivalled imagination, and a mastery of the pen to produce work—art!—that is without question distinct and beautiful.

Over the first half of the 20th century, Mr. Cady was renowned as a magazine illustrator (*St. Nicholas*, *Life*, the *Saturday Evening Post*, the *Ladies Home Journal*, and other popular publications were home to his work), and as a comic strip artist: Cady joined forces with Mr. Burgess and his forest creatures to produce a strip which Peter Rabbit (who is the leading character in the second adventure story in this book). Their strips appeared regularly in the *New York Herald Tribune*, and soon Mr. Cady was writing them as well as drawing them. He did this for nearly 30 years, during which time his Peter Rabbit feature was nationally syndicated.

Born in Gardner, Massachusetts in 1877, Harrison Cady—like his friend Thornton Burgess—lived to a "ripe old age." He died at 93 in 1970.

We are happy to have his work, and that of Mr. Burgess, live on in this book.

About this Book

THE STORIES INCLUDED in the second volume of *The National Review Treasury of Classic Bedtime Stories* come from original "Bedtime Stories" books that were published from 1913 to 1920. This book contains the final ten of Mr. Burgess's 20 Bedtime adventures, and came about thusly: The pages of the original books were scanned and processed. Each page—at first only an image—was next converted into text files that could be edited and formatted. Elizabeth Capano did much of this cumbersome work, for which we thank her. Once this had been completed, the stories were proofread—our thanks to Tim Wolff and Elena Koly for their efforts and expertise—then corrected, while pictures were checked for quality.

Luba Myts, the Art Director of *National Review*, gained possession of all these files and made sense of the madness. Her efforts have resulted in this handsome volume. Luba designed the book's layout and its cover art, and handled the myriad of "pre-press" chores that are unpleasant, but unavoidable—all this in addition to her day-to-day responsibilities with the magazine. We bow to her, and as well to our colleagues and friends at the Intercollegiate Studies Institute—Jeff Nelson, Doug Schneider, Jeremy Beer, Jennifer Connelly. It is a joy to work with such good people in our joint venture of publishing good books.

Thanks are also due to Kevin Longstreet and Russell Jenkins of *NR*'s Publishing Deparetment, who helped out in many ways large and small, and to *NR* CEO Ed Capano, now recently retired, who for many years diligently oversaw *National Review*'s book-publishing forays.

Happy and enjoyable reading!

Jack Fowler
Publisher, *National Review*
October 2006

The Adventures of Buster Bear

CHAPTER ONE: BUSTER BEAR GOES FISHING

BUSTER BEAR YAWNED as he lay on his comfortable bed of leaves and watched the first early morning sunbeams creeping through the Green Forest to chase out the Black Shadows. Once more he yawned, and slowly got to his feet and shook himself. Then he walked over to a big pine tree, stood up on his hind legs, reached as high up on the trunk of the tree as he could, and scratched the bark with his great claws. After that he yawned until it seemed as if his jaws would crack, and then sat down to think what he wanted for breakfast.

While he sat there, trying to make up his mind what would taste best, he was listening to the sounds that told of the waking of all the little people who live in the Green Forest. He heard Sammy Jay way off in the distance screaming, "Thief! Thief!" and grinned. "I wonder," thought Buster, "if someone has stolen Sammy's breakfast, or if he has stolen the breakfast of someone else. Probably he is the thief himself."

He heard Chatterer the Red Squirrel scolding as fast as he could make his tongue go and working himself into a terrible rage. "Must be that Chatterer got out of bed the wrong way this morning," thought he.

He heard Blacky the Crow cawing at the top of his lungs, and he knew by the sound that Blacky was getting into mischief of some kind. He heard the sweet voices of happy little singers, and they were good to hear. But most of all he listened to a merry, low, silvery laugh that never stopped but went on and on, until he just felt as if he must laugh too. It was the voice of the Laughing Brook. And as Buster listened it suddenly came to him just what he wanted for breakfast.

"I'm going fishing," said he in his deep grumbly-rumbly voice to no one in particular. "Yes, Sir, I'm going fishing. I want some fat trout for my breakfast."

He shuffled along over to the Laughing Brook, and straight to a little pool of which he knew, and as he drew near he took the greatest care not to make the teeniest, weeniest bit of noise. Now it just happened that early as he was, someone was before Buster Bear. When he came in sight of the little pool, who should he see but another fisherman there, who had already caught a fine fat trout. Who was it?

Why, Little Joe Otter to be sure. He was just climbing up the bank with the fat trout in his mouth. Buster Bear's own mouth watered as he saw it. Little Joe sat down on the bank and prepared to enjoy his breakfast. He hadn't seen Buster Bear, and he didn't know that he or anyone else was anywhere near.

Buster Bear tiptoed up very softly until he was right behind Little Joe Otter. "Woof, woof!" said he in his deepest, most grumbly-rumbly voice. "That's a very fine looking trout. I wouldn't mind if I had it myself."

Little Joe Otter gave a frightened squeal and without even turning to see who was speaking dropped his fish and dived head-first into the Laughing Brook. Buster Bear sprang forward and with one of his big paws caught the fat trout just as it was slipping back into the water.

"Here's your trout, Mr. Otter," said he, as Little Joe put his head out of water to see who had frightened him so. "Come and get it."

But Little Joe wouldn't. The fact is, he was afraid to. He snarled at Buster Bear and called him a thief and everything bad he could think of. Buster didn't seem to mind. He chuckled as if he thought it all a great joke and repeated his invitation to Little Joe to come and get his fish. But Little Joe just turned his back and went off down the Laughing Brook in a great rage.

"It's too bad to waste such a fine fish," said Buster thoughtfully. "I wonder what I'd better do with it." And while he was wondering, he ate it all up. Then he started down the Laughing Brook to try to catch some for himself.

CHAPTER TWO: LITTLE JOE OTTER GETS EVEN WITH BUSTER BEAR

LITTLE JOE OTTER was in a terrible rage. It was a bad beginning for a beautiful day and Little Joe knew it. But who wouldn't be in a rage if his breakfast was taken from him just as he was about to eat it? Anyway, that is what Little Joe told Billy Mink. Perhaps he didn't tell it quite exactly as it was, but you know he was very badly frightened at the time.

"I was sitting on the bank of the Laughing Brook beside one of the little pools," he told Billy Mink, "and was just going to eat a fat trout I had caught, when who should come along but that great big bully, Buster Bear. He took that fat trout away from me and ate it just as if it belonged to him! I hate him! If I live long enough I'm going to get even with him!"

Of course that wasn't nice talk and anything but a nice spirit, but Little Joe Otter's temper is sometimes pretty short, especially when he is hungry, and this time he had had no breakfast, you know.

Buster Bear hadn't actually taken the fish away from Little Joe. But looking at the matter as Little Joe did, it amounted to the same thing. You see, Buster knew perfectly well when he invited Little Joe to come back and get it that Little Joe wouldn't dare do anything of the kind.

"Where is he now?" asked Billy Mink.

"He's somewhere up the Laughing Brook. I wish he'd fall in and get drowned" snapped Little Joe.

Billy Mink just had to laugh. The idea of great big Buster Bear getting drowned in the Laughing Brook was too funny. There wasn't water enough in it anywhere except down in the Smiling Pool, and that was on the Green Meadows, where Buster had never been known to go. "Let's go see what he is doing," said Billy Mink.

At first Little Joe didn't want to, but at last his curiosity got the better of his fear, and he agreed. So the two lit-

"Here's your trout, Mr. Otter."

tle brown-coated scamps turned down the Laughing Brook, taking the greatest care to keep out of sight themselves. They had gone only a little way when Billy Mink whispered: "Sh-h! There he is."

Sure enough, there was Buster Bear sitting close beside a little pool and looking into it very intently.

"What's he doing?" asked Little Joe Otter, as Buster Bear sat for the longest time without moving.

Just then one of Buster's big paws went into the water as quick as a flash and scooped out a trout that had ventured too near.

"He's fishing!" exclaimed Billy Mink.

And that is just what Buster Bear was doing, and it was very plain to see that he was having great fun. When he had eaten the trout he had caught, he moved along to the next little pool.

"They are *our* fish!" said Little Joe fiercely. "He has no business catching *our* fish!"

"I don't see how we are going to stop him," said Billy Mink.

"I do!" cried Little Joe, into whose head an idea had just popped. "I'm going to drive all the fish out of the little pools and muddy the water all up. Then we'll see how many fish he will get! Just you watch me get even with Buster Bear."

Little Joe slipped swiftly into the water and swam straight to the little pool that Buster Bear would try next. He frightened the fish so that they fled in every direction. Then he stirred up the mud until the water was so dirty that Buster couldn't have seen a fish right under his nose. He did the same thing in the next pool and the next. Buster Bear's fishing was spoiled for that day.

CHAPTER THREE: BUSTER BEAR IS GREATLY PUZZLED

BUSTER BEAR HADN'T enjoyed himself so much since he came to the Green Forest to live. His fun began when he surprised Little Joe Otter on the bank of a little pool in the Laughing Brook and Little Joe was so frightened that he dropped a fat trout he had just caught. It had seemed like a great joke to Buster Bear, and he had chuckled over it all the time he was eating the fat trout. When he had finished it, he started on to do some fishing himself.

Presently he came to another little pool. He stole up to it very, very softly, so as not to frighten the fish. Then he sat down close to the edge of it and didn't move. Buster learned a long time ago that a fisherman must be patient unless, like Little Joe Otter, he is just as much at home in the water as the fish themselves, and can swim fast enough to catch them by chasing them. So he didn't move so much as an eye lash. He was so still that he looked almost like the stump of an old tree. Perhaps that is what the fish thought he was, for pretty soon, two or three swam right in close to where he was sitting. Now Buster Bear may be big and clumsy looking, but there isn't anything that can move much quicker than one of those big paws of his when he wants it to. One of them moved now, and quicker than a wink had scooped one of those foolish fish out on to the bank.

Buster's little eyes twinkled, and he smacked his lips as he moved on to the next little pool, for he knew that it was of no use to stay longer at the first one. The fish were so frightened that they wouldn't come back for a long, long time. At the next little pool the same thing happened. By this time Buster Bear was in fine spirits. It was fun to catch the fish, and it was still more fun to eat them. What finer breakfast could anyone have than fresh-caught trout? No wonder he felt good! But it takes more than three trout to fill Buster Bear's stomach, so he kept on to the next little pool.

But this little pool, instead of being beautiful and clear so that Buster could see right to the bottom of it and so tell if there were any fish there, was so muddy that he couldn't see into it at all. It looked as if someone had just stirred up all the mud at the bottom.

"Huh!" said Buster Bear. "It's of no use to try to fish here. I would just waste my time. I'll try the next pool."

So he went on to the next little pool. He found this just as muddy as the other. Then he went on to another, and this was no better. Buster sat down and scratched his head. It was puzzling. Yes, Sir, it was puzzling. He looked this way and he looked that way suspiciously, but there was no one to be seen. Everything was still save for the laughter of the Laughing Brook. Somehow, it seemed to Buster as if the Brook were laughing at him.

"It's very curious," muttered Buster, "very curious indeed. It looks as if my fishing is spoiled for today. I don't understand it at all. It's lucky I caught what I did. It looks as if somebody is trying to—ha!" A sudden thought had popped into his head. Then he began to chuckle and finally to laugh. "I do believe that scamp Joe Otter is trying to get even with me for eating that fat trout!"

And then, because Buster Bear always enjoys a good joke even when it is on himself, he laughed until he had to hold his sides, which is a whole lot better than going off in a rage as Little Joe Otter had done. "You're pretty smart, Mr. Otter! You're pretty smart, but there are other people who are smart too," said Buster Bear, and still chuckling, he went off to think up a plan to get the best of Little Joe Otter.

CHAPTER FOUR: LITTLE JOE OTTER SUPPLIES BUSTER BEAR WITH A BREAKFAST

Getting even just for spite doesn't always pay.
Fact is, it is very apt to work the other way.

THAT IS JUST how it came about that Little Joe Otter furnished Buster Bear with the best breakfast he had had for a long time. He didn't mean to do it. Oh, my, no! The truth is, he thought all the time that he was preventing Buster Bear from getting a breakfast. You see he wasn't well enough acquainted with Buster to know that Buster is quite as smart as he is, and perhaps a little bit smarter. Spite and selfishness were at the bottom of it. You see Little Joe and Billy Mink had had all the fishing in the Laughing Brook to themselves so long that they thought no one else had any right to fish there. To be sure Bobby Coon caught a few little fish there, but they didn't mind Bobby. Farmer Brown's boy fished there too, sometimes, and this always made Little Joe and Billy Mink very angry, but they were so afraid of him that they didn't dare do anything about it. But when they discovered that Buster Bear was a fisherman, they made up their minds that something had got to be done. At least, Little Joe did.

"He'll try it again tomorrow morning," said Little Joe. "I'll keep watch, and as soon as I see him coming, I'll drive out all the fish, just as I did today. I guess that'll teach him to let our fish alone."

So the next morning Little Joe hid before daylight close by the little pool where Buster Bear had given him such a fright. Sure enough, just as the Jolly Sunbeams began to creep through the Green Forest, he saw Buster Bear coming straight over to the little pool. Little Joe slipped into the water and chased all the fish out of the little pool, and stirred up the mud on the bottom so that the water was so muddy that the bottom couldn't be seen at all. Then he hurried down to the next little pool and did the same thing.

Now Buster Bear is very smart. You know he had guessed the day before who had spoiled his fishing. So this morning he only went far enough to make sure that if Little Joe were watching for him, as he was sure he would be, he would see him coming. Then, instead of keeping on to the little pool, he hurried to a place way down the Laughing Brook, where the water was very shallow, hardly over his feet, and there he sat chuckling to himself. Things happened just as he had expected. The frightened fish Little Joe chased out of the little pools up above swam down the Laughing Brook, because, you know, Little Joe was behind them, and there was nowhere else for them to go. When they came to the place where Buster was waiting, all he had to do was to scoop them out on to the bank. It was great fun. It didn't take Buster long to catch all the fish he could eat. Then he saved a nice fat trout and waited.

By and by along came Little Joe Otter, chuckling to think how he had spoiled Buster Bear's fishing. He was so intent on looking behind him to see if Buster was coming that he didn't see Buster waiting there until he spoke.

"I'm much obliged for the fine breakfast you have given me," said Buster in his deepest, most grumbly-rumbly voice. "I've saved a fat trout for you to make up for the one I ate yesterday. I hope we'll go fishing together often."

Then he went off laughing fit to kill himself. Little Joe couldn't find a word to say. He was so surprised and angry that he went off by himself and sulked. And Billy Mink, who had been watching, ate the fat trout.

CHAPTER FIVE: GRANDFATHER FROG'S COMMON SENSE

THERE IS NOTHING quite like common sense to smooth out troubles. People who have plenty of just plain common sense are often thought to be very wise. Their neighbors look up to them and are forever running to them for advice, and they are very much respected. That is the way with Grandfather Frog. He is very old and very wise. Anyway, that is what his neighbors think. The truth is, he simply has a lot of common sense, which after all is the very best kind of wisdom.

Now when Little Joe Otter found that Buster Bear had been too smart for him and that instead of spoiling Buster's fishing in the Laughing Brook he had really made it easier for Buster to catch all the fish he wanted, Little Joe went off down to the Smiling Pool in a great rage.

Billy Mink stopped long enough to eat the fat fish Buster had left on the bank and then he too went down to the Smiling Pool.

When Little Joe Otter and Billy Mink reached the Smiling Pool, they climbed up on the Big Rock, and there Little Joe sulked and sulked, until finally Grandfather Frog asked what the matter was. Little Joe wouldn't tell, but Billy Mink told the whole story. When he told how Buster had been too smart for Little Joe, it tickled him so that Billy had to laugh in spite of himself. So did Grandfather Frog. So did Jerry Muskrat, who had been listening. Of course this made Little Joe angrier than ever. He said a lot of unkind things about Buster Bear and about Billy Mink and Grandfather Frog and Jerry Muskrat, because they had laughed at the smartness of Buster.

"He's nothing but a great big bully and thief!" declared Little Joe.

"Chug-a-rum! He may be a bully, because great big people are very apt to be bullies, and though I haven't seen him, I guess Buster Bear is big enough from all I have heard, but I don't see how he is a thief," said Grandfather Frog.

"Didn't he catch my fish and eat them?" snapped Little Joe. "Doesn't that make him a thief?"

"They were no more your fish than mine," protested Billy Mink.

"Well, *our* fish, then! He stole *our* fish, if you like that any better. That makes him just as much a thief, doesn't it?" growled Little Joe.

Grandfather Frog looked up at jolly, round, bright Mr. Sun and slowly winked one of his great, goggly eyes. "There comes a foolish green fly," said he. "Who does he belong to?"

"Nobody!" snapped Little Joe. "What have foolish green flies got to do with my—I mean *our* fish?"

"Nothing, nothing at all," replied Grandfather Frog mildly. "I was just hoping that he would come near enough for me to snap him up; then he would belong to me. As long as he doesn't, he doesn't belong to anyone. I suppose that if Buster Bear should happen along and catch him, he would be stealing from me, according to Little Joe."

"Of course not! What a silly idea! You're getting foolish in your old age," retorted Little Joe.

"Can you tell me the difference between the fish that you haven't caught and the foolish green flies that I haven't caught?" asked Grandfather Frog.

Little Joe couldn't find a word to say.

"You take my advice, Little Joe Otter," continued Grandfather Frog, "and always make friends with those who are bigger and stronger and smarter than you are. You'll find it pays."

CHAPTER SIX: LITTLE JOE OTTER TAKES GRANDFATHER FROG'S ADVICE

Who makes an enemy a friend,
To fear and worry puts an end.

LITTLE JOE OTTER found that out when he took Grandfather Frog's advice. He wouldn't have admitted that he was afraid of Buster Bear. No one ever likes to admit being afraid, least of all Little Joe Otter. And really Little Joe has a great deal of courage. Very few of the little people of the Green Forest or the Green Meadows would willingly quarrel with him, for Little Joe is a great fighter when he has to fight. As for all those who live in or along the Laughing Brook or in the Smiling Pool, they let Little Joe have his own way in everything.

Now having one's own way too much is a bad thing. It is apt to make one selfish and thoughtless of other people and very hard to get along with. Little Joe Otter had his way too much. Grandfather Frog knew it and shook his head very soberly when Little Joe had been disrespectful to him.

"You take my advice, Little Joe Otter,"
continued Grandfather Frog.

"Too bad. Too bad! Too bad! Chug-a-rum! It is too bad that such a fine young fellow as Little Joe should spoil a good disposition by such selfish heedlessness. Too bad," said he.

So, though he didn't let on that it was so, Grandfather Frog really was delighted when he heard how Buster Bear had been too smart for Little Joe Otter. It tickled him so that he had hard work to keep a straight face. But he did and was as grave and solemn as you please as he advised Little Joe always to make friends with anyone who was bigger and stronger and smarter than he. That was good common sense advice, but Little Joe just sniffed and went off declaring that he would get even with Buster Bear yet. Now Little Joe is good-natured and full of fun as a rule, and after he had reached home and his temper had cooled off a little, he began to see the joke on himself—how when he had worked so hard to frighten the fish in the little pools of the Laughing Brook so that Buster Bear should not catch any, he had all the time been driving them right into Buster's paws. By and by he grinned. It was a little sheepish grin at first, but at last it grew into a laugh.

"I believe," said Little Joe as he wiped tears of laughter from his eyes, "that Grandfather Frog is right, and that the best thing I can do is to make friends with Buster Bear. I'll try it tomorrow morning."

So very early the next morning Little Joe Otter went to the best fishing pool he knew of in the Laughing Brook, and there he caught the biggest trout he could find. It was so big and fat that it made Little Joe's mouth water, for you know fat trout are his favorite food. But he didn't take so much as one bite. Instead he carefully laid it on an old log where Buster Bear would be sure to see it if he should come along that way. Then he hid near by, where he could watch. Buster was late that morning. It seemed to Little Joe that he never would come. Once he nearly lost the fish. He had turned his head for just a minute, and when he looked back again, the trout was nowhere to be seen. Buster couldn't have stolen up and taken it, because such a big fellow couldn't possibly have gotten out of sight again.

Little Joe darted over to the log and looked on the other side. There was the fat trout, and there also was Little Joe's smallest cousin, Shadow the Weasel, who is a great thief and altogether bad. Little Joe sprang at him angrily, but Shadow was too quick and darted away. Little Joe put the fish back on the log and waited. This time he didn't take his eyes off it. At last, when he was almost ready to give up, he saw Buster Bear shuffling along towards the Laughing Brook. Suddenly Buster stopped and sniffed. One of the Merry Little Breezes had carried the scent of that fat trout over to him. Then he came straight over to where the fish lay, his nose wrinkling, and his eyes twinkling with pleasure.

"Now I wonder who was so thoughtful as to leave this fine breakfast ready for me," said he out loud.

"Me," said Little Joe in a rather faint voice. "I caught it especially for you."

"Thank you," replied Buster, and his eyes twinkled more than ever. "I think we are going to be friends."

"I—I hope so," replied Little Joe.

CHAPTER SEVEN: FARMER BROWN'S BOY HAS NO LUCK AT ALL

FARMER BROWN'S BOY tramped through the Green Forest, whistling merrily. He always whistles when he feels light-hearted, and he always feels light-hearted when he goes fishing. You see, he is just as fond of fishing as is Little Joe Otter or Billy Mink or Buster Bear. And now he was making his way through the Green Forest to the Laughing Brook, sure that by the time he had followed it down to the Smiling Pool he would have a fine lot of trout to take home. He knew every pool in the Laughing Brook where the trout love to hide, did Farmer Brown's boy, and it was just the kind of a morning when the trout should be hungry. So he whistled as he tramped along, and his whistle was good to hear.

When he reached the first little pool he bailed his hook very carefully and then, taking the greatest care to keep out of sight of any trout that might be in the little pool, he began to fish. Now Farmer Brown's boy learned a long time ago that to be a successful fisherman one must have a great deal of patience, so though he didn't get a bite right away as he had expected to, he wasn't the least bit discouraged. He kept very quiet and fished and fished, patiently waiting for a foolish trout to take his hook. But he didn't get so much as a nibble. "Either the trout have lost their appetite or they have grown very wise," muttered Farmer Brown's boy, as after a long time he moved on to the next little pool.

There the same thing happened. He was very patient, very, very patient, but his patience brought no reward, not so much as the faintest kind of a nibble. Farmer Brown's boy trudged on to the next pool, and there was a puzzled frown on his freckled face. Such a thing never had happened before. He didn't know what to make of it. All the night before he had dreamed about the delicious dinner of fried trout he would have the next day, and now—well, if he didn't catch some trout pretty soon, that splendid dinner would never be anything but a dream.

"If I didn't know that nobody else comes fishing here, I should think that some-body had been here this very morning and caught all the fish or else frightened them so that they are all in hiding," said he, as he trudged on to the next little pool. "I never had such bad luck in all my life before. Hello! What's this?"

There, on the bank beside the little pool, were the heads of three trout. Farmer Brown's boy scowled down at them more puzzled than ever. "Somebody *has* been fishing here, and they have had better luck than I have," thought he. He looked up the Laughing Brook and down the Laughing Brook and this way and that way, but no one was to be seen. Then he picked up one of the little heads and looked at it sharply. "It wasn't cut off with a knife; it was bitten off!" he exclaimed. "I wonder now if Billy Mink is the scamp who has spoiled my fun."

Thereafter he kept a sharp lookout for signs of Billy Mink, but though he found two or three more trout heads, he saw no other signs and he caught no fish. This puzzled him more than ever. It didn't seem possible that such a little fellow as Billy Mink could have caught or frightened all the fish or have eaten so many. Besides, he didn't remember ever having known Billy to leave heads around that way. Billy sometimes catches more fish than he can eat, but then he usually hides them. The farther he went down the Laughing Brook, the more puzzled Farmer Brown's boy grew. It made him feel very queer. He would have felt still more queer if he had known that all the time two other fishermen who had been before him were watching him and chuckling to themselves. They were Little Joe Otter and Buster Bear.

CHAPTER EIGHT: FARMER BROWN'S BOY FEELS HIS HAIR RISE

'Twas just a sudden odd surprise
Made Farmer Brown's boy's hair to rise.

THAT'S A FUNNY thing for hair to do—rise up all of a sudden—isn't it? But that is just what the hair on Farmer Brown's boy's head did the day he went fishing in the Laughing Brook and had no luck at all. There are just two things that make hair rise—anger and fear. Anger sometimes makes the hair on the back and neck of Bowser the Hound and of some other little people bristle and stand up, and you know the hair on the tail of Black Pussy stands on end until her tail looks twice as big as it really is. Both anger and fear make it do that. But there is only one thing that can make the hair on the head of Farmer Brown's boy rise, and as it isn't anger, of course it must be fear.

It never had happened before. You see, there isn't much of anything that Farmer Brown's boy is really afraid of. Perhaps he wouldn't have been afraid this time if it hadn't been for the surprise of what he found. You see when he had found the heads of those trout on the bank he knew right away that someone else had been fishing, and that was why he couldn't catch any; but it didn't seem possible that little Billy Mink could have eaten all those trout, and Farmer Brown's boy didn't once think of Little Joe Otter, and so he was very, very much puzzled.

He was turning it all over in his mind and studying what it could mean, when he came to a little muddy place on the bank of the Laughing Brook, and there he saw something that made his eyes look as if they would pop right out of his head, and it was right then that he felt his hair rise. Anyway, that is what he said when he told about it afterward. What was it he saw? What do you think? Why, it was a footprint in the soft mud. Yes, Sir, that's what it was, and all it was. But it was the biggest footprint Farmer Brown's boy ever had seen, and it looked as if it had been made only a few minutes before. It was the footprint of Buster Bear.

Now Farmer Brown's boy didn't know that Buster Bear had come down to the Green Forest to live. He never had heard of a Bear being in the Green Forest. And so he was so surprised that he had hard work to believe his own eyes, and he had a queer feeling all over—a little chilly feeling, although it was a warm day. Somehow, he didn't feel like meeting Buster Bear. If he had had his terrible gun with him, it might have been different. But he didn't, and so he suddenly made up his mind that he didn't want to fish any more that day. He had a funny feeling, too, that he was being watched, although he couldn't see anyone. He *was* being watched. Little Joe Otter and Buster Bear were watching him and taking the greatest care to keep out of his sight.

All the way home through the Green Forest, Farmer Brown's boy kept looking behind him, and he didn't draw a long breath until he reached the edge of the Green Forest. He hadn't run, but he had wanted to.

"Huh!" said Buster Bear to Little Joe Otter, "I believe he was afraid!" And Buster Bear was just exactly right.

CHAPTER NINE: LITTLE JOE OTTER HAS GREAT NEWS TO TELL

LITTLE JOE OTTER was fairly bursting with excitement. He could hardly contain himself. He felt that he had the greatest news to tell since Peter Rabbit had first found the tracks of Buster Bear in the Green Forest. He couldn't keep it to himself a minute longer than he had to. So he hurried to the Smiling Pool, where he was sure he would find Billy Mink and Jerry Muskrat and Grandfather Frog and Spotty the Turtle, and he hoped that perhaps some of the little people who live in the Green Forest might be there too. Sure enough, Peter Rabbit was there on one side of the Smiling Pool, making faces at Reddy Fox, who was on the other side, which, of course, was not at all nice of Peter. Mr. and Mrs. Redwing were there, and Blacky the Crow was sitting in the Big Hickory tree.

Little Joe Otter swam straight to the Big Rock and climbed up to the very highest part. He looked so excited, and his eyes sparkled so, that everyone knew right away that something had happened.

"Hi!" cried Billy Mink. "Look at Little Joe Otter! It must be that for once he has been smarter than Buster Bear."

Little Joe made a good-natured face at Billy Mink and shook his head. "No,

Billy," said he, "you are wrong, altogether wrong. I don't believe anybody can be smarter than Buster Bear."

Reddy Fox rolled his lips back in an unpleasant grin. "Don't be too sure of that!" he snapped. "I'm not through with him yet."

"Boaster! Boaster!" cried Peter Rabbit.

Reddy glared across the Smiling Pool at Peter. "I'm not through with you either, Peter Rabbit!" he snarled. "You'll find it out one of these fine days!"

"Reddy, Reddy, smart and sly, Couldn't catch a buzzing fly!"

taunted Peter.

"Chug-a-rum!" said Grandfather Frog in his deepest, gruffest voice. "We know all about that. What we want to know is what Little Joe Otter has got on his mind."

"It's news—great news!" cried Little Joe.

"We can tell better how great it is when we hear what it is," replied Grandfather Frog testily. "What is it?"

Little Joe Otter looked around at all the eager faces watching him, and then in the slowest, most provoking way, he drawled: "Farmer Brown's boy is afraid of Buster Bear."

For a minute no one said a word. Then Blacky the Crow leaned down from his perch in the Big Hickory tree and looked very hard at Little Joe as he said:

"I don't believe it. I don't believe a word of it. Farmer Brown's boy isn't afraid of anyone who lives in the Green Forest or on the Green Meadows or in the Smiling Pool, and you know it. We are all afraid of him."

Little Joe glared back at

Reddy glanced across the Smiling Pool at Peter.

Blacky. "I don't care whether you believe it or not; it's true," he retorted. Then he told how early that very morning he and Buster Bear had been fishing together in the Laughing Brook, and how Farmer Brown's boy had been fishing there too, and hadn't caught a single trout because they had all been caught or frightened before he got there. Then he told how Farmer Brown's boy had found a footprint of Buster Bear in the soft mud, and how he had stopped fishing right away and started for home, looking behind him with fear in his eyes all the way.

"Now tell me that he isn't afraid!" concluded Little Joe. "For once he knows just how we feel when he comes prowling around where we are. Isn't that great news? Now we'll get even with *him!*"

"I'll believe it when I see it for myself!" snapped Blacky the Crow.

CHAPTER TEN: BUSTER BEAR BECOMES A HERO

THE NEWS THAT Little Joe Otter told at the Smiling Pool—how Farmer Brown's boy had run away from Buster Bear without even seeing him—soon spread all over the Green Meadows and through the Green Forest, until everyone who lives there knew about it. Of course, Peter Rabbit helped spread it. Trust Peter for that! But everybody else helped too. You see, they had all been afraid of Farmer Brown's boy for so long that they were tickled almost to pieces at the very thought of having someone in the Green Forest who could make Farmer Brown's boy feel fear as they had felt it. And so it was that Buster Bear became a hero right away to most of them.

A few doubted Little Joe's story. One of them was Blacky the Crow. Another was Reddy Fox. Blacky doubted because he knew Farmer Brown's boy so well that he couldn't imagine him afraid. Reddy doubted because he didn't want to believe. You see, he was jealous of Buster Bear, and at the same time he was afraid of him. So Reddy pretended not to believe a word of what Little Joe Otter had said, and he agreed with Blacky that only by seeing Farmer Brown's boy afraid could he ever be made to believe it. But nearly everybody else believed it, and there was great rejoicing. Most of them were afraid of Buster, very much afraid of him, because he was so big and strong. But they were still more afraid of Farmer Brown's boy, because they didn't know him or understand him, and because in the past he had tried to catch some of them in traps and had hunted some of them with his terrible gun.

So now they were very proud to think that one of their own number actually had frightened him, and they began to look on Buster Bear as a real hero. They tried in ever so many ways to show him how friendly they felt and went quite out of their way to do him favors. Whenever they met one another, all they could talk about was the smartness and the greatness of Buster Bear.

"Now I guess Farmer Brown's boy will keep away from the Green Forest, and we won't have to be all the time watching out for him," said Bobby Coon, as he washed his dinner in the Laughing Brook, for you know he is very neat and particular.

"And he won't dare set any more traps for me," gloated Billy Mink.

"Ah wish Brer Bear would go up to Farmer Brown's henhouse and scare Farmer Brown's boy so that he would keep away from there. It would be a favor to me which Ah cert'nly would appreciate," said Unc' Billy Possum when he heard the news.

"Let's all go together and tell Buster Bear how much obliged we are for what he has done," proposed Jerry Muskrat.

"That's a splendid idea!" cried Little Joe Otter. "We'll do it right away."

"Caw, caw caw!" broke in Blacky the Crow. "I say, let's wait and see for ourselves if it's all true."

"Of course it's true!" snapped Little Joe Otter. "Don't you believe I'm telling the truth?"

"Certainly, certainly. Of course no one doubts your word," replied Blacky, with the utmost politeness. "But you say yourself that Farmer Brown's boy didn't see Buster Bear, but only his footprint. Perhaps he didn't know whose it was, and if he had he wouldn't have been afraid. Now I've got a plan by which we can see for ourselves if he really is afraid of Buster Bear."

"What is it?" asked Sammy Jay eagerly.

Blacky the Crow shook his head and winked. "That's telling," said he. "I want to think it over. If you meet me at the Big Hickory tree at sun-up tomorrow morning, and get everybody else to come that you can, perhaps I will tell you."

CHAPTER ELEVEN: BLACKY THE CROW TELLS HIS PLAN

Blacky is a dreamer!
Blacky is a schemer!
His voice is strong;
When things go wrong
Blacky is a screamer!

IT'S A FACT Blacky the Crow is forever dreaming and scheming and almost always it is of mischief. He is one of the smartest and cleverest of all the little people of the Green Meadows and the Green Forest, and all the others know it. Blacky likes excitement. He wants something going on. The more exciting it is, the better he likes it. Then he has a chance to use that harsh voice of his, and how he does use it!

So now, as he sat in the top of the Big Hickory tree beside the Smiling Pool and looked down on all the little people gathered there, he was very happy. In the first place he felt very important, and you know Blacky dearly loves to feel important. They had all come at his invitation to listen to a plan for seeing for themselves if it were really true that Farmer Brown's boy was afraid of Buster Bear.

On the Big Rock in the Smiling Pool sat Little Joe Otter, Billy Mink, and Jerry Muskrat. On his big, green lily-pad sat Grandfather Frog. On another lily-pad sat Spotty the Turtle. On the bank on one side of the Smiling Pool were Peter Rabbit, Jumper the Hare, Danny Meadow Mouse, Johnny Chuck, Jimmy Skunk, Unc' Billy Possum, Striped Chipmunk and Old Mr. Toad. On the other side of the Smiling Pool were Reddy Fox, Digger the Badger, and Bobby Coon. In the Big Hickory tree were Chatterer the Red Squirrel, Happy Jack the Gray Squirrel, and Sammy Jay.

Blacky waited until he was sure that no one else was coming. Then he cleared his throat very loudly and began to speak.

"Friends," said he.

Everybody grinned, for Blacky has played so many sharp tricks that no one is really his friend unless it is that other mischief-maker, Sammy Jay, who, you know, is Blacky's cousin. But no one said anything, and Blacky went on.

"Little Joe Otter has told us how he saw Farmer Brown's boy hurry home when he found the footprint of Buster Bear on the edge of the Laughing Brook, and how all the way he kept looking behind him, as if he were afraid. Perhaps he was, and then again perhaps he wasn't. Perhaps he had something else on his mind. You have made a hero of Buster Bear, because you believe Little Joe's story. Now I don't say that I don't believe it, but I do say that I will be a lot more sure that Farmer Brown's boy is afraid of Buster when I see him run away myself. Now here is my plan:

"Tomorrow morning, very early, Sammy Jay and I will make a great fuss near the edge of the Green Forest. Farmer Brown's boy has a lot of curiosity, and he will be sure to come over to see what it is all about. Then we will lead him to where Buster Bear is. If he runs away, I will be the first to admit that Buster Bear is as great a hero as some of you seem to think he is. It is a very simple plan, and if you will all hide where you can watch, you will be able to see for yourselves if Little Joe Otter is right. Now what do you say?"

Right away everybody began to talk at the same time. It was such a simple plan that everybody agreed to it. And it promised to be so exciting that everybody promised to be there, that is, everybody but Grandfather Frog and Spotty the Turtle, who didn't care to go so far away from the Smiling Pool. So it was agreed that Blacky should try his plan the very next morning.

CHAPTER TWELVE: FARMER BROWN'S BOY AND
BUSTER BEAR GROW CURIOUS

EVER SINCE IT was light enough to see at all, Blacky the Crow had been sitting in the top of the tallest tree on the edge of the Green Forest nearest to Farmer Brown's house, and never for an instant had he taken his eyes from Farmer Brown's back door. What was he watching for? Why, for Farmer Brown's boy to come out on his way to milk the cows. Meanwhile, Sammy Jay was slipping silently through the Green Forest, looking for Buster Bear, so that when the time came he could let his cousin, Blacky the Crow, know just where Buster was.

By and by the back door of Farmer Brown's house opened, and out stepped Farmer Brown's boy. In each hand he carried a milk pail. Right away Blacky began to scream at the top of his lungs. "Caw, caw, caw!" shouted Blacky. "Caw, caw, caw!" And all the time he flew about among the trees near the edge of the Green Forest as if so excited that he couldn't keep still. Farmer Brown's boy looked over there as if he wondered what all that fuss was about, as indeed he did, but he didn't start to go over and see. No, Sir, he started straight for the barn.

Blacky didn't know what to make of it. You see, smart as he is and shrewd as he is, Blacky doesn't know anything about the meaning of duty, for he never has to work excepting to get enough to eat. So, when Farmer Brown's boy started for the barn instead of for the Green Forest, Blacky didn't know what to make of it. He screamed harder and louder than ever, until his voice grew so hoarse he couldn't scream any more, but Farmer Brown's boy kept right on to the barn.

"I'd like to know what you're making such a fuss about, Mr. Crow, but I've got to feed the cows and milk them first," said he.

Now all this time the other little people of the Green Forest and the Green Meadows had been hiding where they could see all that went on. When Farmer Brown's boy disappeared in the barn, Chatterer the Red Squirrel snickered right out loud. "Ha, ha, ha! This is a great plan of yours, Blacky! Ha, ha, ha!" he shouted. Blacky couldn't find a word to say. He just hung his head, which is something Blacky seldom does.

"Perhaps if we wait until he comes out again, he will come over here," said Sammy Jay, who had joined Blacky. So it was decided to wait. It seemed as if Farmer Brown's boy never would come out, but at last he did. Blacky and Sammy Jay at once began to scream and make all the fuss they could. Farmer Brown's boy took the two pails of milk into the house, then out he came and started straight for the Green Forest. He was so curious to know what it all meant that he couldn't wait another minute.

Now there was someone else with a great deal of curiosity also. He had heard the screaming of Blacky the Crow and Sammy Jay, and he had listened until he couldn't stand it another minute. He just had to know what it was all about. So at the same time Farmer Brown's boy started for the Green Forest, this other listener started towards the place where Blacky and Sammy were making such a racket. He walked very softly so as not to make a sound. It was Buster Bear.

CHAPTER THIRTEEN: FARMER BROWN'S BOY AND BUSTER BEAR MEET

If you should meet with Buster Bear
While walking through the wood,
What would you do? Now tell me true.
I'd run the best I could.

THAT IS WHAT Farmer Brown's boy did when he met Buster Bear, and a lot of the little people of the Green Forest and some from the Green Meadows saw him. When Farmer Brown's boy came hurrying home from the Laughing Brook without any fish one day and told about the great footprint he had seen in a muddy place on the bank deep in the Green Forest, and had said he was sure that it was the footprint of a Bear, he had been laughed at. Farmer Brown had laughed and laughed.

"Why," said he, "there hasn't been a Bear in the Green Forest for years and years and years, not since my own grandfather was a little boy, and that, you know, was a long, long, long time ago. If you want to find Mr. Bear, you will have to go to the Great Woods. I don't know who made that footprint, but it certainly couldn't have been a Bear. I think you must have imagined it."

Then he had laughed some more, all of which goes to show how easy it is to be mistaken, and how foolish it is to laugh at things you really don't know about. Buster Bear *had* come to live in the Green Forest, and Farmer Brown's boy *had* seen his footprint. But Farmer Brown laughed so much and made fun of him so much, that at last his boy began to think that he must have been mistaken after all. So when he heard Blacky the Crow and Sammy Jay making a great fuss near the edge of the Green Forest, he never once thought of Buster Bear, as he started over to see what was going on.

When Blacky and Sammy saw him coming, they moved a little farther in to the Green Forest, still screaming in the most excited way. They felt sure that Farmer Brown's boy would follow them, and they meant to lead him to where Sammy had seen Buster Bear that morning. Then they would find out for sure if what Little Joe Otter had said was true—that Farmer Brown's boy really was afraid of Buster Bear.

Now all around, behind trees and stumps, and under thick branches, and even in tree tops, were other little people watching with round, wide-open eyes to see what would happen. It was very exciting, the most exciting thing they could remember.

You see, they had come to believe that Farmer Brown's boy wasn't afraid of anybody or anything, and as most of them were very much afraid of him, they had hard work to believe that he would really be afraid of even such a great, big, strong fellow as Buster Bear. Everyone was so busy watching Farmer Brown's boy that no one saw Buster coming from the other direction. You see, Buster walked very softly. Big as he is, he can walk without making the teeniest, weeniest sound. And that is how it happened that no one saw him or heard him until just as Farmer Brown's boy stepped out from behind one side of a thick little hemlock tree, Buster Bear stepped out from behind the other side of that same little tree, and there they were face to face! Then everybody held their breath, even Blacky the Crow and Sammy Jay. For just a little minute it was so still there in the Green Forest that not the least little sound could be heard. What was going to happen?

CHAPTER FOURTEEN: A SURPRISING THING HAPPENS

BLACKY THE CROW and Sammy Jay, looking down from the top of a tall tree, held their breath. Happy Jack the Gray Squirrel and his cousin, Chatterer the Red Squirrel, looking down from another tree, held *their* breath. Unc' Billy Possum, sticking his head out from a hollow tree, held *his* breath. Bobby Coon, looking through a hole in a hollow stump in which he was hiding, held *his* breath. Reddy Fox, lying flat down behind a heap of brush, held *his* breath. Peter Rabbit, sitting bolt upright under a thick hemlock branch, with eyes and ears wide open, held *his* breath. And all the other little people who happened to be where they could see did the same thing.

You see, it was the most exciting moment there ever was in the Green Forest. Farmer Brown's boy had just stepped out from behind one side of a little hemlock tree and Buster Bear had just stepped out from behind the opposite side of the little hemlock tree and neither had known that the other was anywhere near. For a whole minute they stood there face to face, gazing into each other's eyes, while everybody watched and waited, and it seemed as if the whole Green Forest was holding its breath.

Then something happened. Yes, Sir, something happened. Farmer Brown's boy opened his mouth and yelled! It was such a sudden yell and such a loud yell that it startled Chatterer so that he nearly fell from his place in the tree, and it made Reddy Fox jump to his feet ready to run. And that yell was a yell of fright. There was no doubt about it, for with the yell Farmer Brown's boy turned and ran for home, as no one ever had seen him run before. He ran just as Peter Rabbit runs when he has got to reach the dear Old Briar-patch before Reddy Fox can catch him, which, you know, is as fast as he can run. Once he stumbled and fell, but he scrambled to his feet in a twinkling, and away he went without once turning his head to see if Buster Bear was after him. There wasn't any doubt that he was afraid, very much afraid.

Everybody leaned forward to watch him. "What did I tell you? Didn't I say that he was afraid of Buster Bear?" cried Little Joe Otter, dancing about with excitement.

"You were right, Little Joe! I'm sorry that I doubted it. See him go! Caw, caw, caw!" shrieked Blacky the Crow.

For a minute or two everybody forgot about Buster Bear. Then there was a great crash which made everybody turn to look the other way. What do you think they saw? Why, Buster Bear was running away too, and he was running twice as fast as Farmer Brown's boy!

He bumped into trees and crashed through bushes and jumped over logs, and in almost no time at all he was out of sight. Altogether it was the most surprising thing that the little people of the Green Forest ever had seen.

Buster Bear was running away too.

Sammy Jay looked at Blacky the Crow, and Blacky looked at Chatterer, and Chatterer looked at Happy Jack, and Happy Jack looked at Peter Rabbit, and Peter looked at Unc' Billy Possum, and Unc' Billy looked at Bobby Coon, and Bobby looked at Johnny Chuck, and Johnny looked at Reddy Fox, and Reddy looked at Jimmy Skunk, and Jimmy looked at Billy Mink, and Billy looked at Little Joe Otter, and for a minute nobody could say a word. Then Little Joe gave a funny little gasp.

"Why, why-e-e!" said he, "I believe Buster Bear is afraid too!"

Unc' Billy Possum chuckled. "Ah believe yo' are right again, Brer Otter," said he. "It cert'nly does look so. If Brer Bear isn't scared, he must have remembered something important and has gone to attend to it in a powerful hurry."

Then everybody began to laugh.

CHAPTER FIFTEEN: BUSTER BEAR IS A FALLEN HERO

A FALLEN HERO is someone to whom everyone has looked up as very brave and then proves to be less brave than he was supposed to be. That was the way with Buster Bear. When Little Joe Otter had told how Farmer Brown's boy had been afraid at the mere sight of one of Buster Bear's big footprints, they had at once made a hero of Buster. At least some of them had. As this was the first time, the very first time, that they had ever known anyone who lives in the Green Forest to make Farmer Brown's boy run away, they looked on Buster Bear with a great deal of respect and were very proud of him.

But now they had seen Buster Bear and Farmer Brown's boy meet face to face; and while it was true that Farmer Brown's boy had run away as fast as ever he could, it was also true that Buster Bear had done the same thing. He had run even faster than Farmer Brown's boy, and had hidden in the most lonely place he could find in the very deepest part of the Green Forest. It was hard to believe, but it was true. And right away everybody lost a great deal of the respect for Buster which they had felt. It is always that way. They began to say unkind things about him. They said them among themselves, and some of them even said them to Buster when they met him, or said them so that he would hear them.

Of course Blacky the Crow and Sammy Jay, who, because they can fly, have nothing to fear from Buster, and who always delight in making other people uncomfortable, never let a chance go by to tell Buster and everybody else within hearing what they thought of him. They delighted in flying about through the Green Forest until they had found Buster Bear and then from the safety of the tree tops screaming at him.

> *"Buster Bear is big and strong;*
> *His teeth are big; his claws are long;*
> *In spite of these he runs away*
> *And hides himself the livelong day!"*

A dozen times a day Buster would hear them screaming this. He would grind his teeth and glare up at them, but that was all he could do. He couldn't get at them. He just had to stand it and do nothing. But when impudent little Chatterer the Red Squirrel shouted the same thing from a place just out of reach in a big pine tree, Buster could stand it no longer. He gave a deep, angry growl that made little shivers run over Chatterer, and then suddenly he started up that tree after Chatterer. With a frightened little shriek Chatterer scampered to the top of the tree. He hadn't known that Buster could climb. But Buster is a splendid climber, especially when the tree is big and stout as this one was, and now he went up after Chatterer, growling angrily.

How Chatterer did wish that he had kept his tongue still! He ran to the very top of the tree, so frightened that his teeth chattered, and when he looked down and saw Buster's great mouth coming nearer and nearer, he nearly tumbled down with terror. The worst of it was there wasn't another tree near enough for him to jump to. He was in trouble this time, was Chatterer, sure enough! And there was no one to help him.

CHAPTER SIXTEEN: CHATTERER THE RED SQUIRREL JUMPS FOR HIS LIFE

IT ISN'T VERY often that Chatterer the Red Squirrel knows fear. That is one reason that he is so often impudent and saucy. But once in a while a great fear takes possession of him, as when he knows that Shadow the Weasel is looking for him. You see, he knows that Shadow can go wherever he can go. There are very few of the little people of the Green Forest and the Green Meadows who do not know fear at some time or other, but it comes to Chatterer as seldom as to anyone, because he is very sure of himself and his ability to hide or run away from danger.

But now as he clung to a little branch near the top of a tall pine tree in the Green Forest and looked down at the big sharp teeth of Buster Bear drawing nearer and nearer, and listened to the deep, angry growls that made his hair stand on end, Chatterer was too frightened to think. If only he had kept his tongue still instead of saying hateful things to Buster Bear! If only he had known that Buster could climb a tree! If only he had chosen a tree near enough to other trees for him to jump across! But he *had* said hateful things, he *had* chosen to sit in a tree which stood quite by itself, and Buster Bear *could* climb! Chatterer was in the worst kind of trouble, and there was no one to blame but himself. That is usually the case with those who get into trouble.

Nearer and nearer came Buster Bear, and deeper and angrier sounded his voice. Chatterer gave a little frightened gasp and looked this way and looked that way. What should he do? What *could* he do! The ground seemed a terrible distance below. If only he had wings like Sammy Jay! But he hadn't.

"G-r-r-r-r!" Growled Buster Bear. "I'll teach you manners! I'll teach you to treat your betters with respect! I'll swallow you whole, that's what I'll do. G-r-r-r-r!"

"Oh!" cried Chatterer.

"G-r-r-r-r! I'll eat you all up to the last hair on your tail!" Growled Buster, scrambling a little nearer.

"Oh! Oh!" cried Chatterer, and ran out to the very tip of the little branch to which he had been clinging. Now if Chatterer had only known it, Buster Bear couldn't reach him way up there, because the tree was too small at the top for such a big fellow as Buster. But Chatterer didn't think of that. He gave one more frightened look down at those big teeth, then he shut his eyes and jumped—jumped straight out for the far-away ground.

It was a long, long, long way down to the ground, and it certainly looked as if such a little fellow as Chatterer must be killed. But Chatterer had learned from Old Mother Nature that she had given him certain things to help him at just such times, and one of them is the power to spread himself very flat. He did it now. He spread his arms and legs out just as far as he could, and that kept him from falling as fast and as hard as he otherwise would have done, because being spread out so flat that way, the air held him up a little. And then there was his tail, that funny little tail he is so fond of jerking when he scolds. This helped him too. It helped him keep his balance and keep from turning over and over.

Down, down, down he sailed and landed on his feet. Of course, he hit the ground pretty hard, and for just a second he quite lost his breath. But it was only for a second, and then he was scurrying off as fast as a frightened Squirrel could. Buster Bear watched him and grinned.

"I didn't catch him that time," he growled, "but I guess I gave him a good fright and taught him a lesson."

CHAPTER SEVENTEEN: BUSTER BEAR GOES BERRYING

BUSTER BEAR IS a great hand to talk to himself when he thinks no one is around to overhear. It's a habit. However, it isn't a bad habit unless it is carried too far. Any habit becomes bad, if it is carried too far. Suppose you had a secret, a real secret, something that nobody else knew and that you didn't want anybody else to know. And suppose you had the habit of talking to yourself. You might, without thinking, you know, tell that secret out loud to yourself, and someone might, just might happen to overhear! Then there wouldn't be any secret. That is the way that a habit which isn't bad in itself can become bad when it is carried too far.

Now Buster Bear had lived by himself in the Great Woods so long that this habit of talking to himself had grown and grown. He did it just to keep from being lonesome. Of course, when he came down to the Green Forest to live, he brought all his habits with him. That is one thing about habits—you always take them with you wherever you go. So Buster brought this habit of talking to himself down to the Green Forest, where he had many more neighbors than he had in the Great Woods.

"Let me see, let me see, what is there to tempt my appetite?" said Buster in his deep, grumbly-rumbly voice. "I find my appetite isn't what it ought to be. I need a change. Yes, Sir, I need a change. There is something I ought to have at this time of year, and I haven't got it. There is something that I used to have and don't have now. Ha! I know! I need some fresh fruit. That's it—fresh fruit! It must be about berry time now, and I'd forgotten all about it. My, my, my, how good some berries would taste! Now if I were back up there in the Great Woods I could have all I could eat. Um-m-m-m! Makes my mouth water just to think of it. There ought to be some up in the Old Pasture. There ought to be a lot of 'em up there. If I wasn't afraid that someone would see me, I'd go up there."

Buster sighed. Then he sighed again. The more he thought about those berries he felt sure were growing in the Old Pasture, the more he wanted some. It seemed to him that never in all his life had he wanted berries as he did now. He wandered about uneasily. He was hungry—hungry for berries and nothing else. By and by he began talking to himself again.

"If I wasn't afraid of being seen, I'd go up to the Old Pasture this very minute. Seems as if I could taste those berries." He licked his lips hungrily as he spoke. Then his face brightened. "I know what I'll do! I'll go up there at the very first peep of day tomorrow. I can eat all I want and get back to the Green Forest before there is any danger that Farmer Brown's boy or anyone else I'm afraid of will see me. That's just what I'll do. My, I wish tomorrow morning would hurry up and come."

Now though Buster didn't know it, someone had been listening, and that some-one was none other than Sammy Jay. When at last Buster lay down for a nap, Sammy flew away, chuckling to himself. "I believe I'll visit the Old Pasture tomor-row morning myself," thought he. "I have an idea that something interesting may happen if Buster doesn't change his mind."

Sammy was on the lookout very early the next morning. The first Jolly Little Sunbeams had only reached the Green Meadows and had not started to creep into the Green Forest, when he saw a big, dark form steal out of the Green Forest where it joins the Old Pasture. It moved very swiftly and silently, as if in a great hurry. Sammy knew who it was: it was Buster Bear, and he was going berrying. Sammy waited a little until he could see better. Then he too started for the Old Pasture.

CHAPTER EIGHTEEN: SOMEBODY ELSE GOES BERRYING

ISN'T IT FUNNY how two people will often think of the same thing at the same time, and neither one know that the other is thinking of it? That is just what happened the day that Buster Bear first thought of going berrying. While he was walking around in the Green Forest, talking to himself about how hungry he was for some berries and how sure he was that there must be some up in the Old Pasture, someone else was thinking about berries and about the Old Pasture too.

"Will you make me a berry pie if I will get the berries tomorrow?" asked Farmer Brown's boy of his mother.

Of course Mrs. Brown promised that she would, and so that night Farmer Brown's boy went to bed very early that he might get up early in the morning, and all night long he dreamed of berries and berry pies. He was awake even before jolly, round, red Mr. Sun thought it was time to get up, and he was all ready to start for the Old Pasture when the first Jolly Little Sunbeams came dancing across the Green Meadows. He carried a big tin pail, and in the bottom of it, wrapped up in a piece of paper, was a lunch, for he meant to stay until he filled that pail, if it took all day.

Now the Old Pasture is very large. It lies at the foot of the Big Mountain, and even extends a little way up on the Big Mountain. There is room in it for many people to pick berries all day without even seeing each other, unless they roam about a great deal. You see, the bushes grow very thick there, and you cannot see very far in any direction. Jolly, round, red Mr. Sun had climbed a little way up in the sky by the time Farmer Brown's boy reached the Old Pasture, and was smiling down on all the Great World, and all the Great World seemed to be smiling back. Farmer Brown's boy started to whistle, and then he stopped.

"If I whistle," thought he, "everybody will know just where I am, and will keep out of sight, and I never can get acquainted with folks if they keep out of sight."

You see, Farmer Brown's boy was just beginning to understand something that Peter Rabbit and the other little people of the Green Meadows and the Green Forest learned almost as soon as they learned to walk—that if you don't want to be seen, you mustn't be heard. So he didn't whistle as he felt like doing, and he tried not to make a bit of noise as he followed an old cow-path towards a place where he knew the berries grew thick and oh, so big, and all the time he kept his eyes wide open, and he kept his ears open too.

That is how he happened to hear a little cry, a very faint little cry. If he had been whistling, he wouldn't have heard it at all. He stopped to listen. He never had heard a cry just like it before. At first he couldn't make out just what it was or where it came from. But one thing he was sure of, and that was that it was a cry of fright. He stood perfectly still and listened with all his might. There it was again—

"Help! Help! Help"—and it was very faint and sounded terribly frightened. He waited a minute or two, but heard nothing more. Then he put down his pail and began a hurried look here, there, and everywhere. He was sure that it had come from somewhere on the ground, so he peered behind bushes and peeped behind logs and stones, and then just as he had about given up hope of finding where it came from, he went around a little turn in the old cow-path, and there right in front of him was little Mr. Gartersnake, and what do you think he was doing? Well, I don't like to tell you, but he was trying to swallow one of the children of Stickytoes the Tree Toad. Of course Farmer Brown's boy didn't let him. He made little Mr. Gartersnake set Master Stickytoes free and held Mr. Gartersnake until Master Stickytoes was safely out of reach.

CHAPTER NINETEEN: BUSTER BEAR HAS A FINE TIME

BUSTER BEAR WAS having the finest time he had had since he came down from the Great Woods to live in the Green Forest. To be sure, he wasn't in the Green Forest now, but he wasn't far from it. He was in the Old Pasture, one edge of which touches one edge of the Green Forest. And where do you think he was, in the Old Pasture? Why, right in the middle of the biggest patch of the biggest blueberries he ever had seen in all his life! Now if there is any one thing that Buster Bear had rather have above another, it is all the berries he can eat, unless it be honey. Nothing can quite equal honey in Buster's mind. But next to honey give him berries. He isn't particular what kind of berries. Raspberries, blackberries, or blueberries, either kind, will make him perfectly happy.

"Um-m-m, my, my, but these are good!" he mumbled in his deep grumbly-rumbly voice, as he sat on his haunches stripping off the berries greedily. His little eyes twinkled with enjoyment, and he didn't mind at all if now and then he got leaves and some green berries in his mouth with the big ripe berries. He didn't try to get them out. Oh, my, no! He just chomped them all up together and patted his stomach from sheer delight. Now Buster had reached the Old Pasture just as jolly, round, red Mr. Sun had crept out of bed, and he had fully made up his mind that he would be back in the Green Forest before Mr. Sun had climbed very far up in the blue, blue sky. You see, big as he is and strong as he is, Buster Bear is very shy and bashful, and he has no desire to meet Farmer Brown, or Farmer Brown's boy, or any other of those two-legged creatures called men. It seems funny, but he actually is afraid of them. And he had a feeling that he was a great deal more likely to meet one of them in the Old Pasture than deep in the Green Forest.

So when he started to look for berries, he made up his mind that he would eat what he could in a great hurry and get back to the Green Forest before Farmer

Brown's boy was more than out of bed. But when he found those berries he was so hungry that he forgot his fears and everything else. They tasted so good that he just had to eat and eat and eat. Now you know that Buster is a very big fellow, and it takes a lot to fill him up. He kept eating and eating and eating, and the more he ate the more he wanted. You know how it is.

So he wandered from one patch of berries to another in the Old Pasture, and never once thought of the time. Somehow, time is the hardest thing in the world to remember, when you are having a good time.

Jolly, round, red Mr. Sun climbed higher and higher in the blue, blue sky. He looked down on all the Great World and saw all that was going on. He saw Buster Bear in the Old Pasture, and smiled as he saw what a perfectly glorious time Buster was having. And he saw something else in the Old Pasture that made his smile still broader. He saw Farmer Brown's boy filling a great tin pail with blueberries, and he knew that Farmer Brown's boy didn't know that Buster Bear was anywhere about, and he knew that Buster Bear didn't know that Farmer Brown's boy was anywhere about, and somehow he felt very sure that he would see something funny happen if they should chance to meet.

"Um-m-m, um-m-m," mumbled Buster Bear with his mouth full, as he moved along to another patch of berries. And then he gave a little gasp of surprise and delight. Right in front of him was a shiny thing just full of the finest, biggest, bluest berries! There were no leaves or green ones there. Buster blinked his greedy little eyes rapidly and looked again. No, he wasn't dreaming. They were real berries, and all he had got to do was to help himself. Buster looked sharply at the shiny thing that held the berries. It seemed perfectly harmless. He reached out a big paw and pushed it gently. It tipped over and spilled out a lot of the

Buster blinked his greedy little eyes rapidly.

berries. Yes, it was perfectly harmless. Buster gave a little sigh of pure happiness. He would eat those berries to the last one, and then he would go home to the Green Forest.

CHAPTER TWENTY: BUSTER BEAR CARRIES OFF THE PAIL OF FARMER BROWN'S BOY

THE QUESTION IS, did Buster Bear steal Farmer Brown's boy's pail? To steal is to take something which belongs to someone else. There is no doubt that he stole the berries that were in the pail when he found it, for he deliberately ate them. He knew well enough that someone must have picked them—for whoever heard of blueberries growing in tin pails? So there is no doubt that when Buster took them, he stole them. But with the pail it was different. He took the pail, but he didn't mean to take it. In fact, he didn't want that pail at all.

You see it was this way: When Buster found that big tin pail brimming full of delicious berries in the shade of that big bush in the Old Pasture, he didn't stop to think whether or not he had a right to them. Buster is so fond of berries that from the very second that his greedy little eyes saw that pailful, he forgot everything but the feast that was waiting for him right under his very nose. He didn't think anything about the right or wrong of helping himself. There before him were more berries than he had ever seen together at one time in all his life, and all he had to do was to eat and eat and eat. And that is just what he did do. Of course he upset the pail, but he didn't mind a little thing like that. When he had gobbled up all the berries that rolled out, he thrust his nose into the pail to get all that were left in it. Just then he heard a little noise, as if someone were coming. He threw up his head to listen, and somehow, he never did know just how, the handle of the pail slipped back over his ears and caught there.

This was bad enough, but to make matters worse, just at that very minute he heard a shrill, angry voice shout, "Hi, there! Get out of there!" He didn't need to be told whose voice that was. It was the voice of Farmer Brown's boy. Right then and there Buster Bear nearly had a fit. There was that awful pail fast over his head so that he couldn't see a thing. Of course, that meant that he couldn't run away, which was the thing of all things he most wanted to do, for big as he is and strong as he is, Buster is very shy and bashful when human beings are around. He growled and whined and squealed. He tried to back out of the pail and couldn't. He tried to shake it off and couldn't. He tried to pull it off, but somehow he couldn't get hold of it. Then there was another yell. If Buster hadn't been so frightened himself, he might have recognized that second yell as one of fright, for that is what it was. You see Farmer Brown's boy had just discovered Buster Bear. When he had yelled the first time, he had supposed that it was one of the young cattle who live in the Old Pasture all summer, but when he saw Buster, he was just as badly frightened as Buster himself. In fact, he was too surprised and frightened even to run. After that second yell he just stood still and stared.

Buster clawed at that awful thing on his head more frantically than ever. Suddenly it slipped off, so that he could see. He gave one frightened look at Farmer Brown's boy, and then with a mighty "Woof!" he started for the Green Forest as fast as his legs could take him, and this was very fast indeed, let me tell you. He didn't stop to pick out a path, but just crashed through the bushes as if they were nothing at all, just nothing at all. But the funniest thing of all is this—he took that pail with him!

Yes, Sir, Buster Bear ran away with the big tin pail of Farmer Brown's boy! You see when it slipped off his head, the handle was still around his neck, and there he was running away with a pail hanging from his neck! He didn't want it. He would have given anything to get rid of it. But he took it because he couldn't help it. And that brings us back to the question, did Buster steal Farmer Brown's boy's pail? What do you think?

CHAPTER TWENTY-ONE: SAMMY JAY MAKES THINGS WORSE

"THIEF, THIEF, THIEF! Thief, thief, thief!" Sammy Jay was screaming at the top of his lungs, as he followed Buster Bear across the Old Pasture towards the Green Forest. Never had he screamed so loud, and never had his voice sounded so excited. The little people of the Green Forest, the Green Meadows, and the Smiling Pool are so used to hearing Sammy cry thief that usually they think very little about it. But every blessed one who heard Sammy this morning stopped whatever he was doing and pricked up his ears to listen.

Sammy's cousin, Blacky the Crow, just happened to be flying along the edge of the Old Pasture, and the minute he heard Sammy's voice, he turned and flew over to see what it was all about. Just as soon as he caught sight of Buster Bear running for the Green Forest as hard as ever he could, he understood what had excited Sammy so. He was so surprised that he almost forgot to keep his wings moving. Buster Bear had what looked to Blacky very much like a tin pail hanging from his neck! No wonder Sammy was excited. Blacky beat his wings fiercely and started after Sammy.

And so they reached the edge of the Green Forest, Buster Bear running as hard as ever he could, Sammy Jay flying just behind him and screaming, "Thief, thief, thief!" at the top of his lungs, and behind him Blacky the Crow, trying to catch up and yelling as loud as he could, "Caw, caw, caw! Come on, everybody! Come on!"

Poor Buster! It was bad enough to be frightened almost to death as he had been up in the Old Pasture when the pail had caught over his head just as Farmer Brown's boy had yelled at him. Then to have the handle of the pail slip down around his neck so that he couldn't get rid of the pail but had to take it with him as he ran, was making a bad matter worse. Now to have all his neighbors of the Green Forest see him in such a fix and make fun of him, was more than he could stand. He felt humiliated. That is just another way of saying shamed. Yes, Sir, Buster felt that he was shamed in the eyes of his neighbors, and he wanted nothing so much as to get away by himself, where no one could see him, and try to get rid of that dreadful pail. But Buster is so big that it is not easy for him to find a hiding place. So, when he reached the Green Forest, he kept right on to the deepest, darkest, most lonesome part and crept under the thickest hemlock tree he could find.

But it was of no use. The sharp eyes of Sammy Jay and Blacky the Crow saw him. They actually flew into the very tree under which he was hiding, and how they did scream! Pretty soon Ol' Mistah Buzzard came dropping down out of the blue, blue sky and took a seat on a convenient dead tree, where he could see all that went on. Ol' Mistah Buzzard began to grin as soon as he saw that tin pail on Buster's neck. Then came others—Redtail the Hawk, Scrapper the Kingbird, Redwing the Blackbird, Drummer the Woodpecker, Welcome Robin, Tommy Tit the Chickadee, Jenny Wren, Redeye the Vireo, and ever so many more. They came from the Old Orchard, the Green Meadows, and even down by the Smiling Pool, for the voices of Sammy Jay and Blacky the Crow carried far, and at the sound of them everybody hurried over, sure that something exciting was going on.

Presently Buster heard light footsteps, and peeping out, he saw Billy Mink and Peter Rabbit and Jumper the Hare and Prickly Porky and Reddy Fox and Jimmy Skunk. Even timid little Whitefoot the Wood Mouse was where he could peer out and see without being seen. Of course, Chatterer the Red Squirrel and Happy Jack the Gray Squirrel were there. There they all sat in a great circle around him, each where he felt safe, but where he could see, and every one of them laughing and making fun of Buster.

"Thief, thief, thief!" screamed Sammy until his throat was sore. The worst of it was Buster knew that everybody knew that it was true. That pail was proof of it.

"I wish I never had thought of berries," growled Buster to himself.

CHAPTER TWENTY-TWO: BUSTER BEAR HAS A FIT OF TEMPER

A temper is a bad, bad thing when once it gets away.
There's nothing quite at all like it to spoil a pleasant day.

BUSTER BEAR WAS in a terrible temper. Yes, Sir, Buster Bear was having the worst fit of temper ever seen in the Green Forest. And the worst part of it all was that all his neighbors of the Green Forest and a whole lot from the Green Meadows and the Smiling Pool were also there to see it. It is bad enough to give way to temper when you are all alone, and there is no one to watch you, but when you let temper get the best of you right where others see you, oh, dear, dear, it certainly is a sorry sight.

Now ordinarily Buster is one of the most good-natured persons in the world. It takes a great deal to rouse his temper. He isn't one tenth so quick tempered as Chatterer the Red Squirrel, or Sammy Jay, or Reddy Fox. But when his temper is aroused and gets away from him, then watch out! It seemed to Buster that he had had all that he could stand that day and a little more. First had come the fright back there in the Old Pasture. Then the pail had slipped down behind his ears and held fast, so he had run all the way to the Green Forest with it hanging about his neck. This was bad enough, for he knew just how funny he must look, and besides, it was very uncomfortable. But to have Sammy Jay call everybody within hearing to come and see him was more than he could stand. It seemed to Buster as if everybody who lives in the Green Forest, on the Green Meadows, or around the Smiling Brook, was sitting around his hiding place, laughing and making fun of him. It was more than any self-respecting Bear could stand.

With a roar of anger Buster Bear charged out of his hiding place. He rushed this way and that way! He roared with all his might! He was very terrible to see. Those who could fly, flew. Those who could climb, climbed. And those who were swift of foot, ran. A few who could neither fly nor climb nor run fast, hid and lay shaking and trembling for fear that Buster would find them. In less time than it takes to tell about it, Buster was alone. At least, he couldn't see anyone.

Then he vented his temper on the tin pail. He cuffed at it and pulled at it, all the time growling angrily. He lay down and clawed at it with his hind

Those who could fly, flew. Those who could climb, climbed. And those who were swift of foot, ran.

feet. At last the handle broke, and he was free! He shook himself. Then he jumped on the helpless pail. With a blow of a big paw he sent it clattering against a tree. He tried to bite it. Then he once more knocked it this way and that way, until it was pounded flat, and no one would ever have guessed that it had once been a pail.

Then, and not till then, did Buster recover his usual good nature. Little by little, as he thought it all over, a look of shame crept into his face. "I—I guess it wasn't the fault of that thing. I ought to have known enough to keep my head out of it," he said slowly and thoughtfully.

"You got no more than you deserve for stealing Farmer Brown's boy's berries," said Sammy Jay, who had come back and was looking on from the top of a tree. "You ought to know by this time that no good comes of stealing."

Buster Bear looked up and grinned, and there was a twinkle in his eyes. "You ought to know, Sammy Jay," said he. "I hope you'll always remember it."

"Thief, thief, thief!" screamed Sammy, and flew away.

CHAPTER TWENTY-THREE: FARMER BROWN'S BOY LUNCHES ON BERRIES

When things go wrong in spite of you
To smile's the best thing you can do—
To smile and say, "I'm mighty glad
They are no worse; they're not so bad!"

THAT IS WHAT Farmer Brown's boy said when he found that Buster Bear had stolen the berries he had worked so hard to pick and then had run off with the pail. You see, Farmer Brown's boy is learning to be something of a philosopher, one of those people who accept bad things cheerfully and right away see how they are better than they might have been.

When he had first heard someone in the bushes where he had hidden his pail of berries, he had been very sure that it was one of the cows or young cattle who live in the Old Pasture during the summer. He had been afraid that they might stupidly kick over the pail and spill the berries, and he had hurried to drive whoever it was away. It hadn't entered his head that it could be anybody who would eat those berries.

When he had yelled and Buster Bear had suddenly appeared, struggling to get off the pail which had caught over his head, Farmer Brown's boy had been too frightened to even move. Then he had seen Buster tear away through the brush even more frightened than he was, and right away his courage had begun to come back.

"If he is so afraid of me, I guess I needn't be afraid of him," said he. "I've lost my berries, but it is worth it to find out that he is afraid of me. There are plenty more on the bushes, and all I've got to do is to pick them. It might be worse."

He walked over to the place where the pail had been, and then he remembered that when Buster ran away he had carried the pail with him, hanging about his neck. He whistled. It was a comical little whistle of chagrin as he realized that he had nothing in which to put more berries, even if he picked them. "It's worse than I thought," cried he. "That bear has cheated me out of that berry pie my mother promised me." Then he began to laugh, as he thought of how funny Buster Bear had looked with the pail about his neck, and then because, you know, he is learning to be a philosopher, he once more repeated, "It might have been worse. Yes, indeed, it might have been worse. That bear might have tried to eat me instead of the berries. I guess I'll go eat that lunch I left back by the spring, and then I'll go home. I can pick berries some other day."

Chuckling happily over Buster Bear's great fright, Farmer Brown's boy tramped back to the spring where he had left two thick sandwiches on a flat stone when he started to save his pail of berries. "My, but those sandwiches will taste good," thought he. "I'm glad they are big and thick. I never was hungrier in my life. Hello!" This he exclaimed right out loud, for he had just come in sight of the flat stone where the sandwiches should have been, and they were not there. No, Sir, there wasn't so much as a crumb left of those two thick sandwiches. You see, Old Man Coyote had found them and gobbled them up while Farmer Brown's boy was away.

But Farmer Brown's boy didn't know anything about Old Man Coyote. He rubbed his eyes and stared everywhere, even up in the trees, as if he thought those sandwiches might be hanging up there. They had disappeared as completely as if they never had been, and Old Man Coyote had taken care to leave no trace of his visit. Farmer Brown's boy gaped foolishly this way and that way. Then, instead of growing angry, a slow smile stole over his freckled face. "I guess someone else was hungry too," he muttered. "Wonder who it was? Guess this Old Pasture is no place for me today. I'll fill up on berries and then I'll go home."

So Farmer Brown's boy made his lunch on blueberries and then rather sheepishly he started for home to tell of all the strange things that had happened to him in the Old Pasture. Two or three times, as he trudged along, he stopped to scratch his head thoughtfully. "I guess," said he at last, "that I'm not so smart as I thought I was, and I've got a lot to learn yet."

This is the end of the adventures of Buster Bear in this book because—guess why. Because Old Mr. Toad insists that I must write a book about his adventures, and Old Mr. Toad is such a good friend of all of us that I am going to do it.

The Adventures of Old Mr. Toad

CHAPTER ONE: JIMMY SKUNK IS PUZZLED

OLD MOTHER WEST WIND had just come down from the Purple Hills and turned loose her children, the Merry Little Breezes, from the big bag in which she had been carrying them. They were very lively and very merry as they danced and raced across the Green Meadows in all directions, for it was good to be back there once more. Old Mother West Wind almost sighed as she watched them for a few minutes. She felt that she would like to join them. Always the springtime made her feel this way—young, mad, carefree, and happy. But she had work to do. She had to turn the windmill to pump water for Farmer Brown's cows, and this was only one of many mills standing idle as they waited for her. So she puffed her cheeks out and started about her business.

Jimmy Skunk sat at the top of the hill that overlooks the Green Meadows and watched her out of sight. Then he started to amble down the Lone Little Path to look for some beetles. He was ambling along in his lazy way, for you know he never hurries, when he heard someone puffing and blowing behind him. Of course he turned to see who it was, and he was greatly surprised when he discovered Old Mr. Toad. Yes, Sir, it was Old Mr. Toad, and he seemed in a great hurry. He was quite short of breath, but he was hopping along in the most determined way as if he were in a great hurry to get somewhere.

Now it is a very unusual thing for Mr. Toad to hurry, very unusual indeed. As a rule he hops a few steps and then sits down to think it over. Jimmy had never before seen him hop more than a few steps unless he was trying to get away from danger, from Mr. Blacksnake for instance. Of course the first thing Jimmy thought of was Mr. Blacksnake, and he looked for him. But there was no sign of Mr. Blacksnake nor of any other danger. Then he looked very hard at Old Mr. Toad, and he saw right away that Old Mr. Toad didn't seem to be frightened at all, only very determined, and as if he had something important on his mind.

"Well, well," exclaimed Jimmy Skunk, "whatever has got into those long hind legs of yours to make them work so fast?"

Old Mr. Toad didn't say a word, but simply tried to get past Jimmy and keep on his way. Jimmy put out one hand and turned Old Mr. Toad right over on his back, where he kicked and struggled in an effort to get on his feet again, and looked very ridiculous.

"Don't you know that it isn't polite not to speak when you are spoken to?" demanded Jimmy severely, though his eyes twinkled.

"I—I beg your pardon. I didn't have any breath to spare," panted Old Mr. Toad. "You see I'm in a great hurry."

"Yes, I see," replied Jimmy. "But don't you know that it isn't good for the health to hurry so? Now, pray, what are you in such a hurry for? I don't see anything to run away from."

"I'm not running away," retorted Old Mr. Toad indignantly. "I've business to attend to at the Smiling Pool, and I'm late as it is."

"Business!" exclaimed Jimmy as if he could hardly believe his ears. "What business have you at the Smiling Pool?"

"That is my own affair," retorted Old Mr. Toad, "but if you really want to know, I'll tell you. I have a very important part in the spring chorus, and I'm going down there to sing. I have a very beautiful voice."

That was too much for Jimmy Skunk. He just lay down and rolled over and over with laughter. The idea of anyone so homely, almost ugly-looking, as Mr. Toad thinking that he had a beautiful voice! "Ha, ha, ha! Ho, ho, ho!" roared Jimmy.

When at last he stopped because he couldn't laugh any more, he discovered that Old Mr. Toad was on his way again. Hop, hop, hipperty-hop, hop, hop, hipperty-hop went Mr. Toad. Jimmy watched him, and he confessed that he was puzzled.

CHAPTER TWO: JIMMY SKUNK CONSULTS HIS FRIENDS

JIMMY SKUNK SCRATCHED his head thoughtfully as he watched Old Mr. Toad go down the Lone Little Path, hop, hop, hipperty-hop, towards the Smiling Pool. He certainly was puzzled, was Jimmy Skunk. If Old Mr. Toad had told him that he could fly, Jimmy would not have been more surprised, or found it harder to believe than that Old Mr. Toad had a beautiful voice. The truth is, Jimmy didn't believe it. He thought that Old Mr. Toad was trying to fool him.

Presently Peter Rabbit came along. He found Jimmy Skunk sitting in a brown study. He had quite forgotten to look for fat beetles, and when he forgets to do that you may make up your mind that Jimmy is doing some hard thinking.

"Hello, old Striped-coat, what have you got on your mind this fine morning?" cried Peter Rabbit.

"Him," said Jimmy simply, pointing down the Lone Little Path.

"Do you see anything queer about him?" he asked.

Peter looked. "Do you mean Old Mr. Toad?" he asked.

Jimmy nodded. "Do you see anything queer about him?" he asked in his turn.

Peter stared down the Lone Little Path. "No," he replied, "except that he seems in a great hurry."

"That's just it," Jimmy returned promptly. "Did you ever see him hurry unless he was frightened?"

Peter confessed that he never had.

"Well, he isn't frightened now, yet just look at him go," retorted Jimmy. "Says he has got a beautiful voice, and that he has to take part in the spring chorus at the Smiling Pool and that he is late."

Peter looked very hard at Jimmy to see if he was fooling or telling the truth. Then he began to laugh. "Old Mr. Toad sing! The very idea!" he cried. "He can sing about as much as I can, and that is not at all."

Jimmy grinned. "I think he's crazy, if you ask me," said he. "And yet he was just as earnest about it as if it were really so. I think he must have eaten something that has gone to his head. There's Unc' Billy Possum over there. Let's ask him what he thinks."

So Jimmy and Peter joined Unc' Billy, and Jimmy told the story about Old Mr. Toad all over again. Unc' Billy chuckled and laughed just as they had at the idea of Old Mr. Toad's saying he had a beautiful voice. But Unc' Billy has a shrewd little head on his shoulders. After a few minutes he stopped laughing.

"Ah done learn a right smart long time ago that Ah don' know all there is to know about mah neighbors," said he. "We-uns done think of Brer Toad as ugly-lookin' fo' so long that we-uns may have overlooked something. Ah don' reckon Brer Toad can sing, but Ah 'lows that perhaps he thinks he can. What do you-alls say to we-uns going down to the Smiling Pool and finding out what he really is up to?"

"The very thing!" cried Peter, kicking up his heels. You know Peter is always ready to go anywhere or do anything that will satisfy his curiosity.

Jimmy Skunk thought it over for a few minutes, and then he decided that as he hadn't anything in particular to do, and as he might find some fat beetles on the way, he would go too. So off they started after Old Mr. Toad, Peter Rabbit in the lead as usual, Unc' Billy Possum next, grinning as only he can grin, and in the rear Jimmy Skunk, taking his time and keeping a sharp eye out for fat beetles.

CHAPTER THREE: THE HUNT FOR OLD MR. TOAD

NOW, THOUGH OLD MR. TOAD was hurrying as fast as ever he could and was quite out of breath, he wasn't getting along very fast compared with the way Peter Rabbit or Jimmy Skunk or Unc' Billy Possum could cover the ground. You see he cannot make long jumps like his cousin, Grandfather Frog, but only little short hops.

So Peter and Jimmy and Unc' Billy took their time about following him. They stopped to hunt for fat beetles for Jimmy Skunk, and at every little patch of sweet clover for Peter Rabbit to help himself. Once they wasted a lot of time while Unc' Billy Possum hunted for a nest of Carol the Meadow Lark, on the chance that he would find some fresh eggs there. He didn't find the nest for the very good reason that Carol hadn't built one yet. Peter was secretly glad. You know he doesn't eat eggs, and he is always sorry for his feathered friends when their eggs are stolen.

Half way across the Green Meadows they stopped to play with the Merry Little Breezes, and because it was very pleasant there, they played longer than they realized. When at last they started on again, Old Mr. Toad was out of sight. You see all the time he had kept right on going, hop, hop, hipperty-hop.

"Never mind," said Peter, "we can catch up with him easy enough, he's such a slow-poke."

But even a slow-poke who keeps right on doing a thing without wasting any time always gets somewhere sooner or later, very often sooner than those who are naturally quicker, but who waste their time. So it was with Old Mr. Toad. He kept right on, hop, hop, hipperty-hop, while the others were playing, and so it happened that when at last Peter and Jimmy and Unc' Billy reached the Smiling Pool, they hadn't caught another glimpse of Old Mr. Toad.

"Do you suppose he hid somewhere and we passed him?" asked Peter.

Unc' Billy shook his head. "Ah don' reckon so," said he. "We-uns done been foolin' away our time, an' Brer Toad done stole a march on us. Ah reckons we-uns will find him sittin' on the bank here somewhere."

So right away the three separated to look for Old Mr. Toad. All along the bank of the Smiling Pool they looked. They peeped under old leaves and sticks. They looked in every place where Old Mr. Toad might have hidden, but not a trace of him did they find.

> "Tra-la-la-lee! Oka-chee! Oka-chee!
> Happy am I as I can be!"

sang Mr. Redwing, as he swayed to and fro among the bulrushes.

"Say, Mr. Redwing, have you seen Old Mr. Toad?" called Peter Rabbit.

"No," replied Mr. Redwing. "Is that whom you fellows are looking for? I wondered if you had lost something. What do you want with Old Mr. Toad?"

Peter explained how they had followed Old Mr. Toad just to see what he really was up to. "Of course we know that he hasn't any more voice than I have," declared Peter, "but we are curious to know if he really thinks he has, and why he should be in such a hurry to reach the Smiling Pool. It looks to us as if the spring has made Old Mr. Toad crazy."

"Oh, that's it, is it?" replied Mr. Redwing, his bright eyes twinkling. "Some people don't know as much as they might. I've been wondering where Old Mr. Toad was, and I'm ever so glad to learn that he hasn't forgotten that he has a very important part in our beautiful spring chorus." Then once more Mr. Redwing began to sing.

CHAPTER FOUR: PETER RABBIT FINDS OLD MR. TOAD

IT ISN'T OFTEN that Peter Rabbit is truly envious, but sometimes in the joyousness of spring he is. He envies the birds because they can pour out in beautiful song the joy that is in them. The only way he can express his feelings is by kicking his long heels, jumping about, and such foolish things. While that gives Peter a great deal of satisfaction, it doesn't add to the joy of other people as do the songs of the birds, and you know to give joy to others is to add to your own joy. So there are times when Peter wishes he could sing.

He was wishing this very thing now, as he sat on the bank of the Smiling Pool, listening to the great spring chorus.

> "Tra-la-la-lee! Oka-chee! Oka-chee!
> There's joy in the spring for you and for me."

sang Redwing the Blackbird from the bulrushes.

From over in the Green Meadows rose the clear lilt of Carol the Meadow Lark, and among the alders just where the Laughing Brook ran into the Smiling Pool a flood of happiness was pouring from the throat of Little Friend the Song Sparrow. Winsome Bluebird's sweet, almost plaintive, whistle seemed to fairly float in the air, so that it was hard to say just where it did come from, and in the top of the Big Hickory tree, Welcome Robin was singing as if his heart were bursting with joy. Even Sammy Jay was adding a beautiful, bell-like note instead of his usual harsh scream. As for the Smiling Pool, it seemed as if the very water itself sang, for a mighty chorus of clear piping voices from unseen singers rose from all around its banks. Peter knew who those singers were, although look as he would he could see none of them. They were hylas, the tiny cousins of Stickytoes the Tree Toad.

Listening to all these joyous voices, Peter forgot for a time what had brought him to the Smiling Pool. But Jimmy Skunk and Unc' Billy Possum didn't forget. They were still hunting for Old Mr. Toad.

"Well, old Mr. Dreamer, have you found him yet?" asked Jimmy Skunk, stealing up behind Peter and poking him in the back.

Peter came to himself with a start. "No," said he. "I was just listening and wishing that I could sing, too. Don't you ever wish you could sing, Jimmy?"

"No," replied Jimmy. "I never waste time wishing I could do things it was never meant I should do. It's funny where Old Mr. Toad is. He said that he was coming down here to sing, and Redwing the Blackbird seemed to be expecting him. I've looked everywhere I can think of without finding him, but I don't believe in giving up without another try. Stop your dreaming and come help us hunt."

So Peter stopped his dreaming and joined in the search. Now there was one place where neither Peter nor Jimmy nor Unc' Billy had thought of looking. That was in the Smiling Pool itself. They just took it for granted that Old Mr. Toad was somewhere on the bank. Presently Peter came to a place where the bank was very low and the water was shallow for quite a little distance out in the Smiling Pool. From out of that shallow water came the piping voice of a hyla, and Peter stopped to stare, trying to see the tiny singer.

Suddenly he jumped right up in the air with surprise. There was a familiar-looking head sticking out of the water. Peter had found Old Mr. Toad!

CHAPTER FIVE: OLD MR. TOAD'S MUSIC BAG

Never think that you have learned all there is to know.
That's the surest way of all Ignorance to show.

"I'VE FOUND OLD MR. TOAD!" cried Peter Rabbit, hurrying after Jimmy Skunk.

"Where?" demanded Jimmy.

"In the water," declared Peter. "He's sitting right over there where the water is shallow, and he didn't notice me at all. Let's get Unc' Billy, and then creep over to the edge of the Smiling Pool and watch to see if Old Mr. Toad really does try to sing."

So they hunted up Unc' Billy Possum, and the three stole very softly over to the edge of the Smiling Pool, where the bank was low and the water shallow. Sure enough, there sat Old Mr. Toad with just his head out of water. And while they were watching him, something very strange happened.

"What—what's the matter with him?" whispered Peter, his big eyes looking as if they might pop out of his head.

"If he don't watch out, he'll blow up and bust!" exclaimed Jimmy.

"Listen!" whispered Unc' Billy Possum. "Do mah ol' ears hear right? 'Pears to me that that song is coming right from where Brer Toad is sitting."

"If he don't watch out, he'll blow up and bust!" exclaimed Jimmy.

It certainly did appear so, and of all the songs that glad spring day there was none sweeter. Indeed there were few as sweet. The only trouble was the song was so very short. It lasted only for two or three seconds. And when it ended, Old Mr. Toad looked quite his natural self again; just as commonplace, almost ugly, as ever. Peter looked at Jimmy Skunk, Jimmy looked at Unc' Billy Possum, and Unc' Billy looked at Peter. And no one had a word to say. Then all three looked back at Old Mr. Toad.

And even as they looked, his throat began to swell and swell and swell, until it was no wonder that Jimmy Skunk had thought that he was in danger of blowing up. And then, when it stopped swelling, there came again those beautiful little notes, so sweet and tremulous that Peter actually held his breath to listen. There was no doubt that Old Mr. Toad was singing just as he had said he was going to, and it was just as true that his song was one of the sweetest if not the sweetest of all the chorus from and around the Smiling Pool. It was very hard to believe, but Peter and Jimmy and Unc' Billy both saw and heard, and that was enough. Their respect for Old Mr. Toad grew tremendously as they listened.

"How does he do it?" whispered Peter.

"With that bag under his chin, of course," replied Jimmy Skunk. "Don't you see it's only when that is swelled out that he sings? It's a regular music bag. And I didn't know he had any such bag there at all."

"I wish," said Peter Rabbit, feeling of his throat, "that I had a music bag like that in my throat."

And then he joined in the laugh of Jimmy and Unc' Billy, but still with something of a look of wistfulness in his eyes.

CHAPTER SIX: PETER DISCOVERS SOMETHING MORE

There are stranger things in the world today
Than ever you dreamed could be.
There's beauty in some of the commonest things
If only you've eyes to see.

EVER SINCE PETER RABBIT was a little chap and had first run away from home, he had known Old Mr. Toad, and never once had Peter suspected that he could sing. Also he had thought Old Mr. Toad almost ugly-looking, and he knew that most of his neighbors thought the same way. They were fond of Old Mr. Toad, for he was always good-natured and attended strictly to his own affairs; but they liked to poke fun at him, and as for there being anything beautiful about him, such a thing never entered their heads.

Now that they had discovered that he really has a very beautiful voice, they began to look on him with a great deal more respect. This was especially so with Peter. He got in the habit of going over to the Smiling Pool every day, when the way was clear, just to sit on the bank and listen to Old Mr. Toad.

"Why didn't you ever tell us before that you could sing?" he asked one day, as Old Mr. Toad looked up at him from the Smiling Pool.

"What was the use of wasting my breath?" demanded Old Mr. Toad. "You wouldn't have believed me if I had. You didn't believe me when I did tell you."

Peter knew that this was true, and he couldn't find any answer ready. At last he ventured another question. "Why haven't I ever heard you sing before?"

"You have," replied Old Mr. Toad tartly. "I sang right in this very place last spring, and the spring before, and the spring before that. You've sat on that very bank lots of times while I was singing. The trouble with you, Peter, is that you don't use your eyes or your ears."

Peter looked more foolish than ever. But he ventured another question. It wouldn't be Peter to let a chance for questions go by. "Have I ever heard you singing up on the meadows or in the Old Orchard?"

"No," replied Old Mr. Toad, "I only sing in the springtime. That's the time for singing. I just *have* to sing then. In the summer it is too hot, and in the winter I sleep. I always return to my old home to sing. You know I was born here. All my family gathers here in the spring to sing, so of course I come too."

Old Mr. Toad filled out his queer music bag under his chin and began to sing again. Peter watched him. Now it just happened that Old Mr. Toad was facing him, and so Peter looked down straight into his eyes. He never had looked into Mr. Toad's eyes before, and now he just stared and stared, for it came over him that those eyes were very beautiful, very beautiful indeed.

"Oh!" he exclaimed, "what beautiful eyes you have, Mr. Toad!"

"So I've been told before," replied Old Mr. Toad. "My family always has had beautiful eyes. There is an old saying that every Toad has jewels in his head, but of course he hasn't, not real jewels. It is just the beautiful eyes. Excuse me, Peter, but I'm needed in that chorus." Old Mr. Toad once more swelled out his throat and began to sing.

Peter watched him a while longer, then hopped away to the dear Old Briar-patch, and he was very thoughtful.

"Never again will I call anybody homely and ugly until I know all about him," said Peter, which was a very wise decision. Don't you think so?

CHAPTER SEVEN: A SHADOW PASSES OVER THE SMILING POOL

Here's what Mr. Toad says; heed it well, my dear:
"Time to watch for clouds is when the sky is clear."

HE SAYS THAT that is the reason that he lives to a good old age, does Old Mr. Toad. I suppose he means that when the sky is cloudy, everybody is looking for rain and is prepared for it, but when the sun is shining, most people forget that there is such a thing as a storm, so when it comes suddenly very few are prepared for it. It is the same way with danger and trouble. So Old Mr. Toad very wisely watches out when there seems to be the least need of it, and he finds it always pays.

It was a beautiful spring evening. Over back of the Purple Hills to which Old Mother West Wind had taken her children, the Merry Little Breezes, and behind which jolly, round, red Mr. Sun had gone to bed, there was still a faint, clear light. But over the Green Meadows and the Smiling Pool the shadows had drawn a curtain of soft dusk which in the Green Forest became black. The little stars looked down from the sky and twinkled just to see their reflections twinkle back at them from the Smiling Pool. And there and all around it was perfect peace. Jerry Muskrat swam back and forth, making little silver lines on the surface of the Smiling Pool and squeaking contentedly, for it was the hour which he loves best. Little Friend the Song Sparrow had tucked his head under his wing and gone to sleep among the alders along the Laughing Brook and Redwing the Blackbird had done the same thing among the bulrushes. All the feathered songsters who had made joyous the bright day had gone to bed.

But this did not mean that the glad spring chorus was silent. Oh, my, no! No indeed! The Green Meadows were silent, and the Green Forest was silent, but as if to make up for this, the sweet singers of the Smiling Pool, the hylas and the frogs and Old Mr. Toad, were pouring out their gladness as if they had not been singing most of the departed day. You see it was the hour they love best of all, the hour which seems to them just made for singing, and they were doing their best to tell Old Mother Nature how they love her, and how glad they were that she had brought back sweet Mistress Spring to waken them from their long sleep.

It was so peaceful and beautiful there that it didn't seem possible that danger of any kind could be lurking near. But Old Mr. Toad, swelling out that queer music bag in his throat and singing with all his might, never once forgot that wise saying of his, and so he was the first to see what looked like nothing so much as a little detached bit of the blackness of the Green Forest floating out towards the Smiling Pool. Instantly he stopped singing. Now that was a signal. When he stopped singing, his nearest neighbor stopped singing, then the next one and the next, and in a minute there wasn't a sound from the Smiling Pool save the squeak of Jerry Muskrat hidden among the bulrushes. That great chorus stopped as abruptly as the electric lights go out when you press a button.

Back and forth over the Smiling Pool, this way and that way, floated the shadow, but there was no sign of any living thing in the Smiling Pool. After a while the shadow floated away over the Green Meadows without a sound.

"Hooty the Owl didn't get one of us that time," said Old Mr. Toad to his nearest neighbor with a chuckle of satisfaction. Then he swelled out his music bag and began to sing again. And at once, as abruptly as it had stopped, the great chorus began again as joyous as before, for nothing had happened to bring sadness as might have but for the watchfulness of Old Mr. Toad.

CHAPTER EIGHT: OLD MR. TOAD'S BABIES

The Smiling Pool's a nursery
Where all the sunny day,
A thousand funny babies
Are taught while at their play.

REALLY THE SMILING POOL is a sort of kindergarten, one of the most interesting kindergartens in the world. Little Joe Otter's children learn to swim there. So do Jerry Muskrat's babies and those of Billy Mink, the Trout and Minnow babies, and a lot more. And there you will find the children and grandchildren of Grandfather Frog and Old Mr. Toad.

Peter Rabbit had known for a long time about the Frog babies, but though he knew that Old Mr. Toad was a cousin to Grandfather Frog, he hadn't known anything about Toad babies, except that at a certain time in the year he was forever running across tiny Toads, especially on rainy days, and each little Toad was just like Old Mr. Toad, except for his size.

Peter had heard it said that Toads rain down from the sky, and sometimes it seems as if this must be so. Of course he knew it couldn't be, but it puzzled him a great deal. There wouldn't be a Toad in sight. Then it would begin to rain, and right away there would be so many tiny Toads that it was hard work to jump without stepping on some.

He remembered this as he went to pay his daily call on Old Mr. Toad in the Smiling Pool and listen to his sweet song. He hadn't seen any little Toads this year, but he remembered his experiences with them in other years, and he meant to ask about them.

Old Mr. Toad was sitting in his usual place, but he wasn't singing. He was staring at something in the water. When Peter said "Good morning," Old Mr. Toad didn't seem to hear him. He was too much interested in what he was watching. Peter stared down into the water to see what was interesting Old Mr. Toad so much, but he saw nothing but a lot of wriggling tadpoles.

"What are you staring at so, Mr. Sobersides?" asked Peter, speaking a little louder than before.

Old Mr. Toad turned and looked at Peter, and there was a look of great pride in his face.

"I'm just watching my babies. Aren't they lovely?" said he.

Peter stared harder than ever, but he couldn't see anything that looked like a baby Toad.

"Where are they?" asked he. "I don't see any babies but those of Grandfather

Frog, and if you ask me, I always did think tadpoles about the homeliest things in the world."

Old Mr. Toad grew indignant. "Those are not Grandfather Frog's children; they're mine!" he sputtered. "And I'll have you know that they are the most beautiful babies in the world!"

Peter drew a hand across his mouth to hide a smile. "I beg your pardon, Mr. Toad," said he. "I—I thought all tadpoles were Frog babies. They all look alike to me."

"Well, they're not," declared Old Mr. Toad. "How anyone can mistake my babies for their cousins I cannot understand. Now mine are beautiful, while—"

"Chug-arum!" interrupted the great deep voice of Grandfather Frog. "What are you talking about? Why, your babies are no more to be compared with my babies for real beauty than nothing at all! I'll leave it to Peter if they are."

But Peter wisely held his tongue. To tell the truth, he couldn't see beauty in any of them. To him they were all just wriggling pollywogs. They were more interesting now, because he had found out that some of them were Toads and some were Frogs, and he hadn't known before that baby Toads begin life as tadpoles, but he had no intention of being drawn into the dispute now waxing furious between Grandfather Frog and Old Mr. Toad.

CHAPTER NINE: THE SMILING POOL KINDERGARTEN

Play a little, learn a little,
Grow a little too;
That's what every pollywoggy
Tries his best to do.

OF COURSE THAT'S what a kindergarten is for. And you may be sure that the babies of Grandfather Frog and Old Mr. Toad and Stickytoes the Tree Toad did all of these things in the kindergarten of the Smiling Pool. They looked considerably alike, did these little cousins, for they were all pollywogs to begin with. Peter Rabbit came over every day to watch them. Always he had thought pollywogs just homely, wriggling things, not the least bit interesting, but since he had discovered how proud of them were Grandfather Frog and Old Mr. Toad, he had begun to wonder about them and then to watch them.

"There's one thing about them, and that is they are not in danger the way my babies are," said Peter, talking to himself as is his way when there is no one else to talk to. Just then a funny little black pollywog wriggled into sight, and while Peter was watching him, a stout-jawed water-beetle suddenly rushed from among the water grass, seized the pollywog by his tail, and dragged him down. Peter stared. Could it be that that ugly-looking bug was as dangerous an enemy to the baby Toad as Reddy Fox is to a baby Rabbit? He began to suspect so, and a little later he knew so, for there was that same little pollywog trying hard to swim and making bad work of it, because he had lost half of his long tail.

That set Peter to watching sharper than ever, and presently he discovered that pollywogs have to keep their eyes open quite as much as do baby Rabbits, if they would live to grow up. There were several kinds of queer, ugly-looking bugs forever darting out at the wriggling pollywogs. Hungry-looking fish lay in wait for them, and Longlegs the Blue Heron seemed to have a special liking for them. But the pollywogs were spry, and seemed to have learned to watch out. They seemed to Peter to spend all their time swimming and eating and growing. They grew so fast that it seemed to him that he could almost *see* them grow. And just imagine how surprised Peter was to discover one day that that very pollywog which he had seen lose his tail had grown a *new* one. That puzzled Peter more than anything he had seen in a long time.

"Why, I couldn't do that!" he exclaimed right out loud.

"Do what?" demanded Jerry Muskrat, who happened along just then.

"Why, grow a new tail like that pollywog," replied Peter, and told Jerry all that he had seen. Jerry laughed.

"You'll see queerer things than that if you watch those pollywogs long enough," said he. "They are a queer lot of babies, and very interesting to watch if you've got the time for it. I haven't. This Smiling Pool is a great kindergarten, and there's something happening here every minute. There's no place like it."

"Are those great big fat pollywogs Grandfather Frog's children, or Old Mr. Toad's?" asked Peter,

"Grandfather Frog's last year's children," replied Jerry. "They'll grow into real Frogs this summer, if nothing happens to them."

"Where are Old Mr. Toad's last year's children?" asked Peter.

"Don't ask me," replied Jerry. "They hopped away last summer. Never saw anything like the way those Toad youngsters grow. Those Toad pollywogs you see now will turn into real Toads, and be leaving the Smiling Pool in a few weeks. People think Old Mr. Toad is slow, but there is nothing slow about his children. Look at that little fellow over there; he's begun to grow legs already."

Peter looked, and sure enough there was a pollywog with a pair of legs sprouting out. They were his fore legs, and they certainly did make him look funny. And only a few days before there hadn't been a sign of legs.

"My gracious!" exclaimed Peter. "What a funny sight! I thought my babies grew fast, but these beat them."

CHAPTER TEN: THE LITTLE TOADS
START OUT TO SEE THE WORLD

The world is a wonderful great big place
And in it the young must roam,
To learn what their elders have long since learned—
There's never a place like home.

IT HAD BEEN some time since Peter Rabbit had visited the Smiling Pool to watch the pollywogs. But one cloudy morning he happened to think of them, and decided that he would run over there and see how they were getting along. So off he started, lipperty-lipperty-lip. He wondered if those pollywog children of Old Mr. Toad would be much changed. The last time he saw them some of them had just begun to grow legs, although they still had long tails.

He had almost reached the Smiling Pool when great big drops of rain began to splash down. And with those first raindrops something funny happened. Anyway, it seemed funny to Peter. Right away he was surrounded by tiny little Toads. Everywhere he looked he saw Toads, tiny little Toads just like Old Mr. Toad, only so tiny that one could have sat comfortably on a ten-cent piece and still had plenty of room.

Peter's big eyes grew round with surprise as he stared. Where had they all come from so suddenly? A minute before he hadn't seen a single one, and now he could hardly move without stepping on one. It seemed, it really seemed, as if each raindrop turned into a tiny Toad the instant it struck the ground. Of course Peter knew that that couldn't be, but it was very puzzling. And all those little Toads were bravely hopping along as if they were bound for some particular place.

Peter watched them for a few minutes, then he once more started for the Smiling Pool. On the very bank whom should he meet but Old Mr. Toad. He looked rather thin, and his back was to the Smiling Pool. Yes, Sir, he was hopping away from the Smiling Pool where he had been all the spring, singing in the great chorus. Peter was almost as surprised to see him as he had been to see the little Toads, but just then he was most interested in those little Toads.

"Good morning, Old Mr. Toad," said Peter in his most polite manner. "Can you tell me where all these little Toads came from?"

"Certainly," replied Old Mr. Toad. "They came from the Smiling Pool, of course. Where did you suppose they came from?"

"I—I didn't know. There wasn't one to be seen, and then it began to rain, and right away they were everywhere. It—it almost seemed as if they had rained down out of the sky."

"Can you tell me where all these little Toads came from?"

Old Mr. Toad chuckled. "They've got good sense, if I must say it about my own children," said he. "They know that wet weather is the only weather for Toads to travel in. They left the Smiling Pool in the night while it was damp and comfortable, and then, when the sun came up, they hid, like sensible children, under anything they could find, sticks, stones, pieces of bark, grass. The minute this shower came up, they knew it was good traveling weather and out they popped."

"But what did they leave the Smiling Pool for?" Peter asked.

"To see the Great World," replied Old Mr. Toad. "Foolish, very foolish of them, but they would do it. I did the same thing myself when I was their age. Couldn't stop me any more than I could stop them. They don't know when they're well off, but young folks never do. Fine weather, isn't it?"

CHAPTER ELEVEN: OLD MR. TOAD'S QUEER TONGUE

Old Mother Nature doth provide for all her children, large or small.
Her wisdom foresees all their needs and makes provision for them all.

IF YOU DON'T believe it, just you go ask Old Mr. Toad, as Peter Rabbit did, how such a slow-moving fellow as he is can catch enough bugs and insects to keep him alive.

Perhaps you'll learn something just as Peter did. Peter and Old Mr. Toad sat in the rain watching the tiny Toads, who, you know, were Mr. Toad's children, leaving their kindergarten in the Smiling Pool and starting out to see the Great World.

When the last little Toad had passed them, Old Mr. Toad suddenly remembered that he was hungry, very hungry indeed.

"Didn't have time to eat much while I was in the Smiling Pool," he explained. "Couldn't eat and sing too, and while I was down there, I was supposed to sing. Now that it is time to quit singing, I begin to realize that I've got a stomach to look out for as well as a voice. See that bug over there on that leaf? Watch him."

Peter looked, and sure enough there was a fat bug crawling along on an old leaf. He was about two inches from Old Mr. Toad, and he was crawling very fast. And right while Peter was looking at him he disappeared. Peter turned to look at Old Mr. Toad. He hadn't budged. He was sitting exactly where he had been sitting all the time, but he was smacking his lips, and there was a twinkle of satisfaction in his eyes. Peter opened his eyes very wide. "Wha—what—" he began.

"Nice bug," interrupted Old Mr. Toad. "Nicest bug I've eaten for a long time."

"But I didn't see you catch him!" protested Peter, looking at Old Mr. Toad as if he suspected him of joking.

"Anything wrong with your eyes?" inquired Old Mr. Toad.

"No," replied Peter just a wee bit crossly. "My eyes are just as good as ever."

"Then watch me catch that fly over yonder," said Old Mr. Toad. He hopped towards a fly which had lighted on a blade of grass just ahead. About two inches from it he stopped, and so far as Peter could see, he sat perfectly still. But the fly disappeared, and it wasn't because it flew away, either. Peter was sure of that. As he told Mrs. Peter about it afterwards, "It was there, and then it wasn't, and that was all there was to it."

Old Mr. Toad chuckled. "Didn't you see that one go, Peter?" he asked.

Peter shook his head. "I wish you would stop fooling me," said Peter. "The joke is on me, but now you've had your laugh at my expense, I wish you would tell me how you do it. Please, Mr. Toad."

Now when Peter said please that way, of course Old Mr. Toad couldn't resist him. Nobody could.

"Here comes an ant this way. Now you watch my mouth instead of the ant and see what happens," said Old Mr. Toad.

Peter looked and saw a big black ant coming. Then he kept his eyes on Old Mr. Toad's mouth. Suddenly there was a little flash of red from it, so tiny and so quick that Peter couldn't be absolutely sure that he saw it. But when he looked for the ant, it was nowhere to be seen. Peter looked at Old Mr. Toad very hard.

"Do you mean to tell me, Mr. Toad, that you've got a tongue long enough to reach way over to where that ant was?" he asked.

Old Mr. Toad chuckled again. With every insect swallowed he felt better natured. "You've guessed it, Peter," said he. "Handy tongue, isn't it?"

"I think it's a very queer tongue," retorted Peter, "and I don't understand it at all. If it's so long as all that, where do you keep it when it isn't in use? I should think you'd have to swallow it to get it out of the way, or else leave it hanging out of your mouth."

"Ha, ha, ha, ha, ha!" laughed Old Mr. Toad. "My tongue never is in the way, and it's the handiest tongue in the world. I'll show it to you."

CHAPTER TWELVE: OLD MR. TOAD SHOWS HIS TONGUE

To show one's tongue, as you well know, is not considered nice to do;
But if it were like Mr. Toad's, I'd want to show it—wouldn't you?

I'M QUITE SURE you would. You see, if it were like Old Mr. Toad's, it would be such a wonderful tongue that I suspect you would want everybody to see it. Old Mr. Toad thinks his tongue the most satisfactory tongue in the world. In fact, he is quite sure that without it he couldn't get along at all, and I don't know as he could. And yet very few of his neighbors know anything about that tongue and how different it is from most other tongues. Peter Rabbit didn't until Old Mr. Toad showed him after Peter had puzzled and puzzled over the mysterious way in which bugs and flies disappeared whenever they happened to come within two inches or less of Old Mr. Toad.

What Peter couldn't understand was what Old Mr. Toad did with a tongue that would reach two inches beyond his mouth. He said as much.

"I'll show you my tongue, and then you'll wish you had one just like it," said Old Mr. Toad, with a twinkle in his eyes.

He opened his big mouth and slowly ran his tongue out its full length. "Why! Why-ee!" exclaimed Peter. "It's fastened at the wrong end!"

"No such thing!" replied Old Mr. Toad indignantly. "If it was fastened at the other end, how could I run it out so far?"

"But mine and all other tongues that I ever have seen are fastened way down in the throat," protested Peter. "Yours is fastened at the other end, way in the very front of your mouth. I never heard of such a thing."

"There are a great many things you have never heard of, Peter Rabbit," replied Old Mr. Toad dryly. "Mine is the right way to have a tongue. Because it is fastened way up in the front of my mouth that way, I can use the whole of it. You see it goes out its full length. Then, when I draw it in with a bug on the end of it, I just turn it over so that the end that was out goes way back in my throat and takes the bug with it to just the right place to swallow."

Peter thought this over for a few minutes before he ventured another question.

"I begin to understand," said he, "but how do you hold on to the bug with your tongue?"

"My tongue is sticky, of course, Mr. Stupid," replied Old Mr. Toad, looking very much disgusted. "Just let me touch a bug with it, and he's mine every time."

Peter thought this over. Then he felt of his own tongue. "Mine isn't sticky," said he very innocently.

Old Mr. Toad laughed right out. "Perhaps if it was, you couldn't ask so many questions," said he. "Now watch me catch that fly." His funny little tongue darted out, and the fly was gone.

"It certainly is very handy," said Peter politely. "I think we are going to have more rain, and I'd better be

His funny tongue darted out, and the fly was gone.

getting back to the dear Old Briar-patch. Very much obliged to you, Mr. Toad. I think you are very wonderful."

"Not at all," replied Old Mr. Toad. "I've simply got the things I need in order to live, just as you have the things you need. I couldn't get along with your kind of a tongue, but no more could you get along with mine. If you live long enough, you will learn that Old Mother Nature makes no mistakes. She gives each of us what we need, and each one has different needs."

CHAPTER THIRTEEN: PETER RABBIT IS IMPOLITE

PETER RABBIT COULDN'T get Old Mr. Toad off his mind. He had discovered so many interesting things about Old Mr. Toad that he was almost on the point of believing him to be the most interesting of all his neighbors. And his respect for Old Mr. Toad had become very great indeed. Of course. Who wouldn't respect anyone with such beautiful eyes and such a sweet voice and such a wonderful tongue?

Yet at the same time Peter felt very foolish whenever he remembered that all his life he had been acquainted with Old Mr. Toad without really knowing him at all. There was one comforting thought, and that was that most of his neighbors were just as ignorant regarding Old Mr. Toad as Peter had been.

"Funny," mused Peter, "how we can live right beside people all our lives and not really know them at all. I suppose that is why we should never judge people hastily. I believe I will go hunt up Old Mr. Toad and see if I can find out anything more."

Off started Peter, lipperty-lipperty-lip. He didn't know just where to go, now that Old Mr. Toad had left the Smiling Pool, but he had an idea that he would not be far from their meeting place of the day before, when Old Mr. Toad had explained about his wonderful tongue. But when he got there, Peter found no trace of Old Mr. Toad. You see, it had rained the day before, and that is just the kind of weather that a Toad likes best for traveling. Peter ought to have thought of that, but he didn't. He hunted for a while and finally gave it up and started up the Crooked Little Path with the idea of running over for a call on Johnny Chuck in the Old Orchard.

Jolly, round, bright Mr. Sun was shining his brightest, and Peter soon forgot all about Old Mr. Toad. He scampered along up the Crooked Little Path, thinking of nothing in particular but how good it was to be alive, and occasionally kicking up his heels for pure joy. He had just done this when his ears caught the sound of a queer noise a little to one side of the Crooked Little Path. Instantly Peter stopped and sat up to listen. There it was again, and it seemed to come from under an old piece of board. It was just a little, rustling sound, hardly to be heard.

"There's someone under that old board," thought Peter, and peeped under. All he could see was that there was something moving. Instantly Peter was all curiosity. Whoever was there was not very big. He was sure of that. Of course that meant that he had nothing to fear. So what do you think Peter did? Why, he just pulled that old board over. And when he did that, he saw, whom do you think? Why, Old Mr. Toad, to be sure.

But such a sight as Old Mr. Toad was! Peter just stared. For a full minute he couldn't find his voice. Old Mr. Toad was changing his clothes! Yes, Sir, that is just what Old Mr. Toad was doing. He was taking off his old suit, and under it was a brand new one. But such a time as he was having! He was opening and shutting his big mouth, and drawing his hind legs under him, and rubbing them against his body. Then Peter saw a strange thing. He saw that Old Mr. Toad's old suit had split in several places, and he was getting it off by sucking it into his mouth!

In a few minutes his hind legs were free of the old suit, and little by little it began to be pulled free from his body. All the time Old Mr. Toad was working very hard to suck it at the corners of his big mouth. He glared angrily at Peter, but he couldn't say anything because his mouth was too full. He looked so funny that Peter just threw himself on the ground and rolled over and over with laughter. This made Old Mr. Toad glare more angrily than ever, but he couldn't say anything, not a word.

When he had got his hands free by pulling the sleeves of his old coat off inside out, he used his hands to pull the last of it over his head. Then he gulped very hard two or three times to swallow his old suit, and when the last of it had disappeared, he found his voice.

"Don't you know that it is the most impolite thing in the world to look at people when they are changing their clothes?" he sputtered.

CHAPTER FOURTEEN: OLD MR. TOAD DISAPPEARS

Admit your fault when you've done wrong,
And don't postpone it over long.

PETER RABBIT DIDN'T blame Old Mr. Toad a bit for being indignant because Peter had watched him change his suit. It wasn't a nice thing to do. Old Mr. Toad had looked very funny while he was struggling out of his old suit, and Peter just couldn't help laughing at him. But he realized that he had been very impolite, and he very meekly told Old Mr. Toad so.

"You see, it was this way," explained Peter. "I heard something under that old board, and I just naturally turned it over to find out what was there."

"Hump!" grunted Old Mr. Toad.

"I didn't have the least idea that you were there," continued Peter. "When I found who it was, and what you were doing, I couldn't help watching because it was so interesting, and I couldn't help laughing because you really did look so funny. But I'm sorry, Mr. Toad. Truly I am. I didn't mean to be so impolite. I promise never to do it again. I don't suppose, Mr. Toad, that it seems at all wonderful to you that you can change your suit that way, but it does to me. I had heard that you swallowed your old suits, but I never half believed it. Now I know it is so and just how you do it, and I feel as if I had learned something worth knowing. Do you know, I think you are one of the most interesting and wonderful of all my neighbors, and I'll never laugh at or tease you again, Mr. Toad."

"Hump!" grunted Old Mr. Toad again, but it was very clear that he was a little flattered by Peter's interest in him and was rapidly recovering his good nature.

"There is one thing I don't understand yet," said Peter, "and that is where you go to sleep all winter. Do you go down into the mud at the bottom of the Smiling Pool the way Grandfather Frog does?"

"Certainly not!" retorted Old Mr. Toad. "Use your common sense, Peter Rabbit. If I had spent the winter in the Smiling Pool, do you suppose I would have left it to come way up here and then have turned right around and gone back there to sing? I'm not so fond of long journeys as all that."

"That's so." Peter looked foolish. "I didn't think of that when I spoke."

"The trouble with you, and with a lot of other people, is that you speak first and do your thinking afterward, when you do any thinking at all," grunted Old Mr. Toad. "Now if I wanted to, I could disappear right here."

"You mean that you would hide under that old board just as you did before," said Peter, with a very wise look.

"Nothing of the sort!" snapped Old Mr. Toad. "I could disappear and not go near that old board, not a step nearer than I am now."

Peter looked in all directions carefully, but not a thing could he see under which Old Mr. Toad could possibly hide except the old board, and he had said he wouldn't hide under that. "I don't like to doubt your word, Mr. Toad," said he, "but you'll have to show me before I can believe that."

Old Mr. Toad's eyes twinkled. Here was a chance to get even with Peter for watching him change his suit. "If you'll turn your back to me and look straight down the Crooked Little Path for five minutes, I'll disappear," said he. "More than that, I give you my word of honor that I will not hop three feet from where I am sitting."

"All right," replied Peter promptly, turning his back to Old Mr. Toad. "I'll look down the Crooked Little Path for five minutes and promise not to peek."

So Peter sat and gazed straight down the Crooked Little Path. It was a great temptation to roll his eyes back and peep behind him, but he had given his word that he wouldn't, and he didn't. When he thought the five minutes were up, he turned around. Old Mr. Toad was nowhere to be seen. Peter looked hastily this way and that way, but there was not a sign of Old Mr. Toad. He had disappeared as completely as if he never had been there.

CHAPTER FIFTEEN: OLD MR. TOAD GIVES PETER A SCARE

If you play pranks on other folks you may be sure that they,
Will take the first chance that they get a joke on you to play.

OLD MR. TOAD was getting even with Peter for laughing at him. While Peter's back had been turned, Old Mr. Toad had disappeared.

It was too much for Peter. Look as he would, he couldn't see so much as a chip under which Old Mr. Toad might have hidden, excepting the old board, and Old

Mr. Toad had given his word of honor that he wouldn't hide under that. Nevertheless, Peter hopped over to it and turned it over again, because he couldn't think of any other place to look. Of course, Old Mr. Toad wasn't there. Of course not. He had given his word that he wouldn't hide there, and he always lives up to his word. Peter should have known better than to have looked there.

Old Mr. Toad had also said that he would not go three feet from the spot where he was sitting at the time, so Peter should have known better than to have raced up the Crooked Little Path as he did. But if Old Mr. Toad had nothing to hide under, of course he must have hopped away, reasoned Peter. He couldn't hop far in five minutes, that was sure, and so Peter ran this way and that way a great deal farther than it would have been possible for Old Mr. Toad to have gone. But it was a wholly useless search, and presently Peter returned and sat down on the very spot where he had last seen Old Mr. Toad. Peter never had felt more foolish in all his life. He began to think that Old Mr. Toad must be bewitched and had some strange power of making himself invisible.

For a long time Peter sat perfectly still, trying to puzzle out how Old Mr. Toad had disappeared, but the more he puzzled over it, the more impossible it seemed. And yet Old Mr. Toad had disappeared. Suddenly Peter gave a frightened scream and jumped higher than he ever had jumped before in all his life. A voice, the voice of Old Mr. Toad himself, had said, "Well, now are you satisfied?" *And that voice had come from right under Peter!* Do you wonder that he was frightened? When he turned to look, there sat Old Mr. Toad right where he himself had been sitting a moment before. Peter rubbed his eyes and stared very foolishly.

"Wh—wh—where did you come from?" he stammered at last.

Old Mr. Toad grinned. "I'll show you," said he. And right while Peter was looking at him, he began to sink down into the ground until only the top of his head could be seen. Then that disappeared. Old Mr. Toad had gone down, and the sand had fallen right back over him. Peter just had to rub his eyes again. He had to! Then, to make sure, he began to dig away the sand where Old Mr. Toad had been sitting. In a minute he felt Old Mr. Toad, who at once came out again.

Old Mr. Toad's beautiful eyes twinkled more than ever. "I guess we are even now, Peter," said he.

Peter nodded. "More than that, Mr. Toad. I think you have a little the best of it," he replied. "Now won't you tell me how you did it?"

Old Mr. Toad held up one of his stout hind feet, and on it was a kind of spur. "There's another just like that on the other foot," said he, "and I use them to dig with. You go into a hole head-first, but I go in the other way. I make my hole in soft earth and back into it at the same time, this way." He began to work his stout hind feet, and as he kicked the earth out, he backed in at the same time. When he was deep enough, the earth just fell back over him, for you see it was very loose and not packed down at all. When he once more reappeared, Peter thanked him. Then he asked one more question.

"Is that the way you go into winter quarters?"

Old Mr. Toad nodded. "And it's the way I escape from my enemies."

CHAPTER SIXTEEN: JIMMY SKUNK IS SURPRISED

JIMMY SKUNK AMBLED along the Crooked Little Path down the hill. He didn't hurry because Jimmy doesn't believe in hurrying. The only time he ever hurries is when he sees a fat beetle trying to get out of sight. Then Jimmy *does* hurry. But just now he didn't see any fat beetles, although he was looking for them. So he just ambled along as if he had all the time in the world, as indeed he had. He was feeling very good-natured, was Jimmy Skunk. And why shouldn't he? There was everything to make him feel good-natured. Summer had arrived to stay. On every side he heard glad voices. Bumble the Bee was humming a song. Best of all, Jimmy had found three beetles that very morning, and he knew that there were more if he could find them. So why shouldn't he feel good?

Jimmy had laughed at Peter Rabbit for being so anxious for Summer to arrive, but he was just as glad as Peter that she had come, although he wouldn't have said so for the world. His sharp little eyes twinkled as he ambled along, and there wasn't much that they missed. As he walked he talked, quite to himself of course, because there was nobody near to hear, and this is what he was saying:

> "Beetle, beetle, smooth and smug,
> You are nothing but a bug.
> Bugs were made for Skunks to eat,
> So come out from your retreat.

"Hello! There's a nice big piece of bark over there that looks as if it ought to have a dozen fat beetles under it. It's great fun to pull over pieces of bark and see fat beetles run all ways at once. I'll just have to see what is under that piece."

Jimmy tiptoed softly over to the big piece of bark, and then as he made ready to turn it over, he began again that foolish little verse.

> "Beetle, beetle, smooth and smug,
> You are nothing but a bug."

As he said the last word, he suddenly pulled the piece of bark over.

"Who's a bug?" asked a funny voice, and it sounded rather cross. Jimmy Skunk nearly tumbled over backward in surprise, and for a minute he couldn't find his tongue. There, instead of the fat beetles he had been so sure of, sat Old Mr. Toad, and he didn't look at all pleased.

"Who's a bug?" he repeated.

Instead of answering, Jimmy Skunk began to laugh. "Who's a bug?" demanded Old Mr. Toad, more crossly than before.

"There isn't any bug, Mr. Toad, and I beg your pardon," replied Jimmy, remembering his politeness. "I just thought there was. You see, I didn't know you were under that piece of bark. I hope you will excuse me, Mr. Toad. Have you seen any fat beetles this morning?"

"No," said Old Mr. Toad grumpily, and yawned and rubbed his eyes.

"Why," exclaimed Jimmy Skunk, "I believe you have just waked up!"

"What if I have?" demanded Old Mr. Toad.

"Oh, nothing, nothing at all, Mr. Toad," replied Jimmy Skunk, "only you are the second one I've met this morning who had just waked up."

"Who was the other?" asked Old Mr. Toad.

"Mr. Blacksnake," replied Jimmy. "He inquired for you."

Old Mr. Toad turned quite pale. "I—I think I'll be moving along," said he.

CHAPTER SEVENTEEN: OLD MR. TOAD'S MISTAKE

IF IS A very little word to look at, but the biggest word you have ever seen doesn't begin to have so much meaning as little "if." If Jimmy Skunk hadn't ambled down the Crooked Little Path just when he did; if he hadn't been looking for fat beetles; if he hadn't seen that big piece of bark at one side and decided to pull it over; if it hadn't been for all these "ifs," why Old Mr. Toad wouldn't have made the mistake he did, and you wouldn't have had this story. But Jimmy Skunk did amble down the Crooked Little Path, he did look for beetles, and he did pull over that big piece of bark. And when he had pulled it over, he found Old Mr. Toad there.

Old Mr. Toad had crept under that piece of bark because he wanted to take a nap. But when Jimmy Skunk told him that he had seen Mr. Blacksnake that very morning, and that Mr. Blacksnake had asked after Old Mr. Toad, the very last bit of sleepiness left Old Mr. Toad. Yes, Sir, he was wide awake right away. You see, he knew right away why Mr. Blacksnake had asked after him. He knew that Mr. Blacksnake has a fondness for Toads. He turned quite pale when he heard that Mr. Blacksnake had asked after him, and right then he made his mistake. He was in such a hurry to get away from that neighborhood that he forgot to ask Jimmy Skunk just where he had seen Mr. Blacksnake. He hardly waited long enough to say good-bye to Jimmy Skunk, but started off as fast as he could go.

Now it just happened that Old Mr. Toad started up the Crooked Little Path, and it just happened that Mr. Blacksnake was coming down the Crooked Little Path. Now when people are very much afraid, they almost always seem to think that danger is behind instead of in front of them. It was so with Old Mr. Toad. Instead of watching out in front as he hopped along, he kept watching over his shoulder, and that was his second mistake. He was so sure that Mr. Blacksnake was somewhere behind him that he didn't look to see where he was going, and you know that people who don't look to see where they are going are almost sure to go head-first right into trouble.

Old Mr. Toad went hopping up the Crooked Little Path as fast as he could, which wasn't very fast because he never can hop very fast. And all the time he kept looking behind for Mr. Blacksnake. Presently he came to a turn in the Crooked Little Path, and as he hurried around it, he almost ran into Mr. Blacksnake himself. It was a question which was more surprised. For just a wee second they stared at each other. Then Mr. Blacksnake's eyes began to sparkle.

"Good morning, Mr. Toad. Isn't this a beautiful morning? I was just thinking about you," said he.

But poor Old Mr. Toad didn't say good morning. He didn't say anything. He couldn't, because he was too scared. He just gave a frightened little squeal, turned around, and started down the Crooked Little Path twice as fast as he had come up. Mr. Blacksnake grinned and started after him, not very fast because he knew that he wouldn't have to run very fast to catch Old Mr. Toad, and he thought the exercise would do him good.

And this is how it happened that summer morning that jolly, bright Mr. Sun, looking down from the blue, blue sky and smiling to see how happy everybody seemed, suddenly discovered that there was one of the little meadow people who wasn't happy, but instead was terribly, terribly unhappy. It was Old Mr. Toad hopping down the Crooked Little Path for his life, while after him, and getting nearer and nearer, glided Mr. Blacksnake.

CHAPTER EIGHTEEN: JIMMY SKUNK IS JUST IN TIME

JIMMY SKUNK AMBLED slowly along, chuckling as he thought of what a hurry Mr. Toad had been in, when he had heard that Mr. Blacksnake had asked after him. It had been funny, very funny indeed, to see Mr. Toad try to hurry.

Suddenly Jimmy stopped chuckling. Then he stopped ambling along the Crooked Little Path. He turned around and looked back, and as he did so he scratched his head thoughtfully. He had just happened to think that Old Mr. Toad had gone up the Crooked Little Path, and it was up the Crooked Little Path that Mr. Blacksnake had shown himself that morning.

"If he's still up there," thought Jimmy, "Old Mr. Toad is hopping right straight into the very worst kind of trouble. How stupid of him not to have asked me where Mr. Blacksnake was! Well, it's none of my business. I guess I'll go on."

But he had gone on down the Crooked Little Path only a few steps when he stopped again. You see, Jimmy is really a very kind-hearted little fellow, and somehow he didn't like to think of what might happen to Old Mr. Toad.

"I hate to go way back there," he grumbled, for you know he is naturally rather lazy. "Still, the Green Meadows wouldn't be quite the same without Old Mr. Toad. I should miss him if anything happened to him. I suppose it would be partly my fault, too, for if I hadn't pulled over that piece of bark, he probably would have stayed there the rest of the day and been safe."

"Maybe he won't meet Mr. Blacksnake," said a little voice inside of Jimmy.

"And maybe he will," said Jimmy right out loud. And with that, he started back up the Crooked Little Path, and strange to say Jimmy hurried.

He had just reached a turn in the Crooked Little Path when who should run right plump into him but poor Old Mr. Toad. He gave a frightened squeal and fell right over on his back, and kicked foolishly as he tried to get on his feet again. But he was all out of breath, and so frightened and tired that all he could do was to kick and kick. He hadn't seen Jimmy at all, for he had been looking behind him, and he didn't even know who it was he had run into.

Right behind him came Mr. Blacksnake. Of course he saw Jimmy, and he stopped short and hissed angrily.

"What were you going to do to Mr. Toad?" demanded Jimmy.

"None of your business!" hissed Mr. Blacksnake. "Get out of my way, or you'll be sorry."

Jimmy Skunk just laughed and stepped in front of poor Old Mr. Toad. Mr. Blacksnake coiled himself up in the path and darted his tongue out at Jimmy in the most impudent way. Then he tried to make himself look very fierce. Then he jumped straight at Jimmy Skunk with his mouth wide open, but he took great care not to jump quite far enough to reach Jimmy. You see, he was just trying to scare Jimmy. But Jimmy didn't scare. He knows all about Mr. Blacksnake and that really he is a coward. So he suddenly gritted his teeth in a way not at all pleasant to hear and started for Mr. Blacksnake. Mr. Blacksnake didn't wait. No, Sir, he didn't wait. He suddenly turned and glided back up the Crooked Little Path, hissing angrily. Jimmy followed him a little way, and then he went back to Old Mr. Toad.

"Oh," panted Mr. Toad, "you came just in time! I couldn't have hopped another hop."

"I guess I did," replied Jimmy. "Now you get your breath and come along with me." And Old Mr. Toad did.

CHAPTER NINETEEN: OLD MR. TOAD GETS HIS STOMACH FULL

Pray do not tip your nose in scorn at things which others eat,
For things to you not good at all to others are most sweet.

THERE ARE ANTS, for instance. You wouldn't want to eat them even if you were dreadfully hungry. But Old Mr. Toad and Buster Bear think there is nothing much nicer. Now Buster Bear had found Old Mr. Toad catching ants, one at a time, as he kept watch beside their home, and it had pleased Buster to find someone else who liked ants. Right away he invited Old Mr. Toad to dine with him. But poor Old Mr. Toad was frightened almost to death when he heard the deep, grumbly-rumbly voice of Buster Bear, for he had been so busy watching the ants that he hadn't seen Buster coming.

He fell right over on his back, which wasn't at all dignified, and made Buster Bear laugh. That frightened Mr. Toad more than ever. You see he didn't have the least doubt in the world that Buster Bear meant to eat him, and when Buster invited him to dinner, he was sure that that was just a joke on Buster's part.

But there was no way to escape, and after a little bit Old Mr. Toad thought it best to be polite, because, you know, it always pays to be polite. So he said in a very faint voice that he would be pleased to dine with Buster. Then he waved his feet feebly, trying to get on his feet again. Buster Bear laughed harder than ever. It was a low, deep, grumbly-rumbly laugh, and sent cold shivers all over poor Old Mr. Toad. But when Buster reached out a great paw with great cruel-looking claws Mr. Toad quite gave up. He didn't have strength enough left to even kick. He just closed his eyes and waited for the end.

What do you think happened? Why, he was rolled over on to his feet so gently that he just gasped with surprise. It didn't seem possible that such a great paw could be so gentle.

"Now," said Buster Bear in a voice which he tried to make sound pleasant, but which was grumbly-rumbly just the same, "I know where there is a fine dinner waiting for us just a little way from here. You follow me, and we'll have it in no time."

So Buster Bear led the way, and Old Mr. Toad followed as fast as he could, because he didn't dare not to. Presently Buster stopped beside a big decayed old log. "If you are ready, Mr. Toad, we will dine now," said he.

Old Mr. Toad didn't see anything to eat. His heart sank again, and he shook all over. "I—I'm not hungry," said he in a very faint voice.

Buster Bear didn't seem to hear. He hooked his great claws into the old log and gave a mighty pull. Over rolled the log, and there were ants and ants and ants, hurrying this way and scurrying that way, more ants than Mr. Toad had seen in all his life before!

"Help yourself," said Buster Bear politely.

Old Mr. Toad didn't wait to be told twice. He forgot all about his fright. He forgot all about Buster Bear. He forgot that he wasn't hungry. He forgot his manners. He jumped right in among those ants, and for a little while he was the busiest Toad ever seen. Buster Bear was busy too. He swept his long tongue this way, and he swept it that way, and each time he drew it back into his mouth, it was covered with ants. At last Old Mr. Toad couldn't hold another ant. Then he remembered Buster Bear and looked up a little fearfully. Buster was smacking his lips, and there was a twinkle in each eye.

"Good, aren't they?" said he.

"The best I ever ate," declared Old Mr. Toad with a sigh of satisfaction.

"Come dine with me again," said Buster Bear, and somehow this time Old Mr. Toad didn't mind that his voice sounded grumbly-rumbly.

"Thank you, I will," replied Old Mr. Toad.

CHAPTER TWENTY: OLD MR. TOAD IS PUFFED UP

OLD MR. TOAD hopped slowly down the Lone Little Path. He usually does hop slowly, but this time he hopped slower than ever. You see, he was so puffed up that he couldn't have hopped fast if he had wanted to, and he didn't want to. In the first place his stomach was so full of ants that there wasn't room for another one. No, Sir, Old Mr. Toad couldn't have swallowed another ant if he had tried. Of course they made his stomach stick out, but it wasn't the ants that puffed him out all over. Oh, my, no! It was pride. That's what it was—pride. You know nothing can puff anyone up quite like foolish pride.

Old Mr. Toad was old enough to have known better. It is bad enough to see young and foolish creatures puffed up with pride, but it is worse to see anyone as old as Old Mr. Toad that way. He held his head so high that he couldn't see his own feet, and more than once he stubbed his toes. Presently he met his old friend, Danny Meadow Mouse. He tipped his head a little higher, puffed himself out a little more, and pretended not to see Danny.

"Hello, Mr. Toad," said Danny.

Mr. Toad pretended not to hear. Danny looked puzzled. Then he spoke again, and this time he shouted: "Hello, Mr. Toad! I haven't seen you for some time."

It wouldn't do to pretend not to hear this time. "Oh, how do you do, Danny?"

said Old Mr. Toad with a very grand air, and pretending to be much surprised. "Sorry I can't stop, but I've been dining with my friend, Buster Bear, and now I must get home." When he mentioned the name of Buster Bear, he puffed himself out a little more.

Danny grinned as he watched him hop on down the Lone Little Path. "Can't talk with common folks any more," he muttered. "I've heard that pride is very apt to turn people's heads, but I never expected to see Old Mr. Toad proud."

Mr. Toad kept on his way, and presently he met Peter Rabbit. Peter stopped to gossip, as is his way. But Old Mr. Toad took no notice of him at all. He kept right on with his head high, and all puffed out. Peter might have been a stick or a stone for all the notice Old Mr. Toad took of him. Peter looked puzzled. Then he hurried down to tell Danny Meadow Mouse about it.

"Oh," said Danny, "he's been to dine with Buster Bear, and now he has no use for his old friends."

Pretty soon along came Johnny Chuck, and he was very much put out because he had been treated by Old Mr. Toad just as Peter Rabbit had. Striped Chipmunk told the same story. So did Unc' Billy Possum. It was the same with all of Old Mr. Toad's old friends and neighbors, excepting Bobby Coon, who, you know, is Buster Bear's little cousin. To him Old Mr. Toad was very polite and talked a great deal about Buster Bear, and thought that Bobby must be very proud to be related to Buster.

At first everybody thought it a great joke to see Old Mr. Toad so puffed up with pride, but after a little they grew tired of being snubbed by their old friend and neighbor, and began to say unpleasant things about him. Then they decided that

"Can't talk with common folks any more," he muttered.

what Old Mr. Toad needed was a lesson, so they put their heads together and planned how they would teach Old Mr. Toad how foolish it is for anyone to be puffed up with pride.

CHAPTER TWENTY-ONE: OLD MR. TOAD RECEIVES ANOTHER INVITATION

THE FRIENDS AND neighbors of Old Mr. Toad decided that he needed to be taught a lesson. At first, you know, everyone had laughed at him, because he had grown too proud to speak to them, but after a little they grew tired of being treated so, and some of them put their heads together to think of some plan to teach Old Mr. Toad a lesson and what a very, very foolish thing false pride is. The very next day Jimmy Skunk went into the Green Forest to look for Buster Bear. You know Jimmy isn't afraid of Buster. He didn't have to look long, and when he had found him, the very first thing he did was to ask Buster if he had seen any fat beetles that morning. You know Jimmy is very fond of fat beetles, and the first thing he asks anyone he may happen to meet is if they have seen any.

Buster Bear grinned and said he thought he knew where there might be a few, and he would be pleased to have Jimmy go with him to see. Sure enough, under an old log he found five fat beetles, and these Jimmy gobbled up without even asking Buster if he would have one. Jimmy is usually very polite, but this time he quite forgot politeness. I am afraid he is rather apt to when fat beetles are concerned. But Buster didn't seem to mind. When the last beetle had disappeared Jimmy smacked his lips, and then he told Buster Bear what he had come for. Of course, at first Buster had thought it was for the fat beetles. But it wasn't. No, Sir, it wasn't for the fat beetles at all. It was to get Buster Bear's help in a plan to teach Old Mr. Toad a lesson.

First Jimmy told Buster all about how puffed up Old Mr. Toad was because he had dined with Buster, and how ever since then he had refused even to speak to his old friends and neighbors. It tickled Buster Bear so to think that little homely Old Mr. Toad could be proud of anything that he laughed and laughed, and his laugh was deep and grumbly-rumbly. Then Jimmy told him the plan to teach Old Mr. Toad a lesson and asked Buster if he would help. Buster's eyes twinkled as he promised to do what Jimmy asked.

Then Jimmy went straight to where Old Mr. Toad was sitting all puffed up, taking a sun-bath.

"Buster Bear has just sent word by me to ask if you will honor him by dining with him tomorrow at the rotted chestnut stump near the edge of the Green Forest," said Jimmy in his politest manner.

Now if Old Mr. Toad was puffed up before, just think how he swelled out when he heard that. Jimmy Skunk was actually afraid that he would burst.

"You may tell my friend, Buster Bear, that I shall be very happy to honor him by dining with him," replied Old Mr. Toad with a very grand air.

Jimmy went off to deliver his reply, and Old Mr. Toad sat and puffed himself out until he could hardly breathe. "Honor him by dining with him," said he over and over to himself. "I never was so flattered in my life."

CHAPTER TWENTY-TWO: OLD MR. TOAD LEARNS A LESSON

Pride is like a great big bubble; you'll find there's nothing in it.
Prick it and for all your trouble it has vanished in a minute.

OLD MR. TOAD was so puffed out with pride as he started for the Green Forest to dine with Buster Bear that those who saw him wondered if he wouldn't burst before he got there. Everybody knew where he was going, and this made Old Mr. Toad feel more important and proud than ever. He might not have felt quite so puffed up if he had known just how it had come about that he received this second invitation to dine with Buster Bear. When Jimmy Skunk brought it to him, Jimmy didn't tell him that Buster had been asked to send the invitation, and that it was all part of a plan on the part of some of Old Mr. Toad's old friends and neighbors to teach him a lesson. No, indeed, Jimmy didn't say anything at all about that!

So Old Mr. Toad went hopping along and stumbling over his own feet, because his head was held so high and he was so puffed out that he couldn't see where he was going. He could think of nothing but how important Buster Bear must consider him to invite him to dinner a second time, and of the delicious ants he was sure he would have to eat.

"What very good taste Buster Bear has," thought he, "and how very fortunate it is that he found out that I also am fond of ants."

He was so busy with these pleasant thoughts of the good dinner that he expected to have that he took no notice of what was going on about him. He didn't see his old friends and neighbors peeping out at him and laughing because he looked so foolish and silly. He was dressed in his very best, which was nothing at all to be proud of, for you know Old Mr. Toad has no fine clothes. And being puffed up so, he was homelier than ever, which is saying a great deal, for at best Mr. Toad is anything but handsome.

He was beginning to get pretty tired by the time he reached the Green Forest and came in sight of the rotted old chestnut stump where he was to meet Buster Bear.

Buster was waiting for him. "How do you do this fine day? You look a little tired and rather warm, Mr. Toad," said he.

"I am a little warm," replied Mr. Toad in his most polite manner, although he couldn't help panting for breath as he said it. "I hope you are feeling as well as you are looking, Mr. Bear."

Buster Bear laughed a great, grumbly-rumbly laugh. "I always feel fine when there is a dinner of fat ants ready for me," said he. "It is fine of you to honor me by coming to dine."

Here Mr. Toad put one hand on his stomach and tried to make a very grand bow. Peter Rabbit, hiding behind a near-by tree, almost giggled aloud, he looked so funny.

"I have ventured to invite another to enjoy the dinner with us," continued Buster Bear. Mr. Toad's face fell. You see he was selfish. He wanted to be the only one to have the honor of dining with Buster Bear. "He's a little late," went on Buster, "but I think he will be here soon, and I hope you will be glad to meet him. Ah, there he comes now!"

Old Mr. Toad looked in the direction in which Buster Bear was looking. He gave a little gasp and turned quite pale. All his puffiness disappeared. He didn't look like the same Toad at all. The newcomer was Mr. Blacksnake. "Oh!" cried Old Mr. Toad, and then, without even asking to be excused, he turned his back on Buster Bear and started back the way he had come, with long, frightened hops.

"Ha, ha, ha!" shouted Peter Rabbit, jumping out from behind a tree.

"Ho, ho, ho!" shouted Jimmy Skunk from behind another.

"Hee, hee, hee!" shouted Johnny Chuck from behind a third.

"I am a little warm," replied Mr. Toad
in his most polite manner.

Then Old Mr. Toad knew that his old friends and neighbors had planned this to teach him a lesson.

CHAPTER TWENTY-THREE: OLD MR. TOAD IS VERY HUMBLE

WHEN OLD MR. TOAD saw Mr. Blacksnake and turned his back on Buster Bear and the fine dinner to which Buster had invited him, he had but just one idea in his head, and that was to get out of sight of Mr. Blacksnake as soon as possible. He forgot to ask Buster Bear to excuse him. He forgot that he was tired and hot. He forgot all the pride with which he had been so puffed up. He forgot everything but the need of getting out of sight of Mr. Blacksnake as soon as ever he could. So away went Old Mr. Toad, hop, hop, hipperty-hop, hop, hop, hipperty-hop! He heard Peter Rabbit and Jimmy Skunk and Johnny Chuck and others of his old friends and neighbors shouting with laughter. Yes, and he heard the deep, grumbly-rumbly laugh of Buster Bear. But he didn't mind it. Not then, anyway. He hadn't room for any feeling except fear of Mr. Blacksnake.

But Old Mr. Toad had to stop after a while. You see, his legs were so tired they just wouldn't go any longer. And he was so out of breath that he wheezed. He crawled under a big piece of bark, and there he lay flat on the ground and panted and panted for breath. He would stay there until jolly, round, bright Mr. Sun went to bed behind the Purple Hills. Then Mr. Blacksnake would go to bed too, and it would be safe for him to go home. Now, lying there in the dark, for it was dark under that big piece of bark, Old Mr. Toad had time to think. Little by little he began to understand that his invitation to dine with Buster Bear had been part of a plan by his old friends and neighbors whom he had so snubbed and looked down on when he had been puffed up with pride, to teach him a lesson. At first he was angry, very angry indeed. Then he began to see how foolish and silly he had been, and shame took the place of anger. As he remembered the deep, grumbly-rumbly laughter of Buster Bear, the feeling of shame grew.

"I deserve it," thought Old Mr. Toad. "Yes, Sir, I deserve every bit of it. The only thing that I have to be proud of is that I'm honest and work for my living. Yes, Sir, that's all."

When darkness came at last, and he crawled out to go home, he was feeling very humble. Peter Rabbit happened along just then. Old Mr. Toad opened his mouth to speak, but Peter suddenly threw his head up very high and strutted past as if he didn't see Old Mr. Toad at all. Mr. Toad gulped and went on. Pretty soon he met Jimmy Skunk. Jimmy went right on about his business and actually stepped right over Old Mr. Toad as if he had been a stick or a stone. Old Mr. Toad gulped again and went on. The next day he went down to see Danny Meadow Mouse. He meant to tell Danny how ashamed he was for the way he had treated Danny and his other friends. But Danny brushed right past without even a glance at him. Old Mr. Toad gulped and started up to see Johnny Chuck. The same thing happened again. So it did when he met Striped Chipmunk.

At last Old Mr. Toad gave up and went home, where he sat under a big mullein leaf the rest of the day, feeling very miserable and lonely. He didn't have appetite enough to snap at a single fly. Late that afternoon he heard a little noise and looked up to find all his old friends and neighbors forming a circle around him. Suddenly they began to dance and shout:

> *"Old Mr. Toad is a jolly good fellow!*
> *His temper is sweet, disposition is mellow!*
> *And now that his bubble of pride is quite busted,*
> *We know that he knows that his friends can be trusted."*

Then Old Mr. Toad knew that all was well once more, and presently he began to dance too, the funniest dance that ever was seen.

This is all for now about homely Old Mr. Toad, because I have just got to tell you about another homely fellow—Prickly Porky the Porcupine—who carries a thousand little spears. The next book will tell you all about his adventures.

The Adventures of Prickly Porky

CHAPTER ONE: HAPPY JACK SQUIRREL MAKES A FIND

HAPPY JACK SQUIRREL had had a wonderful day. He had found some big chestnut trees that he had never seen before, and which promised to give him all the nuts he would want for all the next winter. Now he was thinking of going home, for it was getting late in the afternoon. He looked out across the open field where Mr. Goshawk had nearly caught him that morning. His home was on the other side.

"It's a long way 'round," said Happy Jack to himself, "but it is best to be safe and sure."

So Happy Jack started on his long journey around the open field. Now, Happy Jack's eyes are bright, and there is very little that Happy Jack does not see. So, as he was jumping from one tree to another, he spied something down on the ground which excited his curiosity.

"I must stop and see what that is," said Happy Jack. So down the tree he ran, and in a few minutes he had found the queer thing, which had caught his eyes. It was smooth and black and white, and at one end it was very sharp with a tiny little barb. Happy Jack found it out by pricking himself with it.

"Ooch," he cried, and dropped the queer thing. Pretty soon he noticed there were a lot more on the ground.

"I wonder what they are," said Happy Jack. "They don't grow, for they haven't any roots. They are not thorns, for there is no plant from which they could come. They are not alive, so what can they be?"

Now, Happy Jack's eyes are bright, but sometimes he doesn't use them to the very best advantage. He was so busy examining the queer things on the ground that he never once thought to look up in the tops of the trees. If he had, perhaps he would not have been so much puzzled. As it was he just gathered up three or four of the queer things and started on again. On the way he met Peter Rabbit and showed Peter what he had. Now, you know Peter Rabbit is very curious. He just couldn't sit still, but must scamper over to the place Happy Jack Squirrel told him about.

"You'd better be careful, Peter Rabbit, they're very sharp," shouted Happy Jack.

But as usual, Peter was in too much of a hurry to heed what was said to him. Lipperty-lipperty-lip, lipperty-lipperty-lip, went Peter Rabbit through the woods, as fast as his long legs would take him. Then suddenly he squealed and sat down to nurse one of his feet. But he was up again in a flash with another squeal louder than before. Peter Rabbit had found the queer things that Happy Jack Squirrel had told him about. One was sticking in his foot, and one was in the white patch on the seat of his trousers.

CHAPTER TWO: THE STRANGER FROM THE NORTH

THE MERRY LITTLE BREEZES of Old Mother West Wind were excited. Yes, Sir, they certainly were excited. They had met Happy Jack Squirrel and Peter Rabbit, and they were full of the news of the queer things that Happy Jack and Peter Rabbit had found over in the Green Forest. They hurried this way and that way over the Green Meadows and told everyone they met. Finally they reached the Smiling Pool and excitedly told Grandfather Frog all about it.

Grandfather Frog smoothed down his white and yellow waistcoat and looked very wise, for you know that Grandfather Frog is very old.

"Pooh," said Grandfather Frog. "I know what they are."

"What?" cried all the Merry Little Breezes together. "Happy Jack says he is sure they do not grow, for there are no strange plants over there."

Grandfather Frog opened his big mouth and snapped up a foolish green fly that one of the Merry Little Breezes blew over to him.

"Chug-a-rum," said Grandfather Frog. "Things do not have to be on plants in order to grow. Now I am sure that those things grew, and that they did not grow on a plant."

The Merry Little Breezes looked puzzled. "What is there that grows and doesn't grow on a plant?" asked one of them.

"How about the claws on Peter Rabbit's toes and the hair of Happy Jack's tail?" asked Grandfather Frog.

The Merry Little Breezes looked foolish. "Of course," they cried. "We didn't think of that. But we are quite sure that these queer things that prick so are not claws, and certainly they are not hair."

"Don't you be too sure," said Grandfather Frog. "You go over to the Green Forest and look up in the treetops instead of down on the ground; then come back and tell me what you find."

Away raced the Merry Little Breezes to the Green Forest and began to search among the treetops. Presently, way up in the top of a big poplar, they found a stranger. He was bigger than any of the little meadow people, and he had long sharp teeth with which he was stripping the bark from the tree. The hair of his coat was long, and out of it peeped a thousand little spears just like the queer things that Happy Jack and Peter Rabbit had told them about.

"Good morning," said the Merry Little Breezes politely.

"Mornin'," grunted the stranger in the treetop.

"May we ask where you come from?" said one of the Merry Little Breezes politely.

"I come from the North Woods," said the stranger and then went on about his business, which seemed to be to strip every bit of the bark from the tree and eat it.

CHAPTER THREE: PRICKLY PORKY MAKES FRIENDS

THE MERRY LITTLE BREEZES soon spread the news over the Green Meadows and through the Green Forest that a stranger had come from the North. At once all the little meadow people and forest folk made some excuse to go over to the big poplar tree where the stranger was so busy eating. At first he was very shy and had nothing to say. He was a queer fellow, and he was so big, and his teeth were so sharp and so long, that his visitors kept their distance.

"Pooh," exclaimed Reddy Fox.
"Who's afraid of that fellow?"

Reddy Fox, who, you know, is a great boaster and likes to brag of how smart he is and how brave he is, came with the rest of the little meadow people.

"Pooh," exclaimed Reddy Fox. "Who's afraid of that fellow?"

Just then the stranger began to come down the tree. Reddy backed away.

"It looks as if you were afraid, Reddy Fox," said Peter Rabbit.

"I'm not afraid of anything," said Reddy Fox, and swelled himself up to look twice as big as he really is.

"It seems to me I hear Bowser the Hound," piped up Striped Chipmunk.

Now Striped Chipmunk had not heard Bowser the Hound at all when he spoke, but just then there was the patter of heavy feet among the dried leaves, and sure enough there was Bowser himself. My, how everybody did run—everybody but the stranger from the North. He kept on coming down the tree just the same. Bowser saw him and stopped, in surprise. He had never seen anything quite like this big dark fellow.

"Bow, wow, wow!" shouted Bowser in his deepest voice.

Now, when Bowser used that great deep voice of his, he was accustomed to seeing all the little meadow people and forest folk run, but this stranger did not even hurry. Bowser was so surprised that he just stood still and stared. Then he growled his deepest growl. Still the stranger paid no attention to him. Bowser did not know what to make of it.

"I'll teach that fellow a lesson," said Bowser to himself. "I'll shake him, and shake him and shake him until he hasn't any breath left."

By this time the stranger was down on the ground and starting for another tree, minding his own business. Then, something happened. Bowser made a rush at him, and instead of running, what do you suppose the stranger did? He just rolled himself up in a tight ball with his head tucked down in his waistcoat. When he was rolled up that way, all the little spears hidden in the hair of his coat stood right out until he looked like a great chestnut-burr. Bowser stopped short. Then he reached out his nose and sniffed at this queer thing. Slap! The tail of the stranger struck Bowser the Hound right across the side of his face, and a dozen of those little spears were left sticking there just like pins in a pin-cushion.

"Wow! wow! wow! wow" yelled Bowser at the top of his lungs, and started for home with his tail between his legs, and yelling with every jump. Then the stranger unrolled himself and smiled, and all the little meadow people and forest folk who had been watching shouted aloud for joy.

And this is the way that Prickly Porky the Porcupine made friends.

CHAPTER FOUR: PETER RABBIT HAS SOME STARTLING NEWS

LITTLE MRS. PETER RABBIT, who used to be Little Miss Fuzzytail, sat at the edge of the dear Old Briar-patch, anxiously looking over towards the Green Forest. She was worried. There was no doubt about it. Little Mrs. Peter was very much worried. Why didn't Peter come home? She did wish that he would be content to stay close by the dear Old Briar-patch. For her part, she couldn't see why under the sun he wanted to go way over to the Green Forest. He was always having dreadful adventures and narrow escapes over there, and yet, in spite of all she could say, he would persist in going there. She didn't feel easy in her mind one minute while he was out of her sight. To be sure he always turned up all right, but she couldn't help feeling that sometime his dreadful curiosity would get him into trouble that he couldn't get out of, and so every time he went to the Green Forest, she was sure, absolutely sure, that she would never see him again.

Peter used to laugh at her and tell her that she was a foolish little dear, and that he was perfectly able to take care of himself. Then, when he saw how worried she was, he would promise to be very, very careful and never do anything rash or foolish. But he wouldn't promise not to go to the Green Forest. No, Sir, Peter wouldn't promise that. You see, he has so many friends over there, and there is always so much news to be gathered that he just couldn't keep away. Once or twice he had induced Mrs. Peter to go with him, but she had been frightened almost out of her skin every minute, for it seemed to her that there was danger lurking behind every tree and under every bush. It was all very well for Chatterer the Red Squirrel and Happy Jack the Gray Squirrel, who could jump from tree to tree, but she didn't think it a safe and proper place for a sensible Rabbit, and she said so.

This particular morning she was unusually anxious. Peter had been gone all night. Usually he was home by the time Old Mother West Wind came down from the Purple Hills and emptied her children, the Merry Little Breezes, out of her big bag to play all day on the Green Meadows, but this morning Old Mother West Wind had been a long time gone about her business, and still there was no sign of Peter.

"Something has happened. I just know something has happened!" she wailed.

> "Oh, Peter, Peter, Peter Rabbit
> Why will you be so heedless?
> Why will you take such dreadful risks,
> So foolish and so needless?"

"Don't worry. Peter is smart enough to take care of himself," cried one of the Merry Little Breezes, who happened along just in time to overhear her. He'll be home pretty soon. In fact, I think I see him coming now."

Mrs. Peter looked in the direction that the Merry Little Breeze was looking, and sure enough there was Peter. He was heading straight for the dear Old Briar-patch, and he was running as if he were trying to show how fast he could run. Mrs. Peter's heart gave a frightened thump. "It must be that Reddy or Granny Fox or Old Man Coyote is right at his heels," thought she, but look as hard as she would, she could see nothing to make Peter run so.

In a few minutes he reached her side. His eyes were very wide, and it was plain to see that he was bursting with important news.

"What is it, Peter? Do tell me quick! Have you had another narrow escape?" gasped little Mrs. Peter.

Peter nodded while he panted for breath. "There's another stranger in the Green Forest, a terrible looking fellow without legs or head or tail, and he almost caught me!" panted Peter.

CHAPTER FIVE: PETER RABBIT TELLS HIS STORY

WHEN PETER RABBIT could get his breath after his long hard run from the Green Forest to the dear Old Briar-patch, he had a wonderful story to tell. It was all about a stranger in the Green Forest, and to have heard Peter tell about it, you would have thought, as Mrs. Peter did, that it was a very terrible stranger, for it had no legs, and it had no head, and it had no tail. At least, that is what Peter said.

"You see, it was this way," declared Peter. "I had stopped longer than I meant to in the Green Forest, for you know, my dear, I always try to be home by the time jolly, round, red Mr. Sun gets out of bed and Old Mother West Wind gets down on the Green Meadows." Mrs. Peter nodded. "But somehow time slipped away faster than I thought for, or else Mr. Sun got up earlier than usual," continued Peter. Then he stopped. That last idea was a new one, and it struck Peter as a good one. "I do believe that that is just what happened—Mr. Sun must have made a mistake and crawled out of bed earlier than usual," he cried.

Mrs. Peter looked as if she very much doubted it, but she didn't say anything, and so Peter went on with his story.

"I had just realized how light it was and had started for home, hurrying with all my might, when I heard a little noise at the top of the hill where Prickly Porky the Porcupine lives. Of course I thought it was Prickly himself starting out for his breakfast, and I looked up with my mouth open to say hello. But I didn't say hello. No, Sir, I didn't say a word. I was too scared. There, just starting down the hill straight towards me, was the most dreadful creature that ever has been seen in the Green Forest! It didn't have any legs, and it didn't have any head, and it didn't have any tail, and it was coming straight after me so fast that I had all I could do to get out of the way!" Peter's eyes grew very round and wide as he said this. "I took one good look, and then I jumped. My gracious, how I did jump!" he continued. "Then I started for home just as fast as ever I could make my legs go, and here I am, and mighty glad to be here!"

Mrs. Peter had listened with her mouth wide open. When Peter finished, she closed it with a snap and hopped over and felt of his head.

"Are you sick, Peter?" she asked anxiously.

Peter stared at her. "Sick! Me sick! Not a bit of it!" he exclaimed. "Never felt better in my life, save that I am a little tired from my long run. What a silly question! Do I look sick?"

"No-o," replied little Mrs. Peter slowly. "No-o, you don't look sick, but you talk as if there were something the matter with your head. I think you must be just a little light-headed, Peter, or else you have taken a nap somewhere and had a bad dream. Did I understand you to say that this dreadful creature has no legs, and yet that it chased you?"

"That's what I said!" snapped Peter a wee bit crossly, for he saw that Mrs. Peter didn't believe a word of his story.

"Will you please tell me how any creature in the Green Forest or out of it, for that matter, can possibly chase anyone unless it has legs or wings, and you didn't say anything about its having wings," demanded Mrs. Peter.

Peter scratched his head in great perplexity. Suddenly he had a happy thought. "Mr. Blacksnake runs fast enough, but he doesn't have legs, does he?" he asked in triumph.

Little Mrs. Peter looked a bit discomfited.

"No-o," she admitted slowly, "he doesn't have legs; but I never could understand how he runs without them."

"Well, then," snapped Peter, "if he can run without legs, why can't other creatures? Besides, this one didn't run exactly; it rolled. Now I've told you all I'm going to. I need a long nap, after all I've been through, so don't let anyone disturb me."

"I won't," replied Mrs. Peter meekly. "But, Peter, if I were you, I wouldn't tell that story to anyone else."

CHAPTER SIX: PETER HAS TO TELL HIS STORY MANY TIMES

Once you start a story you cannot call it back;
It travels on and on and on and ever on, alack!

THAT IS THE reason why you should always be sure that a story you repeat is a good story. Then you will be glad to have it travel on and on and on, and will never want to call it back. But if you tell a story that isn't true or nice, the time is almost sure to come when you will want to call it back and cannot. You see stories are just like rivers—they run on and on forever. Little Mrs. Peter Rabbit knew this, and that is why she advised Peter not to tell anyone else the strange story he had told her of the dreadful creature without legs or head or tail that had chased him in the Green Forest. Peter knew by that that she didn't believe a word of it, but he was too tired and sleepy to argue with her then, so he settled himself comfortably for a nice long nap.

When Peter awoke, the first thing he thought of was the terrible creature he had seen in the Green Forest. The more he thought about it, the more impossible it seemed, and he didn't wonder that Mrs. Peter had advised him not to repeat it.

"I won't," said Peter to himself. "I won't repeat it to a soul. No one will believe it. The truth is, I can hardly believe it myself. I'll just keep my tongue still."

But unfortunately for Peter, one of the Merry Little Breezes of Old Mother West Wind had heard Peter tell the story to Mrs. Peter, and it was such a wonderful and curious and unbelievable story that the Merry Little Breeze straightway repeated it to everybody he met, and soon Peter Rabbit began to receive callers who wanted to hear the story all over again from Peter himself. So Peter was obliged to repeat it ever so many times, and every time it sounded to him more foolish than before. He had to tell it to Jimmy Skunk and to Johnny Chuck and to Danny Meadow Mouse and to Digger the Badger and to Sammy Jay and to Blacky the Crow and to Striped Chipmunk and to Happy Jack Squirrel and to Bobby Coon and to Unc' Billy Possum and to Old Mr. Toad.

Now, strange to say, no one laughed at Peter, queer as the story sounded. You see, they all remembered how they had laughed at him and made fun of him when he told about the great footprints he had found deep in the Green Forest, and how later it had been proven that he really did see them, for they were made by Buster Bear who had come down from the Great Woods to live in the Green Forest. Then it had been Peter's turn to laugh at them. So now, impossible as this new story sounded, they didn't dare laugh at it.

"I never heard of such a creature," said Jimmy Skunk, "and I can't quite believe that there is such a one, but it is very clear to me that Peter has seen something strange. You know the old saying that he laughs best who laughs last, and I'm not going to give Peter another chance to have the last laugh and say, 'I told you so.'"

"That is very true," replied Old Mr. Toad solemnly. "Probably Peter has seen something out of the ordinary, and in his excitement he has exaggerated it. The thing to do is to make sure whether or not there is a stranger in the Green Forest. Peter says that it came down the hill where Prickly Porky the Porcupine lives. Someone ought to go ask him what he knows about it. If there is such a terrible creature up there, he ought to have seen it. Why don't you go up there and ask him, Jimmy Skunk? You're not afraid of anybody or anything."

"I will," replied Jimmy promptly, and off he started. You see, he felt very much flattered by Old Mr. Toad's remark, and he couldn't very well refuse, for that would look as if he were afraid, after all.

CHAPTER SEVEN: JIMMY SKUNK CALLS ON PRICKLY PORKY

"A PLAGUE UPON Old Mr. Toad!" grumbled Jimmy, as he ambled up the Lone Little Path through the Green Forest on his way to the hill where Prickly Porky lives. "Of course I'm not afraid, but just the same I don't like meddling with things I don't know anything about. I'm not afraid of anybody I know of, because everybody has the greatest respect for me, but it might be different with a creature without legs or head or tail. Whoever heard of such a thing? It gives me a queer feeling inside."

However, he kept right on, and as he reached the foot of the hill where Prickly Porky lives, he looked sharply in every direction and listened with all his might for strange sounds. But there was nothing unusual to be seen. The Green Forest looked just as it always did. It was very still and quiet there save for the cheerful voice of Redeye the Vireo telling over and over how happy he was.

"That doesn't sound as if there were any terrible stranger around here," muttered Jimmy.

Then he heard a queer, grunting sound, a very queer sound, that seemed to come from somewhere on the top of the hill. Jimmy grinned as he listened. "That's Prickly Porky telling himself how good his dinner tastes," laughed Jimmy. "Funny how some people do like to hear their own voices."

The contented sound of Prickly Porky's voice made Jimmy feel very sure that there could be nothing very terrible about just then, anyway, and so he slowly ambled up the hill, for you know he never hurries. It was an easy matter to find the tree in which Prickly Porky was at work stripping off bark and eating it, because he made so much noise.

"Hello!" said Jimmy Skunk.

Prickly Porky took no notice. He was so busy eating, and making so much noise about it, that he didn't hear Jimmy at all.

"Hello!" shouted Jimmy a little louder. "Hello, there! Are you deaf?" Of course this wasn't polite at all, but Jimmy was feeling a little out of sorts because he had had to make this call. This time Prickly Porky looked down.

"Hello yourself, and see how you like it, Jimmy Skunk!" he cried. "Come on up and have some of this nice bark with me." Then Prickly Porky laughed at his own joke, for he knew perfectly well that Jimmy couldn't climb, and that he wouldn't eat bark if he could.

Jimmy made a face at him. "Thank you, I've just dined. Come down here where I can talk to you without straining my voice," he replied.

"Wait until I get another bite," replied Prickly Porky, stripping off a long piece of bark. Then with this to chew on, he came half way down the tree and made himself comfortable on a big limb. "Now, what is it you've got on your mind?" he demanded.

At once Jimmy told him the queer story Peter Rabbit had told. "I've been sent up here to find out if you have seen this legless, headless, tailless creature. Have you?" he concluded.

Prickly Porky slowly shook his head. "No," said he. "I've been right here all the time, and I haven't seen any such creature."

"That's all I want to know," replied Jimmy. "Peter Rabbit's got something the matter with his eyes, and I'm going straight back to the Old Briar-patch to tell him so. Much obliged." With that Jimmy started back the way he had come, grumbling to himself.

CHAPTER EIGHT: PRICKLY PORKY NEARLY CHOKES

HARDLY WAS JIMMY SKUNK beyond sight and hearing after having made his call than Redeye the Vireo, whose home is in a tree just at the foot of the hill where Prickly Porky lives, heard a very strange noise. He was very busy, was Redeye, telling all who would listen how happy he was and what a beautiful world this is. Redeye seems to think that this is his special mission in life, that he was put in the Green Forest for this one special purpose—to sing all day long, even in the hottest weather when other birds forget to sing, his little song of gladness and happiness. It never seems to enter his head that he is making other people happy just by being happy himself and saying so.

At first he hardly noticed the strange noise, but when he stopped singing for a bit of a rest, he heard it very plainly, and it sounded so very queer that he flew up the hill towards the place from which it seemed to come, and there his bright eyes soon discovered Prickly Porky. Right away he saw that Prickly Porky was in some kind of trouble, and that it was he who was making the queer noise. Prickly Porky was on the ground at the foot of a tree, and he was rolling over and kicking and clawing at his mouth, from which a little piece of bark was hanging. It was such a strange performance that Redeye simply stared for a minute. Then in a flash it came to him what it meant. Prickly Porky was choking, and if something wasn't done to help him, he might choke to death!

Now there was nothing that Redeye himself could do to help, for he was too small. He must get help somewhere else, and he must do it quickly. Anxiously he looked this way and that way, but there was no one in sight. Then he remembered that Unc' Billy Possum's hollow tree was not far away. Perhaps Unc' Billy could help. He hoped that Unc' Billy was at home, and he wasted no time in finding out. Unc' Billy was at home, and when he heard that his old friend Prickly Porky was in trouble, he hurried up the hill as fast as ever he could. He saw right away what was the trouble.

"Yo' keep still just a minute, Brer Porky!" he commanded, for he did not dare go very near while Prickly Porky was rolling and kicking around so, for fear that he would get against some of the thousand little spears Prickly Porky carries hidden in his coat. Prickly Porky did as he was told. Indeed, he was so weak from his long struggle that he was glad to. Unc' Billy caught hold of the piece of bark hanging from Prickly Porky's mouth. Then he braced himself and pulled with all his might. For a minute the piece of bark held. Then it gave way so suddenly that Unc' Billy fell over flat on his back. Unc' Billy scrambled to his feet and looked reprovingly at Prickly Porky, who lay panting for breath, and with big tears rolling down his face.

"Ah cert'nly am surprised, Brer Porky; Ah cert'nly am surprised that yo' should be so greedy that yo' choke yo'self," said Unc' Billy, shaking his head.

Prickly Porky grinned weakly and rather foolishly. "It wasn't greed, Unc' Billy. It wasn't greed at all," he replied.

"Then what was it, may Ah ask?" demanded Unc' Billy severely.

Then he braced himself and pulled with all his might.

"I thought of something funny right in the middle of my meal, and I laughed just as I started to swallow, and the piece of bark went down the wrong way," explained Prickly Porky. And then, as if the mere thought of the thing that had made him laugh before was too much for him, he began to laugh again. He laughed and laughed and laughed, until finally Unc' Billy quite lost patience.

"Yo' cert'nly have lost your manners, Brer Porky!" he snapped.

Prickly Porky wiped the tears from his eyes. "Come closer so that I can whisper, Unc' Billy," said he.

A little bit suspiciously

Unc' Billy came near enough for Prickly Porky to whisper, and when he had finished, Unc' Billy was wiping tears of laughter from his own eyes.

CHAPTER NINE: JIMMY SKUNK AND UNC' BILLY POSSUM TELL DIFFERENT STORIES

THE LITTLE PEOPLE of the Green Meadows and the Green Forest didn't know what to believe. First came Peter Rabbit with the strangest kind of a story about being chased by a terrible creature without legs, head, or tail. He said that it had come down the hill where Prickly Porky the Porcupine lives in the Green Forest. Jimmy Skunk had been sent to call on Prickly Porky and ask him if he had seen any strange creature such as Peter Rabbit had told about. Prickly Porky had said that he hadn't seen any stranger in that part of the Green Forest, and Jimmy had straightway returned to the Green Meadows and told all his friends there that Peter Rabbit must have had something the matter with his eyes or else was crazy, for Prickly Porky hadn't been away from home and yet had seen nothing unusual.

At the same time Unc' Billy Possum was going about in the Green Forest telling everybody whom he met that he had called on Prickly Porky, and that Prickly Porky had told him that Peter Rabbit undoubtedly had seen something strange. Of course Jimmy Skunk's story soon spread through the Green Forest, and Unc' Billy Possum's story soon spread over the Green Meadows, and so nobody knew what to believe or think. If Jimmy Skunk was right, why Peter Rabbit's queer story wasn't to be believed at all. If Unc' Billy was right, why Peter's story wasn't as crazy as it sounded.

Of course all this aroused a great deal of talk and curiosity, and those who had the most courage began to make visits to the hill where Prickly Porky lives to see if they could see for themselves anything out of the ordinary. But they always found that part of the Green Forest just as usual and always, if they saw Prickly Porky at all, he seemed to be fast asleep, and no one liked to wake him to ask questions. Little by little they began to think that Jimmy Skunk was right, and that Peter Rabbit's terrible creature existed only in Peter's imagination.

About this time Unc' Billy told of having just such an experience as Peter had. It happened exactly as it did with Peter, very early in the morning, when he was passing the foot of the hill where Prickly Porky lives.

"Ah was just passing along, minding mah own business, when Ah heard a noise up on the hill behind me," said Unc' Billy, "and when Ah looked up, there was something coming straight down at me, and Ah couldn't see any legs or head or tail."

"What did you do, Unc' Billy," asked Bobby Coon.

"What did Ah do? Ah did just what yo'alls would have done—Ah done run!" replied Unc' Billy, looking around the little circle of forest and meadow people, listening with round eyes and open mouths. "Yes, Sah, Ah done run, and Ah didn't turn around until Ah was safe in mah holler tree."

"Pooh!" sneered Reddy Fox, who had been listening. "You're a coward. I wouldn't have run! I would have waited and found out what it was. You and Peter Rabbit would run away from your own shadows."

"You don't dare go there yourself at daybreak tomorrow!" retorted Unc' Billy.

"I do too!" declared Reddy angrily, though he didn't have the least intention of going.

"All right. Ah'm going to be in a tree where Ah can watch tomorrow mo'ning and see if yo' are as brave as yo' talk," declared Unc' Billy.

Then Reddy knew that he would have to go or else be called a coward. "I'll be there," he snarled angrily, as he slunk away.

CHAPTER TEN: UNC' BILLY POSSUM TELLS JIMMY SKUNK A SECRET

Be sure before you drop a friend, that you've done nothing to offend.

A FRIEND IS always worth keeping. Unc' Billy Possum says so, and he knows. He ought to, for he has made a lot of them in the Green Forest and on the Green Meadows, in spite of the pranks he has cut up and the tricks he has played. And when Unc' Billy makes a friend, he keeps him. He says that it is easier and a lot better to keep a friend than to make a new one. And this is the way he goes about it: Whenever he finds that a friend is angry with him, he refuses to be angry himself. Instead, he goes to that friend, finds out what the trouble is, explains it all away, and then does something nice.

Jimmy Skunk and Unc' Billy had been friends from the time that Unc' Billy came up from ol' Virginny to live in the Green Forest. In fact, they had been partners in stealing eggs from the hen-house of Farmer Brown's boy. So when Jimmy Skunk, who had made a special call on Prickly Porky to find out if he had seen the strange creature without head, tail, or legs, told everybody that Prickly Porky had seen nothing of such a creature, he was very much put out and quite offended to hear that Unc' Billy was telling how Prickly Porky had said that Peter might really have some reason for his queer story. It seemed to him that either Prickly Porky had told an untruth or that Unc' Billy was telling an untruth. It made him very angry.

The afternoon of the day when Unc' Billy had dared Reddy Fox to go at sun-up the next morning to the hill where Prickly Porky lives he met Jimmy Skunk coming down the Crooked Little Path. Jimmy scowled and was going to pass without so much as speaking. Unc' Billy's shrewd little eyes twinkled, and he grinned as only Unc' Billy can grin. "Howdy, Brer Skunk," said he.

Jimmy just frowned harder than ever and tried to pass.

"Howdy, Brer Skunk," repeated Unc' Billy Possum. "Yo' must have something on your mind."

Jimmy Skunk stopped. "I have!" he snapped. "I want to know whether it is you or Prickly Porky who has been telling an untruth. He told me that he hadn't seen anything like what Peter Rabbit said chased him, and you've been telling around how he told you that Peter may have had good grounds for that foolish story. If Peter saw that thing, Prickly Porky would know it, for he hasn't been away from home this summer. Why would he tell me that he hasn't seen it if he has?"

"Don' be hasty, Brer Skunk. Don' be hasty," replied Unc' Billy soothingly. "Ah haven't said that Brer Porky told me that he had *seen* the thing that Peter says chased him. He told the truth when he told you that he hadn't *seen* any stranger around his hill. What he told me was that—" Here Unc' Billy whispered.

Jimmy Skunk's face cleared. "That's different," said he.

"Of course it is," replied Unc' Billy. "Yo' see, Peter *did* see something strange, even if Brer Porky didn't. Ah have seen it mahself, and now Ah invites yo' to be over at the foot of Brer Porky's hill at sun-up tomorrow mo'ning and see what happens when Brer Fox tries to show how brave he is. Only don' forget that it's a secret."

Jimmy was chuckling by this time. "I won't forget, and I'll be there," he promised. "I'm glad to know that nobody has been telling untruths, and I beg your pardon, Unc' Billy, for thinking you might have been."

"Don' mention it, Brer Skunk, don' mention it. Ah'll be looking fo' yo' tomorrow mo'ning," replied Unc' Billy, with a sly wink that made Jimmy laugh aloud.

CHAPTER ELEVEN: WHAT HAPPENED TO REDDY FOX

REDDY FOX WISHED with all his might that he had kept his tongue still about not being afraid to meet the strange creature that had given Peter Rabbit such a fright. When he had boasted that he would stop and find out all about it if he happened to meet it, he didn't have the least intention of doing anything of the kind. He was just idly boasting and nothing more. You see, Reddy is one of the greatest boasters in the Green Forest or on the Green Meadows. He likes to strut around and talk big. But like most boasters, he is a coward at heart.

Unc' Billy Possum knew this, and that is why he dared Reddy to go the next morning to the foot of the hill where Prickly Porky the Porcupine lives, and where Peter Rabbit had had his strange adventure, and where Unc' Billy himself claimed to have seen the same strange creature without head, tail, or legs which had so frightened Peter. Unc' Billy had said that he would be there himself up in a tree where he could see whether Reddy really did come or not, and so there was nothing for Reddy to do but to go and make good his foolish boast, if the strange creature should appear. You see, a number of little people had heard him boast and had heard Unc' Billy dare him, and he knew that if he didn't make good, he would never hear the end of it and would be called a coward by everybody.

Reddy didn't sleep at all well that afternoon, and when at dusk he started to hunt for his supper, he found that he had lost his appetite. Instead of hunting, he spent most of the night in trying to think of some good reason for not appearing at Prickly Porky's hill at daybreak. But think as he would, he couldn't think of a single excuse that would sound reasonable. "If only Bowser the Hound wasn't chained up at night, I would get him to chase me, and then I would have the very best kind of an excuse," thought he. But he knew that Bowser *was* chained. Nevertheless he did go up to Farmer Brown's dooryard to make sure. It was just as he expected—Bowser was chained.

Reddy sneaked away without even a look at Farmer Brown's hen-house. He didn't see that the door had carelessly been left open, and even if he had, it would have made no difference. He hadn't a bit of appetite. No, Sir. Reddy Fox wouldn't have eaten the fattest chicken there if it had been right before him. All he could think of was that queer story told by Peter Rabbit and Unc' Billy Possum, and the scrape he had got himself into by his foolish boasting. He just wandered about restlessly, waiting for daybreak and hoping that something would turn up to prevent him from going to Prickly Porky's hill. He didn't dare to tell old Granny Fox about it. He knew just what she would say. It seemed as if he could hear her sharp voice and the very words:

"Serves you right for boasting about something you don't know anything about. How many times have I told you that no good comes of boasting? A wise Fox never goes near strange things until he has found out all about them. That is the only way to keep out of trouble and live to a ripe old age. Wisdom is nothing but knowledge, and a wise Fox always knows what he is doing."

So Reddy wandered about all the long night. It seemed as if it never would pass, and yet he wished it would last forever. The more he thought about it, the more afraid he grew. At last he saw the first beams from jolly, round, red Mr. Sun creeping through the Green Forest. The time had come, and he must choose between making his boast good or being called a coward by everybody. Very, very slowly, Reddy Fox began to walk towards the hill where Prickly Porky lives.

CHAPTER TWELVE: WHAT REDDY FOX SAW AND DID

Who guards his tongue as he would keep
A treasure rich and rare,
Will keep himself from trouble free,
And dodge both fear and care.

THE TROUBLE WITH a great many people is that they remember this too late. Reddy Fox is one of these. Reddy is smart and sly and clever in some ways, but he hasn't learned yet to guard his tongue, and half the trouble he gets into is because of that unruly member. You see it is a boastful tongue and an untruthful tongue and that is the worst combination for making trouble that I know of. It has landed him in all kinds of scrapes in the past, and here he was in another, all on account of that tongue.

Jolly, round, red Mr. Sun had kicked his rosy blankets off and was smiling down on the Great World as he began his daily climb up in the blue, blue sky. The Jolly Little Sunbeams were already dancing through the Green Forest, chasing out the Black Shadows, and Reddy knew that it was high time for him to be over by the hill where Prickly Porky the Porcupine lives. With lagging steps he sneaked along from tree to tree, peering out from behind each anxiously, afraid to go on, and still more afraid not to, for fear that he would be called a coward.

He had almost reached the foot of the hill without seeing anything out of the usual and without any signs of Unc' Billy Possum. He was just beginning to hope that Unc' Billy wasn't there, as he had said he would be, when a voice right over his head said:

"Ah cert'nly am glad to see that yo' are as good as your word, Brer Fox, fo' we need someone brave like yo' to find out what this strange creature is that has been chasing we-uns."

Reddy looked up with a sickly grin. There sat Unc' Billy Possum in a pine tree right over his head. He knew now that there was no backing out; he had got to go on. He tried to swagger and look very bold and brave.

"I told you I'm not afraid. If there's anything queer around here, I'll find out what it is," he once more boasted, but Unc' Billy noticed that his voice sounded just a wee bit trembly.

"Keep right on to the foot of the hill; that's where Ah saw it yesterday. My, Ah'm glad that we've got someone so truly brave!" replied Unc' Billy.

Reddy looked at him sharply, but there wasn't a trace of a smile on Unc' Billy's face, and Reddy couldn't tell whether Unc' Billy was making fun of him or not. So, there being nothing else to do, he went on. He reached the foot of the hill without

Reddy wouldn't have believed that it was alive.

seeing or hearing a thing out of the usual. The Green Forest seemed just as it always had seemed. Redeye the Vireo was pouring out his little song of gladness, quite as if everything was just as it should be. Reddy's courage began to come back. Nothing had happened, and nothing was going to happen. Of course not! It was all some of Peter Rabbit's foolishness. Some day he would catch Peter Rabbit and put an end to such silly tales.

"Ah! What was that?" Reddy's sharp ears had caught a sound up near the top of the hill. He stopped short and looked up. For just a little wee minute Reddy couldn't believe that his eyes saw right. Coming down the hill straight towards him was the strangest thing he ever had seen. He couldn't see any legs. He couldn't see any head. He couldn't see any tail. It was round like a ball, but it was the strangest looking ball that ever was. It was covered with old leaves. Reddy wouldn't have believed that it was alive but for the noises it was making. For just a wee minute he stared, and then, what do you think he did? Why, he gave a frightened yelp, put his tail between his legs, and ran just as fast as he could make his legs go. Yes, Sir, that's just what Reddy Fox did.

CHAPTER THIRTEEN: REDDY FOX IS VERY MISERABLE

WHEN REDDY FOX put his tail between his legs and started away from that terrible creature coming down the hill where Prickly Porky lives, he thought of nothing but of getting as far away as he could in the shortest time that he could, and so, with a little frightened yelp with every jump, he ran as he seldom had run before. He forgot all about Unc' Billy Possum watching from the safety of a big pine tree.

He didn't see Jimmy Skunk poking his head out from behind an old stump and laughing fit to kill himself. When he reached the edge of the Green Forest, he didn't even see Peter Rabbit jump out of his path and dodge into a hollow log.

When Reddy was safely past, Peter came out. He sat up very straight, with his ears pointing right up to the sky and his eyes wide open with surprise as he stared after Reddy. "Why! Why, my gracious, I do believe Reddy has had a fright!" exclaimed Peter. Then, being Peter, he right away began to wonder what could have frightened Reddy so, and in a minute he thought of the strange creature which had frightened him a few days before. "I do believe that was it!" he cried. "I do believe it was. Reddy is coming from the direction of Prickly Porky's, and that was where I got my fright. I—I—"

Peter hesitated. The truth is he was wondering if he dared go up there and see if that strange creature without head, tail, or legs really was around again. He knew it would be a foolish thing to do, for he might walk right into danger. He knew that little Mrs. Peter was waiting for him over in the dear Old Briar-patch and that she would worry, for he ought to be there this very blessed minute. But he was very curious to know what had frightened Reddy so, and his curiosity, which has led him into so many scrapes, grew greater with every passing minute.

"It won't do any harm to go part way up there," thought Peter. "Perhaps I will find out something without going way up there."

So, instead of starting for home as he should have done, he turned back through the Green Forest and, stopping every few hops to look and listen, made his way clear to the foot of the hill where Prickly Porky lives. There he hid under a little hemlock tree and looked in every direction for the strange creature which had frightened him so the last time he was there. But nobody was to be seen but Prickly Porky, Jimmy Skunk, and Unc' Billy Possum rolling around in the leaves at the top of the hill and laughing fit to kill themselves.

"There's no danger here; that is sure," thought Peter shrewdly, "and I believe those fellows have been up to some trick."

With that he boldly hopped up the hill and joined them. "What's the joke?" he demanded.

"Did you meet Reddy Fox?" asked Jimmy Skunk, wiping the tears of laughter from his eyes.

"Did I meet him? Why, he almost ran into me and didn't see me at all. I guess he's running yet. Now, what's the joke?" Peter demanded.

When the others could stop laughing long enough, they gathered around Peter and told him something that sent Peter off into such a fit of laughter that it made his sides ache. "That's a good one on Reddy, and it was just as good a one on me," he declared. "Now who else can we scare?"

All of which shows that there was something very like mischief being planned on the hill where Prickly Porky the Porcupine lives.

CHAPTER FOURTEEN: REDDY FOX TRIES TO KEEP OUT OF SIGHT

NEVER IN ALL his life was Reddy Fox more uncomfortable in his mind. He knew that by this time everybody in the Green Forest, on the Green Meadows, around the Smiling Pool, and along the Laughing Brook, knew how he had put his tail between his legs and run with all his might at the first glimpse of the strange creature which had rolled down the hill of Prickly Porky. And he was right; everybody *did* know it, and everybody *was* laughing about it. Unc' Billy Possum, Jimmy Skunk, Prickly Porky, and Peter Rabbit had seen him run, and you may be sure they told everybody they met about it, and news like that travels very fast.

It wouldn't have been so bad if he hadn't boasted beforehand that if he met the strange creature he would wait for it and find out what it was. As it was, he had run just as Peter Rabbit had run when he saw it, and he had been just as much frightened as Peter had. Now, as he sneaked along trying to find something to eat, for he was hungry, he did his very best to keep out of sight. Usually he is very proud of his handsome red coat, but now he wished that he could get rid of it. It is very hard to keep out of sight when you have bright colored clothes. Presently Sammy Jay's sharp eyes spied him as he tried to crawl up on the young family of Mrs. Grouse. At once Sammy flew over there screaming at the top of his lungs:

> "Reddy Fox is very brave when there's no danger near;
> But where there is, alas, alack! he runs away in fear."

Reddy looked up at Sammy and snarled. It was of no use at all now to try to surprise and catch any of the family of Mrs. Grouse, so he turned around and hurried away, trying to escape from Sammy's sharp eyes. He had gone only a little way when a sharp voice called: "Coward! Coward! Coward!" It was Chatterer the Red Squirrel.

No sooner had he got out of Chatterer's sight than he heard another voice. It was saying over and over:

> "Dee, dee, dee! Oh, me, me!
> Some folks can talk so very brave
> And then such cowards be."

It was Tommy Tit the Chickadee. Reddy couldn't think of a thing to say in reply, and so he hurried on, trying to find a place where he would be left in peace. But nowhere that he could go was he free from those taunting voices. Not even when he had crawled into his house was he free from them, for buzzing around his doorway was Bumble Bee and Bumble was humming:

"Bumble, grumble, rumble, hum! Reddy surely can run some."

Late that afternoon old Granny Fox called him out, and it was clear to see that Granny was very much put out about something. "What is this I hear everywhere I go about you being a coward?" she demanded sharply, as soon as he put his head out of the doorway.

Reddy hung his head, and in a very shamefaced way he told her about the terrible fright he had had and all about the strange creature without legs, head, or tail that had rolled down the hill where Prickly Porky lives.

"Serves you right for boasting!" snapped Granny. "How many times have I told you that no good comes of boasting? Probably somebody has played a trick on you. I've lived a good many years, and I never before heard of such a creature. If there were one, I'd have seen it before now. You go back into the house and stay there. You are a disgrace to the Fox family. I am going to have a look about and find out what is going on. If this is some trick, they'll find that old Granny Fox isn't so easily fooled."

CHAPTER FIFTEEN: OLD GRANNY FOX INVESTIGATES

IN-VEST-I-GATE IS A great big word, but its meaning is very simple. To in-vest-i-gate is to look into and try to find out all about something. That is what old Granny Fox started to do after Reddy had told her about the terrible fright he had had at the hill where Prickly Porky lives.

Now old Granny Fox is very sly and smart and clever, as you all know. Compared with her, Reddy Fox is almost stupid. He may be as sly and smart and clever some day, but he has got a lot to learn before then. Now if it had been Reddy who was going to investigate, he would have gone straight over to Prickly Porky's hill and looked around and asked sly questions, and everybody whom he met would have known that he was trying to find out something.

But old Granny Fox did nothing of the kind. Oh, my, no! She went about hunting her dinner just as usual and didn't appear to be paying the least attention to what was going on about her. With her nose to the ground she ran this way and ran that way as if hunting for a trail. She peered into old hollow logs and looked under little brush piles, and so, in course of time, she came to the hill where Prickly Porky lives.

Now Reddy had told Granny that the terrible creature that had so frightened him had rolled down the hill at him, for he was at the bottom. Granny had heard that the same thing had happened to Peter Rabbit and to Unc' Billy Possum. So instead of coming to the hill along the hollow at the bottom, she came to it from the other way. "If there is anything there, I'll be behind it instead of in front of it," she thought shrewdly.

As she drew near where Prickly Porky lives, she kept eyes and ears wide open, all the time pretending to pay attention to nothing but the hunt for her dinner. No one would ever have guessed that she was thinking of anything else. She ran this way and that way all over the hill, but nothing out of the usual did she see or hear excepting one thing: she did find some queer marks down the hill as if something might have rolled there. She followed these down to the bottom, but there they disappeared.

As she was trotting home along the Lone Little Path through the Green Forest, she met Unc' Billy Possum. No, she didn't exactly meet him, because he saw her before she saw him, and he promptly climbed a tree.

"Ah suppose yo'all heard of the terrible creature that scared Reddy almost out of his wits early this mo'ning," said Unc' Billy.

Granny stopped and looked up. "It doesn't take much to scare the young and innocent, Mr. Possum," she replied. "I don't believe all I hear. I've just been hunting all over the hill where Prickly Porky lives, and I couldn't find so much as a Wood Mouse for dinner. Do you believe such a foolish tale, Mr. Possum?"

Unc' Billy coughed behind one hand. "Yes, Mrs. Fox, Ah confess Ah done have to believe it," he replied. "Yo' see, Ah done see that thing mah own self, and Ah just naturally has to believe mah own eyes."

"Huh! I'd like to see it! Maybe I'd believe it then!" snapped Granny Fox.

"The only time to see it is just at sun-up," replied Unc' Billy. "Anybody that comes along through that hollow at the foot of Brer Porky's hill at sun-up is likely never to forget it. Ah wouldn't do it again. No, Sah, once is enough fo' your Unc' Billy."

"Huh!" snorted Granny and trotted on.

Unc' Billy watched her out of sight and grinned broadly. "As sho' as Brer Sun gets up tomorrow mo'ning, Ol' Granny Fox will be there," he chuckled. "Ah must get word to Brer Porky and Brer Skunk and Brer Rabbit."

CHAPTER SIXTEEN: OLD GRANNY FOX LOSES HER DIGNITY

UNC' BILLY POSSUM had passed the word along to Jimmy Skunk, Peter Rabbit, and Prickly Porky that old Granny Fox would be on hand at sun-up to see for herself the strange creature which had frightened Reddy Fox at the foot of the hill where Prickly Porky lives. How did Unc' Billy know? Well, he just guessed. He is quite as shrewd and clever as Granny Fox herself, and when he told her that the only time the strange creature everybody was talking about was seen was at sun-up, he guessed by the very way she sniffed and pretended not to believe it at all that she would visit Prickly Porky's hill the next morning.

"The ol' lady suspects that there is some trick, and we-uns have got to be very careful," warned Unc' Billy, as he and his three friends put their heads together in the early evening. "She is done bound to come snooping around before sun-up," he continued, "and we-uns must be out of sight, all excepting Brer Porky. She'll come just the way she did this afternoon—from back of the hill instead of along the holler."

Unc' Billy was quite right. Old Granny Fox felt very sure that someone was playing tricks, so she didn't wait until jolly, round, red Mr. Sun was out of bed. She was at the top of the hill where Prickly Porky lives a full hour before sun-up, and there she sat down to wait. She couldn't see or hear anything in the least suspicious. You see, Unc' Billy Possum was quite out of sight, as he sat in the thickest part of a hemlock tree, and Peter Rabbit was sitting perfectly still in a hollow log, and Jimmy Skunk wasn't showing so much as the tip of his nose, as he lay just inside the doorway of an old house under the roots of a big stump. Only Prickly Porky was to be seen, and he seemed to be asleep in his favorite tree. Everything seemed to be just as old Granny Fox had seen it a hundred times before.

At last the Jolly Little Sunbeams began to dance through the Green Forest, chasing out the Black Shadows. Redeye the Vireo awoke and at once began to sing, as is his way, not even waiting to get a mouthful of breakfast. Prickly Porky yawned and grunted. Then he climbed down from the tree he had been sitting in, walked slowly over to another, started to climb it, changed his mind, and began to poke around in the dead leaves. Old Granny Fox arose and slowly stretched. She glanced at Prickly Porky contemptuously. She had seen him act in this stupid, uncertain way dozens of times before. Then slowly, watching out sharply on both sides of her, without appearing to do so, she walked down the hill to the hollow at the foot.

Now old Granny Fox can be very dignified when she wants to be, and she was now. She didn't hurry the least little bit. She carried her big, plumey tail just so. And she didn't once look behind her, for she felt sure that there was nothing out of the way there, and to have done so would have been quite undignified. She had reached the bottom of the hill and was walking along the hollow, smiling to herself to think how easily some people are frightened, when her sharp ears caught a sound on the hill behind her. She turned like a flash and then—well, for a minute old Granny Fox was too surprised to do anything but stare. There, rolling down the hill straight towards her, was the very thing Reddy had told her about.

At first Granny decided to stay right where she was and find out what this thing was, but the nearer it got, the stranger and more terrible it seemed. It was just a great ball all covered with dried leaves, and yet somehow Granny felt sure that it was alive, although she could see no head or tail or legs. The nearer it got, the stranger and more terrible it seemed. Then Granny forgot her dignity. Yes, Sir, she forgot her dignity. In fact, she quite lost it altogether. Granny Fox ran just as Reddy had run!

CHAPTER SEVENTEEN: GRANNY FOX CATCHES PETER RABBIT

Now listen to this little tale
That deals somewhat with folly,
And shows how sometimes one may be
A little bit too jolly.

NO SOONER WAS old Granny Fox out of sight, running as if she thought that every jump might be her last, than Jimmy Skunk came out from the hole under a big stump where he had been hiding, Peter Rabbit came out of the hollow log from which he had been peeping, and Unc' Billy Possum dropped down from the hemlock tree in which he had so carefully kept out of sight, and all three began to dance around Prickly Porky, laughing as if they were trying to split their sides.

"Ho, ho, ho!" shouted Jimmy Skunk. "I wonder what Reddy Fox would have said if he could have seen old Granny go down that hollow!"

"Ha, ha, ha!" shouted Peter Rabbit. "Did you see how her eyes popped out?"

"Hee, hee, hee!" squeaked Unc' Billy Possum in his funny cracked voice. "Ah reckons she am bound to have sore feet if she keeps on running the way she started."

Prickly Porky didn't say a word. He just smiled in a quiet sort of way as he slowly climbed up to the top of the hill.

Now old Granny Fox had been badly frightened. "Who wouldn't have been at seeing a strange creature without head, tail, or legs rolling down hill straight towards them? But Granny was too old and wise to run very far without cause. She was hardly out of sight of the four little scamps who had been watching her when she stopped to see if that strange creature were following her. It didn't take her long to decide that it wasn't. Then she did some quick thinking.

"I said beforehand that there was some trick, and now I'm sure of it," she muttered. "I have an idea that that good-for-nothing old Billy Possum knows something about it, and I'm just going back to find out."

She wasted no time thinking about it, but began to steal back the way she had come. Now, no one is lighter of foot than old Granny Fox, and no one knows better how to keep out of sight. From tree to tree she crawled, sometimes flat on her stomach, until at last she reached the foot of the hill where she had just had such a fright. There was nothing to be seen there, but up at the top of the hill she saw something that made a fierce, angry gleam come into her yellow eyes. Then she smiled grimly. "The last laugh always is the best laugh, and this time I guess it is going to be mine," she said to herself. Very slowly and carefully, so as not to so much as rustle a leaf, she began to crawl around so as to come up on the back side of the hill.

Now what old Granny Fox had seen was Peter Rabbit and Jimmy Skunk and Unc' Billy Possum rolling over and over in the dried leaves, turning somersaults, and shouting and laughing, while Prickly Porky sat looking on and smiling. Granny knew well enough what was tickling them so, and she knew too that they didn't dream but that she was still running away in fright. At last they were so tired with their good time that they just had to stop for a rest.

"Oh, dear, I'm all out of breath," panted Peter, as he threw himself flat on the ground. "That was the funniest thing I ever saw. I wonder who we—"

Peter didn't finish. No, Sir, Peter didn't finish. Instead, he gave a frightened shriek as something red flashed out from under a low-growing hemlock tree close behind him, and two black paws pinned him down, and sharp teeth caught him by the back of the neck. Old Granny Fox had caught Peter Rabbit at last!

CHAPTER EIGHTEEN: A FRIEND IN NEED IS A FRIEND INDEED

The friendship which is truest, best,
Is that which meets the trouble test.

NO ONE REALLY knows who his best friends are until he gets in trouble. When everything is lovely and there is no sign of trouble anywhere, one may have ever and ever so many friends. At least, it may seem so. But let trouble come, and all too often these seeming friends disappear as if by magic, until only a few, sometimes a very few, are left. These are the real friends, the true friends, and they are worth more than all the others put together. Remember that if you are a true friend to anyone, you will stand by him and help him, no matter what happens. Sometimes it is almost worthwhile getting into trouble just to find out who your real friends are.

Peter Rabbit found out who some of his truest friends are when, because of his own carelessness, old Granny Fox caught him. Peter has been in many tight places and had many terrible frights in his life, but never did he feel quite so helpless and hopeless as when he felt the black paws of old Granny Fox pinning him down and Granny's sharp teeth in the loose skin on the back of his neck. All he could do was to kick with all his might, and kicking was quite useless, for Granny took great care to keep out of the way of those stout hind legs of his.

Many, many times Granny Fox had tried to catch Peter, and always before Peter had been too smart for her, and had just made fun of her and laughed at her. Now it was her turn to laugh, all because he had been careless and foolish. You see, Peter had been so sure that Granny had had such a fright when she ran away from the strange creature that rolled down Prickly Porky's hill at her that she wouldn't think of coming back, and so he had just given himself up to enjoying Granny's fright. At Peter's scream of fright, Unc' Billy Possum scampered for the nearest tree, and Jimmy Skunk dodged behind a big stump. You see, it was so sudden that they really didn't know what had happened. But Prickly Porky, whom some people call stupid, made no move to run away. He happened to be looking at Peter when Granny caught him, and so he knew just what it meant. A spark of anger flashed in his usually dull eyes and for once in his life Prickly Porky moved quickly. The thousand little spears hidden in his coat suddenly stood on end and Prickly Porky made a fierce little rush forward.

"Drop him!" he grunted.

Granny Fox just snarled and backed away, dragging Peter with her and keeping him between Prickly Porky and herself.

By this time Jimmy Skunk had recovered himself. You know he is not afraid of anybody or anything. He sprang out from behind the stump, looking a wee bit shame-faced, and started for old Granny Fox. "You let Peter Rabbit go!" he commanded in a very threatening way. Now the reason Jimmy Skunk is afraid of nobody is because he carries

"Drop him!" he grunted.

with him a little bag of very strong perfume which makes everybody sick but himself. Granny Fox knows all about this. For just a minute she hesitated. Then she thought that if Jimmy used it, it would be as bad for Peter as for her, and she didn't believe Jimmy would use it. So she kept on backing away, dragging Peter with her. Then Unc' Billy Possum took a hand, and his was the bravest deed of all, for he knew that Granny was more than a match for him in a fight. He slipped down from the tree where he had sought safety, crept around behind Granny, and bit her sharply on one heel. Granny let go of Peter to turn and snap at Unc' Billy. This was Peter's chance. He slipped out from under Granny's paws and in a flash was behind Prickly Porky.

CHAPTER NINETEEN: JIMMY SKUNK TAKES WORD TO MRS. PETER

WHEN OLD GRANNY FOX found Prickly Porky, with his thousand little spears all pointing at her, standing between her and Peter Rabbit, she was the angriest old Fox ever seen. She didn't dare touch Prickly Porky, for she knew well enough what it would mean to get one of those sharp, barbed little spears in her skin. To think that she actually had caught Peter Rabbit and then lost him was too provoking! It was more than her temper, never of the best, could stand. In her anger she dug up the leaves and earth with her hind feet, and all the time her tongue fairly flew as she called Prickly Porky, Jimmy Skunk, and Unc' Billy Possum everything bad she could think of. Her yellow eyes snapped so that it seemed almost as if sparks of fire flew from them. It made Peter shiver just to look at her.

Unc' Billy Possum, who, by slipping up behind her and biting one of her heels, had made her let go of Peter, grinned down at her from a safe place in a tree. Jimmy Skunk stood grinning at her in the most provoking manner, and she couldn't do a thing about it, because she had no desire to have Jimmy use his little bag of perfume. So she talked herself out and then with many parting threats of what she would do, she started for home. Unc' Billy noticed that she limped a little with the foot he had nipped so hard, and he couldn't help feeling just a little bit sorry for her.

When she had gone, the others turned to Peter Rabbit to see how badly he had been hurt. They looked him all over and found that he wasn't much the worse for his rough experience. He was rather stiff and lame, and the back of his neck was very sore where Granny Fox had seized him, but he would be quite himself in a day or two.

"I must get home now," said he in a rather faint voice. "Mrs. Peter will be sure that something has happened to me and will be worried almost to death."

"Do tell me quickly what has happened to Peter!"

"No, you don't!" declared Jimmy Skunk. "You are going to stay right here where we can take care of you. It wouldn't be safe for you to try to go to the Old Briar-patch now, because if you should meet Old Man Coyote or Reddy Fox or Whitetail the Marshhawk, you would not be able to run fast enough to get away. I will go down and tell Mrs. Peter, and you will make yourself comfortable in the old house behind that stump where I was hiding."

Peter tried to insist on going home, but the others wouldn't hear of it, and Jimmy Skunk settled the matter by starting for the dear Old Briar-patch. He found little Mrs. Peter anxiously looking towards the Green Forest for some sign of Peter.

"Oh!" she cried, "you have come to bring me bad news. Do tell me quickly what has happened to Peter!"

"Nothing much has happened to Peter," replied Jimmy promptly. Then in the drollest way he told all about the fright of Granny Fox when she first saw the terrible creature rolling down the hill and all that happened after, but he took great care to make light of Peter's escape, and explained that he was just going to rest up there on Prickly Porky's hill for that day and would be home the next night. But little Mrs. Peter wasn't wholly satisfied.

"I've begged him and begged him to keep away from the Green Forest," said she, "but now if he is hurt so that he can't come home, he needs me, and I'm going straight up there myself!"

Nothing that Jimmy could say had the least effect, and so at last he agreed to take her to Peter.

And so, hopping behind Jimmy Skunk, timid little Mrs. Peter Rabbit actually went into the Green Forest of which she was so much afraid, which shows how brave love can be sometimes.

CHAPTER TWENTY: A PLOT TO FRIGHTEN OLD MAN COYOTE

Mischief leads to mischief, for it is almost sure
To never, never be content without a little more.

NOW YOU WOULD think that after Peter Rabbit's very, very narrow escape from the clutches of Old Granny Fox that Jimmy Skunk, Unc' Billy Possum, Peter Rabbit, and Prickly Porky would have been satisfied with the pranks they already had played—No, Sir, they were not! You see, when danger is over, it is quickly forgotten. No sooner had Peter been made comfortable in the old house behind the big stump on the hill where Prickly Porky lives than the four scamps began to wonder who else they could scare with the terrible creature without head, legs, or tail which had so frightened Reddy and Old Granny Fox.

"There is Old Man Coyote; he is forever frightening those smaller and weaker than himself. I'd just love to see him run," said Peter Rabbit.

"The very one!" cried Jimmy Skunk. "I wonder if he would be afraid. You know he is even smarter than Granny Fox, and though she was frightened at first, she soon got over it. How do you suppose we can get him over here?"

"We-uns will take Brer Jay into our secret. Brer Jay will tell Brer Coyote that Brer Rabbit is up here on Brer Porky's hill, hurt so that he can't get home," said Unc' Billy Possum. "That's all Brer Jay need to say. Brer Coyote is gwine to come up here hot foot with his tongue hanging out fo' that dinner he's sho' is waiting fo' him here."

"You won't do anything of the kind!" spoke up little Mrs. Peter, who, you know, had bravely left the dear Old Briar-patch and come up here in the Green Forest to take care of Peter. "Peter has had trouble enough already, and I'm not going to let him have any more, so there!"

"Peter isn't going to get into any trouble," spoke up Jimmy Skunk. "Peter and you are going to be just as safe as if you were over in the Old Briar-patch, for you will be in that old house where nothing can harm you. Now, please, Mrs. Peter, don't be foolish. You don't like Old Man Coyote, do you? You'd like to see him get a great scare to make up for the scares he has given Peter and you, wouldn't you?"

Little Mrs. Peter was forced to admit that she would, and after a little more teasing she finally agreed to let them try their plan for giving Old Man Coyote a scare. Sammy Jay happened along just as Jimmy Skunk was starting out to look for him, and when he was told what was wanted of him, he agreed to do his part. You know Sammy is always ready for any mischief. Just as he started to look for Old Man Coyote, Unc' Billy Possum made another suggestion.

"We-uns have had a lot of fun with Reddy and Granny Fox," said he, "and now it seems to me that it is no more than fair to invite them over to see Old Man Coyote and what he will do when he first sees the terrible creature that has frightened them so. Granny knows now that there is nothing to be afraid of, and perhaps she will forget her anger if she has a chance to see Old Man Coyote run away. Yo' know she isn't wasting any love on him. What do yo' alls say?"

Peter and Mrs. Peter said "No!" right away, but Jimmy Skunk and Prickly Porky thought it a good idea, and of course Sammy Jay was willing. After a little, when it was once more pointed out to them how they would be perfectly safe in the old house behind the big stump, Peter and Mrs. Peter agreed, and Sammy started off on his errand.

CHAPTER TWENTY-ONE: SAMMY JAY DELIVERS HIS MESSAGE

SAMMY JAY HAS been the bearer of so many messages that no one knows better than he how to deliver one. He knows when to be polite, and no one can be more polite than he. First he went over to the home of Reddy and Granny Fox and invited them to come over to the hill where Prickly Porky lives and see the terrible creature which had frightened them so give Old Man Coyote a scare. Both Reddy and Granny promptly said they would do nothing of the kind, that probably Sammy was engaged in some kind of mischief, and that anyway they knew that there was no such creature without head, legs, or tail, and though they had been fooled once, they didn't propose to be fooled again.

"All right," replied Sammy, quite as if it made no difference to him. "You admit that smart as you are you were fooled, and we thought you might like to see the same thing happen to Old Man Coyote."

With this he flew on his way to the Green Meadows to look for Old Man Coyote, and as he flew he chuckled to himself. "They'll be there," he muttered. "I know them well enough to know that nothing would keep them away when there is a chance to see someone else frightened, especially Old Man Coyote. They'll try to keep out of sight, but they'll be there."

Sammy found Old Man Coyote taking a sun-bath. "Good morning, Mr. Coyote. I hope you are feeling well," said Sammy in his politest manner.

"Fairly, fairly, thank you," replied Old Man Coyote, all the time watching Sammy sharply out of the corners of his shrewd eyes. "What's the news in the Green Forest?"

"There isn't any, that is, none to amount to anything," declared Sammy. "I never did see such a dull summer. Is there any news down here on the Green Meadows? I hear Danny Meadow Mouse has found his lost baby."

"So I hear," replied Old Man Coyote. "I tried to find it for him. You know I believe in being neighborly."

Sammy grinned, for as he said this, Old Man Coyote had winked one eye ever so little, and Sammy knew very well that if he had found that lost baby, Danny Meadow Mouse would never have seen him again. "By the way," said Sammy in the most matter-of-fact tone, "as I was coming through the Green Forest, I saw Peter Rabbit over on the hill where Prickly Porky lives, and Peter seems to have been in some kind of trouble. He was so lame that he said he didn't dare try to go home to the Old Briar-patch for fear that he might meet someone looking for a Rabbit dinner, and he knew that, feeling as he did, he wouldn't be able to save himself. Peter is going to come to a bad end some day if he doesn't watch out."

"That depends on what you call a bad end," replied Old Man Coyote with a sly grin. "It might be bad for Peter and at the same time be very good for someone else."

Sammy laughed right out. "That's one way of looking at it," said he. "Well, I should hate to have anything happen to Peter, because I have lots of fun quarreling with him and should miss him dreadfully. I think I'll go up to the Old Orchard and see what is going on there."

Off flew Sammy in the direction of the Old Orchard, and once more he chuckled as he flew. He had seen Old Man Coyote's ears prick up ever so little when he had mentioned that Peter was over in the Green Forest so lame that he didn't dare go home. "Old Man Coyote will start for the Green Forest as soon as I am out of sight," thought Sammy. And that is just what Old Man Coyote did.

CHAPTER TWENTY-TWO: OLD MAN COYOTE LOSES HIS APPETITE

HARDLY WAS SAMMY JAY out of sight, flying towards the Old Orchard, before Old Man Coyote started for the Green Forest. He is very sharp, is Old Man Coyote, so sharp that it is not very often that he is fooled. If Sammy Jay had gone to him and told him what a splendid chance he would have to catch Peter Rabbit if he hurried up to the Green Forest right away, Old Man Coyote would have suspected a trick of some kind. Sammy had been clever enough to know this. So he had just mentioned in the most matter-of-fact way that he had seen Peter over on Prickly Porky's hill and that Peter appeared to have been in trouble, so that he was too lame to go to his home in the dear Old Briar-patch. There wasn't even a hint that Old Man Coyote should go over there. This was what made him sure that the news about Peter was probably true.

Now as soon as Sammy was sure that Old Man Coyote couldn't see him, he headed straight for the Green Forest and the hill where Prickly Porky, Jimmy Skunk, Unc' Billy Possum, and Peter and Mrs. Peter Rabbit were waiting. As he flew, he saw Reddy Fox and old Granny Fox stretched flat behind an old log some distance away, but where they could see all that might happen.

"I knew they would be on hand," he chuckled.

When he reached the others, he reported that he had delivered the message to Old Man Coyote, and that he was very sure, in fact he was positive, that Old Man Coyote was already on his way there in the hope that he would be able to catch Peter Rabbit. It was decided that everybody but Peter should get out of sight at once. So Unc' Billy Possum climbed a tree. Jimmy Skunk crawled into a hollow log. Sammy Jay hid in the thickest part of a hemlock tree. Prickly Porky got behind a big stump right at the top of the hill. Little Mrs. Peter, with her heart going pit-a-pat, crept into the old house between the roots of this same old stump, and only Peter was to be seen when at last Old Man Coyote came tiptoeing along the hollow at the foot of the hill, as noiseless as a gray shadow.

He saw Peter almost as soon as Peter saw him, and the instant he saw him, he stopped as still as if he were made of stone. Peter took a couple of steps, and it was very plain to see that he was lame, just as Sammy Jay had said.

"That good-for-nothing Jay told the truth for once," thought Old Man Coyote, with a hungry gleam in his eyes.

Whenever Old Man Coyote thought that Peter was not looking his way, he would crawl on his stomach from one tree to another, always getting a little nearer to Peter. He would lie perfectly still when Peter seemed to be looking towards him. Now of course Peter knew just what was going on, and he took the greatest care not to get more than a couple of jumps away from the old house under the big stump, where Mrs. Peter was hiding and wishing with all her might that she and Peter were back in the dear Old Briar-patch. It was very still in the Green Forest save for the song of happiness of Redeye the Vireo who, if he knew what was going on, made no sign.

My, but it was exciting to those who were watching!

Old Man Coyote had crept half-way up the hill, and Peter was wondering how much nearer he could let him get with safety, when a sudden grunting broke out right behind him. Peter knew what it meant and jumped to one side. Then down the hill, rolling straight towards Old Man Coyote, started the strange, headless, tailless, legless creature that had so frightened Reddy and Granny Fox.

Old Man Coyote took one good look, hesitated, looked again, and then turned tail and started for the Green Meadows as fast as his long legs would take him. It was plain to see that he was afraid, very much afraid. Quite suddenly he had lost his appetite.

CHAPTER TWENTY-THREE: BUSTER BEAR GIVES IT ALL AWAY

IT WAS VERY clear that Old Man Coyote wasn't thinking about his stomach just then, but about his legs and how fast they could go. He had been half-way up the hill when he first saw the terrible creature without head, tail, or legs rolling down straight at him. He stopped only long enough for one good look and then he started for the bottom of the hill as fast as he could make his legs go. Now, it is a very bad plan to run fast down-hill. Yes, Sir, it is a very bad plan. You see, once you are started, it is not the easiest thing in the world to stop. And then again, you are quite likely to stub your toes.

This is what Old Man Coyote did. He stubbed his toes and turned a complete somersault. He looked so funny that the little scamps watching him had all they could do to keep from shouting right out. Old Granny Fox and Reddy Fox, looking on from a safe distance, did laugh. You know they had not been friendly with Old Man Coyote since he came to live on the Green Meadows, and as they had themselves had a terrible fright when they first saw the strange creature, they rejoiced in seeing him frightened.

But Old Man Coyote didn't stop for a little thing like a tumble. Oh, my, no! He just rolled over on to his feet and was off again, harder than before. Now there are very few people who can see behind them without turning their heads as Peter Rabbit can, and Old Man Coyote is not one of them. Trying to watch behind him, he didn't see where he was going, and the first thing he knew he ran bump into—guess who! Why, Buster Bear, to be sure.

Where Buster had come from nobody knew, but there he was, as big as life. When Old Man Coyote ran into him, he growled a deep, provoked growl and whirled around with one big paw raised to cuff whoever had so nearly upset him. Old Man Coyote, more frightened than ever, yelped and ran harder than before, so that by the time Buster Bear saw who it was who had run into him, he was safely out of reach and still running.

Then it was that Buster Bear first saw, rolling down the hill, the strange creature which had so frightened Old Man Coyote. Unc' Billy Possum, Jimmy Skunk, Sammy Jay, Peter Rabbit and Mrs. Peter, watching from safe hiding places, wondered if Buster would run too. If he did, it would be almost too good to be true. But he didn't. He looked first at the strange creature rolling down the hill, then at Old Man Coyote running as hard as ever he could, and his shrewd little eyes began to twinkle. Then he began to laugh.

"Ha, ha, ha! Ho, ho, ho! Ha, ha, ho! I see you are up to your old tricks, Prickly Porky!" he shouted, as the strange creature rolled past, almost over his toes and brought up against a little tree at the foot of the hill.

"I see you are up to your old tricks, Prickly Porky!" he shouted.

Old Man Coyote heard him and stopped short and turned to see what it meant. Very slowly the strange creature unrolled and turned over. There was a head now and a tail and four legs. It was none other than Prickly Porky himself! There was no doubt about it, though he still looked very strange, for he was covered with dead leaves which clung to the thousand little spears hidden in his coat. Prickly Porky grinned.

"You shouldn't have given me away, Buster Bear, just because you have seen me roll down-hill before in the Great Woods where we both came from," said he.

"I think it was high time I did," replied Buster Bear, still chuckling. "You might have scared somebody to death down here where they don't know you."

Then everybody came out of their hiding places, laughing and talking all at once, as they told Buster Bear of the joke they had played on Old Man Coyote, and how it had all grown out of the fright Peter Rabbit had received when he just happened along as Prickly Porky was rolling down-hill just for fun. As for Old Man Coyote, he sneaked away, grinding his teeth angrily. Like a great many other people, he couldn't take a joke on himself.

So Prickly Porky made himself at home in the Green Forest and took his place among the little people who live there. In just the same way Old Man Coyote came as a stranger to the Green Meadows and established himself there. In the next book you may read all about how he came to the Green Meadows and of some of his adventures there and in the Green Forest.

The Adventures of Old Man Coyote

CHAPTER ONE: THE STRANGE VOICE

"LISTEN!" IT WAS Jimmy Skunk speaking. He had just met Peter Rabbit half-way down the Crooked Little Path just where the moonlight was brightest. But he did not need to tell Peter to listen. Peter *was* listening—listening with all his might. He was sitting up very straight, and his long ears were turned in the direction of the strange sound. Just then it came again, a sound such as neither Peter Rabbit nor Jimmy Skunk had ever heard before. Peter's teeth began to chatter.

"Wha—wha—what is it?" he whispered.

"I don't know, unless it is Hooty the Owl gone crazy," replied Jimmy.

"No," said Peter, "it isn't Hooty the Owl. Hooty never could make such a noise as that."

"Maybe it's Dippy the Loon. I've heard him on the Big River, and he sounds just as if he had gone crazy," replied Jimmy.

"No," said Peter, looking behind him nervously. "No, it isn't Dippy the Loon, for Dippy never leaves the water, and that voice came from the Green Meadows. I wouldn't be surprised—" Peter didn't finish, for just then the strange voice sounded again, and it was nearer than before. Never had the Green Meadows or the Green Forest heard anything like it. It sounded something like Hooty the Owl, and Dippy the Loon, and two or three little dogs howling all together, and there was something in the sound that made cold chills run up and down Peter Rabbit's backbone. He crept a little closer to Jimmy Skunk.

"I believe it is Farmer Brown's boy and some of his friends laughing and shouting together," said Jimmy.

"No, it isn't! Farmer Brown's boy and his friends can make some dreadful noises but nothing so dreadful as that. It makes me afraid, Jimmy Skunk," said Peter.

"Pooh! You're afraid of your own shadow!" replied Jimmy Skunk, who isn't afraid of much of anything. "Let's go down there and find out what it is."

Peter's big eyes grew rounder than ever with fright at the very thought. "D-d-don't you think of such a thing, Jimmy Skunk! D-d-don't y-y-you think of such a

So together they went up to Jimmy Skunk's house.

thing!" he chattered. "I know it's something terrible. Oh, dear! I wish I were safe at home in the dear Old Briar-patch."

Again sounded the strange voice, or was it voices? It seemed sometimes as if there were two or three together. Then again it sounded like only one. Each time Peter Rabbit crept a little closer to Jimmy Skunk. Pretty soon even Jimmy began to feel a little uneasy.

"I'm going home," said he suddenly.

"I want to, but I don't dare to," said Peter, shaking all over with fright.

"Pooh! Anyone who can run as fast as you can ought not to be afraid," said Jimmy. "But if you really are afraid, you can come up to my house and stay a while," he added, good-naturedly.

"Oh, thank you, Jimmy Skunk. I believe I will come sit on your doorstep if you don't mind."

So together they went up to Jimmy Skunk's house, and sat on his doorstep in the moonlight, and listened to the strange voice all the long night; and then, when he saw Old Mother West Wind coming down from the Purple Hills in the early dawn, Peter Rabbit became courageous enough to start for his home in the dear Old Briar-patch.

CHAPTER TWO: PETER RABBIT'S RUN FOR LIFE

IT WAS VERY, very early in the morning when Old Mother West Wind came down from the Purple Hills with her big bag and out of it emptied her children, the Merry Little Breezes, to play on the Green Meadows. Peter Rabbit, watching her from the doorstep of Jimmy Skunk's house, felt his courage grow. All the night long he and Jimmy Skunk had sat on the doorstep listening to a strange voice, a terrible voice Peter had thought. But with the first light of the coming day the voice had been heard no more, and now, as Peter watched Old Mother West Wind just as he had done so often before, he began to wonder if that dreadful voice hadn't been a bad dream.

So he bade Jimmy Skunk good-bye, and started for his home in the dear Old Briar-patch. He wanted to run just as fast as he knew how, but he didn't. No, Sir, he didn't. That is, not while he was in sight of Jimmy Skunk. You see, he knew that Jimmy would laugh at him. He wasn't brave enough to be laughed at.

> *The bravest boy is not the one*
> *Who does some mighty deed;*
> *Who risks his very life perchance*
> *To serve another's need.*
> *The bravest boy is he who dares*
> *To face the scornful laugh*
> *For doing what he knows is right,*
> *Though others mock and chaff.*

But as soon as Peter was sure that Jimmy Skunk could no longer see him, he began to hurry, and the nearer he got to the Old Briar-patch, the faster he hurried. He would run a little way as fast as he could, lipperty-lipperty-lip, and then stop and look and listen nervously. Then he would do it all over again. It was one of these times when he was listening that Peter thought he heard a soft footstep behind him. It sounded very much like the footstep of Reddy Fox. Peter crouched down very low and sat perfectly still, holding his breath and straining his ears. There it was again, pit-a-pat, pit-a-pat, very soft and coming nearer. Peter waited no longer. He sprang forward with a great leap and started for the dear Old Briar-Patch as fast as he could go, which, you know, is very fast indeed. As he ran, he saw behind him a fierce, grinning face. It was very much like the face of Reddy Fox, only larger and fiercer and gray instead of red.

Never in all his life had Peter run as he did now, for he knew that he was running for his life. It seemed as if those long legs of his hardly touched the ground. He didn't dare try any of the tricks with which he had so often fooled Reddy Fox, for he didn't know anything about this terrible stranger. He might not be fooled by tricks as Reddy Fox was.

Peter began to breathe hard. It seemed to him that he could feel the hot breath of the fierce stranger. And right down inside, Peter somehow felt sure that this was the owner of the strange voice which had so frightened him in the night. Snap!

That was a pair of cruel jaws right at his very heels. It gave Peter new strength, and he made longer jumps than before. The dear Old Briar-patch, the safe Old Briar-patch, was just ahead. With three mighty jumps, Peter reached the opening of one of his own private little paths and dived in under a bramble bush. And even as he did so, he heard the clash of sharp teeth and felt some hair pulled from his tail. And then, outside the Old Briar-patch, broke forth that same terrible voice Peter had heard in the night.

Peter didn't stop to look at the stranger, but hurried to the very middle of the Old Briar-patch and there he stretched out at full length and panted and panted for breath.

CHAPTER THREE: REDDY FOX MAKES A DISCOVERY

REDDY FOX HAD boasted that he was not afraid of the unknown stranger who had frightened Peter Rabbit so, and whose voice in the night had brought the great fear to the Green Meadows and the Green Forest. But Reddy Fox is always boasting, and a boaster is seldom very brave. Right down deep in his heart Reddy was afraid. What he was afraid of, he didn't know. That is one reason that he was afraid. He is always afraid of things that he doesn't know about. Old Granny Fox had taught Reddy that.

"If you are afraid of things you don't know all about, and just keep away from them, they never will hurt you," said wise Old Granny Fox, and that is one reason that Farmer Brown's boy had never been able to catch her in a trap. But Granny was too smart to boast that she wasn't afraid when she was, while Reddy was forever bragging of how brave he was, when all the time he was one of the greatest cowards among all the little meadow and forest people.

When he had first heard that strange voice, little cold chills had chased each other up and down his backbone, just as they had with nearly all the others who had heard it, and Reddy had not gone hunting that night. But Reddy has a big appetite, and a hungry stomach doesn't let one think of much else. So after a day or two, Reddy grew brave enough to go hunting. Somehow he had a feeling that it was safer to hunt during the day instead of during the night. You see, it was only after jolly, round, red Mr. Sun had gone to bed behind the Purple Hills that that strange voice was heard, and Reddy guessed that perhaps the stranger slept during the day.

So Reddy started out very early in the morning, stepping as softly as he knew how, looking behind every bush and tree, and with his sharp little ears wide open to catch every sound. Every few feet he stopped and sniffed the wind very carefully, for Reddy's nose can tell him of things which his eyes do not see and his ears do not hear. And all the time he was ready to run at the first sign of danger. He had left the Green Forest and was out on the Green Meadows, hoping to catch Danny Meadow Mouse, when that sharp little nose of his was tickled by one of the Merry Little Breezes with a smell that Reddy knew. Reddy turned and went in the direction from which the Merry Little Breeze had come. Just a few steps he went, and then he stopped and sniffed.

"Um-m-m," said Reddy to himself, "that smells to me like chicken. It certainly does smell like chicken!"

Very, very slowly and carefully Reddy moved forward in the direction from which that delicious smell came. Every few steps he stopped and sniffed. Sniff, sniff, sniff! Yes, it certainly was chicken. Reddy's mouth watered. A few more steps and there, a little way in front of him, partly hidden in a clump of tall grass and bushes, lay a half-eaten chicken. Reddy stopped short and sat down to look at it. Then he looked all around it to see if there was anyone about. Then he walked clear around it in a circle, but he was very careful not to go too near. Finally he sat down again where he could smell the chicken. His tongue hung out with longing, and water dripped from the corners of his mouth. His stomach said, "Go get it;" but his head said, "Don't go any nearer; it may be some sort of a trap."

Then Reddy remembered one of the sayings of wise Old Granny Fox:

> *"When you are tempted very much*
> *Just turn your back and go away.*
> *Temptation then can harm you not,*
> *But only those who choose to stay."*

"I hate to do it, but I guess it's the best way," said Reddy Fox and turned his back on the chicken and trotted away.

CHAPTER FOUR: REDDY FOX CONSULTS BOBBY COON

WHEN REDDY FOX had turned his back on the half-eaten chicken that he had found hidden in a bunch of grass and bushes on the Green Meadows it had been the hardest thing to do that Reddy could remember, for his stomach fairly ached, he was so hungry. But there might be danger there, and it was best to be safe. So Reddy turned and trotted away where he could neither see nor smell that chicken. He caught some grasshoppers, and he found a family of fat beetles. They were not very filling, but they were better than nothing. After a while he felt better, and he curled up in a warm sunny spot to rest and think.

"It may be that Farmer Brown's boy has set a trap there," said Reddy to himself.

Then he remembered that the chicken was half-eaten, and he knew that it wasn't likely that Farmer Brown's boy would have a half-eaten chicken unless he had found one that Jimmy Skunk had left near the hen-yard, and for some reason he didn't know, he had a feeling that Jimmy Skunk had not had anything to do with that chicken. The more he thought about it, the more he felt sure that that chicken had something to do with the stranger whose voice had brought so much fear to the Green Meadows. The very thought made him nervous and spoiled his sun-bath.

"I believe I'll run over and see Bobby Coon," said Reddy, and off he started for the Green Forest.

Bobby Coon had been out all night, but he had not been very far away from his hollow tree, because he too had felt little chills of fear when he heard that strange voice, which wasn't the voice of Hooty the Owl or of Dippy the Loon or of a little yelping dog and yet sounded something like all three together. So Bobby's stomach wasn't as full as usual, and he felt cross and uncomfortable. You know it is hard work to feel hungry and pleasant at the same time. He had just begun to doze when he heard Reddy Fox calling softly at the foot of the tree.

"Bobby! Bobby Coon!" called Reddy.

Bobby didn't answer. He kept perfectly still to try to make Reddy think that he was asleep. But Reddy kept right on calling. Finally Bobby scrambled up to the doorway of his house in the big hollow tree and scowled down at Reddy Fox.

"Well, what is it?" he snapped crossly. "You ought to be ashamed of yourself to disturb people who are trying to get a little honest sleep."

Reddy grinned. "I'm very sorry to wake you up, Bobby Coon," said Reddy, "but you see I want your advice. I know that there is no one smarter than you, and I have just discovered something very important about which I want to know what you think."

The scowl disappeared from Bobby Coon's face. He felt very much flattered, just as Reddy meant that he should feel, and he tried to look very important and wise as he said:

"I'm listening, Reddy Fox. What is it that is so important?"

Then Reddy told him about the half-eaten chicken over on the Green Meadows, and how he suspected that the stranger with the terrible voice had had something to do with it. Bobby listened gravely.

"Pooh!" said he. "Probably Jimmy Skunk knows something about it."

"No," replied Reddy, "I'm sure that Jimmy Skunk doesn't know anything about it. Come over with me and see it for yourself."

Bobby began to back down into his house. "You'll have to excuse me this morning, Reddy Fox. You see, I'm very tired and need sleep," said he.

Reddy turned his head aside to hide a smile, for he knew that Bobby was afraid.

"I'm sure it must have been Jimmy Skunk," continued Bobby. "Why don't you go ask him? I never like to meddle with other people's business."

And with that Bobby Coon backed down out of sight in the hollow tree.

CHAPTER FIVE: REDDY FOX VISITS JIMMY SKUNK

"BOBBY COON is afraid! Yes, Sir, Bobby Coon is afraid! He doesn't dare go with me to look at that half-eaten chicken over on the Green Meadows. He's a coward, that's what he is!"

Reddy Fox muttered this to himself as he trotted away from Bobby Coon's big hollow tree in the Green Forest. Reddy was right, and he was wrong. He was right in thinking that Bobby Coon was afraid. Bobby was afraid, but that didn't make him a coward. You see, he couldn't see what good it would do him to go see that half-eaten chicken way out there in the Green Meadows so far away from trees. Bobby is like Happy Jack Squirrel—he never feels really safe unless there is a tree close at hand to climb, for Bobby's legs are not very long, and though he can run fast for a little distance, he soon gets out of breath. Then he climbs the nearest tree. But if there had been any really good reason for going, Bobby would have gone even though he was afraid, and that shows that he wasn't a coward.

But Reddy Fox likes to think himself very brave and everyone else a coward. So he trotted along with his nose turned up in scorn because Bobby Coon was afraid. He was disappointed, too, was Reddy Fox. You see he had hoped to get Bobby to go with him and when they got there that Bobby would go close to the half-eaten chicken and try to find out who had left it on the Green Meadows, and for what reason. Reddy, who is always suspicious, thought that there might be a trap, and if so, Bobby would find it, and then Reddy would know without running any danger himself. That shows how sly he is.

But as long as Bobby wouldn't go, there was nothing for Reddy to do but to try the same plan with Jimmy Skunk, and so he headed straight for Jimmy Skunk's house. Now deep down in his heart Reddy Fox hated Jimmy Skunk, and more than once he had tried to get Jimmy into trouble. But now, as he saw Jimmy sitting on his doorstep, Reddy looked as pleasant as only Reddy can. He smiled as if Jimmy were his very best friend.

"Good morning, Jimmy Skunk. I'm glad to see you," said Reddy. "I hope you are feeling well this morning."

Now Jimmy had had a good breakfast of fat beetles, and he was feeling very good-natured. But he wasn't fooled by Reddy's pleasant ways. To himself he thought, "I wonder what mischief Reddy Fox is up to," but aloud he said:

"Good morning, Reddy Fox. You are looking very fine and handsome this morning. Of course no one who is as big and brave as you are is afraid of the stranger with the terrible voice who has frightened the rest of us so for the last few nights."

Now all the time he was saying this, Jimmy knew perfectly well that Reddy was afraid, and he turned his head to hide a smile as Reddy swelled up to look very big and important and replied:

"Oh, my, no! No, indeed, certainly not! I'm not afraid of anybody or anything. By the way, I saw a strange thing down on the Green Meadows early this morning. It was a half-eaten chicken hidden in a clump of grass and bushes. I wondered if you left it there."

Jimmy Skunk pricked up his ears. "No," said he, "I didn't leave it there. I haven't taken a chicken from Farmer Brown's this spring, and I haven't been up to his hen-house for more than a week. Who do you suppose could have left it there?"

"I haven't the least idea unless—" Reddy looked this way and that to make sure that they were alone—"unless it was the stranger who has frightened everyone but me," he finished in a whisper.

Jimmy pricked his ears up more than ever. "Do you really suppose it could have been?" he asked.

"Come down there with me and see for yourself," replied Reddy. And Jimmy said he would.

CHAPTER SIX: JIMMY SKUNK GOES WITH REDDY FOX

JIMMY SKUNK AND Reddy Fox trotted along down the Crooked Little Path to the Green Meadows. Reddy was impatient and in a hurry. But Jimmy Skunk never hurries, and he didn't now. He just took his time, and Reddy Fox had to keep waiting for him. Reddy was nervous and anxious. He kept turning his head this way and that way. He looked behind every little bush and clump of grass. He cocked his sharp ears at every little sound. He sniffed every little breeze. It was very plain that Reddy Fox was ill at ease.

"Hurry up, Jimmy Skunk! Hurry up!" he urged every few minutes, and he had hard work to make his voice sound pleasant

But Jimmy didn't hurry. Indeed, it seemed as if Jimmy were slower than usual. The more impatient Reddy grew, the slower Jimmy seemed to go. And every time Reddy's back was turned, Jimmy would grin, and his sharp little eyes twinkled with mischief. You see, he knew that despite all his boasting Reddy Fox was afraid, and because he wasn't afraid himself, Jimmy was getting a lot of fun out of watching Reddy. Once, when Reddy had stopped to look over the Green Meadows, Jimmy stole up behind him very softly and suddenly pulled Reddy's tail. Reddy sprang forward with a frightened yelp and started to run as only Reddy can. Then he heard

Jimmy Skunk laughing and knew that Jimmy had played a joke on him. He stopped short and whirled around.

"What are you laughing at, Jimmy Skunk?" he shouted angrily.

"Oh, nothing, nothing at all," replied Jimmy, and his face was as sober as if he never had laughed and never could laugh. Reddy opened his mouth to say something ugly, but suddenly remembered that if he quarreled with Jimmy Skunk, then Jimmy wouldn't go any farther with him. So he gulped down his anger as best he could and grinned sheepishly while he waited for Jimmy to catch up with him.

So at last they came to the bunch of grass and bushes in which Reddy had found the half-eaten chicken early that morning. There it lay just as Reddy had left it. Reddy stopped at a safe distance and pointed it out to Jimmy Skunk. Jimmy looked at it thoughtfully.

"Who do you suppose could have brought it a-way down here on the Green Meadows?" whispered Reddy, as if afraid that someone might overhear him.

Jimmy Skunk scratched his head as if thinking very hard. "It might have been Redtail the Hawk," said he at last.

"That's so. I didn't think of him," replied Reddy.

"But it looks to me as if it were left there in the night, and Redtail never hunts at night because his eyes are for seeing in the daytime and not in the dark," added Jimmy Skunk. "Let's go closer, and perhaps we can tell who left it there."

"Of course. That's a good idea," replied Reddy, starting forward as if he were going to walk right up to the chicken. After a few steps he stopped as if he had a sudden thought. "I tell you what," said he: "one of us had better keep watch to see that no danger is near. I am taller than you and can see over the grass better than you can, so I'll keep watch while you see what you can find out."

Now Jimmy Skunk saw through Reddy's plan right away, but Jimmy wasn't afraid, because he isn't afraid of much of anything, so he agreed. While Reddy kept watch, he carefully made his way to the half-eaten chicken hidden in the clump of grass and bushes. All the time he kept his eyes wide open for traps. But there were no traps there. He was gone a long time, and when at last he came out, his face was very sober.

"Well, was it Redtail the Hawk?" asked Reddy eagerly.

"No," said Jimmy. "No, it wasn't Redtail the Hawk or Hooty the Owl. It was someone with teeth very much like yours, Reddy Fox, only bigger, and with feet very much like yours, only these were bigger too. And the chicken wasn't one of Farmer Brown's at all; it was brought from somewhere farther away than Farmer Brown's, and that shows that it was someone smarter than you, Reddy Fox, because whoever it was knew that if they stole a chicken from Farmer Brown, his boy and Bowser the Hound would come looking for it."

CHAPTER SEVEN: A CALL ON DIGGER THE BADGER

For fox or man the better plan
With unknown danger near,
Is to go home and no more roam
Until the way be clear.

THAT IS WHAT Reddy Fox thinks. The thought popped right into his head when Jimmy Skunk told him that the half-eaten chicken had been left on the Green Meadows by someone with teeth and feet very like Reddy's own but bigger. But Reddy pretended not to believe it. "Pooh!" said he. "How do you know that this stranger has feet like mine, only bigger? You haven't seen him, have you?"

"No," said Jimmy Skunk, shaking his head, "no, I haven't seen him, and I don't need to, to know that. His footprints are right over here in the sand. Come look for yourself, Reddy Fox."

"No, thanks!" said Reddy hastily. "The fact is, I have some very important matters to look after in the Green Forest, and I must hurry along. You'll excuse me, won't you, Jimmy Skunk? If you say that there are footprints like mine, only larger, of course I believe it. I would stop to look at them if I could, but I find that I am already very late. By the way, if you will look a little closer at those footprints, I think you will find that they were made by a dog. I'm sorry I can't wait for you, but you are such a slow walker that I really haven't the time. Let me know if you find out anything about this stranger." And with that off he started for the Green Forest.

Jimmy Skunk grinned, for he knew that Reddy had nothing more important to attend to than to get away as fast as he could from a place which he felt might be dangerous.

"Don't fool yourself, Reddy Fox, by thinking I don't know the footprints of a dog when I see them. Besides, I smelled them, and they don't smell of dog!" shouted Jimmy, before Reddy could get out of hearing.

Jimmy watched Reddy out of sight and chuckled as he saw Reddy keep turning to look over his shoulder as if he expected to find something terrible at his heels. "I'd never run away until I knew what I was running from!" exclaimed Jimmy, with the greatest scorn. "Did you ever see such a coward?"

With Reddy gone, Jimmy's thoughts came back to the queer things which were driving all the happiness from the Green Meadows at the very happiest time of all the year. There was that strange, terrible voice in the night, the voice that was not that of Hooty the Owl or Dippy the Loon or a little yelping dog, yet which sounded something like all three, and which was frightening all the little people until they were afraid to move out of sight of their homes. And here was this half-eaten chicken hidden in the clump of grass and hushes on the Green Meadows by someone with teeth and feet very much like those of Reddy Fox only bigger. It was all very queer, very queer indeed. The more he thought about it, the more Jimmy felt sure that the owner of the terrible voice was the owner of the big teeth and the maker of the strange footprints. He was scratching his head as he puzzled over the matter when he happened to look over to the home of Digger the Badger. Jimmy's eyes brightened.

"Morning," grunted Digger the Badger.

"I believe I'll make a call on Digger. Perhaps he will know something about it," said he, and off he started.

Digger the Badger sat on his doorstep. He has very few friends, for he is grumpy and very apt to be out of sorts. Besides, most of the little Meadow people are afraid of him.

But Jimmy Skunk isn't afraid of anyone but Farmer Brown's boy, and not even of him unless he has his terrible gun. So he walked right up to the doorstep where Digger the Badger was sitting.

"Good morning," said Jimmy politely.

"Morning," grunted Digger the Badger.

"What do you think of the queer doings on the Green Meadows?" asked Jimmy.

"What queer doings?" asked Digger.

Then Jimmy Skunk told all about the strange voice and the strange footprints.

Digger the Badger didn't say a word until Jimmy was through. Then he chuckled.

"Why," said he, "that is only my old friend from the Great West—Old Man Coyote."

CHAPTER EIGHT: OLD MAN COYOTE MAKES HIMSELF AT HOME

IT WAS OUT at last. Digger the Badger had told Jimmy Skunk who it was that had so frightened the little people of the Green Forest and the Green Meadows with his terrible voice, and Jimmy Skunk had straightway sent the Merry Little Breezes of Old Mother West Wind over to the Smiling Pool, up along the Laughing Brook, through the Green Forest, and over the Green Meadows to spread the news that it was Old Man Coyote from the Great West who had come to make his home on the Green Meadows. And that night when they heard his voice, somehow it didn't sound so terrible. You see, they knew who it was, and that made all the difference in the world.

The shivers still might crawl and creep
And chase away good friendly Sleep,
But knowing whom he had to fear
Brought to each heart a bit of cheer.

That may seem a bit queer, but it was so. You see, not knowing what or whom to be afraid of made the little meadow and forest people afraid every minute of the time, afraid to sleep, afraid to put their noses out of their homes, almost afraid to draw a long breath. But now that they knew it was Old Man Coyote who had so frightened them, they felt better, for Digger the Badger, who had known him in the Great West where they had been neighbors, had told Jimmy Skunk what he looked like, and Jimmy Skunk had spread the news so that everybody would know Old Man Coyote when they saw him. So though each one knew that he mustn't give Old Man Coyote a chance to catch him, each felt sure right down in his heart that all he had to do was to be just a little bit smarter than Old Man Coyote, and he would be safe.

Of course it didn't take Old Man Coyote long to learn that he had been found out. He grinned to himself, stretched, and yawned, and then came out from his secret hiding place.

"I think I'll call on my neighbors," said he, and trotted towards the house of Digger the Badger. The Merry Little Breezes saw him first and in a great flutter of excitement they hurried this way and that way to tell everybody that the stranger from the Great West had come out in the light of day. My, my, my! such a scampering as there was for a safe place from which to peep out at Old Man Coyote! He pretended not to notice, and didn't look this way or that way, but trotted on about his own business.

Digger the Badger was sitting on his doorstep, and he grinned when he saw Old Man Coyote coming.

"It's about time you called on your old friend," said he.

It was Old Man Coyote's turn to grin. "That's so, Brother Badger," he replied, "but the fact is, I've been living very quietly."

"Excepting at night," said Digger, showing all his teeth in a rather broad grin. "Your voice certainly has sounded good to me."

"I guess it's the first time," interrupted Old Man Coyote.

"The first time I heard it I thought I was dreaming," continued Digger, just as if he hadn't heard what Old Man Coyote said. "Seems just like home to have you about. But tell me, how does it happen that you have come here out of the Great West?"

"That's too long a story to tell now. Anyway, I might ask you the same thing. But here I am, and I believe I'll stay. I like the Green Meadows and the Green Forest. Now I must be going along to call on the rest of my new neighbors. I hope they'll be glad to see me." Old Man Coyote grinned again when he said this, for no one knew better than he did how very much afraid of him his new neighbors were.

"Come again when you can stop longer," said Digger the Badger.

"I will," replied Old Man Coyote, starting toward the Smiling Pool.

CHAPTER NINE: OLD MAN COYOTE MEETS REDDY FOX

No matter how you feel inside
Hold up your head! Call up your pride!
Stand fast! Look brave! Then none will guess
The fear you feel, but won't confess.

JIMMY SKUNK LEARNED this when he was a very little fellow. Now he isn't afraid of much of anything, but there was a time when he was. Oh, my, yes! There was a time when he first started out to see the world, and before he had found out that all the world is afraid of that little bag of scent he always carries with him, when Jimmy often was as frightened as Peter Rabbit ever is, and you know Peter is very easily frightened. But Jimmy used to think of that little verse, and though sometimes he had to shut his mouth as tightly as he knew how to keep his teeth from chattering with fear, he would hold up his head, stand fast, and look brave. What do you think happened? Why, in a little while people began to say that Jimmy Skunk wasn't afraid of anything, and so no one tried to bother him. Of course when he found this out, Jimmy wasn't afraid.

But Reddy Fox is different. He dearly loves to tell how brave he is. He brags and boasts. But when he finds himself in a place where he is afraid, he shows it. Yes, Sir, he shows it. Reddy Fox has never learned to stand fast and look brave.

When Reddy had first been told that the stranger with the voice which had sound-ed so terrible in the night was Old Man Coyote from the Great West, and that he had decided to make his home on the Green Meadows, Reddy had said: "Pooh! I'm not afraid of him!" and had swelled himself up and strutted back and forth as if he really meant it. But all the time Reddy took care, the very greatest care, to keep out of the way of Old Man Coyote.

Of course, someone told Digger the Badger what Reddy had said, and Digger told Old Man Coyote, who just grinned and said nothing. But he noticed how care-ful Reddy was to keep out of his way, and he made up his mind that he would like to meet Reddy and find out how brave he really was. So one moonlit night he hid behind a big log near one of Reddy's favorite hunting places. Pretty soon Reddy came tiptoeing along, watching for foolish young mice. Just a little while before he had heard the voice of Old Man Coyote way over on the edge of the Old Pasture, so he never once thought of meeting him here. Just as he passed the end of the old log, a deep voice in the black shadow said:

"Good evening, Brother Fox."

Reddy whirled about. His heart seemed to come right up in his throat. It was too late to run, for there was Old Man Coyote right in front of him. Reddy tried to swell himself up just as he so often did before the little people who were afraid of him, but somehow he couldn't.

"Go-good evening, Mr. Coyote," he replied, but his voice sounded very weak. "I hear you've come to make your home on the Green Meadows. I—I hope we will be the best of friends."

"Of course we will," replied Old Man Coyote. "I'm always the best of friends with those who are not afraid of me, and I hear that you are not afraid of anybody."

"N-no, I—I'm not afraid of anybody," said Reddy. "Everybody is afraid of me." All the time he was speaking, he was slowly backing away, and in spite of his bold words, he was shaking with fear. Old Man Coyote saw it and he chuckled to himself.

"I'm not, Brother Fox!" he suddenly snapped, in a deep, horrid sounding voice. "Gr-r-r-r, I'm not!" As he said it, all the hair along his back stood on end, and he showed all his great, cruel-looking teeth.

Instead of holding his ground as Jimmy Skunk would have done, Reddy leaped backward, tripped over his own tail, fell, and then scrambled to his feet with a frightened yelp, and ran as he had never run before in all his life. And as he ran, he heard Old Man Coyote laughing, and all the Green Meadows and the Green Forest heard it:

"Ho, ho, ho! Ha, ha, ha! Hee, hee, hee! Ho, ha, hee, ho! Reddy Fox isn't afraid! Ho, ho!"

Reddy ground his teeth in rage, but he kept on running.

CHAPTER TEN: GRANNY FOX VISITS PRICKLY PORKY

"I've often heard old Granny say:
'He longest lives who runs away.'"

REDDY FOX DIDN'T realize that he was speaking aloud. He was trying to make himself think that he wasn't a coward and that in running away from Old Man Coyote he had done only what everyone of the little meadow and forest people would have done in his place. So, without knowing it, he had spoken aloud.

"But he who runs must leave behind
His self-respect and peace of mind."

The voice came from right over Reddy's head, but he didn't have to look up to know who was there. It was Sammy Jay, of course. Sammy is always on hand when he isn't wanted, and Reddy knew by the look in his eyes that Sammy knew about the meeting with Old Man Coyote.

"What are you waiting around here for?" asked Reddy, with a snarl.

"To tell Old Granny Fox how brave you are," retorted Sammy Jay, his eyes sparkling with mischief, "and how fast you can run."

"You'd better mind your own affairs and leave mine alone. I shall tell Granny all about it myself, anyway," snapped Reddy.

Now when Reddy said that, he didn't tell the truth, for he had no intention of telling Old Granny Fox of how he had run from Old Man Coyote, but hardly were the words out of his mouth when Old Granny Fox herself stepped out from behind a bush. She had been up in the Old Pasture for a week or two and had just come back, so she knew nothing of the fright which Old Man Coyote had given those who live in the Green Meadows and the Green Forest.

"I'm all ready to listen right now, Reddy," said she.

Reddy hung his head. He coughed and cleared his throat and tried to think of some way out of it. But it was of no use. There sat Sammy Jay ready to tell if he didn't, and so, mumbling so low that twice Granny told him to speak louder, Reddy told how he had run, and how Old Man Coyote had laughed at him so that all the little people in the Green Forest and on the Green Meadows had heard.

"Of course he laughed!" snapped Old Granny Fox. "You're a coward, Reddy Fox, just a plain coward. It's all well enough to run away when you know you have to, but to run before there is anything to be afraid of shows you are the biggest kind of a coward. Bah! Get out of my sight!"

Reddy slunk away, muttering to himself and glaring angrily at Sammy Jay, who was chuckling with delight to see Reddy looking so uncomfortable. Old Granny Fox made sure that Reddy was out of sight, and then she sat down to think, and there was a worried pucker in her forehead.

"Old Man Coyote is a wolf," said she, talking to herself, "and a wolf on the Green Meadows and in the Green Forest will mean hard hunting for Reddy and me when food is scarce. It is of no use for me to fight him, for he is bigger and stronger than I am. I'll just have to make all the trouble for him that I can, and then perhaps he'll go away. I wonder if he has ever met Prickly Porky the Porcupine. I believe I'll go over and make Prickly Porky a call right now!"

And as she trotted through the Green Forest on her way to call on Prickly Porky, her thoughts were very busy, very busy indeed. She was planning trouble for Old Man Coyote.

CHAPTER ELEVEN: GRANNY FOX TELLS PRICKLY PORKY A STORY

A little tale which isn't true,
And eager ears to heed it,
Means trouble starts right there to brew
With tattle-tales to feed it.

NO ONE KNOWS how true this is better than does Old Granny Fox. And no one knows better than she how to make trouble for other people by starting little untrue stories. You see, she learned long ago how fast a mean little tale will travel once it has been started, and so when there is someone with whom she is afraid to fight honestly, she uses these little untrue tales instead of claws and teeth, and often they hurt a great deal worse than claws or teeth ever could.

Now you would think that by this time all the little meadow and forest people would have found Old Granny Fox out, and that they wouldn't believe her stories. But the truth is most people are very apt to believe unpleasant things about other people without taking the trouble to find out if they are true, and Old Granny Fox knows this. Besides, she is smart enough to tell these little trouble-making, untrue stories as if she had heard them from someone else. So, of course, someone else gets the blame for starting them. Oh, Granny Fox is smart and sly! Yes, Siree! She certainly is smart and sly.

It was one of her plans to make trouble that was taking her over to see Prickly Porky the Porcupine. She found him as usual in the top of a poplar tree, filling his stomach with tender young bark. Granny strolled along as if she had just happened to pass that way and not as if she had come purposely. She pretended to be very much surprised when she looked up and saw Prickly Porky.

"Good morning, Prickly Porky," she said in her pleasantest voice. "How big and fine and strong and brave you are looking this morning!"

Prickly Porky stopped eating and looked down at her suspiciously, but just the same he felt pleased.

"Huh!" he grunted, then once more he began to eat.

Granny Fox went right on talking. "I said when I heard that story this morning that I didn't believe a word of it I—"

"What story?" Prickly Porky broke in.

"Why, haven't you heard it?" Granny spoke in a tone of great surprise. "Billy Mink told it to me. He said that this stranger, Old Man Coyote, who has come to the Green Meadows and the Green Forest, has been boasting that he is afraid of nobody, but everybody is afraid of him. When somebody asked him if you were afraid of him, he said that you climbed the highest tree you could find if you but saw his shadow. Of course, I didn't believe it, because I know that you are not afraid of anybody. But other people believe it, and they do say that Old Man Coyote is bragging that the first time he meets you on the ground he is going to have Porcupine for dinner."

Prickly Porky had started down the tree before Granny finished speaking, and his usually dull eyes actually looked bright. The fact is, they were bright with anger. Prickly Porky looked positively fierce.

"What are you going to do?" asked Granny Fox, backing away a little.

"Going to give that boaster a chance to try to get his Porcupine dinner," grunted Prickly Porky.

Granny turned aside to grin. "I don't believe you will find him now," said she, "but I heard that he is planning to get you when you go down to the Laughing Brook for a drink this evening."

"Then I'll wait," grunted Prickly Porky.

So Granny Fox bade him good-bye and started on with a wicked chuckle to think how Prickly Porky had believed the story which she had made up.

CHAPTER TWELVE: GRANNY FOX TELLS ANOTHER STORY

Believe all the good that you may hear,
But always doubt the bad.
Pass on the word of kindly cheer;
Forget the tale that's sad.

IF EVERYONE WOULD do that what a different world this would be! My, my, my, yes, indeed! There wouldn't be any place for the Granny Foxes who start untrue stories just to make trouble. But we will have to say this much for Old Granny Fox—she seldom does make trouble just for the sake of trouble. No Sir, Old Granny Fox seldom, very seldom makes trouble, unless she or Reddy Fox have something to gain by it. She is too smart and wise for that.

It was just this way now. You see she felt down in her heart that Old Man Coyote the Wolf had no right on the Green Meadows and in the Green Forest. He was a stranger from the Great West, and she felt that she and Reddy Fox had the best right there, because they had been born there and always had lived there; and she was afraid, very much afraid, that there wouldn't be room for them and for Old Man Coyote. But she wasn't big or strong enough to fight him and drive him away, and so the only thing she could think of was to make him so much trouble that he would leave. She had begun by telling an untrue story to Prickly Porky, a story which had made Prickly Porky very angry with Old Man Coyote, although they had never met. Now she was hurrying down to the Smiling Pool on the banks of which Old Man Coyote was in the habit of taking a sun-bath, she had been told.

All the time he was saying this,
Old Man Coyote was chuckling inside.

Sure enough, when she came in sight of the Smiling Pool, there he lay sprawled out in the sun and talking to Grandfather Frog, who sat on his big green lily-pad well out of reach from the shore. Granny came up on the opposite side of the Smiling Pool from where Old Man Coyote lay.

"How do you do, Mr. Coyote? I have just heard that you have come here to make your home among us, and I am sure we all give you a hearty welcome." Granny said this just as if she really meant it, and all the time she was speaking she was smiling. Old Man Coyote watched her out of half-closed eyes and to himself he thought: "I don't believe a word of it. Granny Fox is too polite, altogether too polite. I wonder what kind of a trick she is trying to play now." But aloud he said, and his voice was just as smooth and soft and pleasant as Granny's:

"I'm very well, thank you, and I am much obliged to you for your hearty welcome. I am sure we shall be the best of friends."

Now all the time he was saying this, Old Man Coyote was chuckling inside, for he knew well enough that they wouldn't be friends, and that Granny Fox didn't want to be friends. You see, he is quite as sharp as she.

"Yes, indeed, I am sure we shall," replied Old Granny Fox. "How big and strong you are, Mr. Coyote! I shouldn't think that you would be afraid of anybody."

Old Man Coyote looked flattered. "I'm not," said he.

Granny Fox raised her eyebrows as if very much surprised. "Is that so?" she exclaimed. "Why I heard that Prickly Porky the Porcupine is boasting that you are afraid of him and don't dare put your foot in the Green Forest when he is about."

Old Man Coyote suddenly jumped to his feet, and there was an ugly gleam in his yellow eyes. Granny Fox was glad that she was on the other side of the Smiling Pool. "I don't know who this Prickly Porky is," said he, "but if you'll be so kind as to tell me where I can find him, I think I will make him a call at once."

"Probably he's taking a nap in a tree-top just now," replied Granny, "but it you really want to meet him, you'll find him getting a drink at the Laughing Brook in the Green Forest late this afternoon. I do hope that you will be careful, Mr. Coyote."

"Careful! Careful!" snorted he. "There won't be any Prickly Porky when I get through with him!"

"Chug-a-rum!" said Grandfather Frog and looked very hard at Old Granny Fox. Granny winked the eye that was nearest to him.

CHAPTER THIRTEEN: THE MEETING AT THE LAUGHING BROOK

The trouble with a quarrel is that when it's once begun
The whole world tries to push it on, and seems to think it fun.

IT USUALLY IS anything but fun for those engaged in it, but their neighbors crowd about and urge them on and do their best to make matters worse. It was just that way when Prickly Porcupine and Old Man Coyote met beside the Laughing Brook. Now until they met here neither had ever seen the other, for you know Old Man Coyote had come out of the Great West, while Prickly Porky had come down from the North Woods. Prickly Porky took one good look and then he grunted, "I'll soon fix him!" What he saw was someone who looked something like a very large gray fox or a dog, and Prickly Porky had put too many foxes and dogs to flight to feel the least bit of fear of the stranger grinning at him and showing all his great teeth.

But Old Man Coyote didn't know what to make of what he saw. Never in all his life had he seen anything like it. He didn't know whether to laugh or to be frightened. About all he could see was what looked like a tremendous great chestnut-burr on legs, which came towards him in little rushes and with a great rattling of the thousand little spears which made him look like a chestnut-burr. Old Man Coyote had never fought with anybody like this, and he didn't know just how to begin. He didn't like the look of the thousand little spears. The nearer they came, the less he liked the look of them. So he backed away a few steps, growling and snarling angrily.

Now it seemed that as if by magic the news that there was trouble between Prickly Porky and Old Man Coyote had spread all over the Green Meadows and through the Green Forest. Everybody who dared to go was on hand to see it. Sammy Jay and his cousin, Blacky the Crow, were there of course, peering down from the top of a pine tree and screaming excitedly. Happy Jack the Gray Squirrel and Chatterer the Red Squirrel actually sat side by side in the same tree, so interested that they forgot for once to quarrel themselves. Unc' Billy Possum and Bobby Coon cut their afternoon nap short and looked on from a safe place in a big chestnut tree. Danny Meadow Mouse and his cousin, Whitefoot the Wood Mouse, shivered with fright, while they peeped out through a crack in a hollow log. Johnny Chuck came as near as he dared and peeped over the trunk of a fallen tree. Billy Mink and Jerry Muskrat quietly swam up the Laughing Brook and crawled out on the farther bank where they could see and still be safe. Of course Reddy and Granny Fox were there, well hidden so that no one should see them.

And what do you think every one of them was wishing? Why, that Prickly Porky would drive Old Man Coyote away from the Green Forest and off of the Green Meadows. You see, every one of them was afraid of Old Man Coyote, and right down in his heart each was hoping that Prickly Porky would be able to send Old Man Coyote off yelping, with his face stuck full of little spears as once upon a time he had sent Bowser the Hound.

CHAPTER FOURTEEN: SLOW WIT AND QUICK WIT

WHEN PRICKLY PORKY the Porcupine and Old Man Coyote the Prairie Wolf met beside the Laughing Brook, it was a case of Slow Wit meeting Quick Wit. You see, Prickly Porky is very slow in everything he does, that is everything but flipping that queer tail of his about when there is an enemy near enough for it to reach. But in everything else he is oh, so slow! He walks as if he had all the time in the world to get to the place he has started for. He climbs in just the same way. And because he never moves quickly, he never thinks quickly. The fact is, he doesn't see any need of hurrying, not even in thinking.

But Old Man Coyote is just the opposite. Yes, Sir, he is just the opposite. No one moves quicker than he does.

He is nimble on his feet, and his wit is just as quick.
His nimble wit and nimble feet are very, very hard to beat.

Digger the Badger, who also comes from the Great West, says that to beat Old Man Coyote in anything, you should start the day before he does and not let him know it.

So here was Slow Wit facing Quick Wit, with most of the little meadow people and forest folk looking on. Suddenly Old Man Coyote sprang forward with his ugliest snarl, a snarl that made everybody but Prickly Porky shiver, even those who were perfectly safe up in the trees.

But Prickly Porky didn't shiver. No, Sir, he just grunted angrily and rattled his thousand little spears.

Now, Old Man Coyote had sprung with that ugly snarl just to try to frighten Prickly Porky, and he had taken care not to spring too close to those rattling spears. When he found that Prickiy Porky wasn't frightened the least little bit, he tried another plan. Perhaps he could get Prickly Porky from behind. As quick as a flash and as light as a feather, he leaped right over Prickly Porky and turned to seize him from behind. But he didn't! Oh, my, no! You see, the thousand little spears covered every inch of Prickly Porky's back.

Slowly and clumsily Prickly Porky turned so as to face his enemy.

"Got fooled that time, didn't you, Mr. Smarty?" he grunted, while his eyes snapped with anger.

Old Man Coyote didn't say anything. He just grinned. But all the time he was using his eyes, and now he discovered that while Prickly Porky was fully protected on his back and sides by the thousand little spears carried in his coat, there wasn't a single little spear in his waistcoat.

"I've got to get him where I can seize him from underneath," thought he, and straightway he began to run in a circle around Prickly Porky while the latter turned slowly round and round, trying to keep his face turned always towards Old Man Coyote. Faster and faster ran Old Man Coyote, and faster and faster turned Prickly Porky. In his slow mind he was trying to understand what it meant, but he couldn't. And for a while the little meadow and forest people looking on were just as much puzzled. It was a most surprising thing. Then suddenly Unc' Billy Possum understood.

"He's trying to make Prickly Porky dizzy," he whispered to Bobby Coon.

"Let's warn Prickly Porky; he'll never think of it himself until it's too late," whispered Bobby Coon.

But before they could do this, the queer performance came to an end. Prickly Porky hadn't discovered what Old Man Coyote was trying to do, but he had become tired of such foolishness, and he suddenly decided to take a rest. So he stopped turning around, and then curled himself up in a ball on the ground, where he looked like a great chestnut-burr. Everybody held their breath to see what Old Man Coyote would do next.

CHAPTER FIFTEEN: PRICKLY PORKY'S TAIL

Who on a prickly porcupine
Makes up his mind that he will dine
Must overcome a thousand quills
Before his stomach Porky fills.
And so it is with you and me;
With everybody whom we see;
With Reddy Fox and Billy Mink,
And all the rest of whom we think
On Meadows Green, in Smiling Pool
Or hidden in the Forest cool:
The thing we've set our hearts upon
Must past a thousand spears be won.

NO ONE KNOWS this better than did Old Man Coyote as he ran around and around Prickly Porky. He had never felt one of those little spears which Prickly Porky rattled so fiercely, and he had no mind to feel one. You see, he didn't like the look of them. When finally Prickly Porky lay down and curled up into a great prickly ball, like a huge chestnut-burr, Old Man Coyote sat down just a little way off to study how he was going to get at Prickly Porky without getting hurt by some of those sharp, barbed little spears.

For a long time he sat and studied and studied, his tongue hanging out of one side of his mouth. Once he looked up at Sammy Jay and Blacky the Crow and winked, but he didn't make a sound. Sammy and Blacky chuckled to themselves and winked back, and for a wonder they didn't make a sound. Somehow that wink made them have more of a friendly feeling for Old Man Coyote. You see, that wink told them that Old Man Coyote was just the same kind of a sly rogue as themselves, and so right away they had a fellow feeling for him.

And none of the little meadow and forest people looking on made a sound. Some of them didn't dare to, and others were so anxious to see what would happen next that they didn't want to. It was so still that the little leaves up in the tree-tops could be heard whispering good night to the Merry Little Breezes, for whom Old Mother West Wind was waiting with her big bag out on the Green Meadows to take them to their home behind the Purple Hills. It was so still that after a while Prickly Porky began to wonder if he were all alone. You see, being curled up that way, he couldn't see and had to trust to his ears. He waited a little longer, and then he uncurled just enough to peep out. There sat Old Man Coyote, and Prickly Porky promptly curled up again.

Now the minute he curled up again something happened. Old Man Coyote looked up at Sammy Jay and Blacky the Crow and winked once more. Then very softly, so softly that he didn't so much as rustle a leaf, he tiptoed around to the other side of Prickly Porky and sat down just as before.

"Now," thought he, "when he peeps out again, he will think I have gone, and then perhaps I can catch him by surprise."

Bobby Coon saw through his plan right away. "Someone ought to warn Prickly Porky," he whispered to Unc' Billy Possum.

Unc' Billy shook his head. "No," he whispered back, "No, Brer Coon! That wouldn't be fair. It's they-all's quarrel and not ours, and though Ah done want to see Brer Porky win just as much as yo' do, Ah reckon it wouldn't be right fo' us to meddle. They-all done got to fight it out themselves."

For a long time nothing happened. Then Old Man Coyote grew tired of waiting. Very carefully he crept nearer and nearer, with his nose stretched out to sniff at that prickly ball on the ground. Everybody held his breath, for everybody remembered what had happened to Bowser the Hound when he came sniffing around Prickly Porky—how Prickly Porky's tail had suddenly slapped Bowser full in the face, filling it with sharp little spears. Now they hoped to see the same thing happen to Old Man Coyote. So they held their breath as they kept their eyes on Old Man Coyote and Prickly Porky's tail.

CHAPTER SIXTEEN: OLD MAN COYOTE'S SMARTNESS

When you meet an adversary
Bold and brave be, also wary.
If the weapons you may hear of,
Teeth and claws, you have no fear of,
Don't be heedless and rush blindly
Lest you be received unkindly,

And, like Prickly Porky, find him
With a dangerous tail behind him.

NOW OLD MAN COYOTE knew nothing about that dangerous tail. He had never heard how Bowser the Hound had been sent yelping home with his face stuck full of those sharp little spears. But Old Man Coyote is wary. Oh, my, yes! He certainly is wary. To be wary, you know, is to be very, very careful where you go and what you do until you know for sure that there is no possible danger. And there is no one more wary than Old Man Coyote, not even wise, sly, Old Granny Fox.

So now, though Prickly Porky, curled up in a ball in front of him, looked harmless enough except for the thousand little spears sticking out all over him, Old Man Coyote was too wary—too smart and too careful—to take any chances as Bowser the Hound had rashly done. And this is why, as he stole forward with his nose stretched out as if to sniff of Prickly Porky, he suddenly stopped just when the little meadow and forest people looking on were holding their breath and hugging themselves with joy and excitement because they expected to see the same thing happen to Old Man Coyote that had happened to Bowser.

Yes, Sir, Old Man Coyote stopped. He studied Prickly Porky a few minutes. Then slowly he walked around him, just studying and studying.

"It looks safe enough to go closer and sniff at him," thought Old Man Coyote, "but I learned a long time ago that you cannot always tell just by looks, and that the most harmless looking thing is sometimes the most dangerous. Now it looks to me as if this stupid Porcupine couldn't hurt a flea so long as

"It looks safe enough to go closer and
sniff him," thought Old Man Coyote.

he keeps curled up this way, but I don't *know*, and I'm not going any nearer until I do know."

He scratched his head thoughtfully, and then he had an idea. He began to dig in the soft earth.

"What under the sun is he doing that for?" whispered Happy Jack Squirrel to his cousin, Chatterer the Red Squirrel.

"I don't know," replied Chatterer, also in a whisper. "We'll probably know in a few minutes."

He had hardly finished when Old Man Coyote threw a little lump of earth so that it hit Prickly Porky. Now, of course Prickly Porky couldn't see what was going on, because, you know, he was curled up with his head tucked down in his waistcoat. But he had been listening as hard as ever he could, and he had heard Old Man Coyote's footsteps very close to him. When the little lump of earth struck him, he thought it was Old Man Coyote himself, and like a flash he slapped that queer tail of his around. Of course it didn't hit anybody, because there was nobody within reach. But it told Old Man Coyote all that he wanted to know.

"Ha, ha, ha!" he laughed. "That's the time I fooled you instead of you fooling me! You've got to get up early to fool me with a trick like that, Mr. Smarty!"

Then what do you think he did? Why, he just scooped earth on to Prickly Porky as fast as he could dig. Prickly Porky stood it for a few minutes, but he didn't want to be buried alive. Besides, now that his trick was found out by the smartness of Old Man Coyote, there was no use in keeping still any longer. So, with a grunt of anger, Prickly Porky scrambled to his feet, and rattling his thousand little spears, rushed at Old Man Coyote, who just jumped to one side, laughing fit to kill himself.

CHAPTER SEVENTEEN: GRANNY FOX IS FOUND OUT

Granny Fox is sly and wise
And seldom taken by surprise,
But wisdom wrongly put to use
Can never find a good excuse.
It ceases then to wisdom be,
But foolishness, as we shall see.

NOW, WITH ALL her smartness and all her cleverness, old Granny Fox had made one great mistake. Yes, Sir, Old Granny Fox had made one great mistake. You see, she had become so used to being thought the smartest and cleverest of all the little people who lived on the Green Meadows and around the Smiling Pool and in the Green Forest, that she had come to believe that there couldn't be anybody anywhere as smart and clever as she. That was because she didn't know Old Man Coyote. And now, as she and Reddy Fox watched from their hiding place the meeting between Old Man Coyote and Prickly Porky, she felt a sudden sharp sting in her pride. Old Man Coyote had proved himself too smart for Prickly Porky. She ground her teeth as she heard him laughing fit to kill himself as he kept out of Prickly Porky's reach, and she ground them still more as she heard him say:

"You will boast that you will drive me out of the Green Forest, will you, Mr. Porcupine? The time to brag will be when you have done it."

Prickly Porky stopped short in the middle of one of his clumsy rushes.

"Boaster and bragger yourself!" he granted. "You don't seem to be dining on Porcupine the first time we meet. Why don't you? Why don't you make your own boast good?'"

Old Man Coyote stopped laughing and pricked up his ears. "What's that?" he demanded. "What's that? Somebody has been filling your ears with something that is very like a lie, Mr. Porcupine."

"I guess you and I are going to be friends," said he.

"No more than they have yours, Mr. Coyote," replied Prickly Porky, letting his thousand little spears drop part way back into his coat. "But Old Granny Fox told me."

"Ha! So it was Granny Fox!" interrupted Old Man Coyote. "So it was Old Granny Fox! Well, it was that same old mischief-maker who told me that—" He stopped and suddenly looked very hard at the very place where Granny and Reddy were hiding. Then he made a long jump in that direction. Granny and Reddy didn't wait for him. They started for home so fast that they looked like nothing but two little red streaks disappearing among the trees.

"Ha, ha, ha! Ho, ho, ho! Hee, hee, hee! Ha, ho, he, ho!" laughed Old Man Coyote, and all the little meadow and forest people who were looking on laughed with him. Then he turned to Prickly Porky.

"I guess you and I are going to be friends," said he.

"I guess we are," replied Prickly Porky, and all his little spears dropped out of sight.

CHAPTER EIGHTEEN: THE CUNNING OF OLD GRANNY FOX

You must get up very early,
You must lie awake at night,
You must have your wits well sharpened
And your eyes must be so bright
That there's nothing can escape them,
Nothing that you do not see,
If ahead of Granny Fox you
Ever get, or hope to be.

HAPPY JACK SQUIRREL made up that verse one day after he had had oh, such a narrow escape from Old Granny Fox. It had made Happy Jack very sober for a while, for Granny had so nearly caught him that she actually had pulled some hair from Happy Jack's tail. All the other little forest and meadow people agreed that Happy Jack was quite right. Most of them had had just such narrow escapes from Old Granny Fox.

You see, it is this way: Old Granny Fox is very, very cunning. To be cunning, you know, is to be sly and smart in doing things in such a way as no one else will think of doing them. Just now, the thing that Granny wanted most of anything in the world was to drive Old Man Coyote away from the Green Meadows and the Green Forest. She couldn't do it openly, because he was bigger and stronger than she, so she had thought and thought and thought, trying to find some plan which might get Old Man Coyote into trouble, so that he would go away and stay away.

Then Reddy Fox told her that he had found the place where Old Man Coyote took a sun-nap every day and a splendid plan came to Granny. At least, it seemed like a splendid plan.

And the more she thought about it, the better it seemed.

But Granny Fox never acts hastily. She is too wise for that. So she studied and studied this plan that she had thought of to make trouble for Old Man Coyote. Finally she was satisfied.

"I believe it will work. I certainly do believe it will work," said she, and called Reddy Fox over to her.

"I want you to make sure that Old Man Coyote takes his sun-nap in the same place every day," said she. "You must see him there yourself. It won't do to take the word of anyone else for it. I want you to steal up every day and make sure that he is there. Be sure you don't tell anyone, not anyone at all, what you are doing, and above all things, don't let *him* get so much as a glimpse of you."

Reddy promised that he would take the greatest care, and so for a week every day he crept to a snug hiding-place behind a thick clump of grass where he could peep through and see Old Man Coyote taking his sun-nap. Then he would tiptoe softly away and hurry to report to Old Granny Fox.

"Good!" she would say. "Go again tomorrow and make sure that he is there."

"But what do you want to know for?" Reddy asked one day, for he was becoming very, very curious.

"Never mind what I want to know for," replied Granny severely. "Do as I tell you, and you will find out soon enough."

You see, Granny Fox was too cunning to let even Reddy know of her plan, for if no one but herself knew it, it couldn't possibly leak out, and that, you know, is the only way to keep a secret.

CHAPTER NINETEEN: BOWSER THE HOUND HAS A VISITOR

BOWSER THE HOUND lay in Farmer Brown's dooryard dozing in the sun. Bowser was dreaming. Yea, Sir, Bowser was dreaming. Farmer Brown's boy, passing through the yard on his way to the cornfield, laughed.

"Sic him, Bowser! Sic him! That's the dog! Don't let him fool you this time," said he.

You see, Bowser was talking in his sleep. He was whining eagerly, and every once in a while breaking out into excited little yelps, and so Farmer Brown's boy knew that he was dreaming that he was hunting, that he was on the trail of Reddy Fox or sly Old Granny Fox. His eyes were shut, and he didn't hear what Farmer Brown's boy said. The latter went off laughing, his hoe on his shoulder, for there was work for him down in the cornfield.

Bowser kept right on getting more and more excited. It was a splendid hunt he was having there in dreamland. Across the Green Meadows, along the edge of the Green Forest, and up through the Old Pasture he ran, all in his dream, you know, and just ahead of him ran Old Granny Fox. Not once was he fooled by her tricks, and she tried every one she knew. For once he was too smart for her, and it made him tingle all over with delight, for he was sure that this time he would catch her.

And then something queer happened. Yes, Sir, it was something very queer indeed. He saw Granny Fox stop just a little way ahead of him. She sat down facing him and began to laugh at him. She laughed and laughed fit to kill herself. It made Bowser very angry. Oh, very angry indeed. No one likes to be laughed at, you know, and to be laughed at by Granny Fox of all people was more than Bowser could stand. He opened his mouth to give a great roar as he sprang at her and then—why, Bowser waked up. Yes, Sir, he really had given a great roar, and had waked himself up with his own voice.

For a few minutes Bowser winked and blinked, for the sun was shining in his eyes. Then he winked and blinked some more, but not because of the sun. Oh, my, no! it wasn't because of the sun that he winked and blinked now. It was because—what do you think? Why, it was because Bowser the Hound couldn't tell whether he was awake or asleep. He thought that he was awake. He was sure that he was awake and yet—well, there sat Old Granny Fox laughing at him, just as he had seen her in his dream. Yes, Sir, there she sat, laughing at him. Poor Bowser! He just didn't know what to think. He rubbed both eyes and looked. There she sat, laughing just as before. Bowser closed his eyes tight and kept them closed for a whole minute. Perhaps when he opened them again, she would be gone. Then he would know that she was only a dream fox, after all.

But no, Sir! When he opened his eyes again, there she sat, laughing harder than ever. Just then a hen came around a corner of the house. Granny Fox stopped laughing. Like a flash she caught the hen, slung her over her shoulder and trotted away, all the time keeping one eye on Bowser.

Then Bowser knew that this was no dream fox, but Old Granny Fox herself, and that she had had the impudence and boldness to steal a hen right under his very nose! He was awake now, was Bowser, very much awake. With a great roar of anger, he sprang to his feet, and started after Granny, and startled the Merry Little Breezes at play on the Green Meadows.

CHAPTER TWENTY: THE CLEVER PLAN OF GRANNY FOX

THE BOLD VISIT of Old Granny Fox to Bowser the Hound in Farmer Brown's dooryard right in broad daylight was all a part of the clever plan Granny had worked out to make trouble for Old Man Coyote. First she had sent Reddy Fox to make sure that Old Man Coyote was taking his usual sun-nap in his usual place. If he were, Reddy was to softly steal away and then hurry to the top of the Crooked Little Path where it comes down the hill. When he got there, he was to bark three times. Granny was to he hidden behind the old stone wall on the edge of Farmer Brown's orchard, and when she heard Reddy bark, she was to do her part, while

Reddy was to hide in a secret place on the edge of the Green Forest and watch what would happen.

It all turned out just as Granny had planned. She had been in hiding behind the old stone wall only a few minutes when she heard Reddy bark three times. Granny grinned. Then she stole up to Farmer Brown's dooryard, and there she found Bowser the Hound fast asleep and dreaming. She was just getting ready to bark to waken him, when he waked himself with his own voice. It was just then that a hen happened to walk around the corner of the house. Granny's eyes sparkled. "Good," said she to herself. "I'll take this hen along with me, and Reddy and I will have a good dinner after I have set Bowser to chasing Old Man Coyote"—for that was what Granny was planning to do. So she caught the hen, threw it over her shoulder, and started off with Bowser the Hound after her, making a great noise with his big voice.

Now, of course Granny knew that she couldn't carry that hen very far and keep ahead of Bowser, so she ran straight across the Old Orchard towards the secret place on the edge of the Green Forest where she knew that Reddy Fox was hiding. When she was sure that Reddy could see her, she gave the hen a toss over into the grass and then raced away towards the Green Meadows. You see, she knew that Bowser would keep on right after her, and when it was safe for him to do so, Reddy would steal out from his hiding place and get the hen, and that is just what did happen.

Away ran Granny, and after her ran Bowser, and all the little meadow and forest people heard his great voice and were glad that he was not after them. But Granny Fox was not worried. You see, she had fooled him so many times that she knew she could do it again. So she kept just a little way ahead of him and gradually led him towards the place where Old Man Coyote took his sun-nap every day. But she was too smart to run straight towards it, "For," said she to herself, "if I do that, he will become alarmed and run away before Bowser is near enough to see him." So she ran in a big circle around the place, feeling sure that Old Man Coyote would lie perfectly still so as not to be seen.

Round and round ran Granny Fox with Bowser after her, and all the time she was making the circles smaller and smaller so as to get nearer and nearer to the napping-place of Old Man Coyote. When she thought that she was near enough, she suddenly started straight for it.

"Now," thought she, "he'll jump and run, and when Bowser sees him, he will forget all about me. He will follow Old Man Coyote, and perhaps he will drive him away from the Green Meadows forever."

Nearer and nearer to the napping place Granny drew. She was almost there. Why didn't Old Man Coyote jump and run? At last she was right to it. She could see just where he had been stretched out, but he wasn't there now. There wasn't a sign of him anywhere! What did it mean? Just then she heard a sound over in the Green Forest that made her grind her teeth with rage.

"Ha, ha, ha! Ho, ho, ho! Hee, hee, hee! Ha, ho, hee, ho!" It was the laughter of Old Man Coyote.

CHAPTER TWENTY-ONE: HOW PETER RABBIT HELPED OLD MAN COYOTE

A kindly word, a kindly deed,
Is like the planting of a seed;
It first sends forth a little root
And by and by bears splendid fruit.

WHEN OLD MAN COYOTE first came to the Green Meadows, to live, he chased Peter Rabbit and gave Peter a terrible fright. After that for some time Peter kept very close to the dear Old Briar-patch, where he always felt perfectly safe. But Peter dearly loves to roam, and Peter is very, very curious, so it wasn't long before he began to grow tired of the Old Briar-patch and longed to go abroad on the Green Meadows and in the Green Forest as he always had done, and find out all that was going on among his neighbors.

Of course Peter heard a great deal, for Sammy Jay and Blacky the Crow would stop almost every day to tell him the latest news about Old Man Coyote. They told him all about how Granny Fox had tried to make trouble between him and Prickly Porky the Porcupine, and how she had been found out. After they had gone, Peter sat very still for a long time, thinking it all over.

"H-m-m," said Peter to himself, "it is very plain to me that Old Man Coyote is smarter than Granny Fox, and that means a great deal to me. Yes, Sir, that means a great deal to me. It means that I have got to watch out for him even sharper than I have to watch out for Granny and Reddy Fox. Dear me, dear me, just as if I didn't have troubles enough as it is!"

As he talked, Peter was sitting on the very edge of the Old Briar-patch, looking towards the place where Sammy Jay had told him that Old Man Coyote took his sun-nap every day. Suddenly he saw something that made him stop thinking about his troubles and sit up a little straighter and open his big eyes a little wider. It was Reddy Fox, creeping very, very slowly and carefully towards the napping place of Old Man Coyote. When he was near enough to see, Reddy lay down in the grass and watched. After a little while he tiptoed back to the Green Forest.

Peter scratched his long left ear with his long right hind foot. "Now what did

*Old Man Coyote stopped and
peeped through the brambles.*

Reddy Fox do that for?" he said, thoughtfully.

The next day and the next day and the day after that, Peter saw Reddy Fox do the same thing, and all the time Peter's curiosity grew and grew and grew. He didn't say anything about it to anyone, but just puzzled and puzzled over it.

That afternoon Peter heard footsteps just outside the Old Briar-patch. Peeping out, he saw Old Man Coyote passing. Peter's curiosity could be kept down no longer.

"How do you do, Mr. Coyote?" said Peter in a very small and frightened sounding voice, but in a very polite manner.

Old Man Coyote stopped and peeped through the brambles. "Hello, Peter Rabbit," said he. "I haven't had the pleasure of meeting you outside of the Old Briar-patch for some time." He grinned when he said this in a way that showed all his long sharp teeth.

"No," replied Peter, "I—I—well, you see, I'm afraid of Old Granny and Reddy Fox."

Old Man Coyote grinned again, for he knew that it was himself Peter really feared. "Pooh, Peter Rabbit! You shouldn't be afraid of them!" said he. "They're not very smart. You ought to be able to keep out of their way."

Peter hopped a little nearer to the edge of the Old Briar-patch. "Tell me, Mr. Coyote, what is Reddy Fox watching you for every day when you take your sun-nap?"

"What's that?" demanded Old Man Coyote sharply. He listened gravely while Peter told him what he had seen. When Peter had finished, Mr. Coyote smiled, and somehow this time he didn't show all those dreadful teeth.

"Thank you, Peter Rabbit," said he. "You have done me a great favor, and I hope I can return it some time. Do you know, I believe that we are going to be friends."

And with that Old Man Coyote went on his way, chuckling to himself.

CHAPTER TWENTY-TWO: WHY THE CLEVER PLAN OF GRANNY FOX FAILED

WHEN OLD MAN COYOTE, chuckling to himself, left Peter Rabbit and the Old Briar-patch, he went straight over to look around the place where he took his sun-nap every day. His sharp eyes soon saw the place where Reddy Fox had been lying in the grass to watch him, for of course the grass was pressed down by the weight of Reddy's body.

"Peter Rabbit told me the truth, sure enough, and I guess I owe him a good turn," muttered Old Man Coyote, as he studied and studied to see why Reddy was watching him every day. You see, he is so sharp and clever himself that he was sure right away that Reddy had some plan in mind to bring him to the same place every day.

But he didn't let on that he knew anything about what was going on. Oh, my, no! The next day he curled up for his sun-nap just as usual, only this time he took care to lie in such a way that he would be looking towards Reddy's hiding place. Then he pretended to go to sleep, but if you had been there and looked into his eyes, you would have found no sleepy-winks there. No, Sir, you wouldn't have found one single sleepy-wink! Instead, his eyes were as bright as if there were no such thing as sleep. He saw Reddy steal out of the Green Forest. Then he closed his eyes all but just a tiny little crack, through which he could see Reddy's hiding place, but all the time he looked as if his eyes were shut tight.

Reddy crept softly as he could, which is very softly indeed, to his hiding place and lay down to watch. Old Man Coyote pretended to be very fast asleep, and every once in a while he would make-believe snore. But all the time he was watching Reddy. After a little while Reddy tiptoed away until he felt sure that it was safe to run. Then he hurried as fast as he could go to report to Old Granny Fox in the Green Forest. Old Man Coyote chuckled as he watched Reddy disappear.

"I don't know what it all means," said he, "but if he and Old Granny Fox think that they are going to catch me napping, they are making one of the biggest mistakes of their lives."

The next day and the next the same thing happened, but the day after that Reddy only stopped long enough to make sure that Old Man Coyote was there just as usual, and then he hurried away to the top of the Crooked Little Path that comes down the hill. There he barked three times. Old Man Coyote watched him go and heard him bark.

"That's some kind of a signal," said he to himself, "and unless I am greatly mistaken, it means mischief. I think I won't take a nap today, for I want to see what is going on."

With that, Old Man Coyote made a very long leap off to one side, then two more, so as to leave no scent to show which way he had gone. Then, chuckling to himself, he hurried to the Green Forest and hid where he could watch Reddy Fox. He saw Reddy hide on the edge of the Green Forest where he could watch Farmer Brown's dooryard, and then he crept up where he could watch too. Of course he saw Old Granny Fox when she led Bowser the Hound down across the Green Meadows, and he guessed right away what her plan was. It tickled him so that he had to clap both hands over his mouth as he watched sly old Granny take Bowser straight over to his napping-place, and when she saw how surprised she was to find him gone he sat up and laughed until all the little people on the Green Meadows and in the Green Forest heard him and wondered what could be tickling Old Man Coyote so.

CHAPTER TWENTY-THREE: OLD MAN COYOTE GETS A GOOD DINNER

WHEN OLD GRANNY FOX found that Old Man Coyote was not at his usual napping-place, she was sure that Reddy Fox must have been very stupid and thought that he saw him there when he didn't. She hurried to the Laughing Brook and waded in it for a little way in order to destroy her scent so that Bowser the Hound would not know in which direction she had gone. You know water is always the friend of little animals who leave scent in their footsteps. Bowser came baying up to the edge of the Laughing Brook, and there he stopped, for his wonderful nose could not follow Granny in the water and he could not tell whether she had gone up or down or across the brook.

But Bowser is not one to give up easily. No, indeed! He had learned many of Granny's tricks, and now he knew well enough what Granny had done. At least, Bowser thought that he knew.

"She'll wade a little way, and then she will come out of the water, so all I have to do is to find the place where she has come out, and there I will find her tracks again," said he, and with his nose to the ground he hurried down one bank of the Laughing Brook.

He went as far as he thought Granny could have waded, but there was no trace of her. Then he crossed the brook, and with his nose still to the ground, ran back to the starting place along the other bank.

"She didn't go down the brook, so she must have gone up," said Bowser, and started up the brook as eagerly as he had gone down. After running as far as he thought Granny could possible have waded, Bowser crossed over and ran back along the other bank to the starting place without finding any trace of Granny Fox. At last, with a foolish and ashamed air, Bowser gave it up and started for home, and all the time Granny Fox was lying in plain sight, watching him. Yes, Sir, she was watching him and laughing to herself. You see, she knew perfectly well that Bowser depends more on his nose than on his eyes, and that when he is running with his nose to the ground, he can see very little about him. So she had simply waded down the Laughing Brook to a flat rock in the middle of it, and on this she had stretched herself out and kept perfectly still. Twice Bowser had gone right past without seeing her. She enjoyed seeing him fooled so much that for the time being she quite forgot about Old Man Coyote and the failure of her clever plan to make trouble for him.

But when Bowser the Hound had gone, Granny remembered. She stopped laughing, and a look of angry disappointment crossed her face as she trotted towards home. But as she trotted along, her face cleared a little. "Anyway, Reddy and I will have a good dinner on that fat hen I caught in Farmer Brown's dooryard," she muttered.

When she reached home, there sat Reddy on the doorstep, but there was no sign of the fat hen, and Reddy looked very uneasy and frightened.

"Where's that fat hen I caught?" demanded Granny crossly.

"I—I—I'm sorry, Granny, but I haven't got it," said Reddy.

"Haven't got it!" snapped Granny. "What's the matter with you, Reddy Fox? Didn't you see me throw it in the grass when I ran past the place where you were hiding, and didn't you know enough to go and get it?"

"Yes," replied Reddy, "I saw you throw it in the grass, and I went out and got it, but on my way home I met someone who took it away from me."

"Took it away from you!" exclaimed Granny. "Who was it? Tell me this instant! Who was it?"

"Old Man Coyote," replied Reddy in a low, frightened voice.

Old Granny Fox simply stared at Reddy. She couldn't find a word to say. Instead of making trouble for Old Man Coyote, she had furnished him with a good dinner. He was smarter than she. She decided then and there that she could not drive Old Man Coyote out of the Green Forest and that she would either have to leave herself or accept him and make the best of it.

But that's what Old Man Coyote had thought all along, for he quite liked his new home and took a good deal of interest in his new neighbors.

One of these whom he found most interesting was Paddy the Beaver. Paddy really is a very wonderful fellow and I will tell you about him in the next book.

The Adventures of Paddy the Beaver

CHAPTER ONE: PADDY THE BEAVER BEGINS WORK

Work, work all the night
While the stars are shining bright;
Work, work all the day;
I have got no time to play.

THIS LITTLE RHYME Paddy the Beaver made up as he toiled at building the dam which was to make the pond he so much desired deep in the Green Forest. Of course it wasn't quite true, that about working all night and all day. Nobody could do that, you know, and keep it up. Everybody has to rest and sleep. Yes, and everybody has to play a little to be at their best. So it wasn't quite true that Paddy worked all day after working all night. But it was true that Paddy had no time to play. He had too much to do. He had had his playtime during the long summer, and now he had to get ready for the long, cold winter.

Now of all the little workers in the Green Forest, on the Green Meadows, and in the Smiling Pool, none can compare with Paddy the Beaver, not even his cousin, Jerry Muskrat. Happy Jack Squirrel and Striped Chipmunk store up food for the long, cold months when rough Brother North Wind and Jack Frost rule, and Jerry Muskrat builds a fine house wherein to keep warm and comfortable, but all this is as nothing to the work of Paddy the Beaver.

As I said before, Paddy had had a long playtime through the summer. He had wandered up and down the Laughing Brook. He had followed it way up to the place where it started. And all the time he had been studying and studying to make sure that he wanted to stay in the Green Forest. In the first place, he had to be sure that there was plenty of the kind of food that he likes. Then he had to be equally sure that he could make a pond near where this particular food grew. Last of all, he had to satisfy himself that if he did make a pond and build a home, he would be reasonably safe in it. And all these things he had done in his playtime. Now he was ready to go to work, and when Paddy begins work, he sticks to it until it is finished. He says that is the only way to succeed, and you know and I know that he is right.

Now Paddy the Beaver can see at night just as Reddy Fox and Peter Rabbit and Bobby Coon can, and he likes the night best, because he feels safest then. But he can see in the daytime too, and when he feels that he is perfectly safe and no one is watching, he works then too. Of course, the first thing to do was to build a dam across the Laughing Brook to make the pond he so much needed. He chose a low, open place deep in the Green Forest, around the edge of which grew many young aspen trees, the bark of which is his favorite food. Through the middle of this open place flowed the Laughing Brook. At the lower edge was just the place for a dam. It would not have to be very long, and when it was finished and the water was stopped in the Laughing Brook, it would just have to flow over the low, open place and make a pond there. Paddy's eyes twinkled when he first saw it. It was right then that he made up his mind to stay in the Green Forest.

So now that he was ready to begin his dam he went up the Laughing Brook to a place where alders and willows grew, and there he began work; that work was the cutting of a great number of trees by means of his big front teeth which were given him for just this purpose. And as he worked, Paddy was happy, for one can never be truly happy who does no work.

CHAPTER TWO: PADDY PLANS A POND

PADDY THE BEAVER was busy cutting down trees for the dam he had planned to build. Up in the woods of the North from which he had come to the Green Forest, he had learned all about tree-cutting and dam-building and canal-digging and house-building. Paddy's father and mother had been very wise in the Beaver world, and Paddy had been quick to learn. So now he knew just what to do and the best way of doing it. You know, a great many people waste time and labor doing things the wrong way, so that they have to be done over again. They forget to be sure they are right, and so they go ahead until they find they are wrong, and all their work goes for nothing.

But Paddy the Beaver isn't this kind. Paddy would never have leaped into the spring with the steep sides without looking, as Grandfather Frog did. So now he carefully picked out the trees to cut. He could not afford to waste time cutting down a tree that wasn't going to be just what he wanted when it was down. When he was sure that the tree was right, he looked up at the top to find out whether, when he had cut it, it would fall clear of other trees. He had learned to do that when he was quite young and heedless. He remembered just how he had felt when, after working hard, oh, so hard, to cut a big tree, he had warned all his friends to get out of the way so that they would not be hurt when it fell, and then it hadn't fallen at all because the top had caught in another tree. He was so mortified that he didn't get over it for a long time.

So now he made sure that a tree was going to fall clear and just where he wanted it. Then he sat up on his hind legs, and with his great broad tail for a brace, began to make the chips fly. You know Paddy has the most wonderful teeth for cutting. They are long and broad and sharp. He would begin by making a deep bite, and then another just a little way below. Then he would pry out the little piece of wood between. When he had cut very deep on one side so that the tree would fall that way, he would work around to the other side. Just as soon as the tree began to lean and he was sure that it was going to fall, he would scamper away so as to be out of danger. He loved to see those tall trees lean forward slowly, then faster and faster, till they struck the ground with a crash.

Just as soon as they were down, he would trim off the branches until the trees where just long poles. This was easy work, for he could take off a good-sized branch with one bite. On many he left their bushy tops. When he had trimmed them to suit him and had cut them into the right lengths, he would tug and pull them down to the place where he meant to build his dam.

There he placed the poles side by side, not across the Laughing Brook like a bridge, but with the big ends pointing up the Laughing Brook, which was quite broad but shallow right there. To keep them from floating away, he rolled stones and piled mud on the bushy ends. Clear across on both sides he laid those poles until the water began to rise. Then he dragged more poles and piled them on top of these and wedged short sticks crosswise between them.

And all the time the Laughing Brook was having harder and harder work to run. Its merry laugh grew less merry and finally almost stopped because, you see, the water could not get through between all those poles and sticks fast enough. It was just about that time that the little people of the Smiling Pool decided that it was time to see just what Paddy was doing, and they started up the Laughing Brook, leaving only Grandfather Frog and the tadpoles in the Smiling Pool, which for a little while would smile no more.

CHAPTER THREE: PADDY HAS MANY VISITORS

PADDY THE BEAVER knew perfectly well that he would have visitors just as soon as he began to build his dam. He expected a lot of them. You see he knew that none of them ever had seen a Beaver at work unless perhaps it was Prickly Porky the Porcupine, who also had come down from the North. So as he worked he kept his ears open, and he smiled to himself as he heard a little rustle here and then a little rustle there. He knew just what those little rustles meant. Each one meant another visitor. Yes, Sir, each rustle meant another visitor, and yet not one had shown himself.

Paddy chuckled. "Seems to me that you are dreadfully afraid to show your-selves," said he in a loud voice, just as if he were talking to nobody in particular. Everything was still. There wasn't so much as a rustle after Paddy spoke. He chuck-led again. He could just *feel* ever so many eyes watching him, though he didn't see a single pair. And he knew that the reason his visitors were hiding so carefully was because they were afraid of him. You see, Paddy was much bigger than most of the little meadow and forest people, and they didn't know what kind of a temper he might have. It is always safest to be very distrustful of strangers. That is one of the very first things taught all little meadow and forest children.

Of course, Paddy knew all about this. He had been brought up that way. "Be sure, and then you'll never be sorry" had been one of his mother's favorite sayings, and he had always remembered it. Indeed, it had saved him a great deal of trouble. So now he was perfectly willing to go right on working and let his hidden visitors watch him until they were sure that he meant them no harm. You see, he himself felt quite sure that none of them was big enough to do him any harm. Little Joe Otter was the only one he had any doubts about, and he felt quite sure that Little Joe wouldn't try to pick a quarrel. So he kept right on cutting trees, trimming off the branches, and hauling the trunks down to the dam he was building. Some of them he floated down the Laughing Brook. This was easier.

Now when the little people of the Smiling Pool, who were the first to find out that Paddy the Beaver had come to the Green Forest, had started up the Laughing Brook to see what he was doing, they had told the Merry Little Breezes where they were going. The Merry Little Breezes had been greatly excited. They couldn't understand how a stranger could have been living in the Green Forest without their knowledge. You see, they quite forgot that they very seldom wandered to the deepest part of the Green Forest.

Of course they started at once, as fast as they could go, to tell all the other lit-tle people who live on or around the Green Meadows, all but Old Man Coyote. For some reason they thought it best not to tell him. They were a little doubtful about Old Man Coyote. He was so big and strong and so sly and smart that all his neigh-bors were afraid of him. Perhaps the Merry Little Breezes had this fact in mind, and knew that none would dare go to call on the stranger if they knew that Old Man Coyote was going too. Anyway, they simply passed the time of day with Old ManCoyote and hurried on to tell everyone else, and the very last one they met was Sammy Jay.

Sammy was terribly put out to think that anything should be going on that he didn't know about first. You know he is very fond of prying into the affairs of other people, and he loves dearly to boast that there is nothing going on in the Green Forest or on the Green Meadows that he doesn't know about. So now his pride was hurt, and he was in a terrible rage as he started after the Merry Little Breezes for the place deep in the Green Forest where they said Paddy the Beaver was at work. He didn't believe a word of it, but he would see for himself.

CHAPTER FOUR: SAMMY JAY SPEAKS HIS MIND

WHEN SAMMY JAY reached the place deep in the Green Forest where Paddy the Beaver was so hard at work, he didn't hide as had the little four-footed people. You see, of course, he had no reason to hide, because he felt perfectly safe. Paddy had just cut a big tree, and it fell with a crash as Sammy came hurrying up. Sammy was so surprised that for a minute he couldn't find his tongue. He had not supposed that anybody but Farmer Brown or Farmer Brown's boy could cut down so large a tree as that, and it quite took his breath away. But he got it again in a minute. He was boiling with anger, anyway, to think that he should have been the last to learn that Paddy had come down from the North to make his home in the Green Forest,

"Mr. Jay seems to have gotten out of the wrong side of his bed this morning."

and here was a chance to speak his mind.

"Thief! thief! thief!" he screamed in his harshest voice.

Paddy the Beaver looked up with a twinkle in his eyes. "Hello, Mr. Jay. I see you haven't any better manners than your cousin who lives up where I come from," said he.

"Thief! thief! thief!" screamed Sammy, hopping up and down, he was so angry.

"Meaning yourself, I suppose," said Paddy. "I never did see an honest Jay, and I don't suppose I ever will."

"Ha, ha, ha!" laughed Peter Rabbit, who had quite forgotten that he was hiding.

"Oh, how do you do, Mr. Rabbit? I'm very glad you have called on me this morning," said Paddy, just as if he hadn't known all the time just where Peter was. "Mr. Jay seems to have gotten out of the wrong side of his bed this morning."

Peter laughed again. "He always does," said he. "If he didn't, he wouldn't be happy. You wouldn't think it to look at him, but he is happy right now. He doesn't know it, but he is. He always is happy when he can show what a bad temper he has."

Sammy Jay glared down at Peter. Then he glared at Paddy. And all the time he still shrieked "Thief!" as hard as ever he could. Paddy kept right on working, paying no attention to Sammy. This made Sammy more angry than ever. He kept coming nearer and nearer until at last he was in the very tree that Paddy happened to be cutting. Paddy's eyes twinkled.

"I'm no thief!" he exclaimed suddenly.

"You are! You are! Thief! Thief!" shrieked Sammy. "You're stealing our trees!"

"They're not your trees," retorted Paddy. "They belong to the Green Forest, and the Green Forest belongs to all who love it, and we all have a perfect right to take what we need from it. I need these trees, and I've just as much right to take them as you have to take the fat acorns that drop in the fall."

"No such thing!" screamed Sammy. You know he can't talk without screaming, and the more excited he gets, the louder he screams. "No such thing! Acorns are food. They are meant to eat. I have to have them to live. But you are cutting down whole trees. You are spoiling the Green Forest. You don't belong here. Nobody invited you, and nobody wants you. You're a thief!"

Then up spoke Jerry Muskrat who, you know, is cousin to Paddy the Beaver.

"Don't you mind him," said he, pointing at Sammy Jay. "Nobody does. He's the greatest trouble-maker in the Green Forest or on the Green Meadows. He would steal from his own relatives. Don't mind what he says, Cousin Paddy."

Now all this time Paddy had been working away just as if no one was around. Just as Jerry stopped speaking, Paddy thumped the ground with his tail, which is his way of warning people to watch out, and suddenly scurried away as fast as he could run. Sammy Jay was so surprised that he couldn't find his tongue for a minute, and he didn't notice anything peculiar about that tree. Then suddenly he felt himself falling. With a frightened scream, he spread his wings to fly, but branches of the tree swept him down with them right into the Laughing Brook.

You see, while Sammy had been speaking his mind, Paddy the Beaver had cut down the very tree in which he was sitting.

Sammy wasn't hurt, but he was wet and muddy and terribly frightened—the most miserable-looking Jay that ever was seen. It was too much for all the little people who were hiding. They just had to laugh. Then they all came out to pay their respects to Paddy the Beaver.

CHAPTER FIVE: PADDY KEEPS HIS PROMISE

PADDY THE BEAVER kept right on working just as if he hadn't any visitors. You see, it is a big undertaking to build a dam. And when that was done there was a house to build and a supply of food for the winter to cut and store. Oh, Paddy the Beaver had no time for idle gossip, you may be sure! So he kept right on building his dam. It didn't look much like a dam at first, and some of Paddy's visitors turned up their noses when they first saw it. They had heard stories of what a wonderful dam-builder Paddy was, and they had expected to see something like the smooth, grass-covered bank with which Farmer Brown kept the Big River from running back on his low lands. Instead, all they saw was a great pile of poles and sticks which looked like anything but a dam.

"Pooh!" exclaimed Billy Mink, "I guess we needn't worry about the Laughing Brook and the Smiling Pool, if that is the best Paddy can do. Why, the water of the Laughing Brook will work through that in no time."

Of course Paddy heard him, but he said nothing, just kept right on working.

"Just look at the way he has laid those sticks!" continued Billy Mink. "Seems as if anyone would know enough to lay them *across* the Laughing Brook instead of just the other way. I could build a better dam than that."

Paddy said nothing; he just kept right on working.

"Yes, Sir," Billy boasted. "I could build a better dam than that. Why, that pile of sticks will never stop the water."

"Is something the matter with your eyesight, Billy Mink?" inquired Jerry Muskrat.

"Of course not!" retorted Billy indignantly. "Why?"

"Oh, nothing much, only you don't seem to notice that already the Laughing Brook is over its banks above Paddy's dam," replied Jerry, who had been studying the dam with a great deal of interest.

Billy looked a wee bit foolish, for sure enough there was a little pool just above the dam, and it was growing bigger.

Paddy still kept at work, saying nothing. He was digging in front of the dam now, and the mud and grass he dug up he stuffed in between the ends of the sticks and patted them down with his hands. He did this all along the front of the dam and on top of it, too, wherever he thought it was needed. Of course this made it harder for the water to work through, and the little pond above the dam began to grow faster. It wasn't a great while before it was nearly to the top of the dam, which at first was very low. Then Paddy brought more sticks. This was easier now, because he could float them down from where he was cutting. He would put them in place on the top of the dam, then hurry for more. Wherever it was needed, he would put in mud. He even rolled a few stones in to help hold the mass.

So the dam grew and grew, and so did the pond above the dam. Of course, it took a good many days to build so big a dam, and a lot of hard work! Every morning the little people of the Green Forest and the Green Meadow would visit it, and every morning they would find that it had grown a great deal in the night, for that is when Paddy likes best to work.

By this time, the Laughing Brook had stopped laughing, and down in the Smiling Pool there was hardly water enough for the minnows to feel safe a minute. Billy Mink had stopped making fun of the dam, and all the little people who live in the Laughing Brook and Smiling Pool were terribly worried.

To be sure, Paddy had warned them of what he was going to do, and had promised that as soon as his pond was big enough, the water would once more run in the Laughing Brook. They tried to believe him, but they couldn't help having just a wee bit of fear that he might not be wholly honest. You see, they didn't know him, for he was a stranger. Jerry Muskrat was the only one who seemed absolutely sure that everything would be all right. Perhaps that was because Paddy is his cousin, and Jerry couldn't help feeling proud of such a big cousin and one who was so smart.

So day by day the dam grew, and the pond grew, and one morning Grandfather Frog, down in what had once been the Smiling Pool, heard a sound that made his heart jump for joy. It was a murmur that kept growing and growing, until at last it was the merry laugh of the Laughing Brook. Then he knew that Paddy had kept his word, and water would once more fill the Smiling Pool.

CHAPTER SIX: FARMER BROWN'S BOY GROWS CURIOUS

NOW IT HAPPENED that the very day before Paddy the Beaver decided that his pond was big enough, and so allowed the water to run in the Laughing Brook once more, Farmer Brown's boy took it into his head to go fishing in the Smiling Pool. Just as usual he went whistling down across the Green Meadows. Somehow, when he goes fishing, he always feels like whistling. Grandfather Frog heard him coming and dived into the little bit of water remaining in the Smiling Pool and stirred up the mud at the bottom so that Farmer Brown's boy shouldn't see him.

Nearer and nearer drew the whistle. Suddenly it stopped right short off. Farmer Brown's boy had come in sight of the Smiling Pool or rather, it was what used to be the Smiling Pool. Now there wasn't any Smiling Pool, for the very little pool left was too small and sickly looking to smile. There were great banks of mud, out of which grew the bulrushes. The lily pads were forlornly stretched out toward the tiny pool of water remaining. Where the banks were steep and high, the holes that Jerry Muskrat and Billy Mink knew so well were plain to see. Over at one side stood Jerry Muskrat's house, wholly out of water.

Somehow, it seemed to Farmer Brown's boy that he must be dreaming. He never, never had seen anything like this before, not even in the very driest weather of the hottest part of the summer. He looked this way and looked that way. The Green Meadows looked just as usual. The Green Forest looked just as usual. The Laughing Brook—ha! What was the matter with the Laughing Brook? He couldn't hear it and that, you know, was very unusual. He dropped his rod and ran over to the Laughing Brook. There wasn't any brook. No, sir, there wasn't any brook; just pools of water with the tiniest of streams trickling between. Big stones over which he had always seen the water running in the prettiest of little white falls were bare and dry. In the little pools frightened minnows were darting about.

Farmer Brown's boy scratched his head in a puzzled way. "I don't understand it," said he. "I don't understand it at all. Something must have gone wrong with the springs that supply the water for the Laughing Brook. They must have failed. Yes, Sir, that is just what must have happened. But I never heard of such a thing happening before, and I really don't see how it could happen. He stared up into the Green Forest just as if he thought he could see those springs. Of course, he didn't think anything of the kind. He was just turning it all over in his mind. "I know what I'll do, I'll go up to those springs this afternoon and find out what the trouble is," he said out loud. "They are way over almost on the other side of the Green Forest, and the easiest way to get there will be to start from home and cut across the Old Pasture up to the edge of the Mountain behind the Green Forest. If I try to follow up the Laughing Brook now, it will take too long, because it winds and twists so. Besides, it is too hard work."

With that, Farmer Brown's boy went back and picked up his rod. Then he started for home across the Green Meadows, and for once he wasn't whistling. You see, he was too busy thinking. In fact, he was so busy thinking that he didn't see Jimmy Skunk until he almost stepped on him, and then he gave a frightened jump and ran, for without a gun he was just as much afraid of Jimmy as Jimmy was of him when he did have a gun.

Jimmy just grinned and went on about his business. It always tickles Jimmy to see people run away from him, especially people so much bigger than himself; they look so silly.

"I should think that they would have learned by this time that if they don't bother me, I won't bother them," he muttered as he rolled over a stone to look for fat beetles. "Somehow, folks never seem to understand me."

CHAPTER SEVEN: FARMER BROWN'S
BOY GETS ANOTHER SURPRISE

ACROSS THE OLD PASTURE to the foot of the Mountain back of the Green Forest tramped Farmer Brown's boy. Ahead of him trotted Bowser the Hound, sniffing and snuffing for the tracks of Reddy or Granny Fox. Of course he didn't find them, for Reddy and Granny hadn't been up in the Old Pasture for a long time. But he did find old Jed Thumper, the big gray Rabbit who had made things so uncomfortable for Peter Rabbit once upon a time and gave old Jed such a fright that he didn't look where he was going and almost ran head-first into Farmer Brown's boy.

"Hi, there, you old cottontail!" yelled Farmer Brown's boy, and this frightened off Jed still more, so that he actually ran right past his own castle of bullbriars without seeing it.

Farmer Brown's boy kept on his way, laughing at the fright of old Jed Thumper. Presently he reached the springs from which came the water that made the very beginning of the Laughing Brook. He expected to find them dry, for way down on the Green Meadows the Smiling Pool was nearly dry, and the Laughing Brook was nearly dry, and he had supposed that of course the reason was that the springs where the Laughing Brook started were no longer bubbling.

But they were! The clear cold water came bubbling up out of the ground just as it always had, and ran off down into the Green Forest in a little stream that would grow and grow as it ran and became the Laughing Brook. Farmer Brown's boy took off his ragged old straw hat and scowled down at the bubbling water just as if it had no business to be bubbling there.

Jimmy just grinned and went on about his business.

Of course, he didn't think just that. The fact is, he didn't know just what he did think. Here were the springs bubbling away just as they always had. There was the little stream starting off down into the Green Forest with a gurgle that by and by would become a laugh, just as it always had. And yet down on the Green Meadows on the other side of the Green Forest there was no longer a Laughing Brook or a Smiling Pool. He felt as if he ought to pinch himself to make sure that he was awake and not dreaming.

"I don't know what it means," said he, talking out loud. "No, Sir, I don't know what it means at all, but I'm going to find out. There's a cause for everything in this world, and when a fellow doesn't know a thing, it is his business to find out all about it. I'm going to find out what has happened to the Laughing Brook, if it takes me a year!"

With that he started to follow the little stream which ran gurgling down into the Green Forest. He had followed that little stream more than once, and now he found it just as he remembered it. The farther it ran, the larger it grew, until at last it became the Laughing Brook, merrily tumbling over rocks and making deep pools in which the trout loved to hide. At last he came to the edge of a little open hollow in the very heart of the Green Forest. He knew what splendid deep holes there were in the Laughing Brook here, and how the big trout loved to lie in them because they were deep and cool. He was thinking of these trout now and wishing that he had brought along his fishing rod. He pushed his way through a thicket of alders and then—Farmer Brown's boy stopped suddenly and fairly gasped! He had to stop because there right in front of him was a pond!

He rubbed his eyes and looked again. Then he stooped down and put his hand in the water to see if it was real. There was no doubt about it. It was real water—a real pond where there never had been a pond before. It was very still there in the heart of the Green Forest. It was always very still there, but it seemed stiller than usual as he tramped around the edge of this strange pond. He felt as if it were all a dream. He wondered if pretty soon he wouldn't wake up and find it all untrue. But he didn't, so he kept on tramping until presently he came to a dam—a splendid dam of logs and sticks and mud. Over the top of it the water was running, and down in the Green Forest below he could hear the Laughing Brook just beginning to laugh once more. Farmer Brown's boy sat down with his elbows on his knees and his chin in his hands. He was almost too much surprised to even think.

CHAPTER EIGHT: PETER RABBIT GETS A DUCKING

FARMER BROWN'S BOY sat with his chin in his hands staring at the new pond in the Green Forest and at the dam which had made it. That dam puzzled him. Who could have built it? What did they build it for? Why hadn't he heard them chopping? He looked carelessly at the stump of one of the trees, and then a still more puzzled look made deep furrows between his eyes. It looked—yes, it looked very much as if teeth, and not an axe, had cut down that tree. Farmer Brown's boy stared and stared, his mouth gaping wide open. He looked so funny that Peter Rabbit, who was hiding under an old pile of brush close by, nearly laughed right out.

But Peter didn't laugh. No, Sir, Peter didn't laugh, for just that very minute something happened. Sniff! Sniff! That was right behind him at the very edge of the old brushpile, and every hair on Peter stood on end with fright.

"Bow, wow, wow!" It seemed to Peter that the great voice was right in his very ears. It frightened him so that he just *had* to jump. He didn't have time to think. And so he jumped right out from under the pile of brush and of course right into plain sight. And the very instant he jumped there came another great roar behind him. Of course it was from Bowser the Hound. You see, Bowser had been following the trail of his master, but as he always stops to sniff at everything he passes, he had been some distance behind. When he came to the pile of brush under which Peter was hiding he had sniffed at that, and of course he had smelled Peter right away.

Now when Peter jumped out so suddenly, he had landed right at one end of the dam. The second roar of Bowser's great voice frightened him still more, and he jumped right up on the dam. There was nothing for him to do now but go across, and it wasn't the best of going. No, indeed, it wasn't the best of going. You see, it was mostly a tangle of sticks. Happy Jack Squirrel or Chatterer the Red Squirrel or Striped Chipmunk would have skipped across it without the least trouble. But Peter Rabbit has no sharp little claws with which to cling to logs and sticks, and right away he was in a peck of trouble. He slipped down between the sticks, scrambled out, slipped again, and then, trying to make a long jump, he lost his balance and—tumbled heels over head into the water.

Poor Peter Rabbit! He gave himself up for lost this time. He could swim, but at best he is a poor swimmer and doesn't like the water. He couldn't dive and keep out of sight like Jerry Muskrat or Billy Mink. All he could do was to paddle as fast as his legs would go. The water had gone up his nose and down his throat so that he choked, and all the time he felt sure that Bowser the Hound would plunge in after him and catch him. And if he shouldn't why Farmer Brown's boy would simply wait for him to come ashore and then catch him.

But Farmer Brown's boy didn't do anything of the kind. No, Sir, he didn't. Instead he shouted to Bowser and called him away. Bowser didn't want to come, but he long ago learned to obey, and very slowly he walked over to where his master was sitting.

"You know it wouldn't be fair, old fellow, to try to catch Peter now. It wouldn't be fair at all, and we never want to do anything unfair, do we?" said he. Perhaps Bowser didn't agree, but he wagged his tail as if he did, and sat down beside his master to watch Peter swim.

It seemed to Peter as if he never, never would reach the shore, though really it was only a very little distance that he had to swim. When he did scramble out, he was a sorry-looking Rabbit. He didn't waste any time, but started for home as fast as he could go, lipperty—lipperty—lip. And Farmer Brown's boy and Bowser the Hound just laughed and didn't try to catch him at all.

"Well, I never!" exclaimed Sammy Jay, who had seen it all from the top of a pine tree. "Well, I never! I guess Farmer Brown's boy isn't so bad, after all."

CHAPTER NINE: PADDY PLANS A HOUSE

PADDY THE BEAVER sat on his dam, and his eyes shone with happiness as he looked out over the shining water of the pond he had made. All around the edge of it grew the tall trees of the Green Forest. It was very beautiful and very still and very lonesome. That is, it would have seemed lonesome to almost anyone but Paddy the Beaver. But Paddy never is lonesome. You see, he finds company in the trees and flowers and all the little plants.

It was still, very, very still. Over on one side was a beautiful rosy glow in the water. It was the reflection from jolly, round, red Mr. Sun. Paddy couldn't see him because of the tall trees, but he knew exactly what Mr. Sun was doing. He was going to bed behind the Purple Hills. Pretty soon the little stars would come out and twinkle down at him. He loves the little stars and always watches for the first one.

Yes, Paddy the Beaver was very happy. He would have been perfectly happy except for one thing. Farmer Brown's boy had found his dam and pond that very afternoon, and Paddy wasn't quite sure what Farmer Brown's boy might do. He had kept himself snugly hidden while Farmer Brown's boy was there, and he felt quite sure that Farmer Brown's boy didn't know who had built the dam. But for this reason he might, he just *might*, try to find out all about it, and that would mean that Paddy would always have to be on the watch.

"But what's the use of worrying over troubles that haven't come yet, and may never come? Time enough to worry when they do come," said Paddy to himself, which shows that Paddy has a great deal of wisdom in his little brown head. "The thing for me to do now is to get ready for winter, and that means a great deal of work," he continued. "Let me see, I've got to build a house, a big, stout, warm house, where I will be warm and safe when my pond is frozen over. And I've got to lay in a supply of food, enough to last me until gentle Sister South Wind comes to prepare the way for lovely Mistress Spring. My, my, I can't afford to be sitting here dreaming when there is so much to be done!"

With that Paddy slipped into the water and swam all around his new pond to make sure of just the best place to build his house. Now, placing one's house in just the right place is a very important matter. Some people are dreadfully careless about this. Jimmy Skunk, for instance, often makes the mistake of digging his house (you know Jimmy makes his house underground) right where everyone who happens along that way will see it. Perhaps that is because Jimmy is so independent that he doesn't care who knows where he lives.

But Paddy the Beaver never is careless. He always chooses just the very best place. He makes sure that it is best before he begins. So now, although he was quite positive just where his house should be, he swam around the pond to make doubly sure. Then, when he was quite satisfied, he swam over to the place he had chosen. It was where the water was quite deep.

"There mustn't be the least chance that the ice will ever get thick enough to close up my doorway, said he, "and I'm sure it never will here. I must make the foundations strong and the walls thick. I must have plenty of mud to plaster with, and inside, up above the water, I must have the snuggest, warmest room where I can sleep in comfort. This is the place to build it, and it is high time I was at work."

With that Paddy swam over to the place where he had cut the trees for his dam, and his heart was light, for he had long ago learned that the surest way to be happy is to be busy.

CHAPTER TEN: PADDY STARTS HIS HOUSE

JERRY MUSKRAT WAS very much interested when he found that Paddy the Beaver, who you know is his cousin, was building a house. Jerry is a house-builder himself, and down deep in his heart he very much doubted if Paddy could build as good a house as he could. His house was down in the Smiling Pool, and Jerry thought it a very wonderful house indeed, and was very proud of it. It was built of mud and sod and little alder and willow twigs and bulrushes. Jerry had spent one winter in it, and he had decided to spend another there after he had fixed it up a little. So, as long as he didn't have to build a brand-new house, he could afford the time to watch his cousin Paddy. Perhaps he hoped that Paddy would ask his advice.

But Paddy did nothing of the kind. He had seen Jerry Muskrat's house, and he had smiled. But he had taken great pains not to let Jerry see that smile. He wouldn't have hurt Jerry's feelings for the world. He is too polite and good-natured to do anything like that. So Jerry sat on the end of an old log and watched Paddy work. The first thing to build was the foundation. This was of mud and grass with sticks worked into it to hold it together. Paddy dug the mud from the bottom of his new pond. And because the pond was new, there was a great deal of grassy sod there, which was just what Paddy needed. It was very convenient.

Jerry watched a little while and then, because Jerry is a worker himself, he just had to get busy and help. Rather timidly he told his big cousin that he would like to have a share in building the new house.

"All right," replied Paddy, "that will be fine. You can bring mud while I am getting the sticks and grass."

So Jerry dived down to the bottom of the pond and dug up mud and piled it on the foundation and was happy. The little stars looked down and twinkled merrily as they watched the two workers. So the foundation grew and grew down under the water. Jerry was very much surprised at the size of it. It was ever and ever so much bigger than the foundation for his own house. You see, he had forgotten how much bigger Paddy is.

Each night Jerry and Paddy worked, resting during the daytime. Occasionally Bobby Coon or Reddy Fox or Unc' Billy Possum or Jimmy Skunk would come to the edge of the pond to see what was going on. Peter Rabbit came every night. But they couldn't see much because, you know, Paddy and Jerry were working under water.

But at last Peter was rewarded. There, just above the water, was a splendid platform of mud and grass and sticks. A great many sticks were carefully laid as soon as the platform was above the water, for Paddy was very particular about this. You see, it was to be the floor for the splendid room he was planning to build. When it suited him, he began to pile mud in the very middle.

Jerry puzzled and puzzled over this. Where was Paddy's room going to be, if he piled up the mud that way? But he didn't like to ask questions, so he kept right on helping. Paddy would dive down to the bottom and then come up with double handfuls of mud, which he held against his chest. He would scramble out onto the platform and waddle over to the pile in the middle, where he would put the mud and pat it down. Then back to the bottom for more.

And so the mud pile grew and grew, until it was quite two feet high. "Now," said Paddy, "I'll build the walls, and I guess you can't help me much with those. I'm going to begin them tomorrow night. Perhaps you will like to see me do it, Cousin Jerry."

"I certainly will," replied Jerry, still puzzling over that pile of mud in the middle.

CHAPTER ELEVEN: PETER RABBIT AND JERRY MUSKRAT ARE PUZZLED

JERRY MUSKRAT WAS more and more sure that his big cousin, Paddy the Beaver, didn't know quite so much as he might about house-building. Jerry would have liked to offer some suggestions, but he didn't quite dare. You see, he was very anxious not to displease his big cousin. But he felt that he simply had got to speak his mind to someone, so he swam across to where he had seen Peter Rabbit almost every night since Paddy began to build. Sure enough, Peter was there, sitting up very straight and staring with big round eyes at the platform of mud and sticks out in the water where Paddy the Beaver was at work.

"Well, Peter, what do you think of it?" asked Jerry

"What is it?" asked Peter innocently. "Is it another dam?"

Jerry threw back his head and laughed and laughed.

Peter looked at him suspiciously. "I don't see anything to laugh at," said he.

"Why, it's a house, you stupid. It's Paddy's new house," replied Jerry, wiping the tears of laughter from his eyes.

"I'm not stupid!" retorted Peter. "How was I to know that that pile of mud and sticks is meant for a house? It certainly doesn't look it. Where is the door?"

"To tell you the truth, I don't think it is much of a house myself," replied Jerry. "It has got a door, all right. In fact it has got three. You can't see them because they

are under water, and there is a passage from each right up through that platform of mud and sticks, which is the foundation of the house. It really is a very fine foundation, Peter; it really is. But what I can't understand is what Paddy is thinking of by building that great pile of mud right in the middle. When he gets his walls built, where will his bedroom be? There won't be any room at all. It won't be a house at all—just a big useless pile of sticks and mud.

Peter scratched his head and then pulled his whiskers thoughtfully as he gazed out at the pile in the water where Paddy the Beaver was at work.

"What is it?" asked Peter innocently.

"It does look foolish, that's a fact," said he. "Why don't you point out to him the mistake he is making, Jerry? You have built such a splendid house yourself that you ought to be able to help Paddy and show him his mistakes."

Jerry had smiled a very self-satisfied smile when Peter mentioned his fine house, but he shook his head at the suggestion that he should give Paddy advice.

"I—I don't just like to," he confessed. "You know, he might not like it and—and it doesn't seem as if it would be quite polite."

Peter sniffed. "That wouldn't trouble me any if he were my cousin," said he.

Jerry shook his head, "No, I don't believe it would," he replied, "but it does trouble me and—and—well, I think I'll wait awhile."

Now all this time Paddy had been hard at work. He was bringing the longest branches which he had cut from the trees out of which he had built his dam, and a lot of slender willow and alder poles. He pushed these ahead of him as he swam. When he reached the foundation of his house, he would lean them against the pile of mud in the middle with their big ends resting on the foundation. So he worked all the way around until by and by the mud pile in the middle couldn't be seen. It was completely covered with sticks, and they were cunningly fastened together at the tops.

CHAPTER TWELVE: JERRY MUSKRAT LEARNS SOMETHING

*If you think you know it all
You are riding for a fall.
Use your ears and use your eyes,
But hold your tongue and you'll be wise.*

JERRY MUSKRAT WILL tell you that is as true as true can be. Jerry knows. He found it out for himself. Now he is very careful what he says about other people or what they are doing. But he wasn't so careful when his cousin, Paddy the Beaver, was building his house. No, Sir, Jerry wasn't so careful then. He thought he knew more about building a house than Paddy did. He was sure of it when he watched Paddy heap up a great pile of mud right in the middle where his room ought to be, and then build a wall of sticks around it. He said as much to Peter Rabbit.

Now it is never safe to say anything to Peter Rabbit that you don't care to have others know. Peter has a great deal of respect for Jerry Muskrat's opinion on house-building. You see, he very much admires Jerry's snug house in the Smiling Pool. It really is a very fine house, and Jerry may be excused for being proud of it. But that doesn't excuse Jerry for thinking that he knows all there is to know about house-building. Of course Peter told everyone he met that Paddy the Beaver was making a foolish mistake in building his house, and that Jerry Muskrat, who ought to know, said so.

So whenever they got the chance, the little people of the Green Forest and Green Meadows would steal up to the shore of Paddy's new pond and chuckle as they looked out at the great pile of sticks and mud which Paddy had built for a house, but in which he had forgotten to make a room. At least they supposed that he had forgotten this very important thing. He must have, for there wasn't any room. It was a great joke. They laughed a lot about it, and they lost a great deal of the respect for Paddy which they had had since he built his wonderful dam.

Jerry and Peter sat in the moonlight talking it over. Paddy had stopped bringing sticks for his wall. He had dived down out of sight, and he was gone a long time. Suddenly Jerry noticed that the water had grown very, very muddy all around Paddy's new house. He wrinkled his brows trying to think what Paddy could be doing. Presently Paddy came up for air. Then he went down again, and the water grew muddier than ever. This went on for a long time. Every little while Paddy would come up for air and a few minutes of rest. Then down he would go, and the water would grow muddier and muddier.

At last Jerry could stand it no longer. He just had to see what was going on. He slipped into the water and swam over to where the water was muddiest. Just as he got there up came Paddy.

"Hello, Cousin Jerry!" said he. "I was just going to invite you over to see what you think of my house inside. Just follow me."

Paddy dived, and Jerry dived after him. He followed Paddy in at one of the three doorways under water and up a smooth hall right into the biggest, nicest bedroom Jerry had ever seen in all his life. He just gasped in sheer surprise. He couldn't do anything else. He couldn't find his tongue to say a word. Here he was in this splendid great room up above the water, and he had been so sure that there wasn't any room at all! He just didn't know what to make of it.

Paddy's eyes twinkled. "Well," said he, "what do you think of it?"

"I—I—think it is splendid, just perfectly splendid! But I don't understand it at all, Cousin Paddy. I—I—Where is that great pile of mud I helped you build in the middle?" Jerry looked as foolish as he felt when he asked this.

"Why, I've dug it all away. That's what made the water so muddy," replied Paddy.

"But what did you build it for in the first place?" Jerry asked.

"Because I had to have something solid to rest my sticks against while I was building my walls, of course," replied Paddy. When I got the tops fastened together for a roof, they didn't need a support any longer, and then I dug it away to make this room. I couldn't have built such a big room any other way. I see you don't know very much about house-building, Cousin Jerry."

"I—I'm afraid I don't," confessed Jerry sadly.

CHAPTER THIRTEEN: THE QUEER STOREHOUSE

EVERYBODY KNEW THAT Paddy the Beaver was laying up a supply of food for the winter, and everybody thought it was queer food. That is, everybody but Prickly Porky the Porcupine thought so. Prickly Porky likes the same kind of food, but he never lays up a supply. He just goes out and gets it when he wants it, winter or summer. What kind of food was it? Why, bark, to be sure. Yes, Sir, it was just bark—the bark of certain kinds of trees.

Now Prickly Porky can climb the trees and eat the bark right there, but Paddy the Beaver cannot climb, and if he would just eat the bark that he can reach from the ground, it would take such a lot of trees to keep him filled up that he would soon spoil the Green Forest. You know, when the bark is taken off a tree all the way around, the tree dies. That is because all the things that a tree draws out of the ground to make it grow and keep it alive are carried up from the roots in the sap, and the sap cannot go up the tree trunks and into the branches when the bark is taken off, because it is up the inside of the bark that it travels. So when the bark is taken from a tree all the way around the trunk, the tree just starves to death.

Now Paddy the Beaver loves the Green Forest as dearly as you and I do, and perhaps even a little more dearly. You see, it is his home. Besides, Paddy never is wasteful. So he cuts down a tree so that he can get all the bark instead of killing a whole lot of trees for a very little bark, as he might do if he were lazy. There isn't a lazy bone in him—not one. The bark he likes best is from the aspen. When he cannot get that, he will eat the bark from the poplar, the alder, the willow, and even the birch. But he likes the aspen so much better that he will work very hard to get it. Perhaps it tastes better because he does have to work so hard for it.

There were some aspen trees growing right on the edge of the pond Paddy had made in the Green Forest. These he cut just as he had cut the trees for his dam. As soon as a tree was down, he would cut it into short lengths, and with these swim out to where the water was deep, close to his new house. He took them one by one and carried the first ones to the bottom, where he pushed them into the mud just enough to hold them. Then, as fast as he brought more, he piled them on the first ones. And so the pile grew and grew.

Jerry Muskrat, Peter Rabbit, Bobby Coon, and the other little people of the Green Forest watched him with the greatest interest and curiosity. They couldn't quite make out what he was doing. It was almost as if he were building the foundation for another house.

"What's he doing, Jerry?" demanded Peter, when he could keep still no longer.

"I don't exactly know," replied Jerry. "He said that he was going to lay in a supply of food for the winter, just as I told you, and I suppose that is what he is doing. But I don't quite understand what he is taking it all out into the pond for. I believe I'll go ask him."

"Do, and then come tell us," begged Peter, who was growing so curious that he couldn't sit still.

So Jerry swam out to where Paddy was so busy. "Is this your food supply, Cousin Paddy?" he asked.

"Yes," replied Paddy, crawling up on the side of his house to rest. "Yes, this is my food supply. Isn't it splendid?"

"I guess it is," replied Jerry, trying to be polite, "though I like lily roots and clams better. But what are you going to do with it? Where is your storehouse?"

"This pond is my storehouse," replied Paddy. "I will make a great pile right here close to my house, and the water will keep it nice and fresh all winter. When the pond is frozen over, all I will have to do is to slip out of one of my doorways down there on the bottom, swim over here and get a stick, and fill my stomach. Isn't it handy?"

CHAPTER FOURTEEN: A FOOTPRINT IN THE MUD

VERY EARLY ONE morning Paddy the Beaver heard Sammy Jay making a terrible fuss over in the aspen trees on the edge of the pond Paddy had made in the Green Forest. Paddy couldn't see because he was inside his house, and it has no window, but he could hear. He wrinkled up his brows thoughtfully.

"Seems to me that Sammy is very much excited this morning," said he, a way he has because he is so much alone. "When he screams like that, Sammy is usually trying to do two things at once—make trouble for somebody and keep somebody else out of trouble; and when you come to think of it, that's rather a funny way of doing. It shows that he isn't all bad, and at the same time he is a long way from being all good. Now, I should say from the sounds that Sammy has discovered Reddy Fox trying to steal up on someone over where my aspen trees are growing. Reddy is afraid of me, but I suspect that he knows that Peter Rabbit has been hanging around here a lot lately, watching me work, and he thinks perhaps he can watch Peter. I shall have to whisper in one of Peter's long ears and tell him to watch out."

After a while he heard Sammy Jay's voice growing fainter and fainter in the Green Forest. Finally he couldn't hear it at all. "Whoever was here has gone away, and Sammy has followed just to torment them," thought Paddy. He was very busy making a bed. He is very particular about his bed, is Paddy the Beaver. He makes it of fine splinters of wood which he splits off with those wonderful great cutting teeth of his. This makes the driest kind of a bed. It requires a great deal of patience and work, but patience is one of the first things a little Beaver learns, and honest work well done is one of the greatest pleasures in the world, as Paddy long ago found out for himself. So he kept at work on his bed for some time after all was still outside.

At last Paddy decided that he would go over to his aspen trees and look them over to decide which ones he would cut the next night. He slid down one of his long halls, out the doorway at the bottom on the pond, and then swam up to the surface, where he floated for a few minutes with just his head out of water. And all the time his eyes and nose and ears were busy looking, smelling, and listening for any sign of danger. Everything was still. Sure that he was quite safe, Paddy swam across to the place where the aspen trees grew, and waddled out on the shore.

Paddy looked this way and looked that way. He looked up in the tree-tops, and he looked off up the hill, but most of all he looked at the ground. Yes, Sir, Paddy just studied the ground. You see, he hadn't forgotten the fuss Sammy Jay had been making there, and he was trying to find out what it was all about. At first he didn't see anything unusual, but by and by he happened to notice a little wet place, and right in the middle of it was something that made Paddy's eyes open wide. It was a footprint! Someone had carelessly stepped in the mud.

"Ha!" exclaimed Paddy, and the hair on his back lifted ever so little, and for a minute he had a prickly feeling all over. The footprint was very much like that of Reddy Fox, only it was larger.

"Ha!" said Paddy again. "That certainly is the foot print of Old Man Coyote! I see I have got to watch out more sharply than I had thought for. All right, Mr. Coyote; now that I know you are about, you'll have to be smarter than I think you are to catch me. You certainly will be back here tonight looking for me, so I think I'll do my cutting right now in the daytime."

CHAPTER FIFTEEN: SAMMY JAY MAKES PADDY A CALL

PADDY THE BEAVER was hard at work. He had just cut down a good-sized aspen tree and now he was gnawing it into short lengths to put in his food pile in the pond. As he worked, Paddy was doing a lot of thinking about the footprint of Old Man Coyote in a little patch of mud, for he knew that meant that Old Man Coyote had discovered his pond, and would be hanging around, hoping to catch Paddy off his guard. Paddy knew it just as well as if Old Man Coyote had told him so. That was why he was at work cutting his food supply in the daytime. Usually he works at night, and he knew that Old Man Coyote knew it.

"He'll try to catch me then," thought Paddy, "so I'll do my working on land now and fool him."

The tree he was cutting began to sway and crack. Paddy cut out one more big chip, then hurried away to a safe place while the tree fell with a crash.

"Thief! thief! thief!" screamed a voice just back of Paddy.

"Hello, Sammy Jay! I see you don't feel any better than usual this morning," said Paddy. "Don't you want to sit up in this tree while I cut it down?"

Sammy grew black in the face with anger, for he knew that Paddy was laughing at him. You remember how only a few days before he had been so intent on calling Paddy bad names that he actually hadn't noticed that Paddy was cutting the very tree in which he was sitting, and so when it fell he had had a terrible fright.

"You think you are very smart, Mr. Beaver, but you'll think differently one of these fine days!" screamed Sammy. "If you knew what I know, you wouldn't be so well satisfied with yourself."

"What do you know?" asked Paddy, pretending to be very much alarmed.

"I'm not going to tell you what I know," retorted Sammy Jay. "You'll find out soon enough. And when you do find out, you'll never steal another tree from our Green Forest. Somebody is going to catch you, and it isn't Farmer Brown's boy either!"

Paddy pretended to be terribly frightened. "Oh, who is it? Please tell me, Mr. Jay," he begged.

Now to be called Mr. Jay made Sammy feel very important. Nearly everybody else called him Sammy. He swelled himself out trying to look as important as he felt, and his eyes snapped with

Paddy pretended to be terribly frightened.

pleasure. He was actually making Paddy the Beaver afraid. At least, he thought he was.

"No, Sir, I won't tell you," he replied. "I wouldn't be you for a great deal, though! Somebody who is smarter than you are is going to catch you, and when he gets through with you, there won't be anything left but a few bones. No, Sir, nothing but a few bones!"

"Oh, Mr. Jay, this is terrible news! Whatever am I to do?" cried Paddy, all the time keeping on at work cutting another tree.

"There's nothing you can do," replied Sammy, grinning wickedly at Paddy's fright. "There's nothing you can do unless you go right straight back to the North where you came from. You think you are very smart, but—"

Sammy didn't finish. Crack! Over fell the tree Paddy had been cutting and the top of it fell straight into the alder in which Sammy was sitting. "Oh! Oh! Help!" shrieked Sammy, spreading his wings and flying away just in time.

Paddy sat down and laughed until his sides ached. "Come make me another call someday, Sammy!" he said. "And when you do, please bring some real news. I know all about Old Man Coyote. You can tell him for me that when he is planning to catch people he should be careful not to leave footprints to give himself away."

Sammy didn't reply. He just sneaked off through the Green Forest, looking quite as foolish as he felt.

CHAPTER SIXTEEN: OLD MAN COYOTE IS VERY CRAFTY

Coyote has a crafty brain;
His wits are sharp his ends to gain.

THERE IS NOTHING in the world more true than that. Old Man Coyote has the craftiest brain of all the little people of the Green Forest or the Green Meadows. Sharp as are the wits of old Granny Fox, they are not quite so sharp as the wits of Old Man Coyote. If you want to fool him, you will have to get up very early in the morning, and then it is more than likely that you will be the one fooled, not he. There is very little going on around him that he doesn't know about. But once in a while something escapes him. The coming of Paddy the Beaver to the Green Forest was one of these things. He didn't know a thing about Paddy until Paddy had finished his dam and his house, and was cutting his supply of food for the winter.

You see, it was this way: When the Merry Little Breezes of Old Mother West Wind first heard what was going on in the Green Forest and hurried around over the Green Meadows and through the Green Forest to spread the news, as is their way, they took the greatest pains not to even hint it to Old Man Coyote because they were afraid that he would make trouble and perhaps drive Paddy away. The place that Paddy had chosen to build his dam was so deep in the Green Forest that Old Man Coyote seldom went that way. So it was that he knew nothing about Paddy, and Paddy knew nothing about him for some time.

But after a while Old Man Coyote noticed that the little people of the Green Meadows were not about as much as usual. They seemed to have a secret of some kind. He mentioned the matter to his friend, Digger the Badger.

Digger had been so intent on his own affairs that he hadn't noticed anything unusual, but when Old Man Coyote mentioned the matter he remembered that Blacky the Crow headed straight for the Green Forest every morning. Several times he had seen Sammy Jay flying in the same direction as if in a great hurry to get somewhere.

Old Man Coyote grinned. "That's all I need to know, friend Digger," said he. "When Blacky the Crow and Sammy Jay visit a place more than once, something interesting is going on there. I think I'll take a stroll up through the Green Forest and have a look around."

With that, off Old Man Coyote started. But he was too sly and crafty to go straight to the Green Forest. He pretended to hunt around over the Green Meadows just as he usually did, all the time working nearer and nearer to the Green Forest. When he reached the edge of it, he slipped in among the trees, and when he felt that no one was likely to see him, he began to run this way and that way with his nose to the ground.

"Ha!" he exclaimed presently, "Reddy Fox has been this way lately."

Pretty soon he found another trail. "So," said he, "Peter Rabbit has been over here a good deal of late, and his trail goes in the same direction as that of Reddy Fox. I guess all I have to do now is to follow Peter's trail, and it will lead me to what I want to find out."

So Old Man Coyote followed Peter's trail, and he presently came to the pond of Paddy the Beaver. "Ha!" said he, as he looked out and saw Paddy's new house. "So there is a newcomer to the Green Forest! I have always heard that Beaver is very good eating. My stomach begins to feel empty this very minute." His mouth began to water, and a fierce, hungry look shone in his eyes.

It was just then that Sammy Jay saw him and began to scream at the top of his lungs so that Paddy the Beaver over in his house heard him. Old Man Coyote knew that it was of no use to stay longer with Sammy Jay about, so he took a hasty look at the pond and found where Paddy came ashore to cut his food. Then, shaking his fist at Sammy Jay, he started straight back for the Green Meadows. "I'll just pay a visit here in the night," said he, "and give Mr. Beaver a surprise while he is at work."

But with all his craft, Old Man Coyote didn't notice that he left a footprint in the mud.

CHAPTER SEVENTEEN: OLD MAN COYOTE IS DISAPPOINTED

OLD MAN COYOTE lay stretched out in his favorite napping place on the Green Meadows. He was thinking of what he had found out up in the Green Forest that morning—that Paddy the Beaver was living there. Old Man Coyote's thoughts seemed very pleasant to himself, though really they were very dreadful thoughts. You see, he was thinking how easy it was going to be to catch Paddy the Beaver, and what a splendid meal he would make. He licked his chops at the thought.

"He doesn't know I know he's here," thought Old Man Coyote. "In fact, I don't believe he even knows that I am anywhere around. Of course he won't be watching for me. He cuts his trees at night, so all I will have to do is to hide right close by where he is at work, and he'll walk right into my mouth. Sammy Jay knows I was up there this morning, but Sammy sleeps at night, so he will not give the alarm. My, my, how good that Beaver will taste!" He licked his chops once more, then yawned and closed his eyes for a nap.

Old Man Coyote waited until jolly, round red Mr. Sun had gone to bed behind the Purple Hills, and the Black Shadows had crept out across the Green Meadows. Then, keeping in the blackest of them, and looking very much like a shadow of himself, he slipped into the Green Forest. It was dark in there, and he made straight for Paddy's new pond, trotting along swiftly without making a sound. When he was near the aspen trees which he knew Paddy was planning to cut, he crept forward very slowly and carefully. Everything was still as still could be.

"Good!" thought Old Man Coyote. "I am here first, and now all I need do is to hide and wait for Paddy to come ashore."

So he stretched himself flat behind some brush close beside the little path Paddy had made up from the edge of the water and waited. It was very still, so still that it seemed almost as if he could hear his heart beat. He could see the little stars twinkling in the sky and their own reflections twinkling back at them from the water of Paddy's pond. Old Man Coyote waited and waited. He is very patient when there is something to gain by it. For such a splendid dinner as Paddy the Beaver would make, he felt that he could well afford to be patient. So he waited and waited, and everything was as still as if no living thing but the trees were there. Even the trees seemed to be asleep.

At last, after a long, long time, he heard just the faintest splash. He pricked up his ears and peeped out on the pond with the hungriest look in his yellow eyes. There was a little line of silver coming straight toward him. He knew that it was made by Paddy the Beaver swimming. Nearer and nearer it drew. Old Man Coyote chuckled way down deep inside, without making a sound. He could see Paddy's head now, and Paddy was coming straight in, as if he hadn't a fear in the world.

Almost to the edge of the pond swam Paddy. Then he stopped. In a few minutes he began to swim again, but this time it was back in the direction of his house, and he seemed to be carrying something. It was one of the little food logs he had cut that day, and he was taking it out to his storehouse. Then back he came for another. And so he kept on, never once coming ashore. Old Man Coyote waited until Paddy had carried the last log to his storehouse and then, with a loud whack on the water with his broad tail, had dived and disappeared in his house.

Then Old Man Coyote arose and started elsewhere to look for his dinner, and in his heart was bitter disappointment.

CHAPTER EIGHTEEN: OLD MAN COYOTE TRIES ANOTHER PLAN

FOR THREE NIGHTS Old Man Coyote had stolen up through the green Forest with the coming of the Black Shadows and had hidden among the aspen trees where Paddy the Beaver cut his food, and for three nights Paddy had failed to come ashore. Each night he had seemed to have enough food logs in the water to keep him busy without cutting more. Old Man Coyote lay there, and the hungry look in his eyes changed to one of doubt and then to suspicion. Could it be that Paddy the Beaver was smarter than he thought? It began to look very much as if Paddy knew perfectly well that he was hiding there each night. Yes, Sir, that's the way it looked. For three nights Paddy hadn't cut a single tree, and yet each night he had plenty of food logs ready to take to his storehouse in the pond.

"That means that he comes ashore in the daytime and cuts his trees," thought Old Man Coyote as, tired and with black anger in his heart, he trotted home the third night. "He couldn't have found out about me himself; he isn't smart enough. It must be that someone has told him. And nobody knows that I have been over there but Sammy Jay. It must be he who has been the tattletale. I think I'll visit Paddy by daylight tomorrow, and then we'll see!"

Now the trouble with some smart people is that they are never able to believe that others may be as smart as they. Old Man Coyote didn't know that the first time he had visited Paddy's pond he had left behind him a footprint in a little patch of soft mud. If he had known it, he wouldn't have believed that Paddy would be smart enough to guess what that footprint meant. So Old Man Coyote laid all the blame at the door of Sammy Jay, and that very morning, when Sammy came flying over the Green Meadows, Old Man Coyote accused him of being a tattletale and threatened the most dreadful things to Sammy if ever he caught him.

Now Sammy had flown down to the green Meadows to tell Old Man Coyote how Paddy was doing all his work on land in the daytime. But when Old Man Coyote began to call him a tattletale and accuse him of having warned Paddy, and to threaten dreadful things, he straightway forgot all his anger at Paddy and turned it all on Old Man Coyote. He called him everything he could think of, and this was a great deal, for Sammy has a wicked tongue. When he hadn't any breath left, he flew over to the Green Forest, and there he hid where he could watch all that was going on.

That afternoon Old Man Coyote tried his new plan. He slipped into the Green Forest, looking this way and that way to be sure that no one saw him. Then very, very softly, he crept up through the Green Forest toward the pond of Paddy the Beaver. As he drew near, he heard a crash, and it made him smile. He knew what it meant. It meant that Paddy was at work cutting down trees. With his stomach almost on the ground, he crept forward little by little, little by little, taking the greatest care not to rustle so much as a leaf. Presently he reached a place where he could see the aspen trees, and there, sure enough, was Paddy, sitting up on his hind legs and hard at work cutting another tree.

Old Man Coyote lay down for a few minutes to watch. Then he wriggled a little nearer. Slowly and carefully he drew his legs under him and made ready for a rush. Paddy the Beaver was his at last! At just that very minute a harsh scream rang out right over his head: "Thief! thief! thief!"

It was Sammy Jay, who had followed him all the way. Paddy the Beaver didn't stop to even look around. He knew what that meant, and he scrambled down his little path to the water as he never had scrambled before. And as he dived with a great splash, Old Man Coyote landed with a great jump on the very edge of the pond.

CHAPTER NINETEEN: PADDY AND SAMMY JAY BECOME FRIENDS

PADDY THE BEAVER floated in his pond and grinned in the most provoking way at Old Man Coyote, who had so nearly caught him. Old Man Coyote fairly danced with anger on the bank. He had felt so sure of Paddy that time that it was hard work to believe that Paddy had really gotten away from him. He bared his long, cruel teeth, and he looked very fierce and ugly.

"Come on in; the water's fine!" called Paddy.

Now, of course this wasn't a nice thing for Paddy to do, for it only made Old Man Coyote all the angrier. You see, Paddy knew perfectly well that he was absolutely safe, and he just couldn't resist the temptation to say some unkind things. He had had to be on the watch for days lest he should be caught, and so he hadn't been able to work quite so well as he could have done with nothing to fear, and he still had a lot of preparations to make for winter. So he told Old Man

Coyote just what he thought of him, and that he wasn't as smart as he thought he was or he never would have left a footprint in the mud to give him away.

When Sammy Jay, who was listening and chuckling as he listened, heard that, he flew down where he would be just out of reach of Old Man Coyote, and then he just turned that tongue of his loose, and you know that some people say that Sammy's tongue is hung in the middle and wags at both ends. Of course this isn't really so, but when he gets to abusing people it seems as if it must be true. He called Old Man Coyote every bad name he could think of. He called him a sneak, a thief, a coward, a bully, and a lot of other things.

"You said I had warned Paddy that you were trying to catch him and that was why you failed to find him at work

"Come on in; the water's fine!" called Paddy.

at night, and all the time you had warned him yourself!" screamed Sammy. "I used to think that you were smart, but I know better now. Paddy is twice as smart as you are."

> "Mr. Coyote is ever so sly;
> Mr. Coyote is clever and spry;
> If you believe all you hear.
> Mr. Coyote is naught of the kind;
> Mr. Coyote is stupid and blind;
> He can't catch a flea on his ear."

Paddy the Beaver laughed till the tears came at Sammy's foolish verse, but it made Old Man Coyote angrier than ever. He was angry with Paddy for escaping from him, and he was angry with Sammy, terribly angry, and the worst of it was he couldn't catch either one, for one was at home in the water and the other was at home in the air and he couldn't follow in either place. Finally he saw it was of no use to stay there to be laughed at, so, muttering and grumbling, he started for the Green Meadows.

As soon as he was out of sight Paddy turned to Sammy Jay.

"Mr. Jay," said he, knowing how it pleased Sammy to be called mister. "Mr. Jay, you have done me a mighty good turn today, and I am not going to forget it. You can call me what you please and scream at me all you please, but you won't get any satisfaction out of it, because I simply won't get angry. I will say to myself, 'Mr. Jay saved my life the other day,' and then I won't mind your tongue."

Now this made Sammy feel very proud and very happy. You know it is very seldom that he hears anything nice said of him. He flew down on the stump of one of the trees Paddy had cut. "Let's be friends," said he.

"With all my heart!" replied Paddy.

CHAPTER TWENTY: SAMMY JAY OFFERS TO HELP PADDY

PADDY SAT LOOKING thoughtfully at the aspen trees he would have to cut to complete his store of food for the winter. All those near the edge of his pond had been cut. The others were scattered about some little distance away. "I don't know," said Paddy out loud. "I don't know."

"What don't you know?" asked Sammy Jay, who, now that he and Paddy had become friends, was very much interested in what Paddy was doing.

"Why," replied Paddy, "I don't know just how I am going to get those trees. Now that Old Man Coyote is watching for me, it isn't safe for me to go very far from my pond. I suppose I could dig a canal up to some of the nearest trees and then float them down to the pond, but it is hard to work and keep watch for enemies at the same time. I guess I'll have to be content with some of these alders growing close to the water, but the bark of aspens is so much better that I—I wish I could get them."

"What's a canal?" asked Sammy abruptly.

"A canal? Why a canal is a kind of ditch in which water can run," replied Paddy.

Sammy nodded. "I've seen Farmer Brown dig one over on the Green Meadows, but it looked like a great deal of work. I didn't suppose that anyone else could do it. Do you really mean that you can dig a canal, Paddy?"

"Of course I mean it," replied Paddy, in a surprised tone of voice. "I have helped dig lots of canals. You ought to see some of them back where I came from."

"I'd like to," replied Sammy. "I think it is perfectly wonderful. I don't see how you do it."

"It's easy enough when you know how," replied Paddy. "If I dared to, I'd show you."

Sammy had a sudden idea. It almost made him gasp. "I tell you what, you work and I'll keep watch!" he cried. "You know my eyes are very sharp."

"Will you?" cried Paddy eagerly. "That would be perfectly splendid. You have the sharpest eyes of anyone whom I know, and I would feel perfectly safe with you on watch. But I don't want to put you to all that trouble, Mr. Jay."

"Of course I will," replied Sammy, "and it won't be any trouble at all. I'll just love to do it." You see, it made Sammy feel very proud to have Paddy say that he had such sharp eyes. "When will you begin?"

"Right away, if you will just take a look around and see that it is perfectly safe for me to come out on land."

Sammy didn't wait to hear more. He spread his beautiful blue wings and started off over the Green Forest straight for the Green Meadows. Paddy watched him go with a puzzled and disappointed air. "That's funny," thought he. "I thought he really meant it, and now off he goes without even saying good-bye."

In a little while back came Sammy, all out of breath. "It's all right," he panted. "You can go to work just as soon as you please."

Paddy looked more puzzled than ever. "How do you know?" he asked. "I haven't seen you looking around."

"I did better than that," replied Sammy. "If Old Man Coyote had been hiding somewhere in the Green Forest, it might have taken me some time to find him. But he isn't. You see, I flew straight over to his home in the Green Meadows to see if he is there, and he is. He's taking a sun-bath and looking as cross as two sticks. I don't think he'll be back here this morning, but I'll keep a sharp watch while you work."

Paddy made Sammy a low bow. "You certainly are smart, Mr. Jay," said he. "I wouldn't have thought of going over to Old Man Coyote's home to see if he was there. I'll feel perfectly safe with you on guard. Now I'll get to work."

CHAPTER TWENTY-ONE: PADDY AND SAMMY JAY WORK TOGETHER

JERRY MUSKRAT HAD been home at the Smiling Pool for several days. But he couldn't stay there long. Oh, my, no! He just had to get back to see what his big cousin, Paddy the Beaver, was doing. So as soon as he was sure that everything was all right at the Smiling Pool he hurried back up the Laughing Brook to Paddy's pond, deep in the Green Forest. As soon as he was in sight of it, he looked eagerly for Paddy. At first he didn't see him. Then he stopped and gazed over at the place where Paddy had been cutting aspen trees for food. Something was going on there,

"Sammy Jay and I are building a canal."

something queer. He couldn't make it out.

Just then Sammy Jay came flying over.

"What's Paddy doing?" Jerry asked.

Sammy Jay dropped down to the top of an alder tree and fluffed out all his feathers in a very important way. "Oh," said he, "Paddy and I are building something!"

"You! Paddy and you! Ha, ha! Paddy and you building something!" Jerry laughed.

"Yes, me!" snapped Sammy angrily. "That's what I said; Paddy and I are building something."

Jerry had begun to swim across the pond by this time, and Sammy was flying across. "Why don't you tell the truth, Sammy, and say that Paddy is building something and you are making him all the trouble you can?" called Jerry.

Sammy's eyes snapped angrily, and he darted down at Jerry's little brown head. "It isn't true!" he shrieked. "You ask Paddy if I'm not helping!"

Jerry ducked under water to escape Sammy's sharp bill. When he came up again, Sammy was over in the little grove of aspen trees where Paddy was at work. Then Jerry discovered something. What was it? Why a little water-path led right up to the aspen trees, and there, at the end of the little water-path, was Paddy the Beaver hard at work. He was digging and piling the earth on one side very neatly. In fact, he was making the water-path longer. Jerry swam right up the little water-path to where Paddy was working. "Good morning, Cousin Paddy," said he. "What are you doing?"

"Oh," replied Paddy, "Sammy Jay and I are building a canal."

Sammy Jay looked down at Jerry in triumph, and Jerry looked at Paddy as if he thought that he was joking.

"Sammy Jay? What's Sammy Jay got to do about it?" demanded Jerry.

"A whole lot," replied Paddy. "You see, he keeps watch while I work. If he didn't, I couldn't work, and there wouldn't be any canal. Old Man Coyote has been trying to catch me, and I wouldn't dare work on shore if it wasn't that I am sure that the sharpest eyes in the Green Forest are watching for danger."

Sammy Jay looked very much pleased indeed and very proud. "So you see, it takes both of us to make this canal; I dig while Sammy watches. So we are building it together," concluded Paddy with a twinkle in his eyes.

"I see," said Jerry slowly. Then he turned to Sammy Jay. "I beg your pardon, Sammy," said he. "I do indeed."

"That's all right," replied Sammy airily. "What do you think of our canal?"

"I think it is wonderful," replied Jerry.

And indeed it was a very fine canal, straight, wide, and deep enough for Paddy to swim in and float his logs out to the pond. Yes, indeed, it was a very fine canal.

CHAPTER TWENTY-TWO: PADDY THE BEAVER FINISHES HIS HARVEST

"Sharp his tongue and sharp his eyes—
Sammy guards against surprise.
If 'twere not for Sammy Jay
I could do no work today."

WHEN SAMMY OVERHEARD Paddy the Beaver say that to Jerry Muskrat, it made him swell up all over with pure pride. You see, Sammy is so used to hearing bad things about himself that to hear something nice like that pleased him immensely. He straightway forgot all the mean things he had said to Paddy when he first saw him—how he had called him a thief because he had cut the aspen trees he needed. He forgot all this. He forgot how Paddy had made him the laughing-stock of the Green Forest and the Green Meadows by cutting down the very tree in which he had been sitting. He forgot everything but that Paddy had trusted him to keep watch and now was saying nice things about him. He made up his mind that he would deserve all the nice things that Paddy could say, and he thought that Paddy was the finest fellow in the world.

Jerry Muskrat looked doubtful. He didn't trust Sammy, and he took care not to go far from the water when he heard that Old Man Coyote had been hanging around. But Paddy worked away just as if he hadn't a fear in the world.

"The way to make people want to be trusted is to trust them," said he to himself. "If I show Sammy Jay that I don't really trust him, he will think it is of no use to try and will give it up. But if I do trust him, and he knows that I do, he'll be the best watchman in the Green Forest."

And this shows that Paddy the Beaver has a great deal of wisdom, for it was just as he thought. Sammy was on hand bright and early every morning. He made sure that Old Man Coyote was nowhere in the Green Forest, and then he settled himself comfortably in the top of a tall pine tree where he could see all that was going on while Paddy the Beaver worked.

Paddy had finished his canal, and a beautiful canal it was, leading straight from his pond up to the aspen trees. As soon as he had finished it, he began to cut the trees. As soon as one was down he would cut it into short lengths and roll them into the canal. Then he would float them out to his pond and over to his storehouse. He took the larger branches, on which there was sweet, tender bark, in the same way, for Paddy is never wasteful.

After a while he went over to his storehouse, which, you know, was nothing but a great pile of aspen logs and branches in his pond close by his house. He studied it very carefully. Then he swam back and climbed up on the bank of his canal.

"Mr. Jay," said he, "I think our work is about finished."

"What!" cried Sammy, "Aren't you going to cut the rest of those aspen trees?"

"No," replied Paddy. "Enough is always enough, and I've got enough to last me all winter. I want those trees for next year. Now I am fixed for the winter. I think I'll take it easy for a while."

Sammy looked disappointed. You see, he had just begun to learn that the greatest pleasure in the world comes from doing things for other people. For the first time since he could remember, someone wanted him around and it gave him such a good feeling down deep inside! Perhaps it was because he remembered that good feeling that the next spring he was so willing and anxious to help poor Mrs. Quack. What he did for her and all about her terrible adventures I will tell you in the next book.

The Adventures of Poor Mrs. Quack

CHAPTER ONE: PETER RABBIT BECOMES ACQUAINTED WITH MRS. QUACK

Make a new acquaintance every time you can;
You'll find it interesting and a very helpful plan.

IT MEANS MORE knowledge. You cannot meet anyone without learning something from him if you keep your ears open and your eyes open. Everyone is at least a little different from everyone else, and the more people you know, the more you may learn. Peter Rabbit knows this, and that is one reason he always is so eager to find out about other people. He had left Jimmy Skunk and Bobby Coon in the Green Forest and had headed for the Smiling Pool to see if Grandfather Frog was awake yet. He had no idea of meeting a stranger there, and so you can imagine just how surprised he was when he got in sight of the Smiling Pool to see someone whom he never had seen before swimming about there. He knew right away who it was. He knew that it was Mrs. Quack the Duck, because he had often heard about her. And then, too, it was very clear from her looks that she was a cousin of the ducks he had seen in Farmer Brown's dooryard. The difference was that while they were big and white and stupid-looking, Mrs. Quack was smaller, brown, very trim, and looked anything but stupid.

Peter was so surprised to see her in the Smiling Pool that he almost forgot to be polite. I am afraid he stared in a very impolite way as he hurried to the edge of the bank. "I suppose," said Peter, "that you are Mrs. Quack, but I never expected to see you unless I should go over to the Big River, and that is a place I never have visited and hardly expect to because it is too far from the dear Old Briar-patch. You are Mrs. Quack, aren't you?"

"Yes," replied Mrs. Quack, "and you must be Peter Rabbit. I've heard of you very often." All the time Mrs. Quack was swimming back and forth and in little circles in the most uneasy way.

"I hope you've heard nothing but good of me," replied Peter.

Mrs. Quack stopped her uneasy swimming for a minute and almost smiled as she looked at Peter. "The worst I have heard is that you are very curious about other people's affairs," said she.

Peter looked a wee, wee bit foolish, and then he laughed right out. "I guess that is true enough," said he. "I like to learn all I can, and how can I learn without being curious? I'm curious right now. I'm wondering what brings you to the Smiling Pool when you never have been here before. It is the last place in the world I ever expected to find you."

"That's why I'm here," replied Mrs. Quack. "I hope others feel the same way. I came here because I just HAD to find some place where people wouldn't expect to find me and so wouldn't come looking for me. Little Joe Otter saw me yesterday on the Big River and told me of this place, and so, because I just had to go somewhere, I came here."

Peter's eyes opened very wide with surprise. "Why," he exclaimed, "I should think you would be perfectly safe on the Big River! I don't see how any harm can possibly come to you out there."

The words were no sooner out of Peter's mouth than a faint bang sounded from way off towards the Big River. Mrs. Quack gave a great start and half lifted her wings as if to fly. But she thought better of it, and then Peter saw that she was trembling all over.

"Did you hear that?" she asked in a faint voice.

Peter nodded. "That was a gun, a terrible gun, but it was a long way from here," said he.

"It was over on the Big River," said Mrs. Quack. "That's why it isn't safe for me over there. That's why I just had to find some other place. Oh, dear, the very sound of a gun sets me to shaking and makes my heart feel as if it would stop beating. Are you sure I am perfectly safe here?"

"Perfectly," spoke up Jerry Muskrat, who had been listening from the top of the Big Rock, where he was lunching on a clam, "unless you are not smart enough to keep out of the clutches of Reddy Fox or Old Man Coyote or Hooty the Owl or Redtail the Hawk."

"I'm not afraid of *them*," declared Mrs. Quack. "It's those two-legged creatures with terrible guns I'm afraid of," and she began to swim about more uneasily than ever.

CHAPTER TWO: MRS. QUACK IS DISTRUSTFUL

JERRY MUSKRAT THINKS there is no place in the world like the Smiling Pool. So, for the matter of that, does Grandfather Frog and also Spotty the Turtle. You see, they have spent their lives there and know little about the rest of the Great

World. When Mrs. Quack explained that all she feared was that a two-legged creature with a terrible gun might find her there, Jerry Muskrat hastened to tell her
that she had nothing to worry about on that account.

"No one hunts here now that Farmer Brown's boy has put away his terrible gun,"
explained Jerry. "There was a time when he used to hunt here and set traps, which
are worse than terrible guns, but that was long ago, before he knew any better."

"Who is Farmer Brown's boy?" demanded Mrs. Quack, looking more anxious
than ever. "Is he one of those two-legged creatures?"

"Yes," said Peter Rabbit, who had been listening with all his ears, "but he is the
best friend we Quaddies have got. He is such a good friend that he ought to be a
Quaddy himself. Why, this last winter he fed some of us when food was scarce, and
he saved Mrs. Grouse when she was caught in a snare, which you know is a kind
of trap. He won't let any harm come to you here, Mrs. Quack."

"I wouldn't trust him, not for one single little minute," declared Mrs. Quack. "I
wouldn't trust one of those two-legged creatures, not *one*. You say he fed some of
you last winter, but that doesn't mean anything good. Do you know what I've
known these two-legged creatures to do?"

"What?" demanded Peter and Jerry together.

"I've known them to scatter food where we Ducks would be sure to find it and
to take the greatest care that nothing should frighten us while we were eating. And
then, after we had got in the habit of feeding in that particular place and had
grown to feel perfectly safe there, they have hidden close by until a lot of us were
feeding together and then fired their terrible guns and killed a lot of my friends and
dreadfully hurt a lot more. I wouldn't trust one of them, not *one!*"

"Oh, how dreadful!" cried Peter, looking quite as shocked as he felt. Then he
added eagerly, "But our Farmer Brown's boy wouldn't do anything like that. You
haven't the least thing to fear from him."

"Perhaps not," said Mrs. Quack, shaking her head doubtfully, "but I wouldn't
trust him. I wouldn't trust him as far off as I could see him. The Smiling Pool is a
very nice place, although it is dreadfully small, but if Farmer Brown's boy is likely
to come over here, I guess I'd better look for some other place, though goodness
knows where I will find one where I will feel perfectly safe."

"You are safe right here, if you have sense enough to stay here," declared Jerry
Muskrat rather testily. "Don't you suppose Peter and I know what we are talking
about?"

"I wish I could believe so," returned Mrs. Quack sadly, "but if you had been
through what I've been through, and suffered what I've suffered, you wouldn't
believe any place safe, and you certainly wouldn't trust one of those two-legged
creatures. Why, for weeks they haven't given me a chance to get a square meal,

and—and—I don't know what has become of Mr. Quack, and I'm all alone!" There was a little sob in her voice and tears in her eyes.

"Tell us all about it," begged Peter. "Perhaps we can help you."

CHAPTER THREE: MRS. QUACK TELLS ABOUT HER HOME

"IT'S A LONG story," said Mrs. Quack, shaking the tears from her eyes, "and I hardly know where to begin."

"Begin at the beginning," said Jerry Muskrat. "Your home is somewhere way up in the Northland where Honker the Goose lives, isn't it?"

Mrs. Quack nodded. "I wish I were there this very minute," she replied, the tears coming again. "But sometimes I doubt if ever I'll get there again. You folks who don't have to leave your homes every year don't know how well off you are or how much you have to be thankful for."

"I never could understand what people want to leave their homes for, anyway," declared Peter.

"We don't leave because we want to, but because we HAVE to," replied Mrs. Quack, "and we go back just as soon as we can. What would you do if you couldn't find a single thing to eat?"

"I guess I'd starve," replied Peter simply.

"I guess you would, and that is just what we would do, if we didn't take the long journey south when Jack Frost freezes everything tight up there where my home is," returned Mrs. Quack. "He comes earlier up there and stays twice as long as he does here, and makes ten times as much ice and snow. We get most of our food in the water or in the mud under the water, as of course you know, and when the water is frozen, there isn't a scrap of anything we can get to eat. We just *have* to come south. It isn't because we want to, but because we must! There is nothing else for us to do."

"Then I don't see what you want to make your home in such a place for," said practical Peter. "I should think you would make it where you can live all the year around."

"I was born up there, and I love it just as you love the dear Old Briar-patch," replied Mrs. Quack simply. "It is home, and there is no place like home. Besides, it is a very beautiful and a very wonderful place in summer. There is everything that Ducks and Geese love. We have all we want of the food we love best. Everywhere is shallow water with tall grass growing in it."

"Huh!" interrupted Peter, "I wouldn't think much of a place like that."

"That's because you don't know what is good," snapped Jerry Muskrat. "It would suit me," he added, with shining eyes.

"There are the dearest little islands just made for safe nesting-places," continued Mrs. Quack, without heeding the interruptions. "And the days are long, and it is easy to hide, and there is nothing to fear, for two-legged creatures with terrible guns never come there."

"If there is nothing to fear, why do you care about places to hide?" demanded Peter.

"Well, of course, we have enemies, just as you do here, but they are natural enemies—Foxes and Minks and Hawks and Owls," explained Mrs. Quack. "Of course, we have to watch out for them and have places where we can hide from them, but it is our wits against their wits, and it is our own fault if we get caught. That is perfectly fair, so we don't mind that. It is only men who are not fair. They don't know what fairness is."

Peter nodded that he understood, and Mrs. Quack went on. "Last summer Mr. Quack and I had our nest on the dearest little island, and no one found it. First we had twelve eggs, and then twelve of the dearest babies you ever saw."

"Maybe," said Peter doubtfully, thinking of his own babies.

"They grew so fast that by the time the cold weather came, they were as big as their father and mother," continued Mrs. Quack. "And they were smart, too. They had learned how to take care of themselves just as well as I could. I certainly was proud of that family. But now I don't know where one of them is."

Mrs. Quack suddenly choked up with grief, and Peter Rabbit politely turned his head away.

CHAPTER FOUR: MRS. QUACK CONTINUES HER STORY

WHEN MRS. QUACK told of her twelve children and how she didn't know where one of them was, Peter Rabbit and Jerry Muskrat knew just how badly she was feeling, and they turned their heads away and pretended that they didn't see her tears. In a few minutes she bravely went on with her story.

"When Jack Frost came and we knew it was time to begin the long journey, Mr. Quack and myself and our twelve children joined with some other Duck families, and with Mr. Quack in the lead, we started for our winter home, which really isn't a home but just a place to stay. For a while we had nothing much to fear. We would fly by day and at night rest in some quiet lake or pond or on some river, with the Great Woods all about us or sometimes great marshes. Perhaps you don't know what marshes are. If the Green Meadows here had little streams of water running every which way through them, and the ground was all soft and muddy and full of water, and the grass grew tall, they would be marshes."

Jerry Muskrat's eyes sparkled. "I would like a place like that!" he exclaimed.

"You certainly would," replied Mrs. Quack. "We always find lots of your relatives in such places."

"Marshes must be something like swamps," ventured Peter Rabbit, who had been thinking the matter over.

"Very much the same, only with grass and rushes in place of trees and bushes," replied Mrs. Quack. "There is plenty to eat and the loveliest hiding-places. In some of these we stayed days at a time. In fact, we stayed until Jack Frost came to drive us out. Then as we flew, we began to see the homes of these terrible two-legged creatures called men, and from that time on we never knew a minute of peace, excepting when we were flying high in the air or far out over the water. If we could have just kept flying all the time or never had to go near the shore, we would have been all right. But we had to eat."

"Of course," said Peter. "Everybody has to eat."

"And we had to rest," said Mrs. Quack.

"Marshes must be something like swamps," ventured Peter Rabbit.

"Certainly," said Peter. "Everybody has to do that."

"And to eat we had to go in close to shore where the water was not at all deep, because it is only in such places that we can get food," continued Mrs. Quack. "It takes a lot of strength to fly as we fly, and strength requires plenty of food. Mr. Quack knew all the best feeding-places, for he had made the long journey several times, so every day he would lead the way to one of these. He always chose the wildest and most lonely looking places he could find, as far as possible from the homes of men, but even then he was never careless. He would lead us around back and forth over the place he had chosen, and we would all look with all our might for signs of danger. If we saw none, we would drop down a little nearer and a little nearer. But with all our watchfulness, we never could be sure, absolutely sure, that all was safe. Sometimes those terrible two-legged creatures would be hiding in the very middle of the wildest, most lonely looking marshes. They would be covered with grass so that we couldn't see them. Then, as we flew over them, would come the bang, bang, bang, bang of terrible guns, and always some of our flock would drop. We would have to leave them behind, for we knew if we wanted to live we must get beyond the reach of those terrible guns. So we would fly our hardest. It was awful, just simply awful!"

Mrs. Quack paused and shuddered, and Peter Rabbit and Jerry Muskrat shuddered in sympathy.

"Sometimes we would have to try three or four feeding-places before we found one where there were no terrible guns. And when we did find one, we would be so tired and frightened that we couldn't enjoy our food, and we didn't dare to sleep without someone on watch all the time. It was like that every day. The farther we got, the worse it became. Our flock grew smaller and smaller. Those who escaped the terrible guns would be so frightened that they would forget to follow their leader and would fly in different directions and later perhaps join other flocks. So it was that when at last we reached the place in the sunny Southland for which we had started, Mr. Quack and I were alone. What became of our twelve children I don't know. I am afraid the terrible guns killed some. I hope some joined other flocks and escaped, but I don't know."

"I hope they did too," said Peter.

CHAPTER FIVE: PETER LEARNS MORE
OF MRS. QUACK'S TROUBLES

It often happens when we know
The troubles that our friends pass through,
Our own seem very small indeed;
You'll always find that this is true.

"MY, YOU MUST have felt glad when you reached your winter home!" exclaimed Peter Rabbit when Mrs. Quack finished the account of her long, terrible journey from her summer home in the far Northland to her winter home in the far Southland.

"I did," replied Mrs. Quack, "but all the time I couldn't forget those to whom terrible things had happened on the way down, and then, too, I kept dreading the long journey back."

"I don't see why you didn't stay right there. I would have," said Peter, nodding his head with an air of great wisdom.

"Not if you were I," replied Mrs. Quack. "In the first place it isn't a proper place in which to bring up young Ducks and make them strong and healthy. In the second place there are more dangers down there for young Ducks than up in the far Northland. In the third place there isn't room for all the Ducks to nest properly. And lastly there is a great longing for our real home, which Old Mother Nature has put in our hearts and which just MAKES us go. We couldn't be happy if we didn't."

"Is the journey back as bad as the journey down?" asked Peter.

"Worse, very much worse," replied Mrs. Quack sadly. "You can see for yourself just how bad it is, for here I am all alone." Tears filled Mrs. Quack's eyes. "It is almost too terrible to talk about," she continued after a minute. "You see, for one thing, food isn't as plentiful as it is in the fall, and we just have to go wherever it is to be found. Those two-legged creatures know where those feeding-grounds are just as well as we do, and they hide there with their terrible guns just as they did when we were coming south. But it is much worse now, very much worse. You see, when we were going the other way, if we found them at one place we could go on to another, but when we are going north we cannot always do that. We cannot go any faster than Jack Frost does. Sometimes we are driven out of a place by the bang, bang of the terrible guns and go on, only to find that we have caught up with Jack Frost, and that the ponds and the rivers are still covered with ice. Then there is nothing to do but to turn back to where those terrible guns are waiting for us. We just *have* to do it."

Mrs. Quack stopped and shivered. "It seems to me I have heard nothing but the noise of those terrible guns ever since we started," said she. "I haven't had a good square meal for days and days, nor a good rest. That is what makes me so dreadfully nervous. Sometimes, when we had been driven from place to place until we had caught up with Jack Frost, there would be nothing but ice excepting in small places in a river where the water runs too swiftly to freeze. We would just have to drop into one of these to rest a little, because we had flown so far that our wings ached as if they would drop off. Then just as we would think we were safe for a little while, there would come the bang of a terrible gun. Then we would have to fly again as long as we could, and finally come back to the same place because there was no other place where we could go. Then we would have to do it all over again until night came. Sometimes I think that those men with terrible guns must hate us and want to kill every one of us. If they didn't, they would have a little bit of pity. They simply haven't any hearts at all."

"It does seem so," agreed Peter. "But wait until you know Farmer Brown's boy! *He's* got a heart!" he added brightly.

"I don't want to know him," retorted Mrs. Quack. "If he comes near here, you'll see me leave in a hurry. I wouldn't trust one of them, not one minute. You don't think he will come, do you?"

Peter sat up and looked across the Green Meadows, and his heart sank. "He's coming now, but I'm sure he won't hurt you, Mrs. Quack," said he.

But Mrs. Quack wouldn't wait to see. With a hasty promise to come back when the way was clear, she jumped into the air and on swift wings disappeared towards the Big River.

CHAPTER SIX: FARMER BROWN'S BOY VISITS THE SMILING POOL

FARMER BROWN'S BOY had heard Welcome Robin singing in the Old Orchard quite as soon as Peter Rabbit had, and that song of "Cheer up! Cheer up! Cheer up! Cheer!" had awakened quite as much gladness in his heart as it had in Peter's heart. It meant that Mistress Spring really had arrived, and that over in the Green Forest and down on the Green Meadows there would soon be shy blue, and just as shy white violets to look for, and other flowers almost if not quite as sweet and lovely. It meant that his feathered friends would soon be busy house-hunting and building. It meant that his little friends in fur would also be doing something very similar, if they had not already done so. It meant that soon there would be a million lovely things to see and a million joyous sounds to hear.

So the sound of Welcome Robin's voice made the heart of Farmer Brown's boy even more happy than it was before, and as Welcome Robin just *had* to sing, so Farmer Brown's boy just *had* to whistle. When his work was finished, it seemed to Farmer Brown's boy that something was calling him, calling him to get out on the Green Meadows or over in the Green Forest and share in the happiness of all the little people there. So presently he decided that he would go down to the Smiling Pool to find out how Jerry Muskrat was, and if Grandfather Frog was awake yet, and if the sweet singers of the Smiling Pool had begun their wonderful spring chorus.

Down the Crooked Little Path cross the Green Meadows he tramped, and as he drew near the Smiling Pool, he stopped whistling lest the sound should frighten some of the little people there. He was still some distance from the Smiling Pool when out of it sprang a big bird and on swift, whistling wings flew away in the direction of the Big River. Farmer Brown's boy stopped and watched until the bird had disappeared, and on his face was a look of great surprise.

"As I live, that was a Duck!" he exclaimed. "That is the first time I've ever known a wild Duck to be in the Smiling Pool. I wonder what under the sun could have brought her over here."

Just then there was a distant bang in the direction of the Big River. Farmer

Brown's boy scowled, and it made his face very angry-looking. "That's it," he muttered. "Hunters are shooting the Ducks on their way north and have driven the poor things to look for any little mudhole where they can get a little rest. Probably that Duck has been shot at so many times on the Big River that she felt safer over here in the Smiling Pool, little as it is."

Farmer Brown's boy had guessed exactly right, as you and I know, and as Peter Rabbit and Jerry Muskrat knew. "It's a shame, a downright shame that anyone should want to shoot birds on their way to their nesting-grounds and that the law should let them if they do want to. Some people haven't any hearts; they're all stomachs. I hope that fellow who shot just now over there on the Big River didn't hit anything, and I wish that gun of his might have kicked a little sense of what is right and fair into his head, but of course it didn't."

He grinned at the idea, and then he continued his way towards the Smiling Pool. He hoped he might find another Duck there, and he approached the Smiling Pool very, very carefully.

But when he reached a point where he could see all over the Smiling Pool, there was no one to be seen save Jerry Muskrat sitting on the Big Rock and Peter Rabbit on the bank on the other side. Farmer Brown's boy smiled when he saw them. "Hello, Jerry Muskrat!" said he. "I wonder how a bite of carrot would taste to you." He felt in his pocket and brought out a couple of carrots. One he put on a little tussock in the water where he knew Jerry would find it. The other he tossed across the Smiling Pool where he felt sure Peter would find it. Presently he noticed two or three feathers on the water close to the edge of the bank. Mrs. Quack had left them there. "I believe that was a Mallard Duck," said he, as he studied them. "I know what I'll do. I'll go straight back home and get some wheat and corn and put it here on the edge of the Smiling Pool. Perhaps she will come back and find it."

And this is just what Farmer Brown's boy did.

CHAPTER SEVEN: MRS. QUACK RETURNS

PETER RABBIT JUST couldn't go back to the dear Old Briar-patch. He just HAD to know if Mrs. Quack would come back to the Smiling Pool. He had seen Farmer Brown's boy come there a second time and scatter wheat and corn among the brown stalks of last summer's rushes, and he had guessed why Farmer Brown's boy had done this. He had guessed that they had been put there especially for Mrs. Quack, and if she should come back as she had promised to do, he wanted to be on hand when she found those good things to eat and hear what she would say.

So Peter stayed over near the Smiling Pool and hoped with all his might that Reddy Fox or Old Man Coyote would not take it into his head to come hunting over there. As luck would have it, neither of them did, and Peter had a very pleasant time gossiping with Jerry Muskrat, listening to the sweet voices of unseen singers in the Smiling Pool—the Hylas, which some people call peepers—and eating the carrot which Farmer Brown's boy had left for him.

Jolly, round, red Mr. Sun was just getting ready to go to bed behind the Purple Hills when Mrs. Quack returned. The first Peter knew of her coming was the whistle of her wings as she passed over him. Several times she circled around, high over the Smiling Pool, and Peter simply stared in open-mouthed admiration at the speed with which she flew. It didn't seem possible that one so big could move through the air so fast. Twice she set her wings and seemed to just slide down almost to the surface of the Smiling Pool, only to start her stout wings in motion once more and circle around again. It was very clear that she was terribly nervous and suspicious. The third time she landed in the water with a splash and sat perfectly still with her head stretched up, looking and listening with all her might.

"It's all right. There's nothing to be afraid of," said Jerry Muskrat.

"Are you sure?" asked Mrs. Quack anxiously. "I've been fooled too often by men with their terrible guns to ever feel absolutely sure that one isn't hiding and waiting to shoot me." As she spoke she swam about nervously.

"Peter Rabbit and I have been here ever since you left, and I guess we ought to know," replied Jerry Muskrat rather shortly. "There hasn't been anybody near here excepting Farmer Brown's boy, and we told you he wouldn't hurt you."

"He brought us each a carrot," Peter Rabbit broke in eagerly.

"Just the same, I wouldn't trust him," replied Mrs. Quack.

"Where is he now?"

Several times she circled over the Smiling Pool.

"He left ever so long ago, and he won't be back tonight," declared Peter confidently.

"I hope not," said Mrs. Quack, with a sigh. "Did you hear the bang of that terrible gun just after I left here?"

"Yes," replied Jerry Muskrat. "Was it fired at you?"

Mrs. Quack nodded and held up one wing. Peter and Jerry could see that one of the long feathers was missing. "I thought I was flying high enough to be safe," said she, "but when I reached the Big River there was a bang from the bushes on the bank, and something cut that feather out of my wing, and I felt a sharp pain in my side. It made me feel quite ill for a while, and the place is very sore now, but I guess I'm lucky that it was no worse. It is very hard work to know just how far those terrible guns can throw things at you. Next time I will fly higher."

"Where have you been since you left us?" asked Peter.

"Right in the middle of the Big River," replied Mrs. Quack. "It was the only safe place. I didn't dare go near either shore, and I'm nearly starved. I haven't had a mouthful to eat today."

Peter opened his mouth to tell her of the wheat and corn left by Farmer Brown's boy and then closed it again. He would let her find it for herself. If he told her about it, she might suspect a trick and refuse to go near the place. He never had seen anyone so suspicious, not even Old Man Coyote. But he couldn't blame her, after all she had been through. So he kept still and waited. He was learning, was Peter Rabbit. He was learning a great deal about Mrs. Quack.

CHAPTER EIGHT: MRS. QUACK HAS A GOOD MEAL AND A REST

There's nothing like a stomach full, to make the heart feel light;
To chase away the clouds of care, and make the world seem bright.

THAT'S A FACT. A full stomach makes the whole world seem different, brighter, better, and more worth living in. It is the hardest kind of hard work to be cheerful and see only the bright side of things when your stomach is empty. But once you fill that empty stomach, everything is changed. It was just that way with Mrs. Quack. For days at a time she hadn't had a full stomach because of the hunters with their terrible guns, and when just before dark that night she returned to the Smiling Pool, her stomach was quite empty.

"I don't suppose I'll find much to eat here, but a little in peace and safety is better than a feast with worry and danger," said she, swimming over to the brown, broken-down bulrushes on one side of the Smiling Pool and appearing to stand on her head as she plunged it under water and searched in the mud on the bottom for food. Peter Rabbit looked over at Jerry Muskrat sitting on the Big Rock, and Jerry winked. In a minute up bobbed the head of Mrs. Quack, and there was both a pleased and a worried look on her face. She had found some of the corn left there by Farmer Brown's boy. At once she swam out to the middle of the Smiling Pool, looking suspiciously this way and that way.

"There is corn over there," said she. "Do you know how it came there?"

"I saw Farmer Brown's boy throwing something over there," replied Peter. "Didn't we tell you that he would be good to you?"

"Quack, quack, quack! I've seen that kind of kindness too often to be fooled by it," snapped Mrs. Quack. "He probably saw me leave in a hurry and put this corn here, hoping that I would come back and find it and make up my mind to stay here a while. He thinks that if I do, he'll have a chance to hide near enough to shoot me. I didn't believe this could be a safe place for me, and now I know it. I'll stay here tonight, but tomorrow I'll try to find some other place. Oh, dear, it's dreadful not to have any place at all to feel safe in." There were tears in her eyes.

Peter thought of the dear Old Briar-patch and how safe he always felt there, and he felt a great pity for poor Mrs. Quack, who couldn't feel safe anywhere. And then right away he grew indignant that she should be so distrustful of Farmer Brown's boy, though if he had stopped to think, he would have remembered that once he was just as distrustful.

"I should think," said Peter with a great deal of dignity, "that you might at least believe what Jerry Muskrat and I, who live here all the time, tell you. We ought to know Farmer Brown's boy if anyone does, and we tell you that he won't harm a feather of you."

"He won't get the chance!" snapped Mrs. Quack.

Jerry Muskrat sniffed in disgust. "I don't doubt you have suffered a lot from men with terrible guns," said he, "but you don't suppose Peter and I have lived as long as we have without learning a little, do you? I wouldn't trust many of those two-legged creatures myself, but Farmer Brown's boy is different. If all of them were like him, we wouldn't have a thing to fear from them. He has a heart. Yes, indeed, he has a heart. Now you take my advice and eat whatever he has put there for you, be thankful, and stop worrying. Peter and I will keep watch and warn you if there is any danger."

I don't know as even this would have overcome Mrs. Quack's fears if it hadn't been for the taste of that good corn in her mouth, and her empty stomach. She couldn't, she just couldn't resist these, and presently she was back among the rushes, hunting out the corn and wheat as fast as ever she could. When at last she could eat no more, she felt so comfortable that somehow the Smiling Pool didn't seem such a dangerous place after all, and she quite forgot Farmer Brown's boy. She found a snug hiding-place among the rushes too far out from the bank for Reddy Fox to surprise her, and then with a sleepy "Good night" to Jerry and Peter, she tucked her head under her wing and soon was fast asleep.

Peter Rabbit tiptoed away, and then he hurried lipperty-lipperty-lip to the dear Old Briar-patch to tell Mrs. Peter all about Mrs. Quack.

CHAPTER NINE: PETER RABBIT MAKES AN EARLY CALL

PETER RABBIT WAS so full of interest in Mrs. Quack and her troubles that he was back at the Smiling Pool before Mr. Sun had kicked off his rosy blankets and begun his daily climb up in the blue, blue sky. You see, he felt that he had heard only a part of Mrs. Quack's story, and he was dreadfully afraid that she would get away before he could hear the rest. With the first bit of daylight, Mrs. Quack swam out from her hiding-place among the brown rushes. It looked to Peter as if she sat up on the end of her tail as she stretched her neck and wings just as far as she could, and he wanted to laugh right out. Then she quickly ducked her head under water two or three times so that the water rolled down over her back, and again Peter wanted to laugh. But he didn't. He kept perfectly still. Mrs. Quack shook herself and then began to carefully dress her feathers. That is, she carefully put back in place every feather that had been rumpled up. She took a great deal of time for this, for Mrs. Quack is very neat and tidy and takes the greatest pride in looking as fine as she can.

Of course it was very impolite of Peter to watch her, but he didn't think of that. He didn't mean to be impolite. And then it was so interesting. "Huh!" said he to himself, "I don't see what anyone wants to waste so much time on their clothes for."

You know, Peter doesn't waste any time on his clothes. In fact, he doesn't seem to care a bit how he looks. He hasn't learned yet that it always pays to be as neat and clean as possible and that you must think well of yourself if you want others to think well of you.

When at last Mrs. Quack had taken a final shower bath and appeared satisfied that she was looking her best, Peter opened his mouth to ask her the questions he was so full of, but closed it again as he remembered people are usually better natured when their stomachs are full, and Mrs. Quack had not yet breakfasted. So he waited as patiently as he could, which wasn't patiently at all. At last Mrs. Quack finished her breakfast, and then she had to clean herself all over again. Finally Peter hopped to the edge of the bank where she would see him.

"Good morning, Mrs. Quack," said he very politely. "I hope you had a good rest and are feeling very well this morning."

"Thank you," replied Mrs. Quack. "I'm feeling as well as could be expected. In fact, I'm feeling better than I have felt for some time in spite of the sore place made by that terrible gun yesterday. You see, I have had a good rest and two square meals, and these are things I haven't had since goodness knows when. This is a very nice place. Let me see, what is it you call it?"

"The Smiling Pool," said Peter.

"That's a good name for it," returned Mrs. Quack. "If only I could be sure that none of those hunters would find me here, and if only Mr. Quack were here, I would be content to stay a while." At the mention of Mr. Quack, the eyes of Mrs. Quack suddenly filled with tears. Peter felt tears of sympathy in his own eyes.

"Where is Mr. Quack?" he asked.

"I don't know," sobbed Mrs. Quack. "I wish I did. I haven't seen him since one of those terrible guns was fired at us over on the Big River yesterday morning a little while before Little Joe Otter told me about the Smiling Pool. Ever since we started for our home in the far North, I have been fearing that something of this kind might happen. I ought to be on my way there now, but what is the use without Mr. Quack? Without him, I would be all alone up there and wouldn't have any home."

"Won't you tell me all that has happened since you started on your long journey?" asked Peter. "Perhaps some of us can help you."

"I'm afraid you can't," replied Mrs. Quack sadly, "but I'll tell you all about it so that you may know just how thankful you ought to feel that you do not have to suffer what some of us do."

CHAPTER TEN: HOW MR. AND MRS. QUACK STARTED NORTH

PETER RABBIT WAS eager to help Mrs. Quack in her trouble, though he hadn't the least idea how he could help and neither had she. How anyone who dislikes water as Peter does could help one who lives on the water all the time was more than either one of them could see. And yet without knowing it, Peter *was* helping Mrs. Quack. He was giving her his sympathy, and sympathy often helps others a great deal more than we even guess. It sometimes is a very good plan to tell your troubles to someone who will listen with sympathy. It was so with Mrs. Quack. She had kept her troubles locked in her own heart so long that it did her good to pour them all out to Peter.

"Mr. Quack and I spent a very comfortable winter way down in the sunny Southland," said she with a far-away look. "It was very warm and nice down there, and there were a great many other Ducks spending the winter with us. The place where we were was far from the homes of men, and it was only once in a long while that we had to watch out for terrible guns. Of course, we had to have our wits with us all the time, because there are Hawks and Owls and Minks down there just as there are up here, but any Duck who can't keep out of their way deserves to furnish one of them a dinner.

"Then there was another fellow we had to watch out for, a queer fellow whom we never see anywhere but down there. It was never safe to swim too near an old log floating in the water or lying on the bank, because it might suddenly open a great mouth and swallow one of us whole."

"What's that?" Peter Rabbit leaned forward and stared at Mrs. Quack with his eyes popping right out. "What's that?" he repeated. "How can an old log have a mouth?"

Mrs. Quack just had to smile, Peter was so in earnest and looked so astonished.

"Of course," said she, "no really true log has a mouth or is alive, but this queer fellow I was speaking of looks so much like an old log floating in the water unless you look at him very sharply, that many a heedless young Duck has discovered the difference when it was too late. Then, too, he will swim under water and come up underneath and seize you without any warning. He has the biggest mouth I've ever seen, with terrible-looking teeth, and could swallow me whole."

By this time Peter's eyes looked as if they would fall out of his head. "What is his name?" whispered Peter.

"It's Old Ally the 'Gator," replied Mrs. Quack. "Some folks call him Alligator and some just 'Gator, but we call him Old Ally. He's a very interesting old fellow. Sometime perhaps I'll tell you more about him. Mr. Quack and I kept out of his reach, you may be sure. We lived quietly and tried to get in as good condition as possible for the long journey back

Old Ally

to our home in the North. When it was time to start, a lot of us got together, just as we did when we came down from the North, only this time the young Ducks felt themselves quite grown up. In fact, before we started there was a great deal of romancing, and each one chose a mate. That was a very happy time, a very happy time indeed, but it was a sad time too for us older Ducks, because we knew what dreadful things were likely to happen on the long journey. It is hard enough to lose father or mother or brother or sister, but it is worse to lose a dear mate."

Mrs. Quack's eyes suddenly filled with tears again. "Oh, dear," she sobbed, "I wish I knew what became of Mr. Quack."

Peter said nothing, but looked the sympathy he felt. Presently Mrs. Quack went on with her story. "We had a splendid big flock when we started, made up wholly of pairs, each pair dreaming of the home they would build when they reached the far North. Mr. Quack was the leader as usual, and I flew right behind him. We hadn't gone far before we began to hear the terrible guns, and the farther we went, the worse they got. Mr. Quack led us to the safest feeding and resting grounds he knew of, and for a time our flock escaped the terrible guns. But the farther we went, the more guns there were." Mrs. Quack paused and Peter waited.

CHAPTER ELEVEN: THE TERRIBLE, TERRIBLE GUNS

"Bang! Bang! Bang! Not a feather spare!
Kill! Kill! Kill! Wound and rip and tear!"

THAT IS WHAT the terrible guns roar from morning to night at Mrs. Quack and her friends as they fly on their long journey to their home in the far North. I don't wonder that she was terribly uneasy and nervous as she sat in the Smiling Pool talking to Peter Rabbit; do you?

"Yes," said she, continuing her story of her long journey from the sunny Southland where she had spent the winter, "the farther we got, the more there were of those terrible guns. It grew so bad that as well as Mr. Quack knew the places where we could find food, and no Duck that ever flew knew them better, he couldn't find one where we could feel perfectly sure that we were safe. The very safest-looking places sometimes were the most dangerous. If you saw a lot of Rabbits playing together on the Green Meadows, you would feel perfectly safe in joining them, wouldn't you?"

Peter nodded. "I certainly would," said he. "If it were safe for them it certainly would be safe for me."

"Well, that is just the way we felt when we saw a lot of Ducks swimming about on the edge of one of those feeding-places. We were tired, for we had flown a long distance, and we were hungry. It was still and peaceful there and not a thing to be seen that looked the least bit like danger. So we went straight in to join those Ducks, and then, just as we set our wings to drop down on the water among them, there was a terrible bang, bang, bang, bang! My heart almost stopped beating. Then how we did fly! When we were far out over the water where we could see that nothing was near us we stopped to rest, and there we found only half as many in our flock as there had been."

"Where were the others?" asked Peter, although he guessed.

"Killed or hurt by those terrible guns," replied Mrs. Quack sadly. "And that wasn't the worst of it. I told you that when we started each of us had a mate. Now we found that of those who had escaped, four had lost their mates. They were heartbroken. When it came time for us to move on, they wouldn't go. They said that if they did reach the nesting-place in the far North, they couldn't have nests or eggs or young because they had no mates, so what was the use? Besides, they hoped that if they waited around they might find their mates. They thought they might not have been killed, but just hurt, and might be able to get away from those hunters. So they left us and swam back towards that terrible place, calling for their lost mates, and it was the saddest sound. I know now just how they felt, for I have lost Mr. Quack, and that's why I'm here." Mrs. Quack drew a wing across her eyes to wipe away the tears.

"But what happened to those Ducks that were swimming about there and made you think it was safe?" asked Peter, with a puzzled look on his face.

"Nothing," replied Mrs. Quack. "They had been fastened out there in the water by the hunters so as to make us think it safe, and the terrible guns were fired at us and not at them. The hunters were hidden under grass, and that is why we didn't see them."

Peter blinked his eyes rapidly as if he were having hard work to believe what he had been told. "Why," said he at last, "I never heard of anything so dreadfully unfair in all my life! Do you mean to tell me that those hunters actually made other Ducks lead you into danger?"

"That's just what I mean," returned Mrs. Quack. "Those two-legged creatures don't know what fairness is. Why, some of them have learned our language and actually call us in where they can shoot us. Just think of that! They tell us in our own language that there is plenty to eat and all is safe, so that we will think that other Ducks are hidden and feeding there, and then when we go to join them, we are shot at! You ought to be mighty thankful, Peter Rabbit, that you are not a Duck."

"I am," replied Peter. He knew that not one of the meadow and forest people who were always trying to catch him would do a thing like that.

"It's all true," said Mrs. Quack, "and those hunters do other things just as unfair. Sometimes awful storms will come up, and we just have to find places where we can rest. Those hunters will hide near those places and shoot at us when we are so tired that we can hardly move a wing. It wouldn't be so bad if a hunter would be satisfied to kill just one Duck, just as Reddy Fox is, but he seems to want to kill *every* Duck. Foxes and Hawks and Owls catch a good many young Ducks, just as they do young Rabbits, but you know how we feel about that. They only hunt when they are hungry, and they hunt fairly. When, they have got enough to make a dinner, they stop. They keep our wits sharp. If we do not keep out of their way, it is our own fault. It is a kind of game—the game of life. I guess it is Old Mother Nature's way of keeping us wide-awake and sharpening our wits, and so making us better fitted to live.

"With these two-legged creatures with terrible guns, it is all different. We don't have any chance at all. If they hunted us as Reddy Fox does, tried to catch us themselves, it would be different. But their terrible guns kill when we are a long way off, and there isn't any way for us to know of the danger. And then, when one of them does kill a Duck, he isn't satisfied, but keeps on killing and killing and killing. I'm sure one would make him a dinner, if that is what he wants.

"And they often simply break the wings or otherwise terribly hurt the ones they shoot at, and then leave them to suffer, unable to take care of themselves. Oh, dear, I'm afraid that is what has happened to Mr. Quack."

Once more poor Mrs. Quack was quite overcome with her troubles and sorrows. Peter wished with all his heart that he could do something to comfort her, but of course he couldn't, so he just sat still and waited until she could tell him just what did happen to Mr. Quack.

CHAPTER TWELVE: WHAT DID HAPPEN TO MR. QUACK

"WHEN DID YOU last see Mr. Quack?" asked Jerry Muskrat, who had been listening while Mrs. Quack told Peter Rabbit about her terrible journey.

"Early yesterday morning," replied Mrs. Quack, the tears once more filling her eyes. "We had reached the Big River over there, just six of us out of the big flock that had started from the sunny Southland. How we got as far as that I don't know. But we did, and neither Mr. Quack nor I had lost a feather from those terrible guns that had banged at us all the way up and that had killed so many of our friends.

"We were flying up the Big River, and everything seemed perfectly safe. We were in a hurry, and when we came to a bend in the Big River, we flew quite close to shore, so as not to have to go way out and around. That was where Mr. Quack made a mistake. Even the smartest people will make mistakes sometimes, you know."

Peter Rabbit nodded. "I know," said he. "I've made them myself." And then he wondered why Jerry Muskrat laughed right out.

"Yes," continued Mrs. Quack, "that is where Mr. Quack made a mistake, a great mistake. I suppose that because not a single gun had been fired at us that morning he thought perhaps there were no hunters on the Big River. So to save time he led us close to shore. And then it happened. There was a bang, bang of a terrible gun, and down fell Mr. Quack just as we had seen so many fall before. It was awful. There was Mr. Quack flying in front of me on swift, strong wings, and there never was a swifter, stronger flier or a handsomer Duck than Mr. Quack, and then all in the wink of an eye he was tumbling helplessly down, down to the water below, and I was flying on alone, for the other Ducks turned off, and I don't know what became of them. I couldn't stop to see what became of Mr. Quack, because if I had, that terrible gun would have killed me. So I kept on a little way and then turned and went back, only I kept out in the middle of the Big River. I dropped down on the water and swam about, calling and calling, but I didn't get any answer, and so I don't know what has become of Mr. Quack. I am afraid he was killed, and if he was, I wish I had been killed myself."

Here Mrs. Quack choked up so that she couldn't say another word. Peter's own eyes were full of tears as he tried to comfort her.

"Perhaps," said he, "Mr. Quack wasn't killed and is hiding somewhere along the Big River. I don't know why I feel so, but I feel sure that he wasn't killed, and that you will find him yet."

"That's why I've waited instead of going on," replied Mrs. Quack between sobs, "though it wouldn't have been of any use to go on without my dear mate. I'm going back to the Big River now to look for him. The trouble is, I don't dare go near the shore, and if he is alive, he probably is hiding somewhere among the rushes along the banks. I think I'll be going along now, but I'll be back tonight if nothing happens to me. You folks who can always stay at home have a great deal to be thankful for."

"It's lucky for me that Mrs. Peter wasn't here to hear her say that," said Peter, as he and Jerry Muskrat watched Mrs. Quack fly swiftly towards the Big River. "Mrs. Peter is forever worrying and scolding because I don't stay in the dear Old Briar-patch. If she had heard Mrs. Quack say that, I never would have heard the last of it. I wish there was something we could do for Mrs. Quack. I'm going back to the dear Old Briar-patch to think it over, and I guess the sooner I start the better, for that looks to me like Reddy Fox over there, and he's headed this way."

So off for home started Peter, lipperty-lipperty-lip, as fast as he could go, and all the way there he was turning over in his mind what Mrs. Quack had told him and trying to think of some way to help her.

CHAPTER THIRTEEN: PETER TELLS ABOUT MRS. QUACK

To get things done, if you'll but try,
You'll always find there is a way.
What you yourself can't do alone,
The chances are another may.

WHEN PETER RABBIT was once more safely back in the dear Old Briar-patch, he told Mrs. Peter all about poor Mrs. Quack and her troubles. Then for a long, long time he sat in a brown study. A brown study, you know, is sitting perfectly still and thinking very hard. That was what Peter did. He sat so still that if you had happened along, you probably would have thought him asleep. But he wasn't asleep. No, indeed! He was just thinking and thinking. He was trying to think of some way to help Mrs. Quack. At last he gave a little sigh of disappointment.

"It can't be done," said he. "There isn't any way."

"What can't be done?" demanded a voice right over his head.

Peter looked up. There sat Sammy Jay. Peter had been thinking so hard that he hadn't seen Sammy arrive.

"What can't be done?" repeated Sammy. "There isn't anything that can't be done. There are plenty of things that you can't do, but what you can't do someone else can. Just tuck that fact away in that empty head of yours and never say can't." You know Sammy dearly loves to tease Peter.

Peter made a good-natured face at Sammy. "Which means, I suppose, that what I can't do you can. You always did have a pretty good opinion of yourself, Sammy," said he.

"Nothing of the kind," retorted Sammy. "I simply mean that nobody can do everything, and that very often two heads are better than one. It struck me that you had something on your mind, and I thought I might be able to help you get rid of it. But of course, if you don't want my help, supposing I could and would give it to you, that is an end of the matter, and I guess I'll be on my way. The Old Briar-patch is rather a dull place anyway."

Peter started to make a sharp retort, but thought better of it. Instead he replied mildly: "I was just trying to think of some way to help poor Mrs. Quack."

"Help Mrs. Quack!" exclaimed Sammy in surprise. "Where under the sun did you get acquainted with Mrs. Quack? What's the matter with her? She always has looked to me quite able to help herself."

"Well, she isn't. That is, she needs others to help her just now," replied Peter, "and I've been most thinking my head off trying to find a way to help her." Then he told Sammy how he had met Mrs. Quack at the Smiling Pool and how terrible

"Just tuck that fact away in that empty head of yours and never say can't."

her long journey up from the sunny Southland had been, and how Mr. Quack had been shot by a hunter with a terrible gun, and how poor Mrs. Quack was quite heartbroken, and how she had gone over to the Big River to look for him but didn't dare go near the places where he might be hiding if he were still alive and hurt so that he couldn't fly, and how cruel and terribly unfair were the men with terrible guns, and all the other things he had learned from Mrs. Quack.

Sammy listened with his head cocked on one side, and for once he didn't interrupt Peter or try to tease him or make fun of him. In fact, as Peter looked up at him, he could see that

Sammy was very serious and thoughtful, and that the more he heard of Mrs. Quack's story the more thoughtful he looked. When Peter finished, Sammy flew down a little nearer to Peter.

"I beg your pardon for saying your head is empty, Peter," said he. "Your heart is right, anyway. Of course, there isn't anything you can do to help Mrs. Quack, but as I told you in the beginning, what you can't do others can. Now I don't say that I can help Mrs. Quack, but I can try. I believe I'll do a little thinking myself."

So Sammy Jay in his turn went into a brown study, and Peter watched him anxiously and a little hopefully.

CHAPTER FOURTEEN: SAMMY JAY'S PLAN TO HELP MRS. QUACK

SAMMY JAY SAT on the lowest branch of a little tree in the dear Old Briar-patch just over Peter Rabbit's head, thinking as hard as ever he could. Peter watched him and wondered if Sammy would be able to think of any plan for helping poor Mrs. Quack. He hoped so. He himself had thought and thought until he felt as if his brains were all mixed up and he couldn't think any more. So he watched Sammy and waited and hoped.

Presently Sammy flitted his wings in a way which Peter knew meant that he had made up his mind. "Did I understand you to say that Mrs. Quack said that if Mr. Quack is alive, he probably is hiding among the rushes along the banks of the Big River?" he asked.

Peter nodded.

"And that she said that she doesn't dare go near the banks because of fear of the terrible guns?"

Again Peter nodded.

"Well, if that's the case, what is the matter with some of us who are not afraid of the terrible guns looking for Mr. Quack?" said Sammy. "I will, for one, and I'm quite sure that my cousin, Blacky the Crow, will, for another. He surely will if he thinks it will spoil the plans of any hunters. Blacky would go a long distance to do that. He hates terrible guns and the men who use them. And he knows all about them. He has very sharp eyes, has Blacky, and he knows when a man has got a gun and when he hasn't. More than that, he can tell better than anyone I know of just how near he can safely go to one of those terrible guns. He is smart, my cousin Blacky is, and if he will help me look for Mr. Quack, we'll find him if he is alive."

"That will be splendid!" cried Peter, clapping his hands. "But aren't you afraid of those terrible guns, Sammy?"

"Not when the hunters are trying for Ducks," replied Sammy. "If there is a Duck anywhere in sight, they won't shoot at poor little me or even at Blacky, though they would shoot at him any other time. You see, they know that shooting at us would frighten the Ducks. Blacky knows all about the Big River. In the winter he often gets considerable food there along its banks. I've been over there a number of times, but I don't know so much about it as he does. Now here is my plan. I'll go find Blacky and tell him all about what we want to do for Mrs. Quack. Then, when Mrs. Quack comes back to the Smiling Pool, if she hasn't found Mr. Quack, we'll tell her what we are going to do and what she must do. She must swim right up the Big River, keeping out in the middle where she will be safe. If there are any hunters hiding along the bank, they will see her, and then they won't shoot at Blacky or me because they will keep hoping that Mrs. Quack will swim in near enough for them to shoot her. Blacky will fly along over one bank of the Big River, and I will do the same over the other bank, keeping as nearly opposite Mrs. Quack as we can. Being up in the air that way and looking down, we will be able to see the hunters and also Mr. Quack, if he is hiding among the rushes. Are you quite sure that Mrs. Quack will come back to the Smiling Pool tonight?"

"She said she would," replied Peter. "Last night she came just a little while before dark, and I think she will do the same thing tonight, to see if any more corn has been left for her. You know Farmer Brown's boy put some there yesterday, and it tasted so good to her that I don't believe she will be able to stay away, even if she wants to. I think your plan is perfectly splendid, Sammy Jay. I do hope Blacky the Crow will help."

"He will. Don't worry about that," replied Sammy. "Hello! There goes Farmer Brown's boy over to the Smiling Pool now."

"Then there will be some more corn for Mrs. Quack. I just know it!" cried Peter. "He is going to see if Mrs. Quack is there, and I just know he has his pockets full of corn."

"I wouldn't mind a little of it myself," said Sammy. "Well, I must go along to hunt up Blacky. Good-bye, Peter."

"Good-bye and good luck," replied Peter. "I've always said you are not half such a bad fellow as you try to make folks think you are, Sammy Jay."

"Thanks," said Sammy, and started for the Green Forest to look for his cousin, Blacky the Crow.

CHAPTER FIFTEEN: THE HUNT FOR MR. QUACK

IN SPITE OF her hopelessness in regard to Mr. Quack, there is no doubt that Mrs. Quack felt better that night after she had eaten the corn left among the rushes of the Smiling Pool by Farmer Brown's boy. Now she had that very comfortable feeling that goes with a full stomach, she could think better. As the Black Shadows crept across the Smiling Pool, she turned over in her mind Sammy Jay's plan for helping her the next day. The more she thought about it, the better it seemed, and she began to feel a little ashamed that she had not appeared more grateful to Sammy when he told her. At the time she had been tired and hungry and discouraged. Now she was beginning to feel rested, and she was no longer hungry. These things made all the difference in the world. As she thought over Sammy's plan, she began to feel a little hope, and when at last she put her head under her wing to go to sleep, she had made up her mind that the plan was worth trying, and that she would do her part.

Bright and early the next morning, Sammy Jay and Blacky the Crow were in the Big Hickory tree near the Smiling Pool ready to start for the Big River to hunt for Mr. Quack. Peter Rabbit had been so afraid that he would miss something that he had stayed near the Smiling Pool all night, so he was on hand to see the start.

It had been agreed that Mrs. Quack was to go to a certain place on the Big

River and then swim up as far as she thought it would be of any use. She was to stay in the middle of the river, where she would be quite safe from hunters with terrible guns, and where also these same hunters would be sure to see her and so not be tempted to shoot at Blacky the Crow if he happened to fly over them. You see, they would hope that Mrs. Quack would swim in near enough to be shot and so would not risk frightening her by shooting at Blacky.

When Mrs. Quack had finished her breakfast, she started for the Big River, and her stout wings moved so swiftly that they made a whistling sound. Sammy Jay and Blacky the Crow followed her, but though they flew as fast as they could, Mrs. Quack had reached the Big River before they had gone half the way. When they did get there, they saw Mrs. Quack out in the middle, swimming about and watching for them. Blacky flew across the river and pretended to be hunting for food along the farther bank, just as every hunter knows he often does. Sammy Jay did the same thing on the other bank.

Mrs. Quack swam slowly up the Big River, keeping in the middle, and Blacky and Sammy followed along up the two banks, all the time using their sharp eyes for all they were worth to find Mr. Quack hiding among the broken-down rushes or under the bushes in the water, for the Big River had overflowed its banks, and in some places bushes and trees were in the water.

Now Sammy Jay dearly loves to hunt for things. Whenever he knows that one of his neighbors in the Green Forest has hidden something, he likes to hunt for it. It isn't so much that he wants what has been hidden, as it is that he wants to feel he is smart enough to find it. When he does find it, he usually steals it, I'm sorry to say. But it is the fun of hunting that Sammy enjoys most. So now Sammy thoroughly enjoyed hunting for Mr. Quack. He peered into every likely hiding-place and became so interested that he quite forgot about the hunters who might be waiting along the bank.

So it happened that he didn't see a boat drawn in among the bushes until he was right over it. Sitting in it was a man with a terrible gun, very intently watching Mrs. Quack out in the middle of the Big River. Sammy was so startled that before he thought he opened his mouth and screamed "Thief! thief! thief!" at the top of his lungs, and flew away with all his might. Mrs. Quack heard his scream and understood just what it meant.

A little later Blacky the Crow discovered another hunter hiding behind the bushes on his side. "Caw! caw! caw!" shouted Blacky, flying out over the water far enough to be safe from that terrible gun he could see.

"Quack! quack!" replied Mrs. Quack, which meant that she understood. And so the hunt went on without a sign of poor Mr. Quack.

CHAPTER SIXTEEN: SAMMY JAY SEES SOMETHING GREEN

FOR ALL THEIR peeking and peering among the broken-down rushes and under the bushes along the banks of the Big River, and no sharper eyes ever peeked and peered, Sammy Jay and Blacky the Crow had found no sign of the missing Mr. Quack.

"I guess Mrs. Quack was right and that Mr. Quack was killed when he was shot," muttered Sammy to himself. "Probably one of those hunters had him for dinner long ago. Hello! There's another hunter up where the Laughing Brook joins the Big River! I guess I won't take any chances. I'd like to find Mr. Quack, but Sammy Jay is a lot more important to me than Mr. Quack, and that fellow just might happen to take it into his head to shoot at me."

So Sammy silently flew around back of the hunter and stopped in a tree where he could watch all that the man did. For some time Sammy sat there watching. The hunter was sitting behind a sort of fence of bushes which quite hid him from anyone who might happen to be out on the Big River. But of course Sammy could see him perfectly, because he was behind him. Out in front of that little fence, which was on the very edge of the water, were a number of what Sammy at first took to be some of Mrs. Quack's relatives. "Why doesn't he shoot them?" thought Sammy. He puzzled over this as he watched them until suddenly it came into his head that he hadn't seen one of them move since he began watching them. The man changed his position, and still those Ducks didn't move, although some of them were so near that they simply couldn't have helped knowing when the hunter moved unless they were more stupid than any one of Sammy's acquaintance.

This was very curious, very curious indeed. Sammy flew a little nearer and then a little nearer, taking the greatest care not to make a sound. Pretty soon he was so near that he could see those Ducks very plainly, and he stared with all his might. He couldn't see any feathers! No, Sir, he couldn't see any feathers! Then he understood.

"Huh!" said he to himself. "Those are not Ducks at all. They are just pieces of wood made to look like Ducks. Now I wonder what they are for."

In a few minutes he found out. He saw the hunter crouch down a little lower and look down the Big River. Sammy looked too. He saw a flock of real Ducks flying swiftly just above the middle of the Big River. Suddenly the leader turned straight towards the place where the hunter was hiding, and the others followed him. He could hear Mrs. Quack calling excitedly out in the middle of the Big River, but the strangers did not heed her. They had their eyes on those wooden Ducks and were coming straight in to join them.

"They think they are real Ducks and so this place is perfectly safe!" thought

Sammy. He saw the hunter make ready to shoot with his terrible gun and then, without stopping to think what might happen to him, he opened his mouth and screamed at the top of his voice. He saw the Ducks suddenly swing out towards the middle of the Big River and knew that they had heard his warning. He saw the hunter suddenly rise and point his gun at the flying Ducks. He heard the bang, bang of the terrible gun, but not one of the flock was hit. The distance was too great. Sammy chuckled happily. Then he remembered that he himself was within easy reach of that terrible gun, and probably the hunter was very angry. In great fright Sammy turned and flew, dodging behind trees and every second expecting to hear again the roar of that terrible gun.

But he didn't, and so when he thought he was safe, he stopped. Now in flying away from the hunter he had followed the Laughing Brook where it winds through a sort of swamp before it joins the Big River. Because there was more water than could be kept between the banks of the Big River, it had crept over the banks, and all the trees of the swamp were standing in water. Just beyond where Sammy was sitting was a pile of brush in the water. A Jolly Little Sunbeam, dancing down through the tree tops, touched something under the edge of the brush, and Sammy's sharp eyes caught a flash of green. Idly he watched it, and presently it moved. Instantly Sammy was all curiosity. He flew over where he could see better.

"Now what can that be?" thought Sammy, as he peered down at the pile of brush and tried to see under it.

CHAPTER SEVENTEEN: MR. QUACK IS FOUND AT LAST

SAMMY JAY'S EYES sparkled as he watched that spot of green under the pile of brush in the swamp through which the Laughing Brook finds its way to join the Big River. All around was water, for you know it was spring, and the melting snows on the hills way up where the Big River has its beginning were pouring more water into the Big River than its banks would hold as it hurried down to the Great Ocean. It just couldn't hurry fast enough to take all that water down as fast as it ran into the Big River, and so the water had crept over the banks in places. It had done this right here in the little swamp where Sammy was.

Sammy sat perfectly still, for he learned long ago that only by keeping perfectly still may one see all that is to be seen. That green spot had moved. He was sure of that. And if it moved, it must be something alive. If it were alive, it must be somebody, and Sammy wanted to know who it was. Try as he would he couldn't remember anyone who wore such glossy green as that. So he sat perfectly still, for he knew that if whoever was hiding under that brush should even guess that he was being watched, he would not come out.

Mr. Quack

So, his eyes sparkling with excitement, Sammy watched. He was impatiently patient. Did you know that it is possible to be impatiently patient? Well, it is. Sammy was just boiling with impatience inside, but he didn't let that impatience spoil the patience of his waiting. He sat there just as still as still, with his eyes fixed on that green spot, and you would never have guessed that he was fairly bursting with impatience to know who it was he was watching. That is what is called self-control. It means the power to make yourself do a certain thing, no matter how much you may want to do something else. It is a splendid thing to have, is self-control.

After what seemed to Sammy a very long time, the green spot moved again. Little by little something reached out from under the pile of brush. It was a head, a very beautiful green head, and it was exactly like Mrs. Quack's head, only hers was a sober brown instead of green. Sammy choked back a little gasp of surprise as a sudden thought popped into his head. Could this be the lost Mr. Quack? He had forgotten that probably Mr. Quack dressed differently from Mrs. Quack, and so of course he had been looking for someone all in brown.

There was the bang of a gun somewhere over on the Big River, and the green head was hastily withdrawn under the bush, but not before Sammy had seen a look of terrible fear in his eyes. "I believe it *is* Mr. Quack!" thought Sammy. "If it is, I'll have the best news ever to tell Mrs. Quack. Just trust Sammy Jay to find anything he goes looking for."

This was just plain boasting, and Sammy knew it. But Sammy always does have a good opinion of himself. It is one of his faults. He quite lost sight of the fact that it was entirely by accident that he had come over to this swamp. Now that he had guessed who this might be, he was less impatient. He waited as still as you please, and at last the green head was slowly stretched out again, and Sammy could see that the neck was green, too, and that around the neck was a white collar. Sammy could keep still no longer.

"Are you Mr. Quack?" he asked eagerly.

The beautiful head disappeared like a flash. Sammy waited a minute or two, before he repeated his question, adding: "You needn't be afraid. There isn't anybody here but me, and I'm your friend. I just want to know if you are Mr. Quack because I've been looking for you for Mrs. Quack. Are you?"

Slowly, looking this way and that way with fear and suspicion in his eyes, a handsome Duck came out from under the pile of brush.

"Yes," said he in a low voice. "I am Mr. Quack. Where is Mrs. Quack?"

"Safe and sound over on the Big River," replied Sammy joyfully. "Oh, I'm so glad I've found you!"

CHAPTER EIGHTEEN: SAMMY JAY SENDS MRS. QUACK TO THE SWAMP

WHEN SAMMY JAY left Mr. Quack in the swamp over by the bank of the Big River, he flew straight back to the Smiling Pool. At first he thought of flying out over the Big River and screaming the news to Mrs. Quack, who, you know, was swimming about out there. But he knew that if he did, she would very likely fly right over where Mr. Quack was, and that wouldn't do at all. No, indeed, that wouldn't do at all. One of the hunters would be sure to see her. So Sammy wisely flew back to the Smiling Pool to wait until Mrs. Quack should come back there for the night.

Of course he told Peter Rabbit all about Mr. Quack, and Peter was so delighted at the thought that Mr. Quack was alive that he capered about in quite the craziest way. "Does Mrs. Quack know yet?" asked Peter.

Sammy shook his head. "I'm going to tell her when she comes back here tonight," he explained. "I was afraid if I told her before then she would fly straight to him and perhaps get them both in trouble."

"Quite right, Sammy! Quite right!" Peter exclaimed. "I wouldn't have thought of that. My, won't she be happy when you do tell her! I wonder what she'll say and what she'll do. I'm going to stay right here so as to see her when she hears the good news. Here comes your cousin, Blacky the Crow. Does he know yet?"

"No," replied Sammy, "but I'm going to tell him as soon as he gets here." They watched Blacky draw nearer and nearer, and as soon as he was within hearing Sammy shouted the news.

"Caw, caw, caw," replied Blacky, hurrying a little faster.

As soon as he reached the Big Hickory tree, Sammy told the whole story over again, and Blacky was quite as glad as the others. While they waited for Mrs. Quack he told how he had hunted and hunted along the farther bank of the Big River and how he had seen the hunters with their terrible guns hiding and had warned Mrs. Quack just where each one was.

Jolly, round, red Mr. Sun was getting ready to go to bed behind the Purple Hills and the Black Shadows were beginning to creep out over the Green Meadows before Mrs. Quack came. In fact, Sammy Jay and Blacky were getting very uneasy. It was almost bedtime for them, for neither of them dared stay out after dark. They had almost made up their minds to leave Peter to tell the news when they saw Mrs. Quack coming swiftly from the direction of the Big River. She looked so sad and discouraged that even Blacky the Crow was sorry for her, and you know Blacky isn't much given to such feelings.

"What's the news, Mrs. Quack?" asked Peter, his eyes dancing.

"There isn't any," replied Mrs. Quack.

"Oh, yes, there is!" cried Sammy Jay, who couldn't possibly keep still any longer.

"What is it?" demanded Mrs. Quack eagerly, and it seemed to Peter that there was a wee bit of hope in her voice.

"Did you happen to notice that just before the Laughing Brook joins the Big River it flows through a little swamp?" asked Sammy.

Mrs. Quack nodded her head rapidly. "What of it?" she demanded.

"Nothing much, only if I were you I would go down there after dark," replied Sammy.

Mrs. Quack looked up at Sammy sharply. "Why should I go down there?" she asked.

"If I tell you, will you wait until I get quite through?" asked Sammy in his turn.

Mrs. Quack promised that she would.

"Well, then," replied Sammy, "this afternoon I found a stranger hiding in there, a stranger with a beautiful green head and neck and a white collar."

"Mr. Quack! Oh, it was Mr. Quack!" cried Mrs. Quack joyfully and lifted her wings as if she would start for the swamp at once.

"Stop!" cried Sammy sharply.

"You said you would wait until I am through. It won't do for you to go there until after dark, because there is a hunter hiding very near Mr. Quack's hiding-place. Wait until it is dark and he has gone home. Then take my advice, and when you have found Mr. Quack, bring him right up here to the Smiling Pool. He can't fly, but he can swim up the Laughing Brook, and this is the safest place for both of you. Now good night and good luck."

CHAPTER NINETEEN: JERRY MUSKRAT'S GREAT IDEA

A friendly friend is a friend indeed
When he proves a friend in the time of need.

MR. AND MRS. QUACK had been so much taken up with each other and with their troubles that they had quite forgotten they were not alone in the Smiling Pool, which they had reached by swimming up the Laughing Brook. So it happened that when Mrs. Quack suggested that if Mr. Quack's wing got strong they might be able to find a lonesome pond not too far away where they could make their home for the summer, they were a little startled to hear a voice say: "I know where there is one, and you will not have to fly at all to get to it." Both jumped a little. You see their nerves had been very much upset for a long time, and the least unexpected thing made them jump. Then both laughed.

"Hello, Jerry Muskrat! We'd forgotten all about you," said Mrs. Quack. "What was that you said?"

Jerry good-naturedly repeated what he had said. Mrs. Quack's face brightened. "Do you really mean it?" she asked eagerly. "Do you really mean that you know of a pond where we could live and not be likely to be seen by these two-legged creatures called men?"

"That's what I said," replied Jerry briefly.

"Oh, Jerry, you're not joking, are you? Tell me you're not joking," begged Mrs. Quack.

"Of course I'm not joking," returned Jerry just a little bit indignantly. I am not the kind of a fellow to joke about people who are in such trouble as you and Mr. Quack seem to be in. The idea came to me while you were talking. I couldn't help overhearing what you were saying, and the minute you mentioned a lonesome pond, the idea came to me, and I think it's a perfectly splendid idea. I know of just the lonesomest kind of a lonesome pond, and you won't have to fly a stroke to get to it. If you are smart enough not to be caught by Reddy Fox or Hooty the Owl or Billy Mink or any of those people who hunt for a living, there isn't any reason I know of why you shouldn't spend the summer there in peace and comfort."

Mrs. Quack's eyes fairly shone with hope and eagerness. "Oh, Jerry, tell us where it is, and we'll start for it right away!" she cried.

Jerry's eyes twinkled. "Of course, the owner of that pond might not like to have neighbors. I hadn't thought of that," said he. "Perhaps he ought to be asked first."

Mrs. Quack's face fell. "Who is the owner?" she asked.

"My cousin, Paddy the Beaver. He made it," replied Jerry proudly.

Mrs. Quack's face lighted up again at once. "I'm sure he won't object," said she.

"We know a great many of the Beaver family. In fact, they are very good neighbors of ours in our home in the far Northland. I didn't suppose there was a Beaver pond anywhere around here. Tell me where it is, Jerry, and I'll go right up there and call on your cousin."

"All you've got to do is to follow the Laughing Brook way back into the Green Forest, and you'll come to Paddy's pond," said he. "He made that pond himself two years ago. He came down from the Great Woods and built a dam across the Laughing Brook way back there in the Green Forest and gave us a great scare here in the Smiling Pool by cutting off the water for a few days. He has got a very nice pond there now. Honker the Goose and his flock spent a night in it on their way south last fall."

Mrs. Quack waited to hear no more. She shot up into the air and disappeared over the tops of the trees in the Green Forest.

"What do you think of my idea?" asked Jerry, as he and Mr. Quack watched her out of sight.

"I think it is great, just simply great," replied Mr. Quack.

CHAPTER TWENTY: HAPPY DAYS FOR MR. AND MRS. QUACK

Whose heart is true and brave and strong,
Who ne'er gives up to grim despair,
Will find some day that skies are blue
And all the world is bright and fair.

IF YOU DON'T believe it, just ask Mr. and Mrs. Quack. They know.

Certainly the world never looked darker for anyone than it did for them when the terrible gun of a hunter broke Mr. Quack's wing on the Big River and ended all their dreams of a home in the far Northland. Then, through the help of Jerry Muskrat, they found the lonely pond of Paddy the Beaver deep in the Green Forest, and there, because their secret had been well kept, presently they found peace and hope and then happiness. You see, the heart of Mrs. Quack was true and brave and strong. She was the kind to make the best of things, and she at once decided that if they couldn't have their home where they wanted it, they would have it where they could have it. She was determined that they should have a home anyway, and Paddy the Beaver's little pond was not such a bad place after all.

So she wasted no time. She examined every inch of the shore of that little pond. At last, a little back from the water, she found a place to suit her, a place so well hidden by bushes that only the sharpest eyes ever would find it. And a little later it would be still harder to find, as she well knew, for all about clumps of tall ferns were springing up, and when they had fully unfolded, not even the keen eyes of Sammy Jay looking down from a near-by tree would be able to discover her secret. There she made a nest on the ground, a nest of dried grass and leaves, and lined it with the softest and most beautiful of wings, down plumed from her own breast. In it she laid ten eggs. Then came long weeks of patient sitting on them, watching the wonder of growing things about her, the bursting into bloom of shy wood flowers, the unfolding of leaves on bush and tree, the springing up in a night of queer mushrooms, which people call toadstools, and all the time dreaming beautiful Duck dreams of the babies which would one day hatch from those precious eggs. She never left them save to get a little food and just enough exercise to keep her well and strong, and when she did leave them, she always carefully pulled soft down over them to keep them warm while she was away.

Mr. Quack knew all about that nest, though he had taken no part in building it and had no share in the care of those eggs. He was very willing that she should do all the work and thought it quite sufficient that he should be on guard to give warning if danger should appear. So he spent the long beautiful days lazily swimming about in the little pond, gossiping with Paddy the Beaver, and taking the best of care of himself. The broken wing healed and grew strong again, for it had not been so badly broken, after all. If he missed the company of others of his kind which he would have had during these long days of waiting had they been able to reach their usual nesting-place in the far Northland, he never mentioned it.

Unknown to them, Farmer Brown's boy discovered where they were. Later he came often to the pond

Those were happy days indeed for Mr. and Mrs. Quack in the pond of Paddy the Beaver.

and was content to sit quietly on the shore and watch Mr. Quack, so that Mr. Quack grew quite used to him and did not fear him at all. In fact, after the first few times, he made no attempt to hide. You see he discovered that Farmer Brown's boy was a friend. Always after he had left, there was something good to eat near where he had been sitting, for Farmer Brown's boy brought corn and oats and sometimes a handful of wheat.

He knew, and Mr. Quack knew that he knew, that somewhere near was a nest, but he did not try to find it much as he longed to, for he knew that would frighten and worry Mrs. Quack.

So the dear, precious secret of Mr. and Mrs. Quack was kept, for not even Paddy the Beaver knew just where that nest was, and in due time, early one morning, Mrs. Quack proudly led forth for their first swim ten downy, funny ducklings. Oh, those were happy days indeed for Mr. and Mrs. Quack in the pond of Paddy the Beaver, and in their joy they quite forgot for a time the terrible journey which had brought them there. But finally the Ducklings grew up, and when Jack Frost came in the fall, the whole family started on the long journey to the sunny Southland.

I hope they got there safely, don't you?

Among those whom Mr. and Mrs. Quack came to know very well while they lived in the pond of Paddy the Beaver was that funny fellow who wears rings on his tail—Bobby Coon.

In the next book I will tell you of some of Bobby's adventures.

The Adventures of Bobby Coon

CHAPTER ONE: BILLY MINK FINDS JOE OTTER

Some dreams are good and some are bad;
Some dreams are light and airy;
Some dreams I think are woven by
The worst kind of a fairy.

DREAMS ARE SUCH queer things, so very real when all the time they are unreal, that sometimes I think they must be the work of fairies—happy dreams the work of good fairies and bad dreams the work of bad fairies.

I guess you've had both kinds. I know I have many times. However, Bobby Coon says that fairies have nothing to do with dreams. Bobby ought to know, for he spends most of the winter asleep, and it is only when you are asleep that you have real dreams.

Bobby had kept awake as long as there was anything to eat, but when Jack Frost froze everything hard, and rough Brother North Wind brought the storm-clouds that covered the Green Forest with snow, Bobby climbed into his warm bed inside the big hollow chestnut tree which he called his, curled up comfortably, and went to sleep. He was so fat that it made him wheeze and puff whenever he tried to hurry during the last few days he was abroad, and this fat helped keep him warm while he slept, and also kept him from waking from hunger.

Bobby didn't sleep right straight through the winter as does Johnny Chuck. Once in a great while he would wake up, especially if the weather had turned rather warm. He would yawn a few times and then crawl up to his doorway and peep out to see how things were looking outside. Sometimes he would climb down from his home and take a little walk for exercise. But he never went far, and soon returned for another long nap.

As it began to get towards the end of winter his naps were shorter. He was no longer fat. In fact, his stomach complained a great deal of being empty. Perhaps you know what it is like to have a stomach complain that way. It is very disturbing. It gave Bobby no peace while he was awake, and when he was asleep it gave him bad dreams. Bobby knew very well that no fairies had anything to do with those dreams; they came from a bothersome, empty, complaining stomach and nothing else.

One day Bobby had the worst dream of all. He had prowled around a little the night before but had found nothing wherewith to satisfy his bothersome stomach.

Sometimes he would climb down from his home and take a little walk for exercise.

So he had gone back to bed very much out of sorts and almost as soon as he was asleep he had begun to dream.

At first the dreams were not so very bad, though bad enough. They were mostly of delicious things to eat which always disappeared just as he was about to taste them. They made him grunt funny little grunts and snarl funny little impatient snarls in his sleep, you know.

But at last he began to have a really, truly, bad dream. It was one of the worst dreams Bobby ever had had. He dreamed that he was walking through the Green Forest, minding his own affairs, when he met a great giant. Being afraid of the great giant, he ran with all his might and hid in a hollow log.

No sooner was he inside that hollow log than up came the great giant and began to beat on that hollow log with a great club.

Every blow made a terrible noise inside that hollow log. It was like being inside a drum with someone beating it. It filled Bobby's ears with a dreadful roaring. It made his head ache as if it would split. If sent cold shivers all over him. It filled him with dreadful fear and despair.

Yes, indeed, it was a bad dream.

A very, very bad dream!

CHAPTER TWO: BOBBY BITES HIS OWN TAIL

"Oh tell me, someone, if you will, am I awake or dreaming still?"

SO CRIED BOBBY COON to no one in particular, because no one was there to hear him. Bobby was in a dreadful state of mind. He couldn't tell for the life of him whether he was awake, or asleep and dreaming, and I cannot think of a much worse state of mind than that, can you?

There was that dreadful dream Bobby had had, the dream of the dreadful giant who had chased him into a hollow log and then beat on that log with a great club, frightening Bobby almost to death, filling his ears with a terrible roaring sound that made his head ache, and sending cold shivers all over him. Bobby was trying to make up his mind to rush out of that hollow log in spite of the dreadful giant, all in his dream you know, when suddenly his eyes flew open and there he was safe in his bed in the hollow chestnut tree which he called his own.

Bobby gave a happy little sigh of relief, for it seemed so good to find that dreadful experience only a dream. "Phew!" he exclaimed. "That was a bad, bad dream!" And then right on top of that he gave a little squeal of fear. There was that awful pounding again! Was he still dreaming? Was he awake? For the life of him Bobby couldn't tell. There was that same dreadful pounding he had heard in the hollow log, but he wasn't in the hollow log; he was safe at home in his own warm bed. Had he somehow reached home without knowing it, in the strange way that things are done in dreams, and had the dreadful giant followed him? That must be it. It must be that he was still dreaming. He wished that he would wake up.

Bobby closed his eyes as tightly as he knew how for a few minutes. Pound, pound, pound, sounded the dreadful blows. Then he opened his eyes. Surely this was his hollow tree, and certainly he felt very much awake. There was the sunlight peeping in at his doorway high overhead. Yet still those dreadful blows sounded—pound, pound, pound. His head ached still, harder than ever. And with every blow he jumped, and a cold shiver ran over him from the roots of his tail to the tip of his nose.

Never in all his life had Bobby known such a mixed-up feeling. "Is this I or isn't it I?" he whimpered. "Am I dreaming and think I'm awake, or am I awake and still dreaming? I know what I'll do; I'll bite my tail, and if I feel it I'll know that I must be awake."

So Bobby took the tip of his tail in his mouth and bit it gently. Then he wondered if he really did feel it or just seemed to feel it. So he bit it again, and this time he bit harder.

"Ouch!" cried Bobby. "That hurt. I must be awake. I'm sure I'm awake. But if

I'm awake, what dreadful thing is happening? Is there a real giant outside pounding on my tree?"

Then Bobby noticed something else. With every blow his house seemed to tremble. At first he thought he imagined it, but when he put his hands against the wall, he felt it tremble. It gave him a horrid sinking feeling inside. He was sure now that he was awake, very much awake. He was sure, too, that something dreadful was happening to his hollow tree, and he couldn't imagine what it could be. And what is more, he was afraid to climb up to his doorway and look out to see.

CHAPTER THREE: BOBBY'S DREADFUL FRIGHT

POOR, POOR BOBBY COON. Now he was sure that he was really and truly awake, he almost wished that he hadn't tried to find out. It would have been some little comfort to have been able to keep his first feeling that maybe it was all a bad dream. But now that he knew positively he was awake, he knew that this terrible pounding, which at first had been part of that bad dream, was also real. The truth is, he could no longer doubt that something terrible was happening to his house, the big hollow chestnut tree he had lived in so long.

With every blow, and the blows followed each other so fast that he couldn't count them, the big tree trembled, and Bobby trembled with it. What could it mean? What could be going on outside? He wanted to climb up to his doorway and look out, but somehow he didn't dare to. He was afraid of what he might see. Yes, Sir, Bobby Coon was afraid to climb up to his doorway and look out for fear he might see something that would frighten him more than he was already frightened, though how he could possibly have been any more frightened I don't know. Yet all the time it didn't seem to him that he could stay where he was another minute. No, Sir, it didn't. He was too frightened to go and too frightened to stay. Now can you think of anything worse than that?

The tree trembled more and more and by and by it began to do more than tremble; with a dreadful, a very dreadful sinking of his heart, Bobby felt his house begin to sway, that is, move a little from side to side. A new fear drove everything else out of his head—the fear that his house might be going to fall! He couldn't believe that this could be true, yet he had the feeling that it was so. He couldn't get rid of it. He had lived in that house a long, long time and never in all that long, long time had he once had such a feeling as now possessed him. Many a time had rough Brother North Wind used all his strength against that big chestnut tree. Sometimes he had made it tremble ever so little, but that was all, and Bobby, curled up in his snug bed, had laughed at rough Brother North Wind. He just couldn't imagine anything really happening to his tree.

But something *was* happening now. There wasn't the smallest doubt about it. The great old tree shivered and shook with every blow. At last Bobby could stand it no longer. He just *had* to know what was happening, and what it all meant. With his teeth chattering with fright, he crawled up to his doorway and looked down. Badly frightened as he was, what he saw frightened him still more. It frightened him so that he let go his hold and tumbled down to his bed. Of course that didn't hurt him, because it was soft, and in a minute he was scrambling up to his doorway again.

"What shall I do? What *can* I do?" whimpered Bobby Coon as he looked down with frightened eyes. "I can't run and I can't stay. What can I do? What can I do?"

Bobby Coon was horribly frightened. There was no doubt about it, he was horribly frightened. Have you guessed what it was that he saw? Well, it was Farmer Brown and Farmer Brown's boy chopping down the big chestnut tree which had been Bobby's home for so long. And looking on was Bowser the Hound.

CHAPTER FOUR: BOWSER FINDS SOMEONE AT HOME

NOW THAT BOBBY COON knew what it was that had frightened him so, he felt no better than before. In fact, he felt worse. Before, he had imagined all sorts of dreadful things, but nothing that he had imagined was as bad as what he now knew to be a fact. His house, the big hollow chestnut tree in which he had lived so long and in which he had gone to sleep so happily at the beginning of winter, was being cut down by Farmer Brown's boy and Farmer Brown himself, and Bowser the Hound was looking on. There was no other tree near enough to jump to. The only way out was down right where those keen axes were at work and where Bowser sat watching. What chance was there for him? None. Not the least chance in the world. At least, that is the way Bobby felt about it. That was because he didn't know Farmer Brown and Farmer Brown's boy.

You see, all this time that Bobby Coon had been having such a dreadful, such a very dreadful time, Farmer Brown and Farmer Brown's boy and Bowser the Hound had known nothing at all about it. Bobby Coon hadn't once entered the heads of any of them. None of them knew that the big chestnut tree was Bobby's home. If Farmer Brown's boy had known it, I suspect that he would have found some good excuse for not cutting it. But he didn't, and so he swung his axe with a will, for he wanted to show his father that he could do a man's work.

Why were they cutting down that big chestnut tree? Well, you see that tree was practically dead, so Farmer Brown had decided that it could be of use in no way now, save as wood for the fires at home. If it were cut down, the young trees springing up around it would have a better chance to grow. It would be better to cut it now than to allow it to stand, growing weaker all the time, until at last it should fall in some great storm and perhaps break down some of the young trees about it.

Now if Bobby Coon had known Farmer Brown and Farmer Brown's boy as Tommy Tit the Chickadee knew them, and as Happy Jack Squirrel knew them, and as some others knew them, he would have climbed right straight down that tree without the teeniest, weeniest bit of fear of them. He would have known that he was perfectly safe. But he didn't know them, and so he felt both helpless and hopeless, and this is a very dreadful feeling indeed.

For a little while he peeped out of his doorway, watching the keen axes and the flying yellow chips. Then he crept miserably back to bed to wait for the worst. He just didn't know what else to do. By and by there was a dreadful crack, and another and another. Farmer Brown shouted. So did Farmer Brown's boy. Bowser the Hound barked excitedly. Slowly the big tree began to lean over. Then it moved faster and faster, and Bobby Coon felt giddy and sick. He felt very sick indeed. Then, with a frightful crash, the tree struck the ground, and for a few minutes Bobby didn't know anything at all. No, Sir, he didn't know a single thing. You see, when the tree hit the ground, Bobby was thrown against the side of his house so hard that all the wind was knocked from his body, and all his senses were knocked from his head. When after a little they returned to him, Bobby discovered that the tree had fallen in such a way that the hole which had been his doorway was partly closed. He was a prisoner in his own house.

He didn't mind this so much as you might expect. He began to hope ever so little. He began to hope that Farmer Brown and his boy wouldn't find that hollow and after a while they would go away. And then Bowser the Hound upset all hope. He came over to the fallen tree and began to sniff along the trunk. When he reached the partly closed hole which was Bobby's doorway, he began to whine and bark excitedly. He would stick his nose in as far as he could, sniff, then lift his head and bark. After that he would scratch frantically at the hole.

"Hello!" exclaimed Farmer Brown's boy, "Bowser has found someone at home! I wonder who it can be."

CHAPTER FIVE: BOBBY COON SHOWS FIGHT

Who for his home doth bravely fight
Is doing what he knows is right.
A coward he, the world would say,
Should he turn tail and run away.

BOBBY COON COULDN'T run away if he wanted to. I suspect that he would have run only too gladly if there had been the least chance to. But there he was, a prisoner in his own house. He couldn't get out if he wanted to, and he didn't want to just then because he knew by the sound of Bowser the Hound's deep sniffs at his doorway, followed by his eager barks that Bowser had discovered that he, Bobby, was at home. He knew that Bowser couldn't get in, and so he was very well content to stay where he was.

But presently Bobby heard the voice of Farmer Brown's boy, and though Bobby didn't understand what Farmer Brown's boy said, his heart sank way down to his toes just the same. At least, that is the way it felt to Bobby. You see, he knew by the sound of that voice, even though he couldn't understand the words, that Farmer Brown's boy had understood Bowser, and now knew that there was someone at home in that hollow tree.

As to that Bobby was quite right. While Farmer Brown's boy couldn't understand what Bowser was saying as he whined and yelped, he did understand perfectly what Bowser meant.

"Who is it, Bowser, old fellow? Is it a Squirrel, or Whitefoot the Wood Mouse, or that sly old scamp, Unc' Billy Possum?" asked Farmer Brown's boy.

"Bow, wow, wow!" replied Bowser, dancing about between sniffs at Bobby's doorway.

"I don't know what that means, but I'm going to find out, Bowser," laughed Farmer Brown's boy, picking up his axe.

"Bow, wow! Bow, wow, wow, wow!" replied Bowser, more excited than ever. First Farmer Brown's boy had Farmer Brown hold Bowser away from the opening. Then with his axe he thumped all along the hollow part of the tree, hoping that this would frighten whoever was inside so that they would try to run out. But Bobby couldn't get out because, as you know, his doorway was partly closed, and he wouldn't have even if he could; he felt safer right where he was. So Farmer Brown's boy thumped in vain. When he found that this was useless, he drove the keen edge of his axe in right at the edge of the hole which was Bobby's doorway. Farmer Brown joined with his axe, and in a few minutes they had slit out a long strip which reached clear to where Bobby was crouching and let the light pour in, so that he had to blink and for a minute or two had hard work to see at all.

Right away Bowser discovered him, and growling savagely, tried to get at him. But the opening wasn't wide enough for Bowser to get more than his nose in, and this Bobby promptly seized in his sharp teeth.

"Yow-w-w! Oh-o-o! Let go! Let go!" yelled Bowser.

"G-r-r-r-r!" growled Bobby, and tried to sink his teeth deeper. Bowser yelled and howled and shook his head and pulled as hard as ever he could, so that at last Bobby had to let go. Farmer Brown's boy hurried up to look in. What he saw was a mouthful of sharp teeth snapping at him. Bobby Coon might have been very much afraid, but he didn't show it. No, Sir, he didn't show it. What he did show was that he meant to fight for his life, liberty, and home. He was very fierce looking, was Bobby Coon, as Farmer Brown's boy peeped in at him.

CHAPTER SIX: SOMETHING IS WRONG WITH BOBBY COON

FARMER BROWN'S BOY chuckled as he peered in at Bobby Coon, and watched Bobby show his teeth, and listened to his snarls and growls. It was very plain that Bobby intended to fight for his life. It might be an entirely hopeless fight, but he would fight just the same.

"Bobby," said Farmer Brown's boy, "you certainly are a plucky little rascal. I know just what you think; you think that my father and I cut this tree down just to get you, and you think that we and Bowser the Hound are going to try to kill you. You are all wrong, Bobby, all wrong. If we had known that this old tree was your house, we wouldn't have cut it down. No, Sir, we wouldn't. And now that we have found out that it is, we are not going to harm so much as a hair of you. I'm going to cut this opening a little larger so that you can get out easily, and then I am going to hold on to Bowser and give you a chance to get away. I hope you know of some other hollow tree near here to which you can go. It's a shame, Bobby, that we didn't know about this. It certainly is, and I'm ever so sorry. Now you just quit your snarling and growling while I give you a chance to get out."

But Bobby continued to threaten to fight whoever came near. You see, he couldn't understand what Farmer Brown's boy said, which was too bad, because it would have lifted a great load from his mind. So he didn't have the least doubt that these were enemies and that they intended to kill him. He didn't believe he had the least chance in the world to escape, but he bravely intended to fight the very best he could, just the same. And this shows that Bobby possessed the right kind of a spirit. It shows that he wasn't a quitter. Furthermore, though no one knew it but himself, Bobby had been badly hurt when that tree fell. The fact is, one of Bobby's legs had been broken. Yet in spite of this, he meant to fight. Yes, Sir, in spite of a broken leg, he had no intention of giving up until he had to.

Farmer Brown's boy swung his axe a few times and split the opening in the hollow tree wider so that Bobby would have no trouble in getting out. All the time Bobby snapped and snarled and gritted his teeth. Then Farmer Brown's boy led Bowser the Hound off to one side and held him. Farmer Brown joined them, and then they waited. Bobby couldn't see them. It grew very still there in the Green Forest. Bobby didn't know just what to make of it. Could it be that he had frightened them away by his fierceness? After a while he began to think that this was so.

He waited just as long as he could be patient and then poked his head out. No one was to be seen, for Farmer Brown and his boy and Bowser the Hound were hidden by a little clump of hemlock trees.

Slowly and painfully Bobby climbed out. That broken leg hurt dreadfully. It was one of his front legs, and of course he had to hold that paw up. That meant that he had to walk on three legs. This was bad enough, but when he started to climb a tree, he couldn't. With a broken leg, there would be no more climbing for Bobby Coon. It was useless for him to look for another hollow tree. All he could do was to look for a hollow log into which he could crawl. Poor

Poor Bobby Coon! What should he do? What could *he do?*

Bobby Coon! What should he do? What *could* he do? For the first time his splendid courage deserted him. You see, he thought he was all alone there, and that no one saw him. So he just crouched right down there at the foot of the tree he had started to climb, and whimpered. He was frightened and very, very miserable, was Bobby Coon, and he was in great pain.

CHAPTER SEVEN: BOBBY HAS A STRANGE JOURNEY

It's funny how you'll often find
That trouble's mostly in your mind.

IT'S A FACT. More than three fourths of the troubles that worry people are not real troubles at all. They are all in the mind. They are things that people are afraid are going to happen, and worry about until they are sure they will happen—and then they do not happen at all. Very, very often things that seem bad turn out to he blessings. All of us do a great deal of worrying for nothing. I know I do. Bobby Coon did when he took his strange journey which I am going to tell you about.

Farmer Brown and Farmer Brown's boy and Bowser the Hound had watched Bobby crawl out of his ruined house and start off to seek a new home. Of course, they had seen right away that something was wrong with Bobby, for he walked on three legs and held the fourth one up.

"The poor little chap," murmured Farmer Brown's boy pityingly. "That leg must have been hurt when the tree fell. I hope it isn't badly hurt. We'll wait a few minutes and see what he does."

So they waited in their hiding-place and watched Bobby. They saw him go to the foot of a tree as if to climb it. They saw him try and fail, because he couldn't climb with only three legs, and they saw him crouch down in a little whimpering heap because he thought he was all alone. It was then that Farmer Brown's boy was sure that Bobby's hurt was really serious.

"We can't let that little fellow go to suffer and perhaps die," said Farmer Brown's boy, and ran forward while Farmer Brown held Bowser.

Bobby heard him coming and promptly faced about ready to fight bravely. When he got near enough, Farmer Brown's boy threw his coat over Bobby and then, in spite of Bobby's frantic struggles, gathered him up and wrapped the coat about him so that he could neither bite nor scratch. Bobby was quite helpless.

"I'm going to take him home, and when I've made him quite comfortable, I'll come back," cried Farmer Brown's boy.

"All right," replied Farmer Brown, with a kindly twinkle in his eyes.

So Farmer Brown's boy started for home, carrying Bobby as gently as he could. Of course Bobby couldn't see where he was being taken, because that coat was over his head, and of course he hadn't understood a word that Farmer Brown's boy had said. But Bobby could imagine all sorts of dreadful things, and he did. He was sure that when this journey ended the very worst that could happen would happen. He was quite hopeless, was Bobby Coon. He kept still because he had to. There was nothing else to do.

All the time he wondered where he was being taken. He was sure that never again would he see the Green Forest. His broken leg pained him dreadfully, but fear of what would happen when this strange journey ended made him almost forget the pain. It was the first time in all his life that Bobby ever had journeyed anywhere save on his own four feet, and quite aside from his fear, it gave him a very queer feeling. He kept wishing it would end quickly, yet at the same time he didn't want it to end because of what he was sure would happen then.

So through the Green Forest, then through the Old Orchard, and finally across the barnyard to the barn Bobby Coon was carried. It was the strangest journey he ever had known and it was the most terrible, though it needn't have been if only he could have known the truth.

CHAPTER EIGHT: FARMER BROWN'S BOY PLAYS DOCTOR

No greater joy can one attain
Than helping ease another's pain.

POOR BOBBY COON! His broken leg pained him a great deal, of course. Broken legs and arms always do pain. They hurt dreadfully when they are broken, they hurt dreadfully after they are broken, and they hurt while they are mending. Among the little people of the Green Forest and the Green Meadows, a broken leg or arm is a great deal worse than it is with us humans. We know how to fix the break so that Mother Nature may mend it and make the leg or arm as good as ever. But with the little people of the Green Forest and the Green Meadows, nothing of that sort is possible, and very, very often a broken limb means an early death. You see, such a break will not mend properly, and the little sufferer becomes a cripple, and cripples cannot long escape their enemies.

So, though he didn't know it at the time, it was a very lucky thing for Bobby Coon that Farmer Brown's boy discovered that broken leg and wrapped him up in his coat and took him home. Bobby didn't think it was lucky—Oh, my, no! Bobby thought it was just the other way about. You see, he didn't know Farmer Brown's boy, except by sight. He didn't know of his gentleness and tender heart. All he knew of men and boys was that most of them seemed to delight in hunting him, in frightening him and trying to kill him. So all through that strange journey in the arms of Farmer Brown's boy, up to Farmer Brown's barn, Bobby was sure, absolutely sure, that he was being taken somewhere to be killed. He didn't have a doubt, not the least doubt, of it.

When they reached the barn, Farmer Brown's boy put Bobby down very gently, but fastened him in the coat so that he couldn't get out. Then he went to the house and presently returned with some neat strips of clean white cloth. Then he took out his knife and made very smooth two thin, flat sticks. When these suited him, he tied Bobby's hind legs together so that he couldn't kick with them. Then he placed Bobby on his side on a board and with a broad strip of cloth bound him to it in such a way that Bobby couldn't move. All the time he talked to Bobby in the gentlest of voices and did his best not to hurt him.

But Bobby couldn't understand, and to be wholly helpless, not to be able to kick or scratch or bite, was the most dreadful feeling he ever had known. He was sure that something worse was about to happen. You see, he didn't know anything about doctors, and so of course he couldn't know that Farmer Brown's boy was playing doctor. Very, very gently Farmer Brown's boy felt of the broken leg. He brought the broken parts together, and when he was sure that they just fitted, he bound them in place on one of the thin, smooth, flat sticks with one of the strips of clean white cloth. Then he put the other smooth flat stick above the break and wound the whole about with strips of cloth so tightly that there was no chance for those two sticks to slip. That was so that the two parts of the broken bone in the leg would be held just where they belonged until they could grow together. When it was done to suit him, he covered the outside with something very, very bitter and bad tasting. This was to keep Bobby from trying to tear off the cloth with his teeth. You see, he knew that if that leg was to become as good as ever it was, it must stay just as he had bound it until Old Mother Nature could heal it.

So Farmer Brown's boy played doctor, and a very gentle and kindly doctor he was, for his heart was full of pity for poor Bobby Coon.

CHAPTER NINE: BOBBY IS MADE MUCH OF

> *There's nothing like a stomach full*
> *To make the world seem brighter;*
> *To banish worry, drive out fear,*
> *And make the heart feel lighter.*

WHILE FARMER BROWN'S boy was playing doctor and doing his best to fix Bobby Coon's broken leg so that it would heal and be as good as ever, poor Bobby was wholly in despair, and nothing is more dreadful than to be wholly in despair. There he was, perfectly helpless, for Farmer Brown's boy had bound him so that he couldn't move. You see, Bobby couldn't understand what it all meant. If he could have understood Farmer Brown's boy, it would have been very different. But he couldn't, and so his mind was all the time full of dreadful fear.

When Farmer Brown's boy had bound that broken leg so that it would be held firmly in place to heal, he made a comfortable bed in a deep box out of which Bobby couldn't possibly climb with that broken leg. In this he put Bobby very gently, after taking off the bands with which he had been bound to the board while the broken leg was being fixed. Then he went to the house and presently returned with more good things to eat than Bobby had seen since cold weather began. These he put in the box with Bobby, and then left him alone.

Now at first Bobby made up his mind that he wouldn't taste so much as a crumb. He would starve rather than live a prisoner, which was what he felt himself to be. But his stomach was empty, the smell of those good things tickled his nose, and in spite of himself he began to nibble. The first thing he knew he had filled his stomach, the first good meal he had had for many weeks, because, you know, he had been asleep most of the winter.

Right away Bobby felt sleepy. A full stomach, you know, almost always makes one feel sleepy. Then, too, Bobby was quite tired out with the fright and strange experience he had been through. So he curled up, and in no time at all he had forgotten all his troubles. And for days and days Bobby slept most of the time. You see, he was finishing out that long winter sleep he was used to. And this, it happens, was the very best thing in the world for Bobby. Being asleep, he wasn't tempted to try to pull off that bandage around the broken leg, and so the leg had just the chance it needed to mend.

Every day Farmer Brown's boy visited Bobby, just as a good doctor should visit a patient, and looked carefully at the bandaged leg to make sure that it was as it should be. And whenever Farmer Brown's boy visited Bobby, he took some goody in his pocket to tempt Bobby's appetite, just as if it needed tempting! Bobby would wake up long enough to eat what had been brought and then would go to sleep again, quite as if he were all alone.

As the weather grew warmer, Bobby grew more wakeful. Of course, he had plenty of time in which to remember and to think. He remembered how dreadfully frightened he had been when Farmer Brown's boy had caught him and brought him to the barn, all because he had not really known Farmer Brown's boy. Now everything was different, so very, very different. It was a fact, an actual fact, that Bobby had learned to know the step of Farmer Brown's boy, and when he heard it coming his way, he was as tickled as once he would have been frightened. You see, Farmer Brown's boy was very, very good to him and made so much of him that I am afraid he was quite spoiling Bobby. Kindness had driven out fear from Bobby's mind, and in its place had come trust. It will do it every time, if given a chance.

CHAPTER TEN: BOBBY LONGS FOR THE GREEN FOREST

NOW THOUGH BOBBY Coon was made a great deal of by Farmer Brown's boy, and was petted and stuffed with good things to eat until it was a wonder that he wasn't made sick, he was really a prisoner. Excepting when Farmer Brown's boy played with him in the house, he was fastened by a long chain. You see, when at last the bandage was taken off, and the leg was found to have healed, Bobby was kept a prisoner that he might get the full use of that leg once more before having to shift for himself. Day by day the strength came back to that leg until it was as good as ever it had been, and still Bobby was kept a prisoner. The truth is, Farmer Brown's boy had grown so fond of Bobby that he couldn't bear to think of parting with him.

At first, Bobby hadn't minded in the least. It was fine to have all the good things to eat he wanted without the trouble of hunting for them, things he never had had before and never could have in the Green Forest. It was fine to have a warm comfortable bed and not a thing in the world to worry about. So for a time Bobby was quite content to be a prisoner. He didn't mind that chain at all, excepting when he wanted to poke his inquisitive little nose into something he couldn't reach.

But as sweet Mistress Spring awakened those who had slept the long winter away—the trees and flowers and insects, and Old Mr. Toad and Johnny Chuck and Striped Chipmunk and all the rest—and as one after another the birds arrived from the sunny Southland, and Bobby heard them singing and twittering, and watched them flying about, a great longing for the Green Forest crept into his heart.

At first he didn't really know what it was that he wanted. It simply made him uneasy. He couldn't keep still. He walked back and forth, back and forth, at the length of his chain. He began to lose his appetite. Then one day Farmer Brown's boy brought him a fish for his dinner, and all in a flash Bobby knew what it was he wanted. He wanted to go back to the Green Forest. He wanted to fish for himself in the Laughing Brook. He wanted to climb trees. He wanted to visit his old neighbors and see what they were doing. He wanted to hunt for bugs under old logs and around old stumps. He wanted to hunt for nests being built, so that later he might steal the eggs from them. Yes, he did just this, I am sorry to say. Bobby is very fond of eggs, and he considers that he has a perfect right to them if he is smart enough to find them. He wanted to be *free*—free to do what he pleased when he pleased and how he pleased. He wanted to go back home to the Green Forest.

"Farmer Brown's boy has been very good to me, and I believe he would let me go if only I could tell him what I want," thought Bobby, "but I can't make him understand what I say any more than I can understand what he says. What a great pity it is that we don't all speak the same language. Then we would all understand each other, and I don't believe we little folks of the Green Forest and the Green Meadows would be hunted so much by these men creatures. There's nothing like common speech to make folks understand one another. I know Farmer Brown's boy would let me go if he only knew; I know he would."

Bobby sat down where be could look over towards the Green Forest and sighed and sighed, and all the longing of his heart crept into his eyes.

CHAPTER ELEVEN: THE HAPPIEST COON EVER

As Jolly Mr. Sun smiles down
And makes the land all bright and fair,
So happiness within the heart
Spreads joy and gladness everywhere.

NOW THOUGH BOBBY Coon couldn't speak the language of Farmer Brown's boy and so tell him how he longed to be free and go back to the Green Forest, he could and he did tell him in another way just what was in his heart. He told him with his eyes, though he didn't know it. You know eyes are sometimes called the windows of the soul. This means simply that as you look out through your eyes and see all that is going on about you, so others may sometimes look right in your eyes and see what is going on within your mind.

Eyes are very wonderful things, and a great deal may be learned from them. Eyes will tell the truth when a tongue is busy telling a wrong story. I guess you know how hard it is when you have done wrong to look mother straight in the face and try to make her believe that you haven't done wrong. That is because your eyes are truthful.

Looking straight into the eyes of fierce wild animals often will fill them with fear. Trainers of lions and other dangerous animals know this and do it a great deal. Fear will show in the eyes when it shows nowhere else. It is the same with happiness and contentment. So it is with sorrow and worry. Just as a thermometer shows just how warm it is or how cold it is, so the eyes show our feelings. So when Bobby Coon sat down and gazed towards the Green Forest and wished that he could tell Farmer Brown's boy how he wanted to go back there, a look of longing grew and grew in Bobby's eyes, and Farmer Brown's boy saw it. What is more, he understood it. His own eyes grew soft.

"You poor little rascal," said he, "I believe you think you are a prisoner and that you want to go back home. Well, I guess there is no reason why you shouldn't now. I'm very fond of you, Bobby. Yes, I am. I'm so fond of you that I hate to have you go, and I guess that I've kept you longer than was necessary. That leg of yours looks to me to be as good as ever, so I really haven't an excuse for keeping you any longer. I think we'll take a walk this afternoon."

If Bobby could have understood what Farmer Brown's boy was saying, it would have made him feel a great deal better. But he didn't understand, and so he continued to stare towards the Green Forest and grow more and more homesick. After dinner, Farmer Brown's boy came out and took off the collar and chain, and picked Bobby up in his arms. This time Bobby didn't have his eyes covered as he did when he had been brought from the Green Forest. Fear no longer made him want to bite and scratch.

Through the Old Orchard straight to the Green Forest they went, and Bobby began to grow excited. What was going to happen? What did it mean? Through the Green Forest straight to the place where Bobby's great hollow tree used to stand went Farmer Brown's boy. When they got there he smoothed Bobby's coat and patted him gently. Then he put him down on the ground.

"Here we are, Bobby," said he. "Now run along and find a new house and be happy. I hope you won't forget me, because I am going to come over often to see you. Just keep out of mischief, and above all keep out of the way of hunters next fall. They shall not hunt here if I can help it, but you know I cannot watch all the time. Good-bye, Bobby, and take care of yourself."

Bobby didn't say good-bye, because he didn't know how. But a great joy came into his eyes, and Farmer Brown's boy saw it and understood. Straight off among the trees Bobby walked. Once he looked back. Farmer Brown's boy was watching him and waved a hand.

"He was good to me. He certainly was good to me," thought Bobby. "I—I believe I really am very fond of him."

Then he went on to look for a new house. All the joy of the springtime was in his heart. He was free! He was home once more in the Green Forest! He no longer feared Farmer Brown's boy!

"I'm the happiest Coon in all the world!" cried Bobby.

CHAPTER TWELVE: BOBBY TRIES THE WRONG HOUSE

"Home again! Home again! Happy am I!
Had I but wings I most surely would fly!"

SO SANG BOBBY COON as he wandered about in the Green Forest after leaving Farmer Brown's boy. At least, he meant it for singing. Of course, it wasn't real singing, for Bobby Coon can no more sing than he can fly. But it did very well to express his happiness, and that was all it was intended to do. Bobby was happy. He was very happy indeed. Indeed he couldn't remember ever having been quite so happy. You see, he never before had understood fully what freedom means. No one can fully understand what a wonderful and blessed thing freedom is until they have lost it and then got it again.

Bobby took long breaths and sniffed and sniffed and sniffed and sniffed the sweet smells of early spring. The Green Forest was full of them, and never had they seemed so good to Bobby. He climbed a tree for nothing under the sun but to know what it felt like to climb once more. Then he climbed down to earth again and went poking around among the leaves just for the fun of poking around. He rolled over and over from sheer joy. Finally he brushed himself off, climbed up on an old stump, and sat down to think things over.

"Of course," said he to himself, "the first thing for me to do is to find a new house. I don't have to have it right away, because there are plenty of places in which I can curl up for a nap, but it is more convenient and much more respectable to have a house. People who sleep anywhere and have no homes are never thought much of by their friends and neighbors. Without a home I can have no self-respect. There's a certain old hollow tree I always did like the looks of. Unc' Billy Possum used to live there, but maybe he has moved. Anyway, he may be out, and if so he will be smarter than I think he is to get me out once I'm inside. I believe I'll look up that tree right away."

Bobby scrambled down from the stump and started down the Lone Little Path. After a while he turned off the Lone Little Path into a hollow and presently came to the tree he had in mind. It was straight, tall, and big. High up was a doorway plenty big enough for Bobby Coon. He sat down and looked up. The longer he looked, the better that tree seemed to him. It would suit for a house first-rate. There were marks on the tree made by claws—the claws of Unc' Billy Possum. Some of them looked quite fresh.

"Looks as if Unc' Billy is still living here," thought Bobby. "Well, I can't help it if he is. If that tree looks as good inside as it does outside, I am afraid Unc' Billy and I will have a falling out. It's everyone for himself in the Green Forest, and I don't think Unc' Billy will care to fight me. I'm bigger and considerably stronger than he, so if he's there, I guess I'll just invite him to move out."

Now, of course, this wasn't at all right of Bobby Coon, but it is the way things are done in the Green Forest, and the people who live there are used to it. The strong take what they want if they can get it, and Bobby knew that Unc' Billy Possum would treat Happy Jack Squirrel the same way, if he happened to want Happy Jack's house. So he climbed up the tree, quite sure that this was the house he would take for his new home. He was half-way up when a sharp voice spoke.

"Haven't yo' made a mistake, Brer Coon?" said the voice. "This isn't your house."

Bobby stopped and looked up. Unc' Billy Possum was grinning down at him from his doorway. Bobby grinned back. "It occurred to me that you might like to move, and as I'm looking for a house, I think this one will suit me very well," said he, and grinned again, for he knew that Unc' Billy would understand just what he meant.

Before Unc' Billy could say a word, another sharp face appeared beside his own, and a voice still sharper than his said: "What's that no 'count Bobby Coon doing in our tree? What's this talk Ah hear about moving? Isn't nobody gwine to move that Ah knows of."

Bobby had forgotten all about old Mrs. Possum, and now as he saw that it was two against one, he suddenly changed his mind.

"Excuse me," said he, "I guess I've got the wrong house."

CHAPTER THIRTEEN: BOBBY MAKES ANOTHER MISTAKE

WHEN BOBBY COON left Unc' Billy Possum's hollow tree, he went fishing. You know he is very fond of fishing. All night long he fished and played along the Laughing Brook, and when at last jolly, round, red Mr. Sun began his daily climb up in the blue, blue sky, Bobby was wet, tired, and sleepy. But he was happy. It did seem so good to be wandering about at his own sweet will in the beautiful Green Forest once more. It struck him now as rather a joke that he hadn't any house to go to. It was a long, long time since he had been without a home.

"I've got to sleep somewhere," said Bobby, rubbing his eyes and yawning, "and the sooner I find a place, the better. I'm so sleepy now I can hardly keep my eyes open. Hello, there's a great big log over there! If it is hollow, it will be just the place for me."

He marched straight over to the old log. It was big, very big, and to Bobby's great joy it was hollow, with an opening at one end. He was just going to crawl in, when Peter Rabbit popped out from behind a tree.

"Hello, Bobby Coon!" cried Peter joyously. "Where have you been? I was over

Before Unc' Billy could say a word, another sharp face appeared beside his own.

where you used to live and found your house gone, and I was afraid something dreadful had happened to you. What did happen, and where have you been?"

Now, tired and sleepy as he was, Bobby had to stop and talk for a few minutes. You see, Peter was the first of his friends Bobby had met to whom he could tell all the wonderful things that had happened to him, and he was fairly aching to tell someone. So he sat down and told Peter how his hollow tree had been cut down, and how his leg had been broken, and how Farmer Brown's boy had taken him home and fixed that leg so that Old Mother Nature could make it as well and sound as ever, and how Farmer Brown's boy had brought him back to the Green Forest and set him free, and how he had been fishing all night and now was looking for a place to get a wink or two of sleep.

"Now, if you'll excuse me, Peter, I'm going to turn in for a nap," Bobby ended, and started to crawl in the end of the hollow log.

"Oh!" cried Peter. "Oh, you mustn't go in there, Bobby!"

But Bobby didn't hear him, or if he did he didn't heed. He kept right on and disappeared. A funny look crept over Peter's face, and presently he began to chuckle. "I think I'll wait a while and see what happens," said he.

Inside that big hollow log, Bobby found it very dry and warm and comfortable. There was a bed of dry leaves there, and it looked very inviting. Now ordinarily Bobby would have examined the inside of that log very thoroughly before going to sleep, but he was so tired and sleepy that he didn't half look around. He didn't go to the farther end at all. He just dropped right down midway, curled up, and in no time at all was fast asleep. It was a mistake, a very great mistake, as Bobby was shortly to find out. Meanwhile, outside sat Peter Rabbit, although it was already past time for him to be home in the dear Old Briar-patch.

CHAPTER FOURTEEN: BOBBY FINDS OUT HIS MISTAKE

If friend of yours a mistake makes
Nor yet has found it out,
I pray that when at last he does
You will not be about.

IT IS BAD enough to find out for yourself that you have made a mistake, but to have other people know it makes you feel a great deal worse. So the kindest thing that anyone can do when they know a friend has made a mistake and it is too late to warn them, is to appear not to know of it at all. So it wasn't nice at all of Peter Rabbit to hang around watching that old hollow log into which Bobby Coon had crawled for a nap.

Presently Peter's long ears caught sounds from inside that hollow log. First there was a rattling and rustling. Then came a series of grunts and squeaks. These were followed by growls and snarls. The latter were from Bobby Coon. He was insisting that he was going to stay right where he was and wouldn't move an inch for anyone. Peter clapped one hand over his mouth to keep from laughing aloud when he heard that, and he fastened his eyes, very big and round with expectation, on the opening in the end of the hollow log. You see, Peter knew all about that log and who lived there. That is what he had tried to tell Bobby Coon. He could hear Bobby declaring:

"I won't move a step, not a single step. You can stay right where you are until I finish my nap. If you come any nearer, I'll—"

Peter didn't hear the rest, if indeed Bobby finished what he had started to say. You see, Bobby was interrupted by a great rattling and rustling and a grunt that sounded both angry and very business-like. Once more Bobby growled and snarled and declared he wouldn't move a step, but Peter noticed that Bobby's voice seemed to come from nearer the open end of the log than before. Again there was a grunt and a rattling and rustling.

Then out of the end of the old log backed Bobby Coon, still growling and snarling and declaring he wouldn't move a step. It was too funny for Peter to hold in any longer. He had to laugh. He couldn't help it. Then the black nose and little dull eyes of Prickly Porky the Porcupine appeared. In each of those little dull eyes there was just a wee spark of anger which made them less dull than usual. It was plain that Prickly Porky was provoked.

As soon as he was out-

The black nose and little dull eyes of Prickly Porky the Porcupine appeared.

side, he made the thousand little spears which he carries hidden in his coat stand on end, and made a quick little rush towards Bobby Coon. Bobby turned tail and ran. The sight of those sharp-pointed little spears was too much for him. He was afraid of them. Everybody is afraid of them, even big Buster Bear. It was these little spears brushing against the inside of the old log that had made the rattling and rustling Peter had heard.

"The impudence of that Coon to walk into my house and go to sleep without so much as asking if he might, and then telling me that I can't come out until he says so! The impudence of him!" grunted Prickly Porky, rattling his thousand little spears.

As for Bobby Coon, he realized now the great mistake he had made in not first finding out whether anyone was at home in that old log before trying to take a nap there. It mortified him to think he had been so careless as to make such a mistake, and it mortified him still more to know that Peter Rabbit had seen all that had happened.

CHAPTER FIFTEEN: ONCE MORE BOBBY TRIES TO SLEEP

> *Did you ever have the Sandman*
> *Fill your eyes all full of sand*
> *And then have to keep them open*
> *When there was no bed at hand?*

IF YOU HAVE had that happen, then you know exactly how Bobby Coon felt when he was obliged to crawl out of Prickly Porky's bed and go hunt for another. He was so very, very sleepy that he felt almost as if he could go to sleep standing right on his feet. This was because he had been up all night and awake most of the day before. Now he wished that instead of spending the night in fishing and playing about the Laughing Brook, he had hunted for a house.

To be sleepy and not able to sleep makes Bobby cross, just as it does most folks. So, as he hurried away from the neighborhood of Prickly Porky and his thousand little spears, he was in a bad temper. Of course, he knew it was his own fault that he was in such a fix, and this didn't make him feel a bit better. In fact, it made him feel worse. It usually is that way.

So he grumbled to himself as he went along. He didn't know where he was going. He was too cross and sleepy and upset to do any thinking. So he went along, aimlessly looking for a place where he might sleep undisturbed. At last he came to a tall stump, a great big old stump that had stood in the Green Forest for years and years. Bobby climbed to the top of it. It was hollow, just as he had hoped. Indeed, it was just a shell. Looking down, Bobby saw with a great deal of satisfaction that the bottom was covered with a great mass of rotted wood. It would make a very comfortable bed. Moreover, it was plain that no one else was using it.

Bobby sighed with satisfaction. It was just the place for a good long nap. He could sleep there all day in perfect comfort. It wouldn't do for a home, because the top was open to the sky, and on a rainy day the inside of that stump would soon be a very wet place indeed. But for a nice long nap on a pleasant day, it would be hard to beat. Bobby sighed again, looked all about to make sure that no one was watching him, and then climbed down inside.

"I guess," muttered Bobby, as he curled up on the bed of rotted wood, which is sometimes called punk, "that at last I shall be allowed to sleep in peace. I never was more sleepy in all my life." He yawned two or three times, changed his position for greater comfort, closed his eyes, and in a twinkling was asleep.

Now, though he thought no one saw him go into that old stump, someone did. That someone was Peter Rabbit. Peter had followed Bobby just out of curiosity. He had hidden behind trees so as to keep out of Bobby's sight. So he had seen Bobby climb the stump and disappear inside.

"I guess," said Peter, "that this time he will sleep in peace. No one is likely to find him there unless it should be that Sammy Jay or Blacky the Crow happens to fly over and so discover him. They wouldn't give him a bit of peace if they should. Hello! There's Blacky's voice now, and he seems to be coming this way. I think I will hang around a while longer."

CHAPTER SIXTEEN: BLACKY THE CROW DISCOVERS BOBBY COON

Blacky the Crow is sharp of eye;
He dearly loves to peek and pry.
I must confess, alas! alack!
Blacky the Crow's an imp in black.

IT IS TRUE, I am sorry to say, that Blacky the Crow never is happier than when he is teasing someone and making them uncomfortable. He is an imp of mischief, is Blacky. Whatever business he has on hand he goes about it with one eye open for a chance to have fun at the expense of someone else. And there is little that those sharp eyes of his miss. He sees all that there is to see. Yes, Sir, you may trust Blacky for that!

It was just the hard luck of Bobby Coon that no sooner was he asleep in that hollow stump in the Green Forest than along came Blacky the Crow, flying above the tree-tops on his way to his nest, but as usual watching sharply for what might be going on below. It just happened that he flew right over that stump, so that he could look right down inside. He saw Bobby Coon curled up there asleep. Yes, indeed, you may be sure he saw Bobby.

Blacky checked himself in his flight and hovered for an instant right above that stump. Mischief fairly danced in his sharp eyes. Then he turned and silently flew down and alighted on the edge of the old stump. For a few minutes he sat there, looking down at Bobby Coon. All the time he was chuckling to himself. Then he flew to the top of a tree and began to call with all his might.

"Caw caw, caw, ca-a-w, caw, caw!" he called. "Caw, ca-a-w, caw!"

Almost right away he was answered, and presently from all directions came hurrying his friends and relatives, each one cawing at the top of his voice and asking Blacky what he had found. Blacky didn't tell them until the last one came hurrying up. Then he told them to go look in the old hollow stump. One after another they flew over it, looking down, and one after another they shouted with glee. Then as many as could find a place on the edge of the old stump did so, while the others sat about in the trees or flew back and forth overhead, and all of them began to caw as hard as ever they could. Such a racket as they made!

Of course, Bobby Coon couldn't sleep. Certainly not. No one could have slept through that racket. He opened his eyes and looked up. He saw a ring of black heads looking down at him and mischief fairly dancing in the sharp eyes watching him. The instant it was known that he was awake, the noise redoubled.

"Ca-a-w, ca-a-w, ca-a-w, caw, caw, ca-a-w, caw, caw, caw!"

Bobby drew back his lips and snarled, and at that his tormentors fairly shrieked with glee. Then Blacky dropped a little stick down on Bobby. Another crow did the same thing. Bobby scrambled to his feet and started to climb up. His tormentors took to the air and screamed louder than ever. Bobby stopped. What was the use of going up where they could get at him? They would pull his fur and make him most uncomfortable, and he knew he couldn't catch one of them to save him. He backed down and sat glaring up at them and telling them what dreadful things he would do to them if ever he should catch one of them.

This delighted Blacky and his friends more than ever. They certainly were having great fun.

Finally Bobby did the wisest thing possible. He once more curled up and took no notice at all of the black imps. Of course, he couldn't go to sleep with such a racket going on, but he pretended to sleep. Now you know there is no fun in trying to tease one who won't show he is teased. After a while Blacky and his friends got tired of screaming. They had had their fun, and one by one they flew about their business until at last the Green Forest was as still as still could be. Bobby sighed thankfully and once more fell asleep.

CHAPTER SEVENTEEN: THE SURPRISE OF TWO COUSINS

PETER RABBIT SHOULD have been back home in the dear Old Briar-patch long ago. He knew that Mrs. Peter was worrying. She always worries when Peter over-stays. But Peter was not giving much thought to Mrs. Peter. In fact, I am afraid he was not giving any thought to her. You see, he was too full of curiosity about Bobby Coon and what might happen to him. He had been sorry for Bobby in a way, yet it had seemed like a great joke that anyone as sleepy as Bobby shouldn't be able to sleep. So I am afraid Peter rather enjoyed the excitement.

When finally Blacky and his friends grew tired and went about their business, Peter began to think of getting back to the dear Old Briar-patch.

"I guess Bobby will sleep in peace now," thought Peter. "I can't think of any-thing more that possibly can happen to disturb him. Poor Bobby. He has had a hard time getting that nap."

Still Peter hung around. He didn't know just why, but he had a feeling that he might miss something if he left, and you know Peter never could forgive himself if he missed anything worth seeing. So he hung around for some time after Blacky and his friends had gone about their business. At last he had just about made up his mind that he would better be starting for home when he was startled by the snapping of a little twig. Peeping out from behind a big tree, Peter stared towards the place from which that sound had come. In a moment he saw a big black form.

"Buster Bear!" gasped Peter. "It's the first time I have seen him this spring. My, how thin he is!"

Peter looked about to make sure that the way was clear for a hasty run if it should be necessary, and then held his breath as Buster drew near. Buster kept stop-ping to look and listen and sniff the air, and suddenly Peter understood.

"He heard those noisy Crows, and he has come to see what it was all about," thought Peter, which was just exactly the case.

Buster knew that it was just about this place that Blacky and his friends had been making such a racket, and his greedy little eyes searched everywhere for some sign of what had been going on. But there was nothing to be seen but a black feath-er at the foot of a tall old stump. By this Buster knew for sure that he had found the place where Blacky and his friends had been, but there was nothing to tell him why they had been there. Buster sat up and blinked thoughtfully. Then as he looked at the old stump, his eyes brightened.

"I don't know what all that fuss was about," he muttered, "and I guess I never will know, but I'm glad I came just the same. That old stump looks to me to be rot-ten and hollow. I have found ant nests in many an old stump like that, and beetles and grubs. I'll just see what this one contains."

Buster walked over to the old stump, hooked his great claws into a crack, and pulled with all his might. Peter Rabbit, watching, held his breath with excitement. There was a sharp cracking sound, and then the whole side of that old stump gave way so suddenly that Buster Bear fell over backwards. As he did so, Bobby Coon rolled out, half awake and frightened almost out of his wits. It was hard to say which was the most surprised of those two cousins, Buster Bear or Bobby Coon.

CHAPTER EIGHTEEN: BUSTER BEAR'S SHORT TEMPER

It's such a very foolish thing,
So silly and so heedless,
To lose your temper when you know
It is so wholly needless.

WHEN BUSTER BEAR scrambled to his feet and saw his cousin, Bobby Coon, scrambling to his feet, Buster straightway lost his temper. It was a foolish thing to do, a very foolish thing to do. There really wasn't the least excuse in the world for it. And yet Buster mustn't be blamed too much. You see, he wasn't really himself. Ordinarily Buster is one of the best-natured people in all the Green Forest. He doesn't begin to be as short-tempered as ever so many others are. In fact, he isn't short-tempered at all.

But just now Buster was hungry. He was so hungry that he couldn't think of anything but his stomach and how empty it was. You see, so early in the spring there was very little for him to eat, and he had to hunt and hunt to find that little. When he had started to tear open that tall old stump, he had hoped that inside he would find either a nest of ants, or some of the worms and insects that like to bury themselves in rotting wood. So when Bobby Coon came rolling out, Buster was so disappointed that he quite lost his temper before he had time to think. He flew into a rage. You see, he just took it for granted that Bobby Coon had been in that hollow stump for the very same purpose that he had torn it open. Now it never does to take things for granted. You know and I know that Bobby Coon had crawled into that stump only to sleep.

Buster didn't know this, and Buster didn't stop to find it out. He growled a terribly deep, ugly-sounding growl that made all of Peter Rabbit's hair stand on end. You know, Peter was close by, hiding behind a big tree to see all that might happen. Then Buster Bear started for his cousin, Bobby Coon, and his little eyes seemed to fairly snap fire.

"I'll teach you to steal an honest Bear's dinner!" he growled in his deep grumbly, rumbly voice.

The whole side of that old stump gave way so suddenly that Buster Bear fell over backwards.

Now this wasn't fair to Bobby, for Bobby had stolen no dinner. Even if he had been hunting for food in that hollow stump, he would have done no injustice to Buster Bear. But Buster didn't stop to think of this.

"You'll pay for it by furnishing me a dinner yourself!" growled Buster.

"But I'm your cousin!" cried Bobby, as he started to run.

"That doesn't make a bit of difference," snapped Buster. "I'm hungry enough to eat my own brother if I had one."

All the time Buster was scrambling after Bobby Coon, and Bobby was running for his life. Now big as he is, Buster can move very fast when he is in a hurry, especially when he is thin and lean. Bobby Coon squealed with fright and scrambled up a big tree faster than he ever had scrambled up a tree before in all his life. Buster growled a deep, grumbly, rumbly growl and started up after him.

"Oh! Oh!" cried Bobby Coon, and you may be sure he was very much awake by this time. There was no thought of sleep in Bobby's head as he scrambled nearly to the top of that big tree. Peter Rabbit stared in horror. Surely Buster Bear would catch Bobby now!

CHAPTER NINETEEN: BOBBY COON GETS A TERRIBLE SHAKING

LEAVE ME ALONE! I've never done you any harm, so leave me alone!" whimpered Bobby Coon, as he climbed the tall tree with Buster Bear scrambling up after him and growling all the way. For a minute or two Bobby wished he had stayed on the ground. You see, he had forgotten that Buster Bear could climb quite as well as he could. Now he was in the tree, and Buster was below him, and it looked very much as if Bobby had trapped himself.

Suddenly he remembered that Buster couldn't go out on little branches as he could, because Buster was too big and heavy. Bobby looked about him, and fear made his eyes quick to see. One branch reached over almost to the top of a slender young tree growing near. If he could get over into that tree, perhaps he could get back to the ground and run for his life. Anyway, it was worth trying. Out along the branch went Bobby as far as he could, and then, with his heart in his mouth, he jumped for the slender young tree. It was a good jump, and he caught hold of a branch of the young tree. Then he turned to see what Buster Bear was about.

Now there is nothing slow about Buster Bear's wits. The moment he saw Bobby run out on that branch, he knew just what was in Bobby's mind.

"Huh!" grunted Buster to himself. "If he thinks he can catch me napping with such an old trick as that, he will have to think again."

He waited only long enough to make sure that Bobby would jump for the other tree, and then Buster went down faster than he had come up. You see, he just dropped for the last half of the distance. So by the time Bobby Coon was half-way down the slender tree, Buster Bear was at the foot of it, waiting for him. Poor Bobby! At first he thought he was no better off than before. There was no other tree he could reach from this one. Now all Buster would have to do would be to climb up and get him. Bobby was about ready to give up in despair.

But Buster didn't climb up. He didn't even try. He just stood there at the foot of the tree and growled. Every growl made a shiver of fright run all over Bobby. Why didn't Buster hurry up and get him? All in a flash it came to Bobby why Buster didn't. He didn't because he couldn't! That was the reason. He couldn't climb that tree because it was too *small* for him to climb. He is such a big fellow that he has to have a good-sized tree to get his arms around. Once more Bobby began to hope.

But Buster Bear isn't one to give up easily. No, Sir, Buster doesn't give up until he has tried all the things he can think of. Now he stood up and took hold of that tree almost as if he were going to try to climb it. At first Bobby thought he was, but in a minute he found out his mistake. Buster began to shake that tree. My, my, my, how he did shake it! He was trying to shake Bobby Coon down.

The very first shake caught Bobby by surprise, and he very nearly lost his hold. Then he saw what Buster was up to, and he held on for dear life. He held on with arms and legs and teeth. Back and forth swung that tree and Bobby with it. It was worse, very much worse, than the hardest wind Bobby ever had been out in. But he grimly held on with claws and teeth, and over and over he said to himself:

"I won't let go. I won't let go. I won't let go." And he didn't.

CHAPTER TWENTY: PETER RABBIT SAVES BOBBY COON

There are heroes who are heroes
First in thought and then in fact.
Others are made into heroes,
Quite by accident, in fact.

REAL HEROES ARE those who do brave deeds, knowing all the time just what they are about, what risks they are taking, what will happen if they fail, and yet do the brave deeds just the same. The other kind of heroes are not real, true heroes at all, but are treated as if they were and are made just as much of as if they were. They are the ones who do what seem to be brave deeds, but which in truth haven't been planned at all and have been done unintentionally. People who in trying to save their own lives happen to save the lives of others always are called heroes and

Then, with his heart in his mouth, he jumped for the slender young tree.

are much looked up to and made of when in truth they are not heroes at all.

Peter Rabbit is this kind of a hero. He saved Bobby Coon's life. At least, Bobby Coon is kind enough to say he did. Anyway, be made it possible for Bobby to escape from angry Buster Bear. So Peter is called a hero and has been made much of. Everybody says that he was very, very brave. But right down in his own heart, Peter knows that he doesn't deserve any of the nice things said about him. True, he did save Bobby Coon, but he didn't do it purposely. No, Sir. Perhaps he might have, if he had thought of it, but he didn't think of it. What he did wasn't the result of thinking and planning at all, but of not thinking; of carelessness and heedlessness, if you please. But it made a hero of Peter in the eyes of his friends and neighbors just the same. You see, it was this way:

When Buster Bear began to shake that slender young tree, trying to shake Bobby Coon out of it, Peter forgot everything but his desire to see what would happen. From where he crouched, behind that big tree, he couldn't clearly see Bobby Coon in the top of the slender young tree. So, quite forgetting that he might be in danger himself, Peter hopped out from behind that big tree to try to find a place where he could see better. In his curiosity and excitement, he heedlessly forgot to watch his steps and trod on a dry stick. It broke with a little snap.

Now, no one in all the Green Forest has keener ears than Buster Bear. In spite of the fact that his attention was all on Bobby Coon, he heard that little snap and whirled like a flash to see what had made it. There sat round-eyed Peter Rabbit, staring with all his might. Without pausing an instant, Buster sprang for Peter. He would make very good eating, as Buster well knew, and a Rabbit on the ground was better than a Coon he couldn't shake out of a tree.

Peter dodged just in time and with a squeal of fear away he went, lipperty-lipperty-lip, twisting, dodging, running with all his might, and after him crashed Buster Bear. How Peter did wish that he hadn't been so curious, but had gone home to the dear Old Briar-patch when he should have! He was too frightened to know when Buster Bear gave up the chase, but kept right on running. As a matter of fact, Buster didn't chase him far. He knew that Peter was too nimble for him to catch in a tail-end race. So presently he gave it up and hurried back. Bobby Coon was nowhere in sight. He had taken the chance to climb down from that tree and run away. By leading Buster off for just those few minutes, Peter had saved Bobby Coon, and though he hadn't done it purposely, he got the credit just the same. He became a hero. This is a funny old world, isn't it?

CHAPTER TWENTY-ONE: BOBBY FINDS A HOME AT LAST

THE VERY INSTANT Buster Bear started after Peter Rabbit, down from that tree scrambled Bobby Coon. Never in all his life had he scrambled down a tree faster. He knew that Buster would not follow Peter far, and so he, Bobby, had no time to lose. He would get just as far from that place as he could before Buster should return.

So while Peter Rabbit was running, lipperty-lipperty-lip, in one direction as fast as ever he could, Bobby Coon was running in the opposite direction, and his black feet were moving astonishingly fast. He didn't know where he was going, but he was on his way somewhere, anywhere, to get out of the neighborhood of Buster Bear. So Bobby took little heed of where he was going, but ran until he was too tired to run any more. His heart was beating thumpity-thump-thump, thumpity-thump-thump, and he was breathing so hard that every breath was a gasp and hurt. He just had to stop. He couldn't run another step.

After a while Bobby's heart stopped going thumpity-thumpity-thump, and he once more breathed easily. He knew that he had escaped. He was safe. He sighed, and that sigh was a happy little sigh. Then he grinned. He was thinking of how hard he had tried to get a chance to sleep that day, and how every time he thought he had found a bed, he had been turned out of it almost as soon as he had closed his eyes. Bobby has a sense of fun, and now he saw the funny side of all his experiences.

"There is one thing sure, and that is being without a home is a more serious matter than I thought it was," said he. "I thought it would be easy enough to find a place to sleep when I wanted to, but I've begun to think that it is about the hardest thing I've ever tried to do. Here I am in a strange part of the Green Forest and homeless. There's no use in going back where I used to live, so I may as well look around here and see what I can find. Perhaps there is an empty house somewhere near. Most anything will do for a while."

So Bobby began to look about for an empty house. Now, of course, he had in mind a hollow tree or log. He always had lived in a hollow tree, and so he preferred one now. But he soon found that hollow trees were few and far between in that part of the Green Forest, and those he did find didn't have hollows big enough for him. The same thing was true of hollow logs. He was getting discouraged when he came to a ledge of rock which was the foundation of a little hill deep in the Green Forest.

In this ledge of rock Bobby discovered a crack big enough for him to squeeze into. Just out of curiosity he did squeeze into it, and then he discovered that after a little it grew wider and formed the snuggest little cave he ever had seen. It was very dry and comfortable in there. All in a flash it came to Bobby that the only thing needed to make this the snuggest kind of a house was a bed of dry leaves, and these were easy to get. Bobby's eyes danced.

"I've found my new home," he declared out loud. "It can't be cut down as my old home was; Buster Bear can't tear it open with his great claws; no one bigger than I can get into it. It's the safest and best house in all the Green Forest, and I'm going to stay right here."

Right then and there Bobby Coon curled up for that sleep he so much needed.

CHAPTER TWENTY-TWO: BOBBY FINDS HE HAS A NEIGHBOR

IN HIS NEW home in the little cave in the ledge of rocks deep in the Green Forest Bobby Coon at last slept peacefully. There was no one to disturb him, and so he made up for all the time he had lost. He slept all the rest of that day, and when he awoke, jolly, round red Mr. Sun had gone to bed behind the Purple Hills, and Mistress Moon had taken his place in the sky.

At first, Bobby couldn't think where he was. He rubbed his eyes and stared hard at the stone walls of his bedroom and wondered where he was and how he came to be there. Then, little by little, he remembered all that had happened—how he had made a mistake in thinking he could take Unc' Billy Possum's home away from him; how he had heedlessly crept into Prickly Porky's house for a nap, only to be driven out by Prickly Porky himself; how he had found a splendid hollow stump but had been discovered there by Blacky the Crow and afterward by Buster Bear; how Buster Bear had chased him and given him a terrible shaking in the top of a slender young tree; how Buster had stopped to chase Peter Rabbit; how he, Bobby, had taken this chance to run until he could run no more and found himself in a strange part of the Green Forest; how he had looked in vain for a hollow tree in which to make a new home, and lastly how he had found this little cave in the ledge of rock. Little by little, all this came back to Bobby, as he lay stretching and yawning.

At last, he scrambled to his feet and began to examine his new house more carefully than he had when he first entered. The more he studied it, the better he liked it. Having no one else to talk to, he talked to himself.

"The first and most important thing to look for in a house is safety," said he. "I used to think a good stout hollow tree was the safest place in the world, but I was mistaken. Men can cut hollow trees down. That is what happened to my old house. But it can't happen here. No, Sir, it can't possibly happen here. Neither can Buster Bear tear it open with his great claws. And the entrance is so narrow that no one of whom I need be afraid can possibly get in here. This is the safest place I've ever seen.

"The next most important thing is dryness. A damp house is bad, very bad. It is uncomfortable, and it is bad for the health. This place is perfectly dry. It will be warm in winter and cool in summer. I can't imagine a more comfortable house. The only thing lacking is a good bed, and that I'll soon make. On the whole, I guess the finding of this new house is worth all I went through. Now I think I'll go out and get acquainted with the neighborhood and see if I have got any near neighbors."

So Bobby went out through the narrow entrance and began to look about to see what he could discover. "I think," said he, "that I'll follow this ledge and see if there are any more caves like mine. I might find a better one, though I doubt it."

He shuffled along, light of heart and brimming over with excitement and curiosity. You know it always is great fun to explore a strange place. He had gone but a little way when he came to a sort of big open cave in the rock. Bobby stopped and peered in. Almost the first thing he saw was a bed. It was a big bed, and it was made of dry leaves and little branches of hemlock. It was a very good bed, and it was clear that someone had been sleeping in it very recently. Bobby's eyes grew very round. Then he sniffed.

That one sniff was enough. Bobby turned and ran back to his new house as fast as his legs would take him. All the pleasure he had taken in his new home was gone. He had discovered that his nearest neighbor was none other than Buster Bear himself!

CHAPTER TWENTY-THREE: BUSTER BEAR FINDS BOBBY COON

BOBBY COON WAS back in his new house, in the little cave in the rocky ledge deep in the Green Forest, and never was he or any member of his family more upset. You see, he had started out in high spirits to see what was to be seen about his new home and to find out who his neighbors might be, and he hadn't much more than started when he discovered that his nearest neighbor was none other than Buster Bear. Wasn't that enough to upset anybody? Anyway, it was enough to upset Bobby Coon, for only a few hours before Buster Bear had tried to catch him and had threatened to eat him. So all desire to spend the night looking about left Bobby the very instant he found Buster Bear's home in that very same rocky ledge in which his own new home was.

"What a dreadful fix, what a dreadful, dreadful fix I'm in," whined Bobby. "Here I've found the best home I've ever had, and now I find that Buster Bear lives almost next door. I don't dare stay here, and I haven't any place to go. Oh, dear, oh, dear, what can a poor little fellow like me do? I wish I were as big as Buster Bear. I do. Then I'd fight him. I would. I'd fight him."

"Who would you fight?" demanded a great, deep, grumbly, rumbly voice from outside his doorway.

Bobby just dropped right down where he was and shook with fright. But he took great care not to make a sound, not the teeniest, weeniest sound. Perhaps Buster Bear didn't know who it was he had overheard. Perhaps, if he kept perfectly still, Buster would think he had been mistaken.

"Who are you in there, anyway?" demanded the deep, grumbly, rumbly voice. "I didn't know anyone was living here. Why don't you come out and be sociable?"

Bobby simply shivered and kept his tongue still. For a minute or two there was no sound from outside. Then there were three long sniffs—sniff, sniff, sniff! They made Bobby shiver more than ever.

"Oh, ho! So it's you, Bobby Coon! It's my little Cousin Bobby!" exclaimed the deep, grumbly, rumbly voice of Buster Bear, followed by a chuckle. "Welcome to the old rock ledge, Bobby. Welcome to the old rock ledge. If I am to have such a near neighbor, I'm glad it is to be you. Come out and shake hands. Don't be so bashful. I won't hurt you."

At that Bobby pricked up his ears a little. He knew that Buster's nose had told him all he wanted to know, and that there was no use to pretend any longer.

"Do you really mean that, Cousin Buster?" he asked in a faint voice.

"Certainly I mean it. Of course. Why not? I usually mean what I say," grumbled Buster Bear.

"That's just the trouble," replied Bobby timidly. "Just a little while ago you tried to catch me and said that you would eat me, and I thought you meant it."

Buster Bear began to chuckle and then to laugh, and his laugh was deep and grumbly rumbly like his voice.

"That's so, Bobby! That's so!" said he. "But that was when my stomach was so empty that it made me lose my temper. Now my stomach is full, and I'm really myself. You know you don't need to be afraid of me when I am myself. Just forget that little affair. I should have, if you hadn't reminded me of it. I'm glad you've decided to be neighborly. You couldn't make your home in a safer place. I'm going to take a nap now. Come over and see me when you feel like it. Be neighborly, Cousin Bobby. Be neighborly."

With this Buster Bear went shuffling along to his own house and bed. As for Bobby Coon, he was soon in the best of spirits again. He decided to remain right there, and he is there this very minute, I suspect, unless he is out getting into mischief or seeking new adventures. Speaking of adventures reminds me of some of Jimmy Skunk's. It will take a whole book to tell you of them, so I am going to devote the next one to Jimmy and his doings.

The Adventures of
Jimmy Skunk

CHAPTER ONE: PETER RABBIT PLANS A JOKE

The Imp of Mischief, woe is me, is always busy as a bee.

THAT IS WHY so many people are forever getting into trouble. He won't keep still. No, Sir, he won't keep still unless he is made to. Once you let him get started there is no knowing where he will stop. Peter Rabbit had just seen Jimmy Skunk disappear inside an old barrel, lying on its side at the top of the hill, and at once the Imp of Mischief began to whisper to Peter. Of course Peter shouldn't have listened. Certainly not. But he did. You know Peter dearly loves a joke when it is on someone else. He sat right where he was and watched to see if Jimmy would come out of the barrel. Jimmy didn't come out, and after a little Peter stole over to the barrel and peeped inside. There was Jimmy Skunk curled up for a nap.

Peter tiptoed away very softly. All the time the Imp of Mischief was whispering to him that this was a splendid chance to play a joke on Jimmy. You know it is very easy to play a joke on anyone who is asleep. Peter doesn't often have a chance to play a joke on Jimmy Skunk. It isn't a very safe thing to do, not if Jimmy is awake. No one knows that better than Peter. He sat down some distance from the barrel but where he could keep an eye on it. Then he went into a brown study, which is one way of saying that he thought very hard. He wanted to play a joke on Jimmy, but like most jokers he didn't want the joke to come back on himself. In fact, he felt that it would be a great deal better for him if Jimmy shouldn't know that he had anything to do with the joke.

As he sat there in a brown study, he happened to glance over on the Green Meadows and there he saw something red. He looked very hard, and in a minute he saw that it was Reddy Fox. Right away, Peter's nimble wits began to plan how he could use Reddy Fox to play a joke on Jimmy. All in a flash an idea came to him, an idea that made him laugh right out. You see, the Imp of Mischief was very, very busy whispering to Peter. "If Reddy were only up here, I believe I could do it, and it would be a joke on Reddy as well as on Jimmy," thought Peter, and laughed right out again.

"What are you laughing at?" asked a voice. It was the voice of Sammy Jay.

Right away a plan for getting Reddy up there flashed into Peter's head. He would get Sammy angry, and that would make Sammy scream. Reddy would be sure to come up there to see what Sammy Jay was making such a fuss about. Sammy, you know, is very quick-tempered. No one knows this better than Peter. So instead of replying politely to Sammy, as he should have done, Peter spoke crossly:

"Fly away, Sammy, fly away! It is no business of yours what I am laughing at," said he.

Right away Sammy's quick temper flared up. He began to call Peter names, and Peter answered back. This angered Sammy still more, and as he always screams when he is angry, he was soon making such a racket that Reddy Fox down on the Green Meadows couldn't help but hear it. Peter saw him lift his head to listen. In a few minutes he began to trot that way. He was coming to find out what that fuss was about. Peter knew that Reddy wouldn't come straight up there. That isn't Reddy's way. He would steal around back of the old stone wall on the edge of the Old Orchard, which was back of Peter, and would try to see what was going on without being seen himself.

"As soon as he sees me he will think that at last he has a chance to catch me," thought Peter. "I shall have to run my very fastest, but if everything goes right, he will soon forget all about me. I do hope that the noise Sammy Jay is making will not waken Jimmy Skunk and bring him out to see what is going on."

So with one eye on the barrel where Jimmy Skunk was taking a nap, and the other eye on the old stone wall behind which he expected Reddy Fox to come stealing up, Peter waited and didn't mind in the least the names that Sammy Jay was calling him.

CHAPTER TWO: PETER MAKES A FLYING JUMP

To risk your life unless there's need is downright foolishness indeed.

NEVER FORGET THAT. Never do such a crazy thing as Peter Rabbit was doing. What was he doing? Why, he was running the risk of being caught by Reddy Fox all for the sake of a joke. Did you ever hear of anything more foolish? Yet Peter was no different from a lot of people who every day risk their lives in the most careless and heedless ways just to save a few minutes of time or for some other equally foolish reason. The fact is, Peter didn't stop to think what dreadful thing might happen if his plans didn't work out as he intended. He didn't once think of little Mrs. Peter over in the dear Old Briar-patch and how she would feel if he never came home again. That's the trouble with thoughtlessness; it never remembers other people.

All the time that Reddy Fox was creeping along behind the old stone wall on the edge of the Old Orchard, Peter knew just where he was, though Reddy didn't know that. If he had known it, he would have suspected one of Peter's tricks.

"He'll peep over that wall, and just as soon as he sees me, he will feel sure that this time he will catch me," thought Peter. "He will steal along to that place where the wall is lowest and will jump over it right there. I must be ready to jump the very second he does."

It all happened just as Peter had expected. While seeming to be paying no attention to anything but to Sammy Jay, he kept his eyes on that low place in the old wall, and presently he saw Reddy's sharp nose, as Reddy peeped over to make sure that he was still there. The instant that sharp nose dropped out of sight, Peter made ready to run for his life. A second later, Reddy leaped over the wall, and Peter was off as hard as he could go, with Reddy almost at his heels. Sammy Jay, who had been so busy calling Peter names that he hadn't seen Reddy at all, forgot all about his quarrel with Peter.

"Go it, Peter! Go it!" he screamed excitedly. That was just like Sammy.

Peter did go it. He had to. He ran with all his might. Reddy grinned as he saw Peter start towards the Green Meadows. It was a long way to the dear Old Briar-patch, and Reddy didn't have any doubt at all that he would catch Peter before he got there. He watched sharply for Peter to dodge and try to get back to the old stone wall. He didn't mean to let Peter do that. But Peter didn't even try. He ran straight for the edge of the hill above the Green Meadows. Then, for the first time, Reddy noticed an old barrel there lying on its side.

"I wonder if he thinks he can hide in that," thought Reddy, and grinned again, for he remembered that he had passed that old barrel a few days before, and that one end was open while the other end was closed. "If he tries that, I will get him without the trouble of much of a chase," thought Reddy, and chuckled.

Lipperty-lipperty-lip ran Peter, lipperty-lipperty-lip, Reddy right at his heels! To Sammy Jay it looked as if in a few more jumps Reddy certainly would catch Peter. "Go it, Peter! Oh, go it! Go it!" screamed Sammy, for in spite of his quarrels with Peter, he didn't want to see him come to any real harm.

Just as he reached the old barrel, Reddy was so close to him that Peter was almost sure that he could feel Reddy's breath. Then Peter made a splendid flying jump right over the old barrel and kept on down the hill, lipperty-lipperty-lip, as fast as ever he could, straight for an old house of Johnny Chuck's of which he knew. When he reached it, he turned to see what was happening behind him, for he knew by the screaming of Sammy Jay and by other sounds that a great deal was happening. In fact, he suspected that the joke which he had planned was working out just as he had hoped it would.

CHAPTER THREE: WHAT HAPPENED AT THE OLD BARREL

PETER RABBIT'S JUMP over the old barrel on the edge of the hill was unexpected to Reddy Fox. In fact, Reddy was so close on Peter's heels that he had no thought of anything but catching Peter. He was running so fast that when Peter made his flying jump over the barrel, Reddy did not have time to jump too, and he ran right smack bang against that old barrel. Now you remember that that barrel was right on the edge of the hill. When Reddy ran against it, he hit it so hard that he rolled it over, and of course that started it down the hill. You know a barrel is a very rolly sort of thing, and once it has started down a hill, nothing can stop it.

It was just so this time. Reddy Fox had no more than picked himself up when the barrel was half way down the hill and going faster and faster. It bounced along over the ground, and every time it hit a little hummock it seemed to jump right up in the air. And all the time it was making the strangest noises. Reddy quite forgot the smarting sore places where he had bumped into the barrel. He simply stood and stared at the runaway.

"As I live," he exclaimed, "I believe there was someone in that old barrel!" There was. You remember that Jimmy Skunk had curled up in there for a nap. Now Jimmy was awake, very much awake. You see, for once in his life he was moving fast, very much faster than ever he had moved before, since he was born. And it wasn't at all comfortable. No, Sir, it wasn't at all a comfortable way in which to travel. He went over and over so fast that it made him dizzy. First he was right side up and then wrong side up, so fast that he couldn't tell which side up he was. And every time that old

Reddy did not have time to jump too, and he ran right smack bang against the old barrel.

barrel jumped when it went over a hummock, Jimmy was tossed up so that he hit whatever part of the barrel happened to be above him. Of course, he couldn't get out, because he was rolled over and over so fast that he didn't have a chance to try.

Now Reddy didn't know who was in the barrel. He just knew by the sounds that someone was. So he started down the hill after the barrel to see what would happen when it stopped. All the time Peter Rabbit was dancing about in the greatest excitement, but taking the greatest care to keep close to that old house of Johnny Chuck's so as to pop into it in case of danger. He saw that Reddy Fox had quite forgotten all about him in his curiosity as to who was in the barrel, and he chuckled as he thought of what might happen when the barrel stopped rolling and Reddy found out. Sammy Jay was flying overhead, screaming enough to split his throat. Altogether, it was quite the most exciting thing Peter had ever seen.

Now it just happened that Old Man Coyote had started to cross the Green Meadows right at the foot of the hill just as the barrel started down. Of course, he heard the noise and looked up to see what it meant. When he saw that barrel rushing right down at him, it frightened him so that he just gave one yelp and started for the Old Pasture like a gray streak. He gave Peter a chance to see just how fast he can run, and Peter made up his mind right then that he never would run a race with Old Man Coyote.

Down at the bottom of the hill was a big stone, and when the barrel hit this, the hoops broke, and the barrel fell all apart. Peter decided that it was high time for him to get out of sight. So he dodged into the old house of Johnny Chuck and lay low in the doorway, where he could watch. He saw Jimmy Skunk lay perfectly still, and a great fear crept into his heart. Had Jimmy been killed? He hadn't once thought of what might happen to Jimmy when he planned that joke. But presently Jimmy began to wave first one leg and then another, as if to make sure that he had some legs left. Then slowly he rolled over and got on to his feet. Peter breathed a sigh of relief.

CHAPTER FOUR: JIMMY SKUNK IS VERY MAD INDEED

> *When Jimmy Skunk is angry*
> *Then everyone watch out!*
> *It's better far at such a time*
> *To be nowhere about.*

JIMMY SKUNK WAS angry this time and no mistake. He was just plain *mad*, and when Jimmy Skunk feels that way, no one wants to be very near him. You know he is one of the very best-natured little fellows in the world ordinarily. He minds his own business, and if no one interferes with him, he interferes with no one. But once he is aroused and feels that he hasn't been treated fairly, look out for him!

And this time Jimmy was mad clear through, as he got to his feet and shook himself to see that he was all there. I don't know that anyone could blame him. To be wakened from a comfortable nap by being rolled over and over and shaken nearly to death as Jimmy had been by that wild ride down the hill in the old barrel was enough to make anyone mad. So he really is not to be blamed for feeling as he did.

Now Jimmy can never be accused of being stupid. He knew that an old barrel which has been lying in one place for a long time doesn't move of its own accord. He knew that that barrel couldn't possibly have started off down the hill unless someone had made it start, and he didn't have a doubt in the world that whoever had done it, had known that he was inside and had done it to make him uncomfortable. So just as soon as he had made sure that he was really alive and quite whole, he looked about to see who could have played such a trick on him.

The first person he saw was Reddy Fox. In fact, Reddy was right close at hand. You see, he had raced down the hill after the barrel to see who was in it when he heard the strange noises coming from it as it rolled and bounded down. If Reddy had known that it was Jimmy Skunk, he would have been quite content to remain at the top of the hill. But he didn't know, and if the truth be known, he had hopes that it might prove to be someone who would furnish him with a good breakfast. So, quite out of breath with running, Reddy arrived at the place where the old barrel had broken to pieces just as Jimmy got to his feet.

Now when Jimmy Skunk is angry, he doesn't bite and he doesn't scratch. You know Old Mother Nature has provided him with a little bag of perfume which Jimmy doesn't object to in the least, but which makes most people want to hold their noses and run. He never uses it, excepting when he is angry or in danger, but when he does use it, his enemies always turn tail and run. That is why he is afraid of no one, and why everyone respects Jimmy and his rights.

He used it now, and he didn't waste any time about it. He threw some of that perfume right in the face of Reddy Fox before Reddy had a chance to turn or to say a word.

"Take that!" snapped Jimmy Skunk. "Perhaps it will teach you not to play tricks on your honest neighbors!"

Poor Reddy! Some of that perfume got in his eyes and made them smart dreadfully. In fact, for a little while he couldn't see at all. And then the smell of it was so strong that it made him quite sick. He rolled over and over on the ground, choking and gasping and rubbing his eyes. Jimmy Skunk just stood and looked on, and there wasn't a bit of pity in his eyes.

"How do you like that?" said he. "You thought yourself very smart, rolling me

"Huh!" said Jimmy Skunk again. "If you were chasing Peter Rabbit, where is he now?"

down hill in a barrel, didn't you? You might have broken my neck."

"I didn't know you were in that barrel, and I didn't mean to roll it down the hill anyway," whined Reddy, when he could get his voice.

"Huh!" snorted Jimmy Skunk, who didn't believe a word of it.

"I didn't. Honestly I didn't," protested Reddy. "I ran against the barrel by accident, chasing Peter Rabbit. I didn't have any idea that anyone was in it."

"Huh!" said Jimmy Skunk again. "If you were chasing Peter Rabbit, where is he now?"

Reddy had to confess he didn't know. He was nowhere in sight, and he certainly hadn't had time to reach the dear Old Briar-patch. Jimmy looked this way and that way, but there was no sign of Peter Rabbit.

"Huh!" said he again, turning his back on Reddy Fox and walking away with a great deal of dignity.

CHAPTER FIVE: REDDY FOX SNEAKS AWAY

TO SNEAK AWAY is to steal away trying to keep out of sight of everybody, and is usually done only by those who for some reason or other are ashamed to be seen. Just as soon as Reddy Fox could see after Jimmy Skunk had thrown that terrible perfume in Reddy's face he started for the Green Forest. He wanted to get away by himself. But he didn't trot with his head up and his big plumey tail carried proudly as is usual with him. No indeed. Instead he hung his head, and his handsome tail was dropped between his legs; he was the very picture of shame. You see that terrible perfume which Jimmy Skunk had thrown at him clung to his red coat and he knew that he couldn't get rid of it, not for a long time anyway. And he knew, too, that wherever he went his neighbors would hold their noses and make fun of him, and that no one would have anything to do with him. So he sneaked away across the Green Meadows towards the Green Forest and he felt too sick and mean and unhappy to even be angry with Sammy Jay, who was making fun of him and saying that he had got no more than he deserved.

Poor Reddy! He didn't know what to do or where to go. He couldn't go home, for old Granny Fox would drive him out of the house. She had warned him time and again never to provoke Jimmy Skunk, and he knew that she never would forgive him if he should bring that terrible perfume near their home. He knew, too, that it would not be long before all the little people of the Green Forest and the Green Meadows would know what had happened to him. Sammy Jay would see to that. He knew just how they would point at him and make fun of him. He would never hear the last of it. He felt as if he never, never would be able to hold his head and his tail up again. Every few minutes he stopped to roll over and over on the ground trying to get rid of that dreadful perfume.

When he reached the Green Forest he hurried over to the Laughing Brook to wash out his eyes. It was just his luck to have Billy Mink come along while he was doing this. Billy didn't need to be told what had happened. "Phew!" he exclaimed, holding on to his nose. Then he turned and hurried beyond the reach of that perfume. There he stopped and made fun of Reddy Fox and said all the provoking things he could think of. Reddy took no notice at all. He felt too miserable to quarrel.

After he had washed his face he felt better. Water wouldn't take away the awful smell, but it did take away the smart from his eyes. Then he tried to plan what to do next.

"The only thing I can do is to get as far away from everybody as I can," thought he. "I guess I'll have to go up to the Old Pasture to live for a while."

So he started for the Old Pasture, keeping as much out of sight as possible. On the way he remembered that Old Man Coyote lived there. Of course it would never do to go near Old Man Coyote's home for if he smelled that awful perfume and discovered that he, Reddy, was the cause of it he would certainly drive him out of the Old Pasture and then where could he go? So Reddy went to the loneliest part of the Old Pasture and crept into an old house that he and Granny had dug there long ago when they had been forced to live in the Old Pasture in the days when Farmer Brown's boy and Bowser the Hound had hunted them for stealing chickens. There he stretched himself out and was perfectly miserable.

"It wouldn't be so bad if I had really been to blame, but I wasn't. I didn't know Jimmy Skunk was in that barrel and I didn't mean to start it rolling down the hill anyway," he muttered. "It was all an accident and—" He stopped and into his yellow eyes crept a look of suspicion. "I wonder," said he slowly, "if Peter Rabbit knew that Jimmy Skunk was there and planned to get me into all this trouble. I wonder."

CHAPTER SIX: PETER RABBIT DOESN'T ENJOY HIS JOKE

ALL THE TIME that Jimmy Skunk was punishing Reddy Fox for rolling him down hill in a barrel, and while Reddy was sneaking away to the Green Forest to get out of sight, Peter Rabbit was lying low in the old house of Johnny Chuck, right near the place where Jimmy Skunk's wild ride had come to an end. It had been a great relief to Peter when he had seen Jimmy Skunk get to his feet, and he knew that Jimmy hadn't been hurt in that wild ride. Lying flat in the doorway of Johnny Chuck's old house, Peter could see all that went on without being seen himself, and he could hear all that was said.

He chuckled as he saw Reddy Fox come up and his eyes were popping right out with excitement as he waited for what would happen next. He felt sure that Reddy Fox was in for something unpleasant, and he was glad. Of course, that wasn't a bit nice of Peter. Right down in his heart Peter knew it, but he had been chased so often by Reddy and given so many dreadful frights, that he felt now that he was getting even. So he chuckled as he waited for what was to happen. Suddenly that chuckle broke right off in the middle, and Peter cried "Ouch!" He had felt a pain as if a hot needle had been thrust into him. It made him almost jump out of the doorway. But he remembered in time that it would never, never do for him to show himself outside, for right away Reddy Fox and Jimmy Skunk would suspect that he had had something to do with that wild ride of Jimmy's in the barrel. So it would not do to show himself now. No, indeed!

All he could do was to kick and squirm and twist his head around to see what was happening. It didn't take long to find out. Even as he looked, he felt another sharp pain which brought another "Ouch!" from him and made him kick harder than ever. Two very angry little insects were just getting ready to sting him again, and more were coming. They were Yellow Jackets, which you know belong to the wasp family and carry very sharp little lances in their tails. The fact is, this old house of Johnny Chuck's had been deserted so long the Yellow Jackets had decided that as no one else was using it, they would, and they had begun to build their home just inside the hall.

Poor Peter! What could he do? He didn't dare go out, and he simply couldn't stay where he was. Whatever he did must be done quickly, for it looked to him as if a regular army of Yellow Jackets was coming, and those little lances they carried were about the most painful things he knew of. By this time he had lost all interest in what was going on outside. There was quite enough going on inside; too much, in fact. He remembered that Johnny Chuck digs his house deep down in the ground. He looked down the long hall. It was dark down there. Perhaps if he went down there, these angry little warriors wouldn't follow him. It was worth trying, anyway.

So Peter scrambled to his feet and scurried down the long hall, and as he ran, he cried "Ouch! Ouch! Oh! Ohoo!" Those sharp little lances were very busy, and there was no way of fighting back. At the end of the long hall was a snug little room, very dark but cool and comfortable. It was just as he had hoped; the Yellow Jackets did not follow him down there. They had driven him away from their home, which was right near the entrance, and they were satisfied.

But what a fix he was in! What a dreadful fix! He ached and smarted all over. My goodness, how he did smart! And to get out he would have to go right past the Yellow Jacket home again.

"Oh, dear, I wish I had never thought of such a joke," moaned Peter, trying in vain to find a comfortable position. "I guess I am served just right."

I rather think he was, don't you?

CHAPTER SEVEN: SAMMY JAY DOES SOME GUESSING

SAMMY JAY IS a queer fellow. Although he is a scamp and dearly loves to make trouble for his neighbors, he is always ready to take their part when others make trouble for them. Many are the times he has given them warning of danger. This is one reason they are quite willing to overlook his own shortcomings. So, though in many ways he is no better than Reddy Fox, he dearly loves to upset Reddy's plans and is very apt to rejoice when Reddy gets into trouble. Of course, being right there, he saw all that happened when Reddy ran against the old barrel at the top of the hill and sent it rolling. He had been quite as much surprised as Reddy to find that there was someone inside, and he had followed Reddy to see who it was. So, of course, he had seen what happened to Reddy.

Now, instead of being sorry for Reddy, he had openly rejoiced. It seems to be just that way with a great many people. They like to see others who are considered very smart get into trouble. So Sammy had laughed and made fun of poor Reddy. In the first place it was very exciting, and Sammy dearly loves excitement. And then it would make such a splendid story to tell, and no one likes to carry tales more than does Sammy Jay. He watched Reddy sneak away to the Green Forest, and Jimmy Skunk slowly walk away in a very dignified manner. Then Sammy flew back to the Old Orchard to spread the news among the little people there. It wasn't until he reached the Old Orchard that he remembered Peter Rabbit. Instead of flying about telling everyone what had happened to Jimmy Skunk and Reddy Fox, he found a comfortable perch in an old apple tree and was strangely silent. The fact is, Sammy Jay was doing some hard thinking. He had suddenly begun to wonder. It had popped into that shrewd little head of his that it was very strange how suddenly Peter Rabbit had disappeared.

"Of course," thought Sammy, "Jimmy Skunk is sure that Reddy rolled that barrel down hill purposely, and I don't wonder that he does think so. But I saw it all, and I know that it was all an accident so far as Reddy was concerned. I didn't know that Jimmy was in that barrel, and Reddy couldn't have known it because he didn't come up here until after I did. But Peter Rabbit may have known. Why did Peter run so that he would have to jump over that barrel when he could have run right past it?

"Of course, he may have thought that if he could make Reddy run right slam bang against that barrel it would stop Reddy long enough to give him a chance to get away. That would have been pretty smart of Peter and quite like him. But somehow I have a feeling that he knew all the time that Jimmy Skunk was taking a nap inside and that something was bound to happen if he was disturbed. The more I think of it, the more I believe that Peter did know and that he planned the whole thing. If he did, it was one of the smartest tricks I ever heard of. I didn't think Peter had it in him. It was rather hard on Jimmy Skunk, but it got rid of Reddy Fox for a while. He won't dare show his face around here for a long time. That means that Peter will have one less worry on his mind. Hello! Here comes Jimmy Skunk. I'll ask him a few questions."

Jimmy came ambling along in his usual lazy manner. He had quite recovered his good nature. He felt that he was more than even with Reddy Fox, and as he was none the worse for his wild ride in the barrel, he had quite forgotten that he had lost his temper.

"Hello, Jimmy. Have you seen Peter Rabbit this morning?" cried Sammy Jay.

Jimmy looked up and grinned. "Yes," said he. "I saw him up here early this morning. Why?"

"Did he see you go into that old barrel?" persisted Sammy.

"I don't know," confessed Jimmy. "He may have. What have you got on your mind, Sammy Jay?"

"Nothing much, only Reddy Fox was chasing him when he ran against that barrel and sent you rolling down the hill," replied Sammy.

Jimmy pricked up his ears. "Then Reddy didn't do it purposely!" he exclaimed.

"No," replied Sammy. "He didn't do it purposely. I am quite sure that he didn't know you were in it. But how about Peter Rabbit? I am wondering. And I'm doing a little guessing, too."

CHAPTER EIGHT: JIMMY SKUNK LOOKS FOR PETER

JIMMY SKUNK LOOKED very hard at Sammy Jay. Sammy Jay looked very hard at Jimmy Skunk. Then Sammy slowly shut one eye and as slowly opened it again. It was a wink.

"You mean," said Jimmy Skunk, "that you guess that Peter Rabbit knew that I was in that barrel, and that he jumped over it so as to make Reddy Fox run against it. Is that it?"

Sammy Jay said nothing, but winked again. Jimmy grinned. Then he looked thoughtful. "I wonder," said he slowly, "if Peter did it so as to gain time to get away from Reddy Fox."

"I wonder," said Sammy Jay.

"And I wonder if he did it just to get Reddy into trouble," continued Jimmy.

"I wonder," repeated Sammy Jay.

"And I wonder if he did it for a joke, a double joke on Reddy and myself," Jimmy went on, scratching his head thoughtfully.

"I wonder," said Sammy Jay once more, and burst out laughing.

Now Jimmy Skunk has a very shrewd little head on his shoulders. "So that is your guess, is it? Well, I wouldn't be a bit surprised if you are right," said he, nodding his head. "I think I will go look for Peter. I think he needs a lesson. Jokes that put other people in danger or make them uncomfortable can have no excuse. My neck might have been broken in that wild ride down the hill, and certainly I was made most uncomfortable. I felt as if everything inside me was shaken out of place and all mixed up. Even now my stomach feels a bit queer, as if it might not be just where it ought to be. By the way, what became of Peter after he jumped over the barrel?"

Sammy shook his head. "I don't know," he confessed. "You see, it was very exciting when that barrel started rolling, and we knew by the sounds that there was someone inside it. I guess Reddy Fox forgot all about Peter. I know I did. And when the barrel broke to pieces against that stone down there, and you and Reddy faced each other, it was still more exciting. After it was over, I looked for Peter, but he was nowhere in sight. He hadn't had time to reach the Old Briar-patch. I really would like to know myself what became of him."

Jimmy Skunk turned and looked down the hill. Then in his usual slow way he started back towards the broken barrel.

"Where are you going?" asked Sammy.

"To look for Peter Rabbit," replied Jimmy. "I want to ask him a few questions."

Jimmy Skunk ambled along down the hill. At first he was very angry as he thought of what Peter had done, and he made up his mind that Peter should be taught a lesson he would never forget. But as he ambled along, the funny side of the whole affair struck him, for Jimmy Skunk has a great sense of humor, and before he reached the bottom of the hill his anger had all gone and he was chuckling.

"I'm sorry if I did Reddy Fox an injustice," thought he, "but he makes so much trouble for other people that I guess no one else will be sorry. He isn't likely to bother anyone for some time. Peter really ought to be punished, but somehow I don't feel so much like punishing him as I did. I'll just give him a little scare and let the scamp off with that. Now, I wonder where he can be. I have an idea he isn't very far away. Let me see. Seems to me I remember an old house of Johnny Chuck's not very far from here. I'll have a look in that."

CHAPTER NINE: JIMMY VISITS JOHNNY CHUCK'S OLD HOUSE

JIMMY SKUNK WAS smiling as he ambled towards the old house of Johnny Chuck near the foot of the hill. There was no one near to see him, and this made him smile still more. You see, the odor of that perfume which he had thrown at Reddy Fox just a little while before was very, very strong there, and Jimmy knew that until that had disappeared no one would come near the place because it was so unpleasant for everyone. To Jimmy himself it wasn't unpleasant at all, and he couldn't understand why other people disliked it so. He had puzzled over that a great deal. He was glad that it was so, because on account of it everyone treated him with respect and took special pains not to quarrel with him.

"I guess it's a good thing that Old Mother Nature didn't make us all alike," said he to himself. "I think there must be something the matter with their noses, and I suppose they think there is something the matter with mine. But there isn't. Not a thing. Hello! There is Johnny Chuck's old house just ahead of me. Now we will see what we shall see."

He walked softly as he drew near to the old house. If Peter was way down inside, it wouldn't matter how he approached. But if Peter should happen to be only just inside the doorway, he might take it into his head to run if he should hear footsteps, particularly if those footsteps were not heavy enough to be those of Reddy or Granny Fox or Old Man Coyote. Jimmy didn't intend to give Peter a chance to do any such thing. If Peter once got outside that old house, his long legs would soon put him beyond Jimmy's reach, and Jimmy knew it. If he was to give Peter the fright that he had made up his mind to give him, he would first have to get him where he couldn't run away. So Jimmy walked as softly as he knew how and approached the old house in such a way as to keep out of sight of Peter, should he happen to be lying so as to look out of the doorway.

At last he reached a position where with one jump he could land right on the doorstep. He waited a few minutes and cocked his head on one side to listen. There wasn't a sound to tell him whether Peter was there or not. Then lightly he jumped over to the doorstep and looked in at the doorway. There was no Peter to be seen.

"If he is here, he is way down inside," thought Jimmy. "I wonder if he really is here. I think I'll look about a bit before I go in."

Now the doorstep was of sand, as Johnny Chuck's doorsteps always are. Almost at once Jimmy chuckled. There were Peter's tracks, and they pointed straight towards the inside of Johnny Chuck's old house. Jimmy looked carefully, but not a single track pointing the other way could he find. Then he chuckled again. "The scamp is here all right," he muttered. "He hid here and watched all that happened and then decided to lie low and wait until he was sure that the way was clear and no one would see him." In this Jimmy was partly right and partly wrong, as you and I know.

He stared down the long dark doorway a minute. Then he made up his mind. "I'll go down and make Peter a call, and I won't bother to knock," he chuckled, and poked his head inside the doorway. But that was as far as Jimmy Skunk went. Yes, Sir, that was just as far as Jimmy Skunk went. You see, no sooner did he start to enter that old house of Johnny Chuck's than he was met by a lot of those Yellow Jackets, and they were in a very bad temper.

Jimmy Skunk knows all about Yellow Jackets and the sharp little lances they carry in their tails; he has the greatest respect for them. He backed out in a hurry and actually hurried away to a safe distance. Then he sat down to think. After a little he began to chuckle again. "I know what happened," said he, talking to himself. "Peter Rabbit popped into that doorway. Those Yellow

Jimmy Skunk knows all about Yellow Jackets and the sharp little lances they carry in their tails.

Jackets just naturally got after him. He didn't dare come out for fear of Reddy Fox and me, and so he went on down to Jimmy Chuck's old bedroom, and he's down there now, wondering how ever he is to get out without getting stung. I reckon I don't need to scare Peter to pay him for that joke. I reckon he's been punished already."

CHAPTER TEN: PETER RABBIT IS MOST UNCOMFORTABLE

IF EVER ANYONE was sorry for having played pranks on other folks, that one was Peter Rabbit. I am afraid it wasn't quite the right kind of sorrow. You see, he wasn't sorry because of what had happened to Jimmy Skunk and Reddy Fox, but because of what had happened to himself. There he was, down in the bedroom of Johnny Chuck's old house, smarting and aching all over from the sharp little lances of the Yellow Jackets who had driven him down there before he had had a chance to see what happened to Reddy Fox. That was bad enough, but what troubled Peter more was the thought that he couldn't get out without once again facing those hot-tempered Yellow Jackets. Peter wished with all his might that he had known about their home in Johnny Chuck's old house before ever he thought of hiding there.

But wishes of that kind are about the most useless things in the world. They wouldn't help him now. He had so many aches and smarts that he didn't see how he could stand a single one more, and yet he couldn't see how he was going to get out without receiving several more. All at once he had a comforting thought. He remembered that Johnny Chuck usually has a back door. If that were the case here, he would be all right. He would find out. Cautiously he poked his head out of the snug bedroom. There was the long hall down which he had come. And there—yes, Sir, there was another hall! It must be the way to the back door. Carefully Peter crept up it.

"Funny," thought he, "that I don't see any light ahead of me."

And then he bumped his nose. Yes, Sir, Peter bumped his nose against the end of that hall. You see, it was an old house, and like most old houses it was rather a tumble-down affair. Anyway, the back door had been blocked with a great stone, and the walls of the back hall had fallen in. There was no way out there. Sadly Peter backed out to the little bedroom. He would wait until night, and perhaps then the Yellow Jackets would be asleep, and he could steal out the front way without getting any more stings. Meanwhile he would try to get a nap and forget his aches and pains.

Hardly had Peter curled up for that nap when he heard a voice. It sounded as if it came from a long way off, but he knew just where it came from. It came from the doorway of that old house. He knew, too, whose voice it was. It was Jimmy Skunk's voice.

"I know where you are, Peter Rabbit," said the voice. "And I know why you are hiding down there. I know, too, how it happened that I was rolled down hill in that barrel. I'm just giving you a little warning, Peter. There are a lot of very angry Yellow Jackets up here, as you will find out if you try to come out before dark. I'm going away now, but I'm going to come back about dark to wait for you. I may want to play a little joke on you to pay you back for the one you played on me."

That put an end to Peter's hope of a nap. He shivered as he thought of what might happen to him if Jimmy Skunk should catch him. What with his aches and pains from the stings of the Yellow Jackets, and fear of being caught by Jimmy Skunk, it was quite impossible to sleep. He was almost ready to face those Yellow Jackets rather than wait and meet Jimmy Skunk. Twice he started up the long hall, but turned back. He just couldn't stand any more stings. He was miserable. Yes, Sir, he was miserable and most uncomfortable in both body and mind.

"I wish I'd never thought of that joke," he half sobbed. "I thought it was a great joke, but it wasn't. It was a horrid, mean joke. Why, oh, why did I ever think of it?"

Meanwhile Jimmy Skunk had gone off, chuckling.

CHAPTER ELEVEN: JIMMY SKUNK KEEPS HIS WORD

Keep your word, whate'er you do,
And to your inmost self be true.

WHEN JIMMY SKUNK shouted down the hall of Johnny Chuck's old house to Peter Rabbit that he would come back at dark, he was half joking. He did it to make Peter uneasy and to worry him. The truth is, Jimmy was no longer angry at all. He had quite recovered his good nature and was very much inclined to laugh himself over Peter's trick. But he felt that it wouldn't do to let Peter off without some kind of punishment, and so he decided to frighten Peter a little. He knew that Peter wouldn't dare come out during the daytime because of the Yellow Jackets whose home was just inside the doorway of that old house; and he knew that Peter wouldn't dare face him, for he would be afraid of being treated as Reddy Fox had been. So that is why he told Peter that he was coming back at dark. He felt that if Peter was kept a prisoner in there for a while, all the time worrying about how he was to get out, he would be very slow to try such a trick again.

As Jimmy ambled away to look for some beetles, he chuckled and chuckled and chuckled. "I guess that by this time Peter wishes he hadn't thought of that joke on Reddy Fox and myself," said he. "Perhaps I'll go back there tonight and perhaps I won't. He won't know whether I do or not, and he won't dare come out."

Then he stopped and scratched his head thoughtfully. Then he sighed. Then he scratched his head again and once more sighed. "I really don't want to go back there tonight," he muttered, "but I guess I'll have to. I said I would, and so I'll have to do it. I believe in keeping my word. If I shouldn't and some day he should find it out, he wouldn't believe me the next time I happened to say I would do a thing. Yes, Sir, I'll have to go back. There is nothing like making people believe that when you say a thing you mean it. There is nothing like keeping your word to make people respect you."

Being naturally rather lazy, Jimmy decided not to go any farther than the edge of the Old Orchard, which was only a little way above Johnny Chuck's old house, where Peter was a prisoner. There Jimmy found a warm, sunny spot and curled up for a nap. In fact, he spent all the day there. When jolly, round, red Mr. Sun went to bed behind the Purple Hills, and the Black Shadows came trooping across the Green Meadows, Jimmy got up, yawned, chuckled, and then slowly ambled down to Johnny Chuck's old house. A look at the footprints in the sand on the doorstep told him that Peter had not come out. Jimmy sat down and waited until it was quite dark. Then he poked his head in at the doorway. The Yellow Jackets had gone to bed for the night.

"Come out, Peter. I'm waiting for you!" he called down the hall, and made his voice sound as angry as he could. But inside he was chuckling. Then Jimmy Skunk calmly turned and went about his business. He had kept his word.

As for Peter Rabbit, that had been one of the very worst days he could recall. He had ached and smarted from the stings of the Yellow Jackets; he had worried all day about what would happen to him if he did meet Jimmy Skunk, and he was hungry. He had had just a little bit of hope, and this was that Jimmy Skunk wouldn't come back when it grew dark. He had crept part way up the hall at the first hint of night and stretched himself out to wait until he could be sure that those dreadful Yellow Jackets had gone to sleep. He had just about made up his mind that it was safe for him to scamper out when Jimmy Skunk's voice came down the hall to him. Poor Peter! The sound of that voice almost broke his heart.

"He has come back. He's kept his word," he half sobbed as he once more went back to Johnny Chuck's old bedroom.

There he stayed nearly all the rest of the night, though his stomach was so empty it ached. Just before it was time for Mr. Sun to rise, Peter ventured to dash out of Johnny Chuck's old house. He got past the home of the Yellow Jackets safely, for they were not yet awake. With his heart in his mouth, he sprang out of the doorway. Jimmy Skunk wasn't there. With a sigh of relief, Peter started for the dear, safe Old Briar-patch, lipperty-lipperty-lip, as fast as he could go.

"I'll never, never play another joke," he said, over and over again as he ran.

CHAPTER TWELVE: JIMMY SKUNK AND UNC' BILLY POSSUM MEET

JIMMY SKUNK AMBLED along down the Lone Little Path through the Green Forest. He didn't hurry. Jimmy never does hurry. Hurrying and worrying are two things he leaves for his neighbors. Now and then Jimmy stopped to turn over a bit of bark or a stick, hoping to find some fat beetles. But it was plain to see that he had something besides fat beetles on his mind.

Up the Lone Little Path through the Green Forest shuffled Unc' Billy Possum. He didn't hurry. It was too warm to hurry. Unlike Jimmy Skunk, he does hurry sometimes, does Unc' Billy, especially when he suspects that Bowser the Hound is about. And sometimes Unc' Billy does worry. You see, there are people who think that Unc' Billy would make a very good dinner. Unc' Billy doesn't think he would. Anyway, he has no desire to have the experiment tried. So occasionally, when he discovers one of these people who think he would make a good dinner, he worries a little.

But just now Unc' Billy was neither hurrying nor worrying. There was no need of doing either, and Unc' Billy never does anything that there is no need of doing. So Unc' Billy shuffled up the Lone Little Path, and Jimmy Skunk ambled down

"Hello, Unc Billy!" said he. "Have you seen any fat beetles this morning?"

the Lone Little Path, and right at a bend in the Lone Little Path they met.

Jimmy Skunk grinned. "Hello, Unc' Billy!" said he. "Have you seen any fat beetles this morning?"

Unc' Billy grinned. "Good mo'nin, Brer Skunk," he replied. "Ah can't rightly say Ah have. Ah had it on mah mind to ask yo' the same thing."

Jimmy sat down and looked at Unc' Billy with twinkling eyes. His grin grew broader and became a chuckle. "Unc' Billy," said he," have you ever in your life combed your hair or brushed your coat?" You know Unc' Billy usually looks as if every hair was trying to point in a different direction from every other hair, while Jimmy Skunk always appears as neat as if he spent half his time brushing and smoothing his handsome black and white coat.

Unc' Billy's eyes twinkled. "Ah reckons Ah did such a thing once or twice when Ah was very small, Brer Skunk," said he, without a trace of a smile. "But it seems to me a powerful waste of time. Ah have mo' important things to worry about. By the way, Brer Skunk, did yo' ever run away from anybody in all your life?"

Jimmy looked surprised at the question. He scratched his head thoughtfully. "Not that I remember of," said he after a little. "Most folks run away from me," he added with a little throaty chuckle. "Those who don't run away always are polite and step aside. It may be that when I was a very little fellow and didn't know much about the Great World and the people who live in it, I might have run away from someone, but if I did, I can't remember it. Why do you ask, Unc' Billy?"

"Oh, no reason in particular, Brer Skunk. No reason in particular. Only Ah wonder sometimes if yo' ever realize how lucky yo' are. If Ah never had to worry about mah hungry neighbors, Ah reckons perhaps Ah might brush mah coat oftener." Unc' Billy's eyes twinkled more than ever.

"Worry," replied Jimmy Skunk sagely, "is the result of being unprepared. Anybody who is prepared has no occasion to worry. Just think it over, Unc' Billy."

It was Unc' Billy's turn to scratch his head thoughtfully. "Ah fear Ah don't quite get your meaning, Brer Skunk," said he.

"Sit down, Unc' Billy, and I'll explain," replied Jimmy.

CHAPTER THIRTEEN: JIMMY SKUNK EXPLAINS

You'll find this true where'er you go
That those prepared few troubles know.

"TO BEGIN WITH, I am not such a very big fellow, am I?" said Jimmy.

"Ah reckons Ah knows a right smart lot of folks bigger than yo', Brer Skunk," replied Unc' Billy, with a grin. You know Jimmy Skunk really is a little fellow compared with some of his neighbors.

"And I haven't very long claws or very big teeth, have I?' continued Jimmy.

"Ah reckons mine are about as long and about as big," returned Unc' Billy, looking more puzzled than ever.

"But you never see anybody bothering me, do you?" went on Jimmy.

"No," replied Unc' Billy.

"And it's the same way with Prickly Porky the Porcupine. You never see anybody bothering him or offering to do him any harm, do you?" persisted Jimmy.

"No," replied Unc' Billy once more.

"Why?" demanded Jimmy.

Unc' Billy grinned broadly. "Ah reckons, Brer Skunk," said he, "that there isn't anybody wants to go fo' to meddle with yo' and Brer Porky. Ah reckons most folks knows what would happen if they did, and that yo' and Brer Porky are folks it's a sight mo' comfortable to leave alone. Leastways, Ah does. Ah ain't aiming fo' trouble with either of yo'. That li'l bag of scent yo' carry is cert'nly most powerful, Brer Skunk, and Ah isn't hankering to brush against those little spears Brer Porky is so free with. Ah knows when Ah's well off, and Ah reckons most folks feel the same way."

Jimmy Skunk chuckled. "One more question, Unc' Billy," said he. "Did you ever know me to pick a quarrel and use that bag of scent without being attacked?"

Unc' Billy considered for a few minutes. "Ah can't say Ah ever did," he replied.

"And you never knew Prickly Porky to go hunting trouble either," declared Jimmy. "We don't either of us go hunting trouble, and trouble never comes hunting us, and the reason is that we both are always prepared for trouble and everybody knows it. Buster Bear could squash me by just stepping on me, but he doesn't try it. You notice he always is very polite when we meet. Prickly Porky and I are armed, for *defense*, but we never use our weapons for *offense*. Nobody bothers us, and we bother nobody. That's the beauty of being prepared."

Unc' Billy thought it over for a few minutes. Then he sighed and sighed again.

"Ah reckons yo' and Brer Porky are about the luckiest people Ah knows," said he. "Yes, Sah, Ah reckons yo' is just that. Ah don't fear anybody mah own size, but Ah cert'nly does have some mighty scary times when Ah meets some people Ah might mention. Ah wish Ol' Mother Nature had done gone and given me something fo' to make people as scary of me as they are of yo'. Ah cert'nly believes in preparedness after seein yo', Brer Skunk. Ah cert'nly does just that very thing. Have yo' found any nice fresh aiggs lately?"

CHAPTER FOURTEEN: A LITTLE SOMETHING ABOUT EGGS

"An egg," says Jimmy Skunk, "is good; it's very good indeed to eat."
"An egg," says Mrs. Grouse, "is dear; 'twill hatch into a baby sweet."

SO IN THE matter of eggs, as in a great many other matters, it all depends on the point of view. To Jimmy Skunk and Unc' Billy Possum eggs are looked on from the viewpoint of something to eat. Their stomachs prompt them to think of eggs. Eggs are good to fill empty stomachs. The mere thought of eggs will make Jimmy and Unc' Billy smack their lips. They say they "love" eggs, but they don't. They "like" them, which is quite different. But Mrs. Grouse and most of the other feathered people of the Green Forest and the Green Meadows and the Old Orchard really do "love" eggs. It is the heart instead of the stomach that responds to the thought of eggs. To them eggs are almost as precious as babies, because they know that some day, some day very soon, those eggs will become babies. There are a few feathered folks, I am sorry to say, who "love" their own eggs, but "like" the eggs of other people—like them just as Jimmy Skunk and Unc' Billy Possum do, to eat. Blacky the Crow is one and his cousin, Sammy Jay, is another.

So in the springtime there is always a great deal of matching of wits between the little people of the Green Forest and the Green Meadows and the Old Orchard. Those who have eggs try to keep them a secret or to build the nests that hold them where none who like to eat them can get them; and those who have an appetite for eggs try to find them.

When Unc' Billy Possum suddenly changed the subject by asking Jimmy Skunk if he had found any nice fresh eggs lately, he touched a subject very close to Jimmy's heart. I should have said, rather, his stomach. To tell the truth, it was a longing for some eggs that had brought Jimmy to the Green Forest. He knew that somewhere there Mrs. Grouse must be hiding a nestful of the very nicest of eggs, and it was to hunt for these that he had come.

"No," replied Jimmy, "I haven't had any luck at all this spring. I've almost forgotten what an egg tastes like. Either I'm growing dull and stupid, or some folks are smarter than they used to be. By the way, have you seen Mrs. Grouse lately?" Jimmy looked very innocent as he asked this.

Unc' Billy chuckled until his sides shook. "Do yo' suppose Ah'd tell yo' if Ah had?" he demanded. "Ah reckons Mrs. Grouse hasn't got any mo' aiggs than Ah could comfortably take care of mahself, not to mention Mrs. Possum." Here Unc' Billy looked back over his shoulder to make sure that old Mrs. Possum wasn't within hearing, and Jimmy Skunk chuckled. "Seems to me, Brer Skunk, yo' might better do your aigg hunting on the Green Meadows and leave the Green Forest to me," continued Unc' Billy. "That would be no mo' than fair. Yo' know Ah never did hanker fo' to get far away from trees, but yo' don't mind. Besides there are mo' aiggs fo' yo' to find on the Green Meadows than there are fo' me to find in the Green Forest. A right smart lot of birds make their nests on the ground there. There is Brer Bob White and Brer Meadowlark and Brer Bobolink and Brer Field Sparrow and Brer—"

"Never mind any more, Unc' Billy," interrupted Jimmy Skunk. "I know all about them. That is, I know all about them I want to know, except where their eggs are. Didn't I just tell you I haven't had any luck at all? That's why I'm over here."

"Well, yo' won't have any mo' luck here unless yo' are a right smart lot sharper than your Unc' Billy, and when it comes to hunting aiggs, Ah don't take mah hat off to anybody, not even to yo', Brer Skunk," replied Unc' Billy.

CHAPTER FIFTEEN: A SECOND MEETING

JIMMY SKUNK COULDN'T think of anything but eggs. The more he thought of them, the more he wanted some. After parting from Unc' Billy Possum in the Green Forest he went back to the Green Meadows and prowled about, hunting for the nests of his feathered neighbors who build on the ground, and having no more luck than he had had before.

Unc' Billy Possum was faring about the same way. He couldn't, for the life of him, stop thinking about those eggs that belonged to Mrs. Grouse. The more he tried to forget about them, the more he thought about them.

"Ah feels it in mah bones that there isn't the least bit of use in hunting fo' them," said he to himself, as he watched Jimmy Skunk amble out of sight up the Lone Little Path. "No, Sah, there isn't the least bit of use. Ah done look every place Ah can think of already. Still, Ah haven't got anything else special on mah mind, and those aiggs cert'nly would taste good. Ah reckons it must be Ah needs those aiggs, or Ah wouldn't have them on mah mind so much. Ah finds it rather painful to carry aiggs on mah mind all the time, but Ah would enjoy carrying them in mah stomach. Ah cert'nly would." Unc' Billy grinned and started to ramble about aimlessly, hoping that chance would lead him to the nest of Mrs. Grouse.

Do what he would, Unc' Billy couldn't get the thought of eggs off his mind, and the more he thought about them the more he wanted some. And that led him to think of Farmer Brown's henhouse. He had long ago resolved never again to go there, but the longing for a taste of eggs was too much for his good resolutions, and as soon as Jolly, round, red Mr. Sun sank to rest behind the Purple Hills, and the Black Shadows came creeping across the Green Meadows and through the Green Forest, Unc' Billy slipped away, taking pains that old Mrs. Possum shouldn't suspect where he was going.

Out from the Green Forest, keeping among the Black Shadows along by the old stone wall on the edge of the Old Orchard, he stole, and so at last he reached Farmer Brown's henhouse. He stopped to listen. There was no sign of Bowser the Hound, and Unc' Billy sighed gently. It was a sigh of relief. Then he crept around a corner of the henhouse towards a certain hole under it he remembered well. Just as he reached it, he saw something white. It moved. It was coming towards him from the other end of the henhouse. Unc' Billy stopped right where he was. He was undecided whether to run or stay. Then he heard a little grunt and decided to stay. He even grinned. A few seconds later up came Jimmy Skunk. It was a white stripe on Jimmy's coat that Unc' Billy had seen.

Jimmy gave a little snort of surprise when he almost bumped into Unc' Billy.

"What are you doing here?" he demanded.

"Just taking a li'l walk fo' the good of mah appetite," replied Unc' Billy, grinning more broadly than ever. "What are yo' doing here, Brer Skunk?"

"The same thing," replied Jimmy. Then he chuckled. "This is an unexpected meeting. I guess you must have had the same thing on your mind all day that I have," he added.

"Ah reckon so," replied Unc' Billy, and both grinned.

CHAPTER SIXTEEN: A MATTER OF POLITENESS

It costs not much to be polite, and, furthermore, it's always right.

UNC' BILLY POSSUM and Jimmy Skunk, facing each other among the Black Shadows close by a hole that led under Farmer Brown's henhouse, chuckled as each thought of what had brought the other there. It is queer how a like thought often brings people together. Unc' Billy had the same longing in his stomach that Jimmy Skunk had, and Jimmy Skunk had the same thing on his mind that Unc' Billy had. More than this, it was the second time that day that they had met. They had met in the morning in the Green Forest and now they had met again among the Black Shadows of the evening at Farmer Brown's henhouse. And it was all on account of eggs. Yes, Sir, it was all on account of eggs.

"Are you just coming out, or are you just going in?" Jimmy inquired politely.

"Ah was just going in, but Ah'll follow yo', Brer Skunk," replied Unc' Billy just as politely.

"Nothing of the kind," returned Jimmy. "I wouldn't for a minute think of going before you. I hope I know my manners better than that."

"Yo' cert'nly are most polite, Brer Skunk. Yo' cert'nly are most polite. Yo' are a credit to your bringing up, but politeness always did run in your family. There is a saying that han'some is as han'some does, and your politeness is as fine as yo' are han'some, Brer Skunk. Ah'll just step one side and let yo' go first just to show that Ah sho'ly does appreciate your friendship," said Unc' Billy.

Jimmy Skunk chuckled. "I guess you've forgotten that other old saying, 'Age before beauty,' Unc' Billy," said he. "So you go first. You know you are older than I. I couldn't think of being so impolite as to go first. I really couldn't think of such a thing."

And so they argued and argued, each insisting in the most polite way that the other should go first. If the truth were known, neither of them was insisting out of politeness at all. No, Sir, politeness had nothing to do with it. Jimmy Skunk wanted Unc' Billy to go first because Jimmy believes in safety first, and it had popped into Jimmy's head that there might, there just might, happen to be a trap inside that hole. If there was, he much preferred that Unc' Billy should be the one to find it out. Yes, Sir, that is why Jimmy Skunk was so very polite.

Unc' Billy wanted Jimmy to go first because he always feels safer behind Jimmy than in front of him. He has great respect for that little bag of scent that Jimmy carries, and he knows that when Jimmy makes use of it, he always throws it in front and never behind him. Jimmy seldom uses it, but sometimes he does if he happens to be startled and thinks danger near. So Unc' Billy preferred that Jimmy should go first. It wasn't politeness at all on the part of Unc' Billy. In both cases it was a kind of selfishness. Each was thinking of himself.

How long they would have continued to argue and try to appear polite if something hadn't happened, nobody knows. But something did happen. There was a sudden loud sniff just around the corner of the henhouse. It was from Bowser the Hound. Right then and there Unc' Billy Possum and Jimmy Skunk forgot all about politeness, and both tried to get through that hole at the same time. They couldn't, because it wasn't big enough, but, they tried hard. Bowser sniffed again, and this time Unc' Billy managed to squeeze Jimmy aside and slip through. Jimmy was right at his heels.

CHAPTER SEVENTEEN: JIMMY SKUNK GETS A BUMP

HARDLY HAD JIMMY SKUNK entered the hole under Farmer Brown's henhouse, following close on the heels of Unc' Billy Possum, than along came Bowser the Hound, sniffing and sniffing in a way that made Unc' Billy nervous. When Bowser reached that hole, of course he smelled the tracks of Unc' Billy and Jimmy, and right away he became excited. He began to dig. Goodness, how he did make the dirt fly! All the time he whined with eagerness.

Unc' Billy wasted no time in squeezing through a hole in the floor way over in one corner, a hole that Farmer Brown's boy had intended to nail a board over long before. Unc' Billy knew that Bowser couldn't get through that, even if he did manage to dig his way under the henhouse. Once through that and fairly in the henhouse, Unc' Billy drew a long breath. He felt safe for the time being, anyway, and he didn't propose to worry over the future.

Jimmy Skunk hurried after Unc' Billy. It wasn't fear that caused Jimmy to hurry. No, indeed, it wasn't fear. He had been startled by the unexpectedness of Bowser's appearance. It was this that had caused him to struggle to be first through that hole under the henhouse. But once through, he had felt a bit ashamed that he had been so undignified. He wasn't afraid of Bowser. He was sorely tempted to turn around and send Bowser about his business, as he knew he very well could. But he thought better of it. Besides, Unc' Billy was already through that hole in the floor, and Jimmy didn't for a minute forget what had brought him there. He had come for eggs, and so had Unc' Billy. It would never do to let Unc' Billy be alone up there for long. So Jimmy Skunk did what he very seldom does—hurried. Yes, Sir, he hurried after Unc' Billy Possum. He meant to make sure of his share of the eggs he was certain were up there.

There was a row of nesting boxes along one side close to the floor. Above these was another row and above these a third row. Jimmy doesn't climb, but Unc' Billy is a famous climber.

"I'll take these lower nests," said Jimmy, and lifted his tail in a way that made Unc' Billy nervous.

"All right," replied Unc' Billy promptly. "All right, Brer Skunk. It's just as yo' say."

With this, Unc' Billy scrambled up to the next row of nests. Jimmy grinned and started to look in the lower nests. He took his time about it, for that is Jimmy's way. There was nothing in the first one and nothing in the second one and nothing in the third one. This was disappointing, to say the least, and Jimmy began to move a little faster. Meanwhile Unc' Billy had hurried from one nest to another in the second row with no better success. By the time Jimmy was half-way along his row Unc' Billy had begun on the upper row, and the only eggs he had found were hard china nest-eggs put there by Farmer Brown's boy to tempt the hens to lay in those particular nests. Disappointment was making Unc' Billy lose his temper. Each time he peeped in a nest and saw one of those china eggs, he hoped it was a real egg, and each time when he found it wasn't he grew angrier.

At last he so lost his temper that when he found another of those eggs he angrily kicked it out of the nest. Now it happened that Jimmy Skunk was just underneath. Down fell that hard china egg squarely on Jimmy Skunk's head. For just a minute Jimmy saw stars. At least, he thought he did. Then he saw the egg, and knew that Unc' Billy had knocked it down, and that it was this that had hit him.

Jimmy was sore at heart because he had found no eggs, and now he had a bump on the head that also was sore. Jimmy Skunk lost his temper, a thing he rarely does.

CHAPTER EIGHTEEN: A SAD, SAD QUARREL

JIMMY SKUNK SAT on the floor of Farmer Brown's henhouse, rubbing his head and glaring up at the upper row of nests with eyes red with anger. Of course it was dark in the henhouse, for it was night, but Jimmy can see in the dark, just as so many other little people who wear fur can. What he saw was the anxious-looking face of Unc' Billy Possum staring down at him.

"You did that purposely!" snapped. Jimmy. "You did that purposely, and you needn't tell me you didn't."

"On mah honor Ah didn't," protested Unc' Billy. "It was an accident, just a sho' 'nuff accident, and Ah'm right sorry fo' it."

"That sounds very nice, but I don't believe a word of it. You did it purposely, and you can't make me believe anything else. Come down here and fight. I dare you to!" Jimmy was getting more and more angry every minute.

Unc' Billy began to grow angry. Of course, it was wholly his fault that that egg had fallen, but it wasn't his fault that Jimmy had happened to be just beneath. He hadn't known that Jimmy was there. He had apologized, and he felt that no one could do more than that. Jimmy Skunk had doubted his word, had refused to believe him, and that made him angry. His little eyes glowed with rage.

"If yo' want to fight, come up here. I'll wait fo' yo' right where Ah am," he sputtered.

This made Jimmy angrier than ever. He couldn't climb up there, and he knew that Unc' Billy knew it. Unc' Billy was perfectly safe in promising to wait for him.

Down fell the egg squarely on Jimmy Skunk's head.

"You're a coward, just a plain no-account coward!" snapped Jimmy. "I'm not going to climb up there, but I'll tell you what I am going to do; I'm going to wait right down here until you come down, if it isn't until next year. Nobody can drop things on my head and not get paid back. I thought you were a friend, but now I know better."

"Wait as long as yo' please. Ah reckons Ah can stay as long as yo' can," retorted Unc' Billy, grinding and snapping his teeth.

"Suit yourself," retorted Jimmy. "I'm going to pay you up for that bump on my head or know the reason why."

And so they kept on quarreling and calling each other names, for the time being quite forgetting that they were where they had no business to be, either of them. It really was dreadful. And it was all because both had been sadly disappointed. They had found no eggs where they had been sure they would find plenty. You see, Farmer Brown's boy had gathered every egg when he shut the biddies up for the night. Did you ever notice what a bad thing for the temper disappointment often is?

CHAPTER NINETEEN: JIMMY SKUNK IS TRUE TO HIS WORD

UNC' BILLY POSSUM was having a bad night of it. When he had grown tired of quarreling with Jimmy Skunk, he had tried to take a nap. He had tried first one nest and then another, but none just suited him. This was partly because he wasn't sleepy. He was hungry and not at all sleepy. He wished with all his heart that he hadn't foolishly yielded to that fit of temper which had resulted in kicking that china nest-egg out of a nest and down on the head of Jimmy Skunk, making Jimmy so thoroughly angry.

Unc' Billy had no intention of going down while Jimmy was there. He thought that Jimmy would soon grow tired of waiting and go away. So for quite a while Unc' Billy didn't worry. But as it began to get towards morning he began to grow anxious. Unc' Billy had no desire to be found in that henhouse when Farmer Brown's boy came to feed the biddies.

Then, too, he was hungry. He had counted on a good meal of eggs, and not one had he found. Now he wanted to get out to look for something else to eat, but he couldn't without facing Jimmy Skunk, and it was better to go hungry than to do that. Yes, Sir, it was a great deal better to go hungry. Several times, when he thought Jimmy was asleep, he tried to steal down. He was just as careful not to make a sound as he could be, but every time Jimmy knew and was waiting for him. Unc' Billy wished that there was no such place as Farmer Brown's henhouse. He wished he had never thought of eggs. He wished many other foolish wishes, but most of all he wished that he hadn't lost his temper and kicked that egg down on Jimmy Skunk's head. When the first light stole in under the door and the biddies began to stir uneasily on their roosts Unc' Billy's anxiety would allow him to keep still no longer.

"Don' yo' think we-uns better make up and get out of here, Brer Skunk?" he ventured.

"I don't mind staying here; it's very comfortable," replied Jimmy, looking up at Unc' Billy in a way that made him most *uncomfortable*. It was plain to see that Jimmy hadn't forgiven him.

For some time Unc' Billy said no more, but he grew more and more restless. You see, he knew it would soon be time for Farmer Brown's boy to come to let the hens out and feed them. At last he ventured to speak again.

"Ah reckons yo' done forget something," said he.

"What is that?" asked Jimmy.

"Ah reckons yo' done fo'get that it's most time fo' Farmer Brown's boy to come, and it won't do fo' we-uns to be found in here," replied Unc' Billy.

"I'm not worrying about Farmer Brown's boy. He can come as soon as he pleases," retorted Jimmy Skunk, and grinned.

That sounded like boasting, but it wasn't. No, Sir, it wasn't, and Unc' Billy knew it. He knew that Jimmy meant it. Unc' Billy was in despair. He didn't dare stay, and he didn't dare go down and face Jimmy Skunk, and there he was. It certainly had been a bad night for Unc' Billy Possum.

CHAPTER TWENTY: FARMER BROWN'S BOY ARRIVES

THE LIGHT CREPT farther under the door of Farmer Brown's henhouse, and by this time the hens were all awake. Furthermore, they had discovered Jimmy Skunk down below and were making a great fuss. They were cackling so that Unc' Billy was sure Farmer Brown's boy would soon hear them and hurry out to find out what the noise was all about.

"If yo' would just get out of sight, Brer Skunk, Ah reckons those fool hens would keep quiet," Unc' Billy ventured.

"I don't mind their noise. It doesn't trouble me a bit," replied Jimmy Skunk, and grinned. It was plain enough to Unc' Billy that Jimmy was enjoying the situation.

But Unc' Billy wasn't. He was so anxious that he couldn't keep still. He paced back and forth along the shelf in front of the upper row of nests and tried to make up his mind whether it would be better to go down and face Jimmy Skunk or to try to hide under the hay in one of the nests, and all the time he kept listening and listening and listening for the footsteps of Farmer Brown's boy.

At last he heard them, and he knew by the sound that Farmer Brown's boy was coming in a hurry. He had heard the noise of the hens and was coming to find out what it was all about. Unc' Billy hoped that now Jimmy Skunk would retreat through the hole in the floor and give him a chance to escape.

"He's coming! Farmer Brown's boy is coming, Brer Skunk! Yo' better get away while yo' can!" whispered Unc' Billy.

"I hear him," replied Jimmy calmly. "I'm waiting for him to open the door for me to go out. It will be much easier than squeezing through that hole."

Unc' Billy gasped. He knew, of course, that it was Jimmy Skunk's boast that he feared no one, but it was hard to believe that Jimmy really intended to face Farmer Brown's boy right in his own henhouse where Jimmy had no business to be. He hoped that at last Jimmy's boldness would get him into trouble. Yes, he did. You see, that might give him a chance to slip away himself. Otherwise, he would be in a bad fix.

The latch on the door rattled. Unc' Billy crept into one of the nests, but frightened as he was, he couldn't keep from peeping over the edge to see what would happen. The door swung open, letting in a flood of light. The hens stopped their noise. Farmer Brown's boy stood in the doorway and looked in. Jimmy Skunk lifted his big plume of a tail just a bit higher than usual and calmly and without the least sign of being in a hurry walked straight towards the open door. Of course Farmer Brown's boy saw him at once.

"So it's you, you black and white rascal!" he exclaimed. "I suppose you expect me to step out of your way, and I suppose I will do just that very thing. You are the most impudent and independent fellow of my acquaintance. That's what you are. You didn't get any eggs, because I gathered all of them last night. And you didn't get a chicken because they were wise enough to stay on their roosts, so I don't know as I have any quarrel with you, and I'm sure I don't want any. Come along out of there, you rascal."

Farmer Brown's boy stepped aside, and Jimmy Skunk calmly and without the least sign of hurry or worry walked out, stopped for a drink at the pan of water in the henyard, walked through the henyard gate, and turned towards the stone wall along the edge of the Old Orchard.

CHAPTER TWENTY-ONE: THE NEST-EGG GIVES UNC' BILLY AWAY

> *'Tis little things that often seem*
> *Scarce worth a passing thought*
> *Which in the end may prove that they*
> *With big results are fraught.*

FARMER BROWN'S BOY watched Jimmy Skunk calmly and peacefully go his way and grinned as he watched him. He scratched his head thoughtfully. "I suppose," said he, "that that is as perfect an example of the value of preparedness as there is. Jimmy knew he was all ready for trouble if I chose to make it, and that because of that I wouldn't make it. So he has calmly gone his way as if he were as much bigger than I as I am bigger than he. There certainly is nothing like being prepared if you want to avoid trouble."

Then Farmer Brown's boy once more turned to the henhouse and entered it. He looked to make sure that no hen had been foolish enough to go to sleep where Jimmy could have caught her, and satisfied of this, he would have gone about his usual morning work of feeding the hens but for one thing. That one thing was the china nest-egg on the floor.

"Hello!" exclaimed Farmer Brown's boy when he saw it. "Now how did that come there? It must be that Jimmy Skunk pulled it out of one of those lower nests."

Now he knew just which nests had contained nest-eggs, and it didn't take but a minute to find that none was missing in any of the lower nests. "That's queer," he muttered. "That egg must have come from one of the upper nests. Jimmy couldn't have got up to those. None of the hens could have kicked it out last night, because they were all on the roosts when I shut them up. They certainly didn't do it this morning, because they wouldn't have dared leave the roosts with Jimmy Skunk here. I'll have to look into this."

So he began with the second row of nests and looked in each. Then he started on the upper row, and so he came to the nest in which Unc' Billy Possum was hiding under the hay and holding his breath. Now Unc' Billy had covered himself up pretty well with the hay, but he had forgotten one thing; he had forgotten his tail. Yes, Sir, Unc' Billy had forgotten his tail, and it hung just over the edge of the nest. Of course, Farmer Brown's boy saw it. He couldn't help but see it.

"Ho, ho!" he exclaimed right away. "Ho, ho! So there was more than one visitor here last night. This henhouse seems to be a very popular place. I see that the first thing for me to do after breakfast is to nail a board over that hole in the floor. So it was you, Unc' Billy Possum, who kicked that nest-egg out. Found it a little hard for your teeth, didn't you? Lost your temper and kicked it out, didn't you? That was foolish, Unc' Billy, very foolish indeed. Never lose your temper over trifles. It doesn't pay. Now I wonder what I'd better do with you."

All this time Unc' Billy hadn't moved. Of course, he couldn't understand what Farmer Brown's boy was saying. Nor could he see what Farmer Brown's boy was doing. So he held his breath and hoped and hoped that he hadn't been discovered. And perhaps he wouldn't have been but for that telltale nest-egg on the floor. That was the cause of all his troubles. First it had angered Jimmy Skunk because as you remember, it had fallen on Jimmy's head. Then it had led Farmer Brown's boy to look in all the nests. It had seemed a trifle, kicking that egg out of that nest, but see what the results were. Truly, little things often are not so little as they seem.

CHAPTER TWENTY-TWO: UNC' BILLY POSSUM'S OLD TRICK

THE FIRST KNOWLEDGE Unc' Billy Possum had that he was discovered came to him through his tail. Yes, Sir, it came to him through his tail. Farmer Brown's boy pinched it. It was rather a mean thing to do, but Farmer Brown's boy was curious. He wanted to see what Unc' Billy would do. And he didn't pinch very hard, not hard enough to really hurt. Farmer Brown's boy is too good-hearted to hurt anyone if he can help it.

Now any other of the Green Forest and Green Meadows people would promptly have pulled their tail away had they been in Unc' Billy's place. But Unc' Billy didn't. No, Sir, Unc' Billy didn't. That tail might have belonged to anyone but him so far as he made any sign. Of course, he felt like pulling it away. Anyone would have in his place. But he didn't move it the tiniest bit, which goes to show that Unc' Billy has great self-control when he wishes.

Farmer Brown's boy pinched again, just a little harder, but still Unc' Billy made no sign. Farmer Brown's boy chuckled and began to pull on that tail. He pulled and pulled until finally he had pulled Unc' Billy out of his hiding-place, and he swung by his tail from the hand of Farmer Brown's boy. There wasn't the least sign of life about Unc' Billy. He looked as if he were dead, and he acted as if he were dead. Anyone not knowing Unc' Billy would have supposed that he *was* dead.

Farmer Brown's boy dropped Unc' Billy on the floor. He lay just as he fell. Farmer Brown's boy rolled him over with his foot, but there wasn't a sign of life in Unc' Billy. He hoped that Farmer Brown's boy really did think him dead. That was what he wanted. Farmer Brown's boy picked him up again and laid him on a box, first putting a board over the hole in the floor and closing the henhouse door. Then he went about his work of cleaning out the henhouse and measuring out the grain for the biddies.

Unc' Billy lay there on the box, and he certainly was pathetic looking. A dead animal or bird is always pathetic looking, and none was ever more so than Unc' Billy Possum as he lay on that box. His hair was all rumpled up, as it usually is. It was filled with dust from the floor and bits of straw. His lips were drawn back and his mouth partly open. His eyes seemed to be closed. As a matter of fact, they were open just a teeny, weeny bit, just enough for Unc' Billy to watch Farmer Brown's boy. But to have looked at him you would have thought him as dead as the deadest thing that ever was.

As he went about his work Farmer Brown's boy kept an eye on Unc' Billy and chuckled. "You old fraud," said he. "You think you are fooling me, but I know you. Possums don't die of nothing in hens' nests. You certainly are a clever old rascal, and the best actor I've ever seen. I wonder how long you will keep it up. I wish I had half as much self-control."

When he had finished his work he picked Unc' Billy up by the tail once more, opened the door, and started for the house with Unc' Billy swinging from his hand and bumping against his legs. Still Unc' Billy gave no sign of life. He wondered where he was being taken to. He was terribly frightened. But he stuck to his old trick of playing dead which had served him so well more than once before.

CHAPTER TWENTY-THREE: UNC' BILLY GIVES HIMSELF AWAY

NEVER HAD UNC' BILLY POSSUM played that old trick of his better than he was playing it now. Farmer Brown's boy knew that Unc' Billy was only pretending to be dead, yet so well did Unc' Billy pretend that it was hard work for Farmer Brown's boy to believe what he knew was the truth—that Unc' Billy was very much alive and only waiting for a chance to slip away.

They were half-way from the henyard to the house when Bowser the Hound came to meet his master. "Now we shall see what we shall see," said Farmer Brown's boy, as Bowser came trotting up. "If Unc' Billy can stand this test, I'll take off my hat to him every time we meet hereafter." He held Unc' Billy out to Bowser, and Bowser sniffed him all over.

Just imagine that! Just think of being nosed and sniffed at by one of whom you were terribly afraid and not so much as twitching an ear! Farmer Brown's boy dropped Unc' Billy on the ground, and Bowser rolled him over and sniffed at him and then looked up at his master, as much as to say: "This fellow doesn't interest me. He's dead. He must be the fellow I saw go under the henhouse last night. How did you kill him?"

Farmer Brown's boy laughed and picked Unc' Billy up by the tail again. "He's fooled you all right, old fellow, and you don't know it," said he to Bowser, as the latter pranced on ahead to the house. The mother of Farmer Brown's boy was in the doorway, watching them approach.

"What have you got there?" she demanded. "I declare if it isn't a Possum! Where did you kill him? Was he the cause of all that racket among the chickens?"

Farmer Brown's boy took Unc' Billy into the kitchen and dropped him on a chair. Mrs. Brown came over to look at him closer. "Poor little fellow," said she. "Poor little fellow. It was too bad he got into mischief and had to be killed. I don't suppose he knew any better. Somehow it always seems wrong to me to kill these little creatures just because they get into mischief when all the time they don't know

Farmer Brown's Boy laughed and picked Unc' Billy up by the tail again.

that they are in mischief." She stroked Unc' Billy gently.

The eyes of Farmer Brown's boy twinkled. He went over to a corner and pulled a straw from his mother's broom. Then he returned to Unc' Billy and began to tickle Unc' Billy's nose. Mrs. Brown looked puzzled. She was puzzled.

"What are you doing that for?" she asked.

"Just for fun," replied Farmer Brown's boy and kept on tickling Unc' Billy's nose. Now Unc' Billy could stand having his tail pinched, and being carried head down, and being dropped on the ground, but this was too much for him; he wanted to sneeze. He had *got* to sneeze. He did sneeze. He couldn't help it, though it were to cost him his life.

"Land of love!" exclaimed Mrs. Brown, jumping back and clutching her skirts in both hands as if she expected Unc' Billy would try to take refuge behind them. "Do you mean to say that that Possum is alive?"

"Seems that way," replied Farmer Brown's boy as Unc' Billy sneezed again, for that straw was still tickling his nose. "I should certainly say it seems that way. The old sinner is no more dead than I am. He's just pretending. He fooled you all right, Mother, but he didn't fool me. I haven't hurt a hair of him. You ought to know me well enough by this time to know that I wouldn't hurt him."

He looked at his mother reproachfully, and she hastened to apologize. "But what could I think?" she demanded. "If he isn't a dead-looking creature, I never have seen one. What are you going to do with him, son?"

"Take him over to the Green Forest after breakfast and let him go," replied Farmer Brown's boy.

This is just what he did do, and Unc' Billy wasted no time in getting home. It was a long time before he met Jimmy Skunk again. When he did, Jimmy was his usual good-natured self, and Unc' Billy was wise enough not to refer to eggs. So we will leave them once more the best of friends, and I will tell you next of the adventures of that dear little friend of ours, Bob White.

The Adventures of Bob White

CHAPTER ONE: A CHEERFUL WORKER

A cheery whistle or a song
Will help the daily work along.

THE LITTLE FEATHERED people of the Green Meadows, the Green Forest and the Old Orchard learned this long ago, and it is one reason why you will so often find them singing with all their might when they are hard at work building their homes in the spring. Most of them sing, but there is one who whistles, and it is such a clear and cheery whistle that it gladdens the hearts of all who hear it. Many and many a time has Farmer Brown's boy stopped to whistle back, and never has he failed to get a response.

A handsome little fellow is this whistler. He is dressed in brown, white and black, and his name is Bob White. Sometimes he is called a Quail and sometimes a Partridge, but if you should ask him he would tell you promptly and clearly that he is Bob White, and he answers to no other name. All the other little people know and love him well, most of them for the cheery sound of his whistle; but a few, like Reddy Fox and Redtail the Hawk, for the good meal he will make them if only they are smart enough to catch him.

Farmer Brown's boy loves him, not only for his cheerful whistle, but because he has found out that Bob White is a worker as well as a whistler, one of the best workers and greatest helpers on the farm. You see, a part of the work of Farmer Brown's boy is to keep down the weeds and destroy the insects that eat up the crops. Now weeds spring up from seeds. If there were no weed-seeds there would be no weeds. In the same way, if there were no insect-eggs there would be no insects. But there are millions and millions of both, and so all summer long Farmer Brown's boy has to fight the weeds and the insects. He is very thankful for any help he may get, and this is one reason he has become so fond of Old Mr. Toad, who helps him keep the garden clear of worms and bugs, and of Tommy Tit the Chickadee and others of the little feathered people who live in the Old Orchard and hunt bugs and their eggs among the apple trees. You know the surest way of winning friends is to help others.

Bob White not only catches worms and bugs, but eats the seeds of weeds, scratching them out where they have hidden in the ground, and filling his little crop with them until he just has to fly to the nearest fence and tell all the world how happy he is to be alive and have a part in the work of the Great World. Not one of all the little people is of greater help to Farmer Brown's boy than Bob White. All the long day he works, and with him works Mrs. Bob and all the little Bobs, scratching up weed-seeds here, picking off bugs there, all the time so happy and cheerful that everybody in the neighborhood is happy and cheerful too. The best of it is Bob White is always just that way. You would think he never had a thing in the world to worry about. But he does have. Yes, indeed! Bob White has plenty to worry about, as you shall hear, but he never allows his troubles to interfere with his cheerfulness if he can help it.

"Bob White! Bob White!" with all his might
He whistles loud and clear.
Because no shame e'er hurt his name
He wants that all shall hear.

One day Peter Rabbit sat listening to it, and it reminded him that he hadn't called on Bob White for some time, and also that there were some things about Bob White that he didn't know. He decided that he would go at once to call on Bob and try to satisfy his curiosity. So off he started, lipperty-lipperty-lip.

CHAPTER TWO: BOB WHITE HAS VISITORS

"Bob White! Bob White! I bid the world good cheer!
Bob White! Bob White! I whistle loud and clear!"

THAT VERY SAME morning Bob White had taken it into his head to come over to live not very far from the dear Old Briar-patch where Peter Rabbit lives. Of course, Peter didn't know that Bob had come over there to live. For that matter, I doubt if Bob White knew it himself. He just happened over that way and liked it, and so finally he made up his mind to look about there for a place to make his home.

Now Peter Rabbit had known Bob White for a long time. Peter, in his roaming about, had met Bob a number of times, and they had passed the time of day. Whenever Peter had heard Bob whistling within a reasonable distance he had made it a point to call on him. Bob is such a cheery fellow that somehow Peter always felt better for just a word or two with him. So when Bob began to whistle that spring morning Peter hurried over, lipperty-lipperty-lip, to call. He didn't have far to go, for Bob was sitting on a fence-post just a little way from the dear Old Briar-patch.

"Good morning," said Peter. "You seem to be very cheerful this morning."

"Why not?" replied Bob White. "I'm always cheerful. It's the only way to get along in this world."

"It must be that you don't have much to worry about," retorted Peter. "Now if you had to run for your life as often as I have to, perhaps you wouldn't find it so easy to be always cheerful."

Bob White's bright little eyes twinkled. "The trouble with a lot of people is that they think that no one has worries but themselves," said he. "Now there is Reddy Fox coming this way. What do you suppose he is coming for?"

"For me!" exclaimed Peter promptly, preparing to scamper back to the Old Briar-patch.

"Nothing of the kind," replied Bob White. "Don't think you are so important, Peter. He doesn't know you are over here at all. He has heard me whistling, and he's coming to see if he can't give me a little surprise. It's me and not you he is after. What's your hurry, Peter?"

"I—I think I'd better be going; I'll call again when you haven't other visitors," shouted Peter over his shoulder.

Hardly had Peter reached the dear Old Briar-patch when Reddy Fox reached the fence where Bob White was sitting. "Good morning," said he, trying to make his voice sound as pleasant as he could, "I'm glad to see you over here. I heard you whistling and hurried over here to welcome you. I hope you will like it here so well that you will make your home here."

"Hello! Here comes Old Man Coyote."

"That is very nice of you," replied Bob White, his eyes twinkling more than ever, for he knew why Reddy hoped he would make his home there. He knew that Reddy hoped to find that home and make a good dinner on Quail some day. "It is very pleasant over here, and I don't know but I will stay. Everybody seems very neighborly. Peter Rabbit has just called."

Reddy looked about him in a very sly way but with a hungry look in his eyes as he said, "Peter always is neighborly. Is he anywhere about now? I should like to pay my respects to him."

"No," replied Bob White. "Peter left in something of a hurry. Hello! Here comes Old Man Coyote. People certainly *are* neighborly here. Why, what's your hurry, Reddy?"

"I have some important matters to attend to over in the Green Forest," replied Reddy, with a hasty glance in the direction of Old Man Coyote. "I hope I'll see you often, Bob White."

"I hope so," replied Bob White politely, and then added under his breath, "but I hope I see you first."

CHAPTER THREE: BOB DECIDES TO BUILD A HOME

OLD MAN COYOTE'S call was very much like that of Reddy Fox. He was very, very pleasant and told Bob White that he was very glad indeed that Bob had come over on the Green Meadows, and he hoped that he would stay. No one could have been more polite than was Old Man Coyote. Bob White was just as polite, but he wasn't fooled. No, indeed. He knew that, just like Reddy Fox, the reason Old Man Coyote was so glad to see him was because he hoped to catch him some fine day. But Bob White didn't let a little thing like that bother him. Ever since he could remember he had been hunted. That was why he had taken the precaution to sit on a fence-post when he whistled. Up there neither Old Man Coyote nor Reddy Fox could reach him. Just after Old Man Coyote left Bob White saw someone else headed his way, and this time he didn't wait. You see it was Redtail the Hawk, and a fence-post was no place to receive a call from him.

Spreading his wings Bob White flew across to the dear Old Briar-patch and dropped in among the brambles close to where Peter Rabbit was sitting. "You did-n't expect me to return your call so soon, did you, Peter?" said he.

"No," replied Peter, "but I'm ever so glad to see you just the same. Did you have a pleasant call from Reddy Fox?"

"Very," replied Bob White with a chuckle. "He was ever so glad to see me. So was Old Man Coyote. I didn't wait to see what Old Redtail would say, but I have a feeling that he would have liked better to have seen me a little nearer. You see,

Peter, you are not the only one who has to keep his eyes open and his wits about him all the time. There are just as many looking for me as for you, but I don't allow that to make me any the less cheerful. Every time I whistle I know that someone is going to come looking for me, but I whistle just the same. I just have to, because in spite of all its troubles life is worth living and full of happiness. Now I've got a secret to tell you."

"What is it?" asked Peter eagerly.

"Promise not to tell a single soul," commanded Bob White.

"Can't I tell Mrs. Peter? I never keep secrets from her you know," replied Peter.

"Well, you may tell her, but she must promise to keep it secret," said Bob.

"I'll promise for her and for myself," declared Peter. "What is it?"

"I've decided to come over here to live," replied Bob White.

"Right here in the Old Briar-patch?" asked Peter excitedly.

"No, but not far from here," replied Bob White. "I'm going back to the Old Pasture after Mrs. Bob, and we are going to build a home right away."

"Goody!" cried Peter, clapping his hands. "Where are you going to build?"

"That," replied Bob White, "is for Mrs. Bob to decide."

"And when she does you'll tell me where it is so that I can come over and call, won't you?" cried Peter.

"That depends," replied Bob White. "You know there are some things it is better not to know."

"No, I don't know," retorted Peter. "I'm your friend, and I don't see what harm it could do for me to know where your home is."

"Without meaning to friends sometimes do the most harm of anyone, especially if they talk too much," replied Bob White. "Now the way is clear and I must hurry back to the Old Pasture to tell Mrs. Bob how nice it is here." And with this away he flew.

"Now what did he mean by friends who talk too much," muttered Peter. "Could he have meant me?"

CHAPTER FOUR: BOB WHITE AND PETER BECOME NEIGHBORS

Who strictly minds his own affairs
And cheerfully doth labor,
He is the one whom I would choose
Always to be my neighbor.

THAT IS JUST the kind of a neighbor Peter Rabbit found Bob White to be. Bob and Mrs. Bob had come down from the Old Pasture and built their home near the dear Old Briar-patch and so become the neighbors of Peter and little Mrs. Peter. Bob was very neighborly. He often dropped in to have a chat with Peter, and Peter was always glad to see him, for he is such a cheerful fellow that Peter always felt better for having him about. It always is that way with cheerful people. They are just like sunshine.

But though Bob and Mrs. Bob had built their home near Peter, he didn't know just where it was. No, Sir, Peter didn't know just where that home of the Bob Whites was. It wasn't because he didn't try to find out. Oh, my, no! Peter could no more have helped trying to find out than he could have helped breathing. That was the curiosity in him. He wasted a great deal of time trying to find Bob White's home, all to no purpose. At first he was rather put out because Bob White wouldn't tell him where it was hidden. But Bob just smiled and told Peter that the reason he wouldn't was because he thought a great deal of Peter and wanted him for a friend always.

"Then," said Peter, "I should think you would tell me where your home is. There ought not to be secrets between friends. I don't think much of a friendship that cannot be trusted."

"How would you feel, Peter, if harm came to me and my family through you?" asked Bob White.

"Dreadfully," declared Peter. "But do you suppose I would let any harm come to you? A nice kind of a friend you must think me!"

"No," replied Bob White soberly, "I don't think you would let any harm come to us if you knew it. But you've lived long enough, Peter, to know that there are eyes and ears and noses watching, listening, smelling everywhere all the time. Now supposing that when you were sure that nobody saw you, somebody *did* see you visit my house. Or supposing Reddy Fox just happened to run across your tracks and followed them to my house. It wouldn't be your fault if something dreadful happened to us, yet you would be the cause of it. You remember what I told you the other day, that there are some things it is better not to know."

Peter looked very thoughtful and pulled his whiskers while he turned this over in his mind. "That is a new idea to me," said he at last. "I never had thought of it before. I certainly never would be able to forgive myself if anything happened to you because of me."

"Of course you wouldn't," replied Bob White. "No more would I ever be able to forgive myself if anything happened to my family because I had told someone where my home is."

Peter nodded. "Of course if I should just happen to *find* your home all by myself, you wouldn't be angry, would you?" he asked.

Bob White laughed. "Of course not," said he. "Just the same I would advise you not to *try* to find it. Then you will have nothing to trouble your mind if you should be followed, and something dreadful did happen to me or mine. You see there are just as many who would like to make a dinner of me as there are who would like to make a dinner of you, and I would a whole lot rather sit on a fence-post and whistle than to fill somebody's stomach."

"And I would a lot rather have you," declared Peter.

CHAPTER FIVE: OTHERS ARE INTERESTED IN BOB WHITE

PETER RABBIT WASN'T the only one who was interested in Bob White and in Bob's hidden home. Oh, my, no! It seemed to Peter that Reddy and Granny Fox were prowling around the dear Old Briar-patch most of the time. At first he didn't understand it. "It isn't me they are after, because they know well enough that they can't catch me here," said he to himself, as he watched them one morning. "It isn't Danny Meadow Mouse, because Danny hasn't been over this way for a

long time. I don't see how it can be Bob White, because he isn't likely to stay on the ground while they are around, and they can't catch him unless he is on the ground."

He was so busy trying to puzzle out what should bring Reddy and Granny that way so often that he neither saw nor heard Jimmy Skunk steal up behind him. "Boo!" said Jimmy, and Peter nearly jumped out of his skin.

"What did you do that for?" demanded Peter indignantly.

"Just to teach you that you shouldn't go to sleep without keeping your ears open," replied Jimmy with a grin.

"I wasn't asleep!" protested Peter crossly. "I was just watch-

"Boo!" said Jimmy, and Peter nearly jumped out of his skin.

ing Reddy and Granny Fox and wondering what brings them over here so much."

"You might just as well have been asleep," replied Jimmy. "Supposing I had been my cousin, Shadow the Weasel."

Peter shivered at the very thought. Jimmy continued: "You are old enough to know, Peter, that it isn't safe to be so interested in one thing that you forget to watch out for other things. As for Reddy and Granny Fox, you ought to know what brings them over this way so much."

"What?" demanded Peter.

"Hasn't Bob White got a nest somewhere around here?" asked Jimmy by way of answer.

"Y-e-s," replied Peter slowly, "I suppose he has. But what of that?"

"Why, Reddy and Granny are looking for it, stupid," replied Jimmy.

Peter stared at Jimmy a minute in a puzzled way. "What do they want of that?" he asked finally. "They don't eat eggs, do they?"

"Eggs hatch out into little birds, don't they?" demanded Jimmy. "If Reddy and Granny can find that nest, they'll wait until the eggs have hatched into birds and then, well, I've heard say that there is nothing more delicious than young Quail. Now do you see?"

Peter did. Of course he did. He understood perfectly. Reddy and Granny had heard Bob White whistling over there every day, and they knew that meant that his home wasn't far away. It was all very plain now.

"By the way, you don't happen to know where that nest is, do you?" asked Jimmy carelessly.

"No, I don't!" exclaimed Peter, and suddenly was glad that he didn't know about that nest. "What do you want to know for?" he demanded suspiciously.

"I'm hungry for some eggs," confessed Jimmy frankly.

"You wouldn't rob Mr. and Mrs. Bob White of their eggs, would you?" cried Peter. "I thought better of you than that, Jimmy Skunk."

Jimmy grinned. "Don't get excited, Peter," said he. "I'm told that Mrs. Bob lays a great many eggs, and if that's the case, she wouldn't miss a few."

"Jimmy Skunk, you're horrid, so there!" declared Peter.

"Don't blame me," retorted Jimmy. "Old Mother Nature gave me a taste for eggs, just as she gave Reddy Fox a taste for Rabbit. You haven't any idea where that nest is, have you?"

"No, I haven't! If I had, I wouldn't tell you," declared Peter.

"Well, so long," replied Jimmy good-naturedly. "I think I'll have a look for it. I don't wish Bob White and his wife the least bit of harm, but I would like two or three of those eggs." And with this Jimmy Skunk ambled out to look for Bob White's nest.

CHAPTER SIX: THE CUNNING OF MR. AND MRS. BOB WHITE

WHEN BOB WHITE brought Mrs. Bob down to the Green Meadows from the Old Pasture in the beautiful springtime, she was as delighted as he had hoped she would be. Very wisely he had not even hinted that he thought there was the place of all places for them to build their home. He knew that she would never be satisfied unless she felt that she was the one who had chosen the place for their home. So Bob didn't so much as hint that he had a home in mind. He didn't even tell her how beautiful it was over on the Green Meadows near the dear Old Briar-patch. He let her find it out for herself.

Now little Mrs. Bob was very anxious to get to housekeeping, and no sooner did she reach the Green Meadows than she made up her mind that here was the place of all places for a home. In the first place it was very beautiful, and Mrs. Bob has an eye for beauty. In the second place there was plenty to eat, one of the most important things to consider when you are likely to have a great many little mouths to feed. In the third place there were plenty of good hiding places, and lastly, Mrs. Bob liked the neighbors.

Bob White took care not to let her see that he was tickled. He gravely pointed out to her the fact that Granny and Reddy Fox, Old Man Coyote and Redtail the Hawk would soon discover that they were living there, and then there would be danger all the time and they would never know what it was to be free from worry.

"Not a bit more than in the Old Pasture where we built last year," snapped Mrs. Bob. "You know as well as I do that wherever we build we will be in danger. It always has been so, and I guess it always will be so. We've been smart enough to fool our enemies before, and I guess we can do it again. I'm not afraid if you are."

Bob hastened to say that he wasn't afraid. He wouldn't have her think that for the world. Oh, my, no! He was just pointing out the dangers so that they might make no mistake.

Mrs. Bob didn't half hear what he was saying. She was too busy poking about, running here, running there, and all the time using her sharp little eyes for all they were worth. Bob waited patiently, a twinkle in his own eyes. He knew that when Mrs. Bob made up her mind that was all there was to it. Presently she called to him in a low voice, and he flew over to join her.

"Here," she announced, "is where we will build."

Bob looked the ground over with a critical eye. "Don't you think, my dear, that this is rather close to the Crooked Little Path?" he asked. "I have noticed that Reddy Fox and Jimmy Skunk use this path a great deal, not to mention Farmer Brown's boy."

"That's what makes it the safest place on the Green Meadows, stupid," declared little Mrs. Bob. "They will never think to look for our home so close to where they pass. These weeds are very thick and will hide our nest completely. This old fallen fence-post will give splendid protection on one side. The Old Briar-patch is so near that in case of need we can get to it in a hurry and there be perfectly safe. You mark my words, Bob White, no one will think of looking here for our nest if you use your common sense and do all your whistling far enough away. Reddy and the others are going to do all their hunting around the place you do your whistling, so it is for you to make this the very safest place in the world. Do you see?"

"Yes, my dear," replied Bob meekly. "You are very clever and cunning. I never should have thought of choosing such a place, but I guess you are quite right."

"I know I am," retorted Mrs. Bob. "Now you fly over to the other side of the Old Briar-patch and whistle while I get busy here. I am anxious to get to work at once."

Bob looked at his little brown wife with admiration. Then he discreetly ran under cover of the weeds and grass until he thought it was safe to take wing, after which he flew to the other side of the dear Old Briar-patch and there began to whistle as only he can.

CHAPTER SEVEN: BOB WHITE FINDS THAT MRS. BOB IS RIGHT

A quarrel you may often stay, by letting others have their way.

AND YOU WILL find, too, that other people are quite as likely to be right as you are. Now while Bob White told Mrs. Bob that he guessed she was right in choosing the place she did for their home he was not at all sure of it in his own mind. It wasn't a place he would have chosen if the matter had been left to him. No, Sir, that place wouldn't have been his choice. He knew of at least half a dozen places which he thought much better and safer. But, after all, this was to be Mrs. Bob's home even more than his, for she was the one who would have to stay there all the long days sitting on those beautiful white eggs they hoped to have soon.

So Bob kept his opinions to himself, and if he worried a little because the new home was so close to the Crooked Little Path along which Reddy and Granny Fox went so often, he said nothing and brought his share of grasses, straw and leaves with which to build the nest. Mrs. Bob was very particular about that nest. Just a common open nest wouldn't do. Perhaps in that wise little head of hers she guessed just what was going on in Bob's mind and how he really didn't approve at all of building there. So she made a very clever little roof or dome of grasses and straw over the nest with a little entrance on one side. When it was all done only the very sharpest eyes ever would discover it.

Of course Bob was proud of it, very proud indeed. "My dear, it's the finest nest I've ever seen," he declared. "I hope, I do hope no one will find it."

Mrs. Bob looked at him sharply. "Why don't you own up that you wish it was somewhere else?" she demanded.

Bob looked a little foolish. "I can't quite get over the idea that this is a very dangerous place," he confessed. "But I've great faith in your judgment, my dear," he hastened to add.

"Then see to it that you are careful when you come over this way and never under any circumstances fly directly here," retorted Mrs. Bob. "Keep away unless I call for you, and when you do come fly over in the long grass back there and then keep out of sight and walk over here under cover of the grass and weeds."

Bob promised he would do just as she had told him to, and to prove it he stole away through the long grass and did not take wing until he was far from the nest. Then he flew over beyond the dear Old Briar-patch and whistled with all his might from sheer happiness.

It wasn't long before there were fifteen beautiful white eggs in the nest in the weeds beside the Crooked Little Path, and then Bob's anxiety increased, you may be sure. Time and time again he saw Reddy Fox or Granny Fox or Jimmy Skunk trot down the Crooked Little Path and he knew that they were coming to look for his nest. But never once did they think of looking in that patch of weeds, for it never entered their heads that anyone would build so close to a path they used so much. But they hunted and hunted everywhere else.

And all the time little Mrs. Bob sat on those white eggs and the color of her cloak was so nearly the color of the brown grasses and leaves that even if they had looked straight at her it isn't at all likely that they would have seen her. Little by little Bob confessed to himself that Mrs. Bob was right. She had chosen the very safest place on the Green Meadows for their home. It was safest because it was the last place anyone would look for it. Then Bob grew less anxious and spent all his spare time in fooling those who were looking for his home.

CHAPTER EIGHT: BOB FOOLS HIS NEIGHBORS

"All's fair in love and war," 'tis said.
Of course this isn't true.
A lot is done that's most unfair
And no one ought to do.

IT IS ALWAYS so when hate rules, and the queer thing is it is also true sometimes when love rules. Love quite often does unfair things and then tries to excuse them.

But Bob White didn't feel that there was anything unfair in trying to fool his neighbors. Not a bit of it. You see, he was doing it for love and war both. He was doing it for love of shy little Mrs. Bob and their home, and for the kind of war that is always going on in the Green Forest and the Green Meadows. Of course, the little people who live there don't call it war, but you know how it is—the big people all the time trying to catch those smaller than themselves, and the little people all the time trying to get the best of the big people.

So Bob White felt that it was perfectly fair and right that he should fool those of his neighbors who were hunting for his home, and so it was. He would sit on a fence-post whistling as only he can whistle, and telling all the world that he, Bob White, was there. Presently he would see Reddy Fox trotting down the Crooked Little Path and pretending that he was just out for a stroll and not at all interested in Bob or his affairs. Then Bob would pretend to look all around as if to see that no danger was near. After that he would fly over to a certain place which looked to be just the kind of a place for a nest, and there he would hide in the grass.

Just as soon as he disappeared, Reddy Fox would grin in that sly way of his and say to himself, "So that's where your nest is! I think I'll have a look over there."

Then he would steal over to where he had seen Bob disappear and poke his sharp nose into every bunch of grass and peek under every little bush. Bob would wait until he heard those soft footsteps very near him, then he would fly up with a great noise of his swift little wings as if he were terribly frightened, and from a distant fence-post he would call in the most anxious sounding voice. Reddy would be sure then that he was near the nest and would hunt and hunt. All the time little Mrs. Bob would be sitting comfortably on those precious eggs in the nest in the weed-patch close beside the Crooked Little Path, chuckling to herself as she listened to Bob's voice. You see, she knew just what he was doing.

It was the same way with Jimmy Skunk and Granny Fox and even Peter Rabbit. All of them hunted and hunted for that nest and watched Bob White and were sure that they knew just where to look for his home, and afterward wondered why it was that they couldn't find it. Jimmy Skunk wanted some of those eggs. Reddy and Granny Fox wanted to catch Mrs. Bob or be ready to gobble up the babies when they should hatch out of those beautiful white eggs. As for Peter Rabbit, he wanted to know where that nest was just out of curiosity. He wouldn't have harmed Mrs. Bob or one of those eggs for the world. But Bob knew that if Peter knew where that nest was he might visit it when someone was watching him, and something dreadful might happen as a result. So he thought it best to fool Peter just as he did the others, and I think it was. Don't you?

CHAPTER NINE: PETER HAS HARD
WORK BELIEVING HIS OWN EYES

When with your eyes you see a thing
Yet can't believe it so,
Pray tell me what you can believe.
I'd really like to know.

THINGS ARE THAT way sometimes. They are so surprising that it doesn't seem that they can be true. Just ask Peter Rabbit, or little Mrs. Peter. Either one will tell you that they have had hard work to believe what their eyes saw. You see, it was this way: Peter knew that somewhere near the dear Old Briar-patch was the home of Bob White. Anyway Bob had said that it was near there, and he himself was never very far away. So Peter didn't doubt that Bob had told him the truth. No one would stay around one place day after day in the beautiful springtime, when everybody was busy housekeeping, unless his home was very near.

But Peter had looked and looked for that home of Bob White's without ever getting so much as a glimpse of it. He had watched Bob White and had visited every place that he saw Bob go to, but Bob had managed to keep his secret and Peter was no wiser than before, though he was thinner from running about so much. Little Mrs. Peter had tried her best to make him see that it was no business of his. You see, she knew just how Mrs. Bob felt about wanting her home a secret, for little Mrs. Peter had had many anxious hours when her own babies were very small.

Finally Peter did give up, but it was because he had looked in every place he could think of and at last had made up his mind that if Bob White really had a nest in the Green Meadows it certainly wasn't near the dear Old Briar-patch. Then one morning a surprising thing happened. Peter was just getting ready to run over to the Laughing Brook when someone right in front of him there in the Old Briar-patch exclaimed:

"Be careful where you step, Peter Rabbit!"

Peter stopped short and looked to see who had spoken. There, under a tangle of brambles, was little Mrs. Bob White. Peter was surprised, for he had not seen her enter the dear Old Briar-patch.

"Oh!" said he. Then he bowed politely. "How do you do, Mrs. Bob White? I'm glad you've decided to make us a call. I hope Bob is very well. I haven't seen him for several days, but I've heard his whistle and it sounds as if he were feeling very fine."

"He is," replied little Mrs. Bob. Then she added anxiously, "Do please be very

*"Oh, Mrs. Peter, do, do be careful
where* you *step!" she cried.*

careful where you step, Peter."

"Why? What's the matter?" asked Peter, looking down at his feet in a puzzled way.

Just then Mrs. Peter, who had heard them talking, came hurrying up. Mrs. Bob White became more anxious than ever. "Oh, Mrs. Peter, do, do be careful where *you* step!" she cried.

Mrs. Peter looked as puzzled as Peter did. Just then little Mrs. Bob uttered the softest, sweetest little call, and all at once it seemed to Peter and Mrs. Peter as if the brown leaves which carpeted the dear Old Briar-patch suddenly came to life and started to run. Peter's eyes almost popped out of his head, and he rubbed them twice to make sure that he really saw what he thought he saw. What was it? Why, a whole family of the funniest little birds scurrying as fast as their small legs could take them to the shelter of Mrs. Bob's wings!

CHAPTER TEN: NEW TENANTS FOR THE BRIAR-PATCH

*Who proves himself a neighbor kind
Will find content and peace of mind.*

"ONE, TWO, THREE, four—oh, dear, they run so fast I can't count them! Aren't they darlings? I'm so glad you brought them over for us to see, Mrs. Bob. How many are there?" cried little Mrs. Peter, as she and Peter watched the tiny little babies of Bob White scamper to the shelter of their mother's wings under the friendly brambles of the dear Old Briar-patch.

"There are fifteen," replied Mrs. Bob White proudly.

"My gracious, what a family!" exclaimed Peter. "I don't see how you keep track of all of them. I should think you would be worried to death."

"They are a great care," confessed little Mrs. Bob White. "That is why I have brought them over to the Old Briar-patch. I hope you and Mrs. Peter will not mind if we live here for a while. Until they can fly it is the safest place I know of."

"We'll be tickled to death to have you here," declared Peter. "We don't own the dear Old Briar-patch, though we've lived here so long we almost feel as if it belongs to us. But of course anyone who wants to is free to live here. I don't know of anyone we would rather have here than you and your family. By the way, I don't see how you could travel far with such little babies. May I ask where you came from?"

Little Mrs. Bob's eyes twinkled. "Certainly," she replied. "We haven't traveled far. We came straight from our home here."

"But where was your home?" Peter asked the question eagerly, for you remember he had spent a great deal of time trying to find that home of the Bob Whites.

"Just over yonder in that little patch of weeds across the Crooked Little Path. You see it was very handy to the Old Briar-patch," replied Mrs. Bob.

"What?" Peter fairly shouted. "Do you mean to say that you have been living so near as all that?"

Mrs. Bob nodded. "I surely have," she replied. "I've been right where I could see you every day as I sat on my eggs."

"But how did you dare build in such a dangerous place? Why, Reddy and Granny Fox passed within a few feet of you every day! I never heard of such a crazy thing!" Peter looked as if he didn't believe it even yet.

"It was the safest place on the Green Meadows," retorted Mrs. Bob. "I should think that by this time you would have learned, Peter Rabbit, that the safest place to hide is the place where no one will look. The proof of it is right here in these babies of mine. Aren't they darlings? I sat there day after day and watched you and Reddy and Granny Fox and Jimmy Skunk hunting for me and had many a good laugh all to myself. I knew that not one of you would dream that I would be so foolishly wise as to build my home where it could be so easily found, and therefore you wouldn't look for it there. And I was right."

Mrs. Peter chuckled. "You were just right, Mrs. Bob," she declared. "It is the smartest thing I ever heard of, my dear. If Peter doesn't feel foolish, he ought to. I told him that it was none of his business where your home was, but he was so curious that he would keep hunting for it. And to think that all the time it was close by! Don't you feel foolish, Peter?"

"Yes, my dear, I certainly do," replied Peter meekly. "But now that I know where it was I am satisfied. And I'm glad that Mrs. Bob has brought her family to live in the dear Old Briar-patch. I think it will be great fun watching those youngsters grow, and I can't help thinking that this is a great deal safer for them than the home they have just left."

"That's why I've brought them here," replied Mrs. Bob. "As long as they were only eggs that was the safest place, but now that they have hatched out and can run about, they wouldn't be safe a minute over there. As it is, I expect it won't be long before they will be wanting to get out in the Great World and then my worries will really begin. Bringing up a large family is a great responsibility."

"It is so," declared Mrs. Peter.

CHAPTER ELEVEN: WATCH YOUR STEP!

Watch your step! Be sure you know
Exactly what lies just before,
Because if you should careless be
'Tis certain you would step no more.

IT WASN'T THAT way with Peter Rabbit. He wasn't afraid that if he didn't watch out he would step no more, not in the Old Briar-patch anyway, but he was afraid, dreadfully afraid, that one of Bob White's babies might step no more. It seemed to Peter that they were always just under foot. It made him nervous. Every time he moved little Mrs. Bob or Mrs. Peter was sure to cry, "Watch your step, Peter!" or "Don't step on one of those darlings!"

So every time he moved Peter looked sharply to see that there wasn't a tiny brown bird hiding under a brown leaf. You know he wouldn't have stepped on one of them for the world. Really there wasn't half as much danger as their fond mother seemed to think, for little as they were those Bob White babies were very spry, and very smart too. But you know how it is with mothers; they seem to be always expecting something dreadful will happen to their babies. So twenty times a day Peter would hear that warning, "Watch your step!"

Still, in spite of this, he was glad that the Bob White family had moved over to the dear Old Briar-patch. It gave him a chance to learn more about the ways of Bob White and his children than he could possibly have learned in any other way. You know, Peter is always anxious to learn, especially about other people. It seemed to him that never had he seen babies grow as did the little Bob Whites. They were everywhere. There were fifteen of them, and Peter often wondered how under the sun their mother kept track of all of them. But she did. One thing he noticed, and this was that they obeyed promptly whenever she called to them. If Redtail the Hawk came sailing lazily over the old Briar-patch, watching with sharp eyes to see if anything was going on down there that he didn't know about, little Mrs. Bob would give a warning, and every one of those youngsters would squat down right where he happened to be and not move until she told him he might. So old Redtail never once suspected that the Bob White family was there. When Mrs. Bob called them to her, they came running on the instant. Such obedience was beautiful to see.

Then, when they were all nestled under her wings, she would tell them about the Great World and all the dangers that they would have to watch out for when they were big enough to go out into it, and how each one was to be met. As they ran this way and that way in the Old Briar-patch, they picked up tiny seeds. Peter had not supposed that there were so many seeds as those little Bob Whites found. You know Peter does not eat tiny seeds, and so he never had noticed them before. Mrs. Bob led them about, showing them what seeds were best and what to leave alone. They didn't have to be shown but once. Often they varied their fare by picking tiny insects from the low-hanging leaves, and once in a while there would be a struggle between two or more for possession of a worm. Peter always liked to watch this. It was very funny.

In a few days there were no bugs or worms to be found in the Old Briar-patch, at least not on or near the ground. The Bob White family had eaten every one.

"I wish they would live here all the time," declared Mrs. Peter. "I don't like bugs and worms. They give me a crawly feeling every time I see them."

But a growing family must have plenty to eat, and at the end of a week Mrs. Bob led her youngsters forth to hunt bugs and worms and seeds on the Green Meadows, but never very far from the Old Briar-patch, so that in case of need they could run back to its friendly shelter. And every night she brought them back there to sleep under the friendly brambles. So after all, it was only for a little while that Peter had to watch his steps, and he was really sorry when he no longer heard that warning every time he moved. You see, he had grown very fond of the little Bob Whites.

CHAPTER TWELVE: THE LITTLE BOB WHITES AT SCHOOL

Everybody goes to school;
That's the universal rule.
Mother Nature long ago
Said it always should be so.

OF COURSE THERE are all kinds of schools, but to one kind or another everybody has to go. A lot of people don't know they are going to school, but they are, just the same. If you should ask them what school they go to, they would tell you they don't go to any. But they do just the same. They go to the hardest school of all, the school of experience. That is the school in which we all learn how to live and take care of ourselves. It is just the same with the little meadow and forest people. The four babies of Johnny and Polly Chuck went to school in the Old Orchard just as soon as they were big enough to run around. It was the same way with the children of Peter Rabbit in the dear Old Briar-patch and the youngsters of Danny and Nanny Meadow Mouse on the Green Meadows and Unc' Billy Possum's lively family in the Green Forest and little Joe Otter's two hopefuls in the Laughing Brook. So of course all the little Bob Whites started in to go to school almost as soon as they were out of their shells.

The very first thing they learned was to mind their parents, which is the very first lesson all little folks must learn. "You see, my dears," explained Mrs. Bob, as they nestled under her wings, "the Great World is full of dangers, especially for little Bob Whites, and so if you want to live to grow up to be as handsome and smart as your father, you must mind instantly when we speak to you."

So as every one of the fifteen little Bob Whites wanted to live to grow up to be as handsome and smart as their father, each one took the greatest care to mind the very second Bob or Mrs. Bob spoke. While they were in the dear Old Briar-patch they were quite safe, but just the same every little while Mrs. Bob would give the danger signal, which meant to squat and keep perfectly still, or another call that meant to come running to her as fast as ever they could. It wasn't until she was sure that they had learned to mind instantly that she led them out on to the Green Meadows among the grasses and the weeds.

Then there was always real danger as she took great pains to tell them. There was danger from the air where old Redtail the Hawk sailed round and round, watching below for heedless and careless little folks. There was danger from Reddy and Granny Fox and Old Man Coyote, prowling about with sharp eyes and keen ears and wonderful noses, all the time hunting for heedless little people. And there was danger from Mr. Blacksnake and some of his cousins, slipping silently through the grass.

So the little Bob Whites learned to be always on the watch as they ran this way and that way, hunting for bugs and worms and seeds. At the least little unknown sound they squatted and waited for Mrs. Bob's signal that all was well. She taught them to know Ol' Mistah Buzzard, who wouldn't hurt a feather of them, from old Redtail the Hawk by the way he sailed and sailed without flapping his wings. Just as soon as they could fly a little, she taught them to make sure just where the nearest bushes or trees were so that they could fly to them in case of sudden danger on the ground. She taught them how to find the safest places in which to spend the night. Oh, there was a great deal for those little Bob Whites to learn! Yes, indeed. And it didn't do to forget a single thing. Forgetting just once might mean a dreadful thing. So they didn't forget. Bob White himself taught them many things, for Bob is wise in the ways of the Great World, and he is the best of fathers. So the little Bob Whites grew and grew until they were too big to nestle under the wings of Mrs. Bob and could fly on swift strong wings. And all the time they were at school without knowing it.

CHAPTER THIRTEEN: FARMER BROWN'S BOY BECOMES THOUGHTFUL

For everything that happens
You've but to look to find
There's bound to be a reason;
So keep that fact in mind.

"SON," SAID FARMER BROWN one morning at the breakfast table, "we've got the finest looking garden anywhere around. I don't remember ever having a garden with so little harm done by bugs and worms. All our neighbors are complaining that bugs and worms are the worst ever this year, and that their gardens are being eaten up in spite of all that they can do. I'm proud of the way in which you've taken care of ours."

Farmer Brown's boy flushed with pleasure. He had worked hard in that garden ever since the seeds were planted. He had fought the weeds and the bugs and worms. But so had some of his neighbors. Yet in spite of this their gardens were nearly ruined. They had worked just as hard as he had, but the worms and the bugs had been too much for them. He couldn't understand why he had succeeded when they had failed. There must be a reason. There is a reason for everything.

After breakfast he put on his old straw hat and started down to the garden to look it over, still puzzling over the reason why his garden was so much better than others. Just on the edge of the garden was an old board. He lifted one end of it and peeped under. Old Mr. Toad looked up at him and blinked sleepily, but in the most friendly way. Mr. Toad's waistcoat was filled out until it looked too tight for comfort. Farmer Brown's boy smiled as he put the board down gently. He knew what made that waistcoat so tight; it was filled with bugs and worms. "There's a part of the reason," muttered Farmer Brown's boy.

A little farther on he discovered Little Friend the Song Sparrow very busy among the berry-bushes. "There's another part of the reason," chuckled Farmer Brown's boy. At the end of a long row he sat down to think it over. There was no doubt that he owed a great deal to Old Mr. Toad and Little Friend and a lot of the feathered folk of the Old Orchard for his fine-looking garden, but he had had their help in other years when his garden had not looked half as well, and yet when there had not been nearly as many bugs and worms as this year. Their help and his own hard work accounted for part of the reason for his fine-looking garden, but he couldn't help but feel that there must be something else he didn't know about.

He was thinking so hard that he sat perfectly still. Presently a pair of bright eyes peeped out at him from under a berry-bush. Then right out in front of him stepped a smart, trim little fellow dressed in brown, gray and white with black trimmings. It was Bob White. He called softly and out ran Mrs. Bob and fifteen children! At a word from Bob they scattered and went to work among the plants.

Farmer Brown's boy held his breath as he watched. They didn't pay the least attention to him because, you know, he sat perfectly still. Some scratched the ground just like the hens at home, and then picked up things so small that he couldn't see what they were. But he knew. He knew that they were tiny seeds. And because all the seeds which he and Farmer Brown had planted were now great strong plants, he knew that these were seeds of weeds.

Bob himself was very busy among the potato-vines. He was near enough for Farmer Brown's boy to see what he was doing. He was eating those striped beetles which Farmer Brown's boy had fought so long and which he had come to hate. "One, two, three, four, five, six, seven, eight, nine, ten, eleven," counted Farmer Brown's boy, and then Bob moved on to where he couldn't be seen. Among the squash-vines he could see Mrs. Bob, and she was picking off bugs as fast as Bob was taking the potato-beetles. What the others were doing he didn't know, but he could guess.

"There's the rest of the reason!" he suddenly exclaimed in triumph. He spoke aloud, and in a twinkling there wasn't a Bob White to be seen.

CHAPTER FOURTEEN: A LITTLE LESSON IN ARITHMETIC

Don't say you "hate" arithmetic, and find it dull and dry.
You'll find it most astonishing if you sincerely try.

FARMER BROWN'S BOY used to feel that way, but he doesn't any more. He never could see any use in puzzling over sums in school. He said that there wasn't anything interesting in it; nothing but hard work. He used to complain about it at home. Farmer Brown would listen a while, then he would say, "If you live long enough, my son, you will find that figures talk and that they tell the most wonderful things." There was always a twinkle in his eyes when he said this.

Now of course Farmer Brown's boy knew that his father didn't mean that figures could speak right out. Of course not. But he never could understand just what he did mean, and he wasn't interested enough to try to find out. So he would continue to scowl over his arithmetic and wish the teacher wouldn't give such hard lessons. And when the long summer vacation began, he just forgot all about figures and sums until after he discovered Bob White and his family helping to rid the garden of bugs and worms and seeds of weeds.

After he discovered them, he went down to the garden every day to watch them. They soon found out that he wouldn't hurt them, and after that they just paid no attention to him at all, but went right on with their business all about him, and that business was the filling of their stomachs with seeds and worms and bugs. One day Bob White ate twelve caterpillars while Farmer Brown's boy was watching him. He got out a stubby pencil and a scrap of paper.

"If every one of those Bob Whites eats twelve of those horrid worms at one meal that would be—let me see." He wrinkled his brows. "There are Bob and Mrs. Bob and fifteen young Bobs and that makes seventeen. Now if each eats twelve, that will make twelve times seventeen." He put down the figures on his bit of paper and worked over them for a few minutes. "That makes 204 caterpillars for one meal," he muttered, "and in one month of thirty days they would eat 6120 if they only ate one meal a day. But they eat ever so many meals a day and that means—" He stopped to stare at the figures on the bit of paper with eyes round with wonder. Then he whistled a little low whistle of sheer astonishment. "No wonder I've got a good garden when those fellows are at work in it!" he exclaimed.

Then he sat down to watch Mrs. Bob catching cabbage-butterflies which he knew were laying the eggs

He counted the number of cabbage-butterflies she caught while she was in sight.

which would hatch out into the worms that spoiled the cabbages. He counted the number she caught while she was in sight. He did the same thing with another of the Bob Whites who was catching cucumber-beetles, and with another who was hunting grasshoppers. Then he did some more figuring on that bit of paper. When he had finished he got up and went straight down to the cornfield where Farmer Brown was at work.

"I know now what you meant when you used to tell me that figures talk," said he. "Why, they've told me more than I ever dreamed! They've told me that the Bob Whites are the best friends we've got, and that the reason that we've got the best garden anywhere around is just because they have made it so. Why, those little brown birds are actually making money for us, and we never guessed it!"

CHAPTER FIFTEEN: FARMER BROWN'S BOY GROWS INDIGNANT

TO BE INDIGNANT is to be angry in a good cause. If you lose your temper and give way to anger because things do not suit you, you are not indignant; you are simply angry. But if anger wells up in your heart because of harm or injustice which is done to someone else, or even to yourself, then you become indignant.

Farmer Brown's boy had spent all his spare time down in the garden watching Bob White and his family. In fact, he had been there so much that all the Bob Whites had come to look on him as harmless if not actually a friend. They just didn't pay him any attention at all, but went about their business as if he were nowhere about. And their business was ridding that garden of bugs and worms and seeds of weeds in order to fill their stomachs. What tickled Farmer Brown's boy was that the bugs and worms of which they seemed the most fond were the very ones which did the most harm to the growing plants.

Over beyond the garden was a field of wheat. You know from wheat comes the flour of which your bread is made. Now there is a certain little bug called the chinch-bug which is such a hungry rascal that when he and a lot of his kind get into a field of wheat, they often spoil the whole crop. They suck the juices from the plants so that they wilt and die. Farmer Brown's boy had heard his neighbors complaining that chinch-bugs were very bad that year, and he knew that they must be by the looks of the wheat on the farms of his neighbors. But Farmer Brown's wheat looked as fine as wheat could look. It was very plain that there were no chinch-bugs there, and he often had wondered why, when they were so bad in the fields of his neighbors.

Farmer Brown's boy noticed that Bob White and his family spent a great deal of time in the wheat-field. One day he noticed Bob picking something from a stem of wheat. He went over to see what it might be. Of course Bob scurried away, but when Farmer Brown's boy looked at that wheat-plant he found some chinch-bugs on it. Then he knew what Bob had been doing. He had been picking off and eating those dreadful little bugs. And he knew, too, why it was that their wheat-field was the best for miles around. It was because Bob White and his family hunted for and ate those bugs as fast as they appeared.

"Hurrah for you! You're the greatest little helpers a farmer ever had!" cried Farmer Brown's boy, and hurried off to tell Farmer Brown what he had found out.

So the summer passed, and the cool crisp days of autumn came. The wheat had been harvested and the vegetables gathered and stored away. Jack Frost had begun to paint the maple trees red and yellow, the garden was bare, and the stubble in the wheat-field a golden brown. The little feathered people who do not like cold weather had flown away to the sunny Southland, led by Ol' Mistah Buzzard. Striped Chipmunk, Chatterer the Red Squirrel, and Happy Jack the Gray Squirrel were busy from morning till night storing away seeds and nuts on which to live through the long cold winter. These were glorious days, and Bob White loved every one of them.

"Son," said Farmer Brown one morning, "those Bob Whites must be fat with the good living they have had. Seeing that we have fed them off the farm all summer, don't you think that it is their turn to feed us? I think broiled Bob White on toast would taste pretty good. The shooting season begins next week, so I suppose you will get out your gun and shoot a few of those Bob Whites for us." There was a twinkle, a kindly twinkle in his eyes as he spoke.

But Farmer Brown's boy didn't see that twinkle. His face grew red. A hot anger filled his heart. He was indignant. He was very indignant to think that his father should ever hint at such a thing. But he didn't forget to be respectful.

"No, sir!" said he. "I wouldn't shoot one of them for anything in the world! They don't owe us anything; we owe them. If it hadn't been for them, we wouldn't have had half a crop of wheat, and our garden would have been just as poor as those of our neighbors. I'm not going to shoot 'em, and I'm not going to let anyone else shoot 'em if I can help it, so there!"

CHAPTER SIXTEEN: FARMER BROWN'S BOY TALKS THINGS OVER

There's nothing to compare with love
In earth or sea or up above.

IF LOVE PREVAILED everywhere there would be no terrible wars, no prisons, no dreadful poverty, no bitter quarrels between those who work and those for whom they work. And on the Green Meadows and in the Green Forest there would be no fear of man and no frightful suffering from traps and terrible guns. Love, that wonderful great thing which is contained in one little word of four letters, could and would bring joy and happiness to every heart for all time if only we would give it a chance.

It was love in the heart of Farmer Brown's boy which made him indignant when Farmer Brown hinted that he might take his gun and shoot Bob White and his family. You see, he had made friends with the Bob Whites and learned to love them, and no one can bear the thought of hurting those they love. He had replied to his father respectfully, but his face had flushed red and in his voice there had been the ring of indignation, which is a certain kind of anger. Farmer Brown actually chuckled when he heard it. Then he turned and held out his big hand.

"Shake hands, son," said he. "I was just trying you out to see what you would say. You know you used to be very fond of hunting, and I was just wondering if your love of killing, or trying to kill, was stronger than your sense of right and justice. Now I know that it isn't, and I'm ever so glad. So you think the Bob Whites have earned our protection?"

Farmer Brown's boy's face flushed again, but this time it was with pleasure.

"Oh, Dad, I'm so glad you don't want them killed to eat!" he cried. "I ought to have known that you were just teasing me. I did like to hunt with my gun once, but that was when I didn't know as much as I do now. It was exciting to try to find the birds and then see if I could hit them. I just thought of them as wild things good to eat and so smart that I had to be a little bit smarter to get them. I never thought of them as having any feelings. But now I know that they love, and fear, and suffer pain, and work, and play, and are glad and sad, just like people. I know because I've watched them. So I don't want to hurt them or allow them to be hurt any more than I would real people. Why I *love* 'em! I wouldn't have anything happen to them for the world. I'm dreadfully afraid something will happen to some of them when the hunting season begins. Can't we do anything for them?"

"We can put up some signs warning all hunters to keep off of our farm and forbidding all shooting," replied Farmer Brown. "Then if Bob White and his family are smart enough to stay on our land I guess they will be safe, but if they go on the land of other people they are likely to be shot unless—" he paused.

"Unless I can get other people who own land near us to put up signs and keep the hunters off and promise not to shoot the Bob Whites themselves!" exclaimed Farmer Brown's boy eagerly.

Farmer Brown smiled. "Exactly, my son," said he. "It is your chance to get even; to do something for the little friends who have done so much for you. Tomorrow is Saturday, and there will be no school. You may have all day in which to see what you can do with the neighbors to save Bob White and his family from the hunters.

Listen! Bob would be a blessing if for nothing but his message of good cheer. But the cheer he puts into the world is the daily help he gives. The man who kills Bob White kills one of our best friends and helpers, and his shot hurts us more than it does poor little Bob. Now let's go over to the barn and see about making those signs."

CHAPTER SEVENTEEN: A BEAUTIFUL DAY MADE DREADFUL

A pity 'tis, aye, 'tis a shame
That rests on all mankind,
That human beings in cruelty
Can sport and pleasure find.

THERE NEVER WAS a more beautiful day than that crisp October one. It was one of those days when you just feel all over how good it is to be alive. Bob White felt it. He tingled all over with the joy of living just as soon as he opened his eyes very early that morning. He whistled for very joy. He loved all the Great World, and he felt that all the Great World loved him. He wanted to tell the Great World so. The Merry Little Breezes of Old Mother West Wind, tumbling out of the big bag in which she had brought them down from the Purple Hills to play all day long on the Green Meadows, danced over to tell him that they loved him. This made Bob still happier.

A certain man tramping along the road toward the home of Farmer Jones was feeling glad, but his gladness was of a different kind. "I guess we are going to have some sport, old fellow," said he to the dog trotting at his heels, and shifted a terrible gun from one shoulder to the other.

Now if Bob White had understood the warning given him by Farmer Brown's boy he never, never would have done as he did. But he didn't understand that warning, and so when he took it into his pretty little head that he wanted to try his wings he led his family straight over to the land of Farmer Jones. He often had been there before, and he saw no reason why he shouldn't go there as often as he pleased. No harm had come from these previous visits. So straight over to the stubble of Farmer Jones' wheat-field he led the way, and soon he and his family were very busy picking up scattered grains of wheat and were happy as you or I would be over a good breakfast.

Right in the midst of it Bob's quick ears heard footsteps. He stretched his neck to peep over the stubble, and suddenly all the gladness and brightness of the day was blotted out. What he saw was a dog with his nose to the ground and he was following the scent that one of Bob's children made as he ran about picking up wheat. Suddenly the dog stopped and stood perfectly still, with one foreleg and nose pointing straight at a certain spot. Bob knew that right at that spot one of his children was squatting close to the ground. As still as a statue stood the dog. From behind him came a man walking slowly and carefully and with a terrible gun held in readiness. When he reached the dog he sent him on. There was nothing for the Bob White squatting there to do but fly. Up into the air he shot on swift wings.

"Bang!" went the terrible gun, and down dropped that little brown bird. At the sound of the terrible gun up jumped all the rest of Bob White's children in terrible fright, for never before had they heard such a dreadful noise. "Bang!" went the gun again, but this time only a few brown feathers floated to the ground. Bob and Mrs. Bob waited until after the second bang before they too took to the air, for they had had experience and knew that after the second bang they were likely to be safe for a while.

The Bob Whites had scattered in all directions as they had been taught to do when in danger. Bob flew straight over to Farmer Brown's wheat-field, and there presently he began to call. One after another of his family answered, all but the one who had fallen at the first shot.

"Got one, anyway," said the hunter, as he loaded his terrible gun, and actually looked happy as he went over to help his dog hunt for the Bob White who had fallen at the first terrible bang.

CHAPTER EIGHTEEN: THE DISAPPOINTED HUNTER

It never does to count upon
A thing until you're sure.
It's often less than you expect,
But very seldom more.

THE HUNTER WHO had shot one of Bob White's children chuckled gleefully as he went forward to pick up the poor little brown bird. He was having what he called sport. It never entered his head to think of how the Bob Whites must feel. He probably didn't think that they had any feelings. He was pleased that he had made a successful shot, and he was pleased to think that he was to have that little brown bird to eat, though of course he didn't need it the least bit in the world, having plenty of other things to eat.

But when he reached the place where he had seen the little Bob White fall, there was no little brown bird there. No, Sir, there was not a sign of that little bird save a few feathers. You see, he hadn't killed the little Bob White as he had supposed, but had broken a wing so that it could not fly. But there was nothing the matter with its legs, and no sooner had it hit the ground than it had run as fast as ever it could through the stubble. So the little Bob White wasn't where the hunter was looking for it at all.

Of course his dog helped him hunt, and with that wonderful nose of his he soon found the scent of that little Bob White and eagerly followed it. It just happened that in that field near where the little Bob White fell was an old home of Johnny Chuck, and all around the entrance to it the sand had been spread out. Now sand does not hold scent. The little Bob White knew nothing about that, for he had not lived long enough to learn all that a Bob White has to learn, but he did see the open doorway. Across the yellow sand he ran and into the doorway and just a little way down the hall, where he hid under some dry, brown leaves which had blown in there. He was almost the color of them himself as he squatted close to the ground and drew his feathers as close to his body as possible. In doing this he was doing a very wise thing, though he didn't know it at the time. You see his feathers drawn tightly against his body that way prevented the scent which might have told the keen nose of that dog where he was.

As it was, the dog lost the scent at the edge of the sand, and neither he nor the hunter once thought to look in that old hole. So while they hunted and hunted, the little Bob White squatted perfectly still, though his broken wing hurt him dreadfully, and the ache of it made his eyes fill with tears. At last the hunter gave up the search. He was too impatient to kill more.

"Must be I just wounded him," said he, without one thought of how dreadful it must be to be wounded. "Probably a fox will get him. Bet I kill the next one!"

With that he sent his dog on to try to find the little Bob White's brothers and sisters, his terrible gun held ready to shoot the instant he should see one of them. He was having great sport, was that hunter, while in the hall of Johnny Chuck's old house lay a little brown Bob White faint with suffering and dreadful fright. It would have been bad enough to simply have such a fright, but to have a broken wing and because of this to feel quite helpless—well, can you imagine anything worse?

CHAPTER NINETEEN: FRIGHTENED, WOUNDED AND ALONE

Oh, cruel is the thoughtless deed
That wounds another without need.

SQUATTING UNDER THE brown dead leaves which had blown into the doorway of the old house made long ago in the wheat-field of Farmer Jones by Johnny Chuck was that poor little Bob White. Tears filled his eyes, tears of fright and pain. He tried to wink them back and to think what he should do next, but he was too

Tears filled his eyes, tears of fright and pain.

bewildered to think. To be bewildered is to be so upset that you cannot understand what has happened or is happening. It was just so with this little Bob White.

With his brothers and sisters he had been happily picking up his breakfast that beautiful October morning. Without the least warning a great dog had threatened to catch him, and he had taken to his swift, strong, little wings. As he did so he had seen a great two-legged creature pointing a stick at him, but he had not feared. All summer long he had seen two-legged creatures like this one, and they had not harmed him. Indeed, he had come to look on them as his friends, for had not Farmer Brown's boy watched him and his brothers and sisters day after day, and not once offered even to frighten them? So he had no fear of this one.

Then from the end of that stick pointed at him had leaped fire and smoke, and there had been a terrible noise. Something had struck him, something that stung, and burned and tore his tender flesh, and one of his swift, strong, little wings had become useless, so that he fell heavily to the ground. Then he had run swiftly until he found this hiding place, and, with his little heart going pit-a-pat, pit-a-pat with terror, had squatted close under the friendly brown leaves while the great dog and the two-legged creature had looked for him. Now they had given him up and gone away. At least, he could not hear them.

What did it all mean? Why had this dreadful thing happened to him? What had he done that the two-legged creature should try to kill him with the terrible fire-stick? Outside the day was as beautiful as ever, but all the joy of it was gone. Instead, it was filled with terror. What should he do now? What *could* he do? Where were his father and mother and brothers and sisters? Were such dreadful things happening to them as had happened to him? Would he ever see them again?

Presently he heard a far-away whistle, a sad, anxious whistle. It was the whistle of his father, Bob White. He was calling his family together. Then he heard answering whistles, and he knew that the others were safe and would soon join Bob White. But he did not dare answer himself. He crawled to the doorway and peeped out. He could see the great dog and the cruel two-legged creature with the terrible fire-stick far away on the other side of the field. He tried to leap into the air and fly as he had been used to doing, but only flopped helplessly. One wing was useless and dragged on the ground. It hurt so that the pain made him faint.

He closed his eyes and lay still for a few minutes, panting. Then a new thought filled him with another terrible fear. If Reddy Fox or Old Man Coyote or Redtail the Hawk should happen along, how could he escape without the use of his wings? If only he were not alone! If only he could reach his father and mother perhaps they could help him. He struggled to his feet and began to walk towards that distant whistle. It was slow work. He was weak and faint, and the drooping wing dragged through the stiff stubble and hurt so that it seemed as if he could not stand it. Often he squatted down and panted with weariness and pain and fright. Then he would go on again. He was terribly thirsty, but there was no water to drink. So at last he crawled under a fence, and then suddenly, right in front of him, was one of those two-legged creatures! Right then and there the little Bob White gave up all hope.

CHAPTER TWENTY: FARMER BROWN'S BOY SPEAKS HIS MIND

You cannot always surely tell
If things be ill or things be well.

WHEN THE POOR suffering, wounded little Bob White crawled under the fence he didn't know it, but he had crawled on to the land of Farmer Brown, where a sign warned all hunters to keep off—that no shooting would be allowed there. And when he looked up and saw right in front of him one of those two-legged creatures like the one with the terrible fire-stick, and at once had given up all hope, he had been too sick at heart and suffering too much to recognize Farmer Brown's boy.

But that is just who it was. You see, Farmer Brown's boy had been so anxious for fear that some hunter would come over on his father's land in spite of the signs, that he had gone down on the Green Meadows just as soon as he had eaten his breakfast. He had seen the hunter on the land of Farmer Jones and had heard him shoot. With all his heart Farmer Brown's boy had hoped that the hunter had missed. Now as he looked down and saw the poor little suffering bird he knew that the hunter had not missed, and fierce anger swelled his heart. He quite forgot that he himself used to hunt with a terrible gun before he had learned to know and to love the little people of the Green Meadows, the Green Forest and the Old Pasture.

He stooped and very tenderly lifted the little Bob White, who closed his eyes and was sure that now all would soon be over.

"You poor little thing! You poor, poor little thing!" said Farmer Brown's boy as he looked at the torn and broken wing. Then he looked across at the hunter and scowled savagely. Just then the hunter saw him and at once started towards him. You see, the hunter thought that perhaps if he offered Farmer Brown's boy money he would allow him to hunt on Farmer Brown's land. He knew that was where Bob White and all his family had flown to. When he reached the fence, he saw the little Bob White in the hands of Farmer Brown's boy.

"Hello!" exclaimed the hunter in surprise, "I guess that's my bird!"

"I guess it's nothing of the sort!" retorted Farmer Brown's boy.

"Oh, yes, it is," replied the hunter. "I shot it a little while ago, but it got away from me. I'll thank you to hand it over to me, young man."

"You'll do nothing of the sort," retorted Farmer Brown's boy. "It may be the bird you shot, more shame to you, but it isn't yours; it's mine. I found it on our land, and it belongs to me if it belongs to anyone."

Now the hunter was tempted to reply sharply, but remembering that he wanted to get this boy's permission to hunt on Farmer Brown's land, he bit the angry reply off short and said instead, "Why don't you wring its neck? If you'll get your father to let me shoot on your land, I'll kill another for you, and then you will have a fine dinner."

Farmer Brown's boy grew red in the face. "Don't you dare put your foot on this side of the fence!" he cried. "I'd have you to know that these Bob Whites are my very best friends. They've worked for me all summer long, and do you suppose I'm going to let any harm come to them now if I can help it? Not much! Look how this poor little thing is suffering. And you call it sport. Bah! The law lets you hunt them, but it's a bad law. It's a horrid law. If they did any harm it would be different. But instead of doing harm they work for us all summer long, and then when the crops which they have helped us save are harvested, we turn around and allow them to be shot! But they can't be shot on this land, and the sooner you get away the better I'll like it."

Instead of getting angry the hunter laughed good-naturedly. "All right, I'll keep off your land, sonny," said he. "But you needn't get so excited. They're only birds, and were made to be shot."

"No more than you were!" retorted Farmer Brown's boy. "And they've got feelings just as you have. This poor little thing is trembling like a leaf in my hand. I'm not going to wring its neck. I'm going to try to cure it." With this Farmer Brown's boy turned his back on the hunter and started for home. And the poor little Bob White, not understanding, had no more hope than before.

CHAPTER TWENTY-ONE: WHAT HAPPENED
TO THE LITTLE BOB WHITE

WITH HIS EYES tightly closed because of the terror in his heart, the little Bob White was being carried by Farmer Brown's boy. Very tender was the way in which he was handled, and after a while he began to take a little comfort in the warmth of the hand which held him. Once in a while Farmer Brown's boy would gently smooth the feathers of the little head and say, "Poor little chap."

Straight home went Farmer Brown's boy. Very, very gently he bathed the wounds of the little Bob White. Then, as gently as he could, he put the broken bones of the wing back in place and bound them there with little strips of thin wood to keep them from slipping. It hurt dreadfully, and the little Bob White didn't know what it all meant. But he had suffered so much already that a little more suffering didn't matter much, and he didn't so much as peep.

When it was all over he was put into a box with a bed of soft clean hay, a little dish of water which he could reach by just stretching out his head, and a handful of wheat, and then he was left alone. He was too sick and weary to want to do anything but squat down in that bed of hay and rest. He was still afraid of what might happen to him, but it was not such a great fear as before, for there had been something comforting in the gentle touch of Farmer Brown's boy. He didn't understand at all what those strange wrappings about his body meant, but a lot of the ache and pain had gone from the broken wing.

So he drank gratefully of the water, for he had been burning with thirst, and then settled himself as comfortably as possible and in no time at all was asleep. Yes, Sir, he was asleep! You see, he was so worn out with fright and pain that he couldn't keep his eyes open. Ever so many times during the day Farmer Brown's boy came to see how he was getting along, and was so very gentle and whistled to him so softly that his little heart no longer went pit-a-pat with fear.

The next morning the little Bob White felt so much better that he was up bright and early and made a good breakfast of the wheat left for him. But it seemed very queer not to be able to move his wings. He couldn't lift them even the teeniest, weeniest bit because, you see, Farmer Brown's boy had bound them to his sides with strips of cloth so that he couldn't even try to fly. This was so that that broken wing might get well and strong again.

Now of course the little Bob White had lived out of doors all his life, and

Farmer Brown's boy knew that he never could be quite happy in the house. So he made a wire pen in the henyard, and in one end he made the nicest little shelter of pine-boughs under which the little Bob White could hide. He put a little dish of clean water in the pen and scattered wheat on the ground, and then he put the little Bob White in there.

As soon as he was left quite alone the little Bob White ran all about to see what his new home was like. You see, there was nothing the matter with his legs.

"I can't get out," thought he, when he had been all around the pen, "but neither can anyone get in, so I am safe and that is something to be thankful for. This two-legged creature is not at all like the one with the terrible fire-stick, and I am beginning to like him. I haven't got to fear Reddy Fox or Old Man Coyote or Redtail the Hawk. I guess that really I am a lot better off than if I were out on the Green Meadows unable to fly. Perhaps, when my wing gets well, I will be allowed to go. I wonder where my father and mother and brothers and sisters are and if any of them were hurt by that terrible fire-stick."

CHAPTER TWENTY-TWO: A JOYOUS DAY FOR THE BOB WHITES

Thrice blessed be the girl or boy
Who fills another's heart with joy.

ONE DAY JUST by chance Bob White flew up in a tree where he could look down in Farmer Brown's henyard, and there he discovered the lost little Bob and talked with him. Then Bob White flew back to the Green Meadows where little Mrs. Bob was anxiously waiting for him, and his heart was light. Mrs. Bob was watching for him and flew to meet him.

"It's all right!" cried Bob. "I found him over in Farmer Brown's henyard." Of course "him" meant the young Bob White who had been given up as killed.

"What?" exclaimed Mrs. Bob. "What is a henyard, and what is he doing there?"

"A henyard is a place where Farmer Brown keeps a lot of big foolish birds," explained Bob, "and little Bob is a prisoner there."

"How dreadful!" cried Mrs. Bob. "If he's a prisoner, how can you say it's all right?"

"Because it is," replied Bob. "He's perfectly safe there, and he wouldn't be if he were here with us. You see, he can't fly. One of his wings was broken by the shot from that terrible gun. Farmer Brown's boy found him and has been very kind to him. He fixed that wing so that I believe it is going to get quite as well as ever. You know quite as well as I do how much chance little Bob would have had over here with a broken wing. Reddy Fox or Redtail the Hawk or someone else would have been sure to get him sooner or later. But up there they can't, because he is in a wire pen. He can't get out, but neither can they get in, and so he is safe. He and Farmer Brown's boy are great friends. With my own eyes I saw him feed from the hand of Farmer Brown's boy. Do you know, I believe that boy is really and truly our friend and can be trusted."

"That is what Peter Rabbit is always saying, but after all we've suffered from them, I can't quite make up my mind that any of those great two-legged creatures are to be trusted," said little Mrs. Bob. "I've got to see for myself."

There he discovered the lost
little Bob and talked with him.

"You shall," declared Bob. "Tomorrow morning you shall go up there and I'll stay here to look after the rest of the youngsters. I am afraid if we left them alone some of them would be careless or foolish enough to go where the hunters with terrible guns would find them."

So the next morning Mrs. Bob went up to visit young Bob, and she saw all that Bob had seen the day before. She returned with a great load off her mind. She knew that Bob was right, and that Farmer Brown's boy had proved himself a true friend from whom there was nothing to fear. The next day Bob and Mrs. Bob took the whole family up there, for Farmer Brown's boy had scattered food for them just outside the henyard where the biddies could not get it, and Bob was smart enough to know that no hunters would dare look for them so close to Farmer Brown's house. Morning after morning they went up there to get their breakfast, and they didn't even fly when Farmer Brown's boy and Farmer Brown himself came out to watch them eat.

Then one morning a wonderful thing happened. Farmer Brown's boy took young Bob out of his pen in the henyard. Young Bob looked quite himself by this time, for the strips of cloth which had bound his broken wing in place had been taken off, and his wing was as good as ever. Farmer Brown's boy took him outside the henyard and gently put him down on the ground.

"There you are! Now go and join your family and in the future keep out of the way of hunters," said he, and laughed to see young Bob scamper over to join his brothers and sisters.

Such a fuss as they made over him! Suddenly Bob White flew up to the top of a post, threw back his head and whistled with all his might, "Bob White! Bob White! Bob White!" You see, he just had to tell all the Great World of the joy in his heart, although this was not the time of year in which he usually whistles.

And this is how it happened that Bob White and his whole family came regularly to Farmer Brown's for their breakfasts, and no hunter ever had another chance to carry fright and suffering and sorrow into their midst.

So this is all about Bob White and his family because Ol' Mistah Buzzard has come all the way up from Ol' Virginny for me to tell you about him and his adventures. I've promised to do it in the very next book.

The Adventures of Ol' Mistah Buzzard

CHAPTER ONE: A GREAT FEAR ON THE GREEN MEADOWS

IT HAD BEEN a bad day on the Green Meadows. Yes, Sir, it had been a very bad day, especially for the littlest folks who live there. From the time jolly, round, red Mr. Sun first began his long climb up the blue, blue sky until it was almost time for him to go to bed behind the Purple Hills there had been great fear on the Green Meadows. And it was all because of a black speck way, way up in the sky, a black speck that kept going round and round and round and round in circles.

Danny Meadow Mouse poked his head out of his doorway and nearly twisted his head off as he watched the black speck go round and round. He shivered and ducked back into his house, only to stick his head out a few minutes later and do it all over again.

Peter Rabbit stuck to the dear Old Briar-patch all that day. He was perfectly safe there, but there wasn't any sweet-clover and he didn't dare go out on the Green Meadows to get any. By noon Peter's neck seemed ready to break from being twisted so much to watch that black speck in the sky.

And it was strangely still on the Green Meadows. The little birds forgot to sing. Mrs. Redwing kept close hidden in the bulrushes on the edge of the Smiling Pool. Even Sammy Jay kept to the Green Forest. Only Blacky the Crow ventured out on the Green Meadows, but Blacky is so big that he is not much afraid of anything, and though once in a while he rolled an eye up at the black speck high in the sky, he went on about his business as usual.

Jimmy Skunk, who fears nothing and nobody, stopped to visit with Johnny Chuck. Johnny was sticking very close to his doorway that morning and every minute or two he rolled one eye up to see where the black speck was.

"I don't know what to make of it," said Johnny Chuck. "It isn't Old White-tail the Marsh Hawk, for he always flies close to the tops of the meadow grasses. It isn't fierce Mr. Goshawk, for he spends most of his time in the Green Forest. It isn't old King Eagle, for he never stays so long in one place. It isn't sharp-eyed old Roughleg, for he has gone back to his home in the Far North. And besides, none of them can fly round and round and round without flapping their wings as that

Unc' Billy Pricked up his ears and listened.

fellow does. I wish he would go away."

But he didn't go away, only just kept sailing round and round over the Green Meadows and sometimes over the Green Forest. Everyone was sure that it was a Hawk, and you know that most of the little meadow and forest folks are terribly afraid of Hawks, but no one could remember ever having seen such a wonderful flier among the Hawks. This big black fellow just sailed and sailed and sailed. Sometimes he shot down almost to the ground and then all the little meadow people scuttled out of sight. None was brave enough to stay and discover who the stranger was.

Now Unc' Billy Possum had been asleep all day and so he hadn't heard of the fright on the Green Meadows. It was just about the time that jolly, round, red Mr. Sun goes to bed when Unc' Billy came crawling out of his snug home in the hollow tree.

Jimmy Skunk happened along just then. He had just seen the stranger glide down and settle for the night on a dead tree in the Green Forest, and he told Unc' Billy Possum all about it. Unc' Billy pricked up his ears as he listened. Then he grew very much excited.

"Ah reckons that that is mah ol' friend, Ol' Mistah Buzzard!" shouted Unc' Billy, as he started for the dead tree in the Green Forest.

CHAPTER TWO: UNC' BILLY MEETS AN OLD FRIEND

UNC' BILLY POSSUM lost no time in getting over to the dead tree in the Green Forest where Jimmy Skunk had seen the stranger go to roost for the night. Unc' Billy wanted to get there before the stranger had gone to sleep, for if it really were his old friend, Ol' Mistah Buzzard, as Unc' Billy felt sure it was, he had just got to say "howdy" that very night.

Now Unc' Billy is seldom caught napping, so though he was very sure that this was his old friend, he didn't intend to run any risk of furnishing a good supper for a hungry Hawk. So as Unc' Billy drew near the dead tree he crept up very quietly and carefully until he was where he could see the stranger clearly. There he sat on a branch of the dead tree. He was dressed in sooty black and he sat like an old man, his head drawn down and his shoulders hunched up. His head was bald and wrinkled.

Unc' Billy took one good look, and then he let out a whoop that made the stranger stretch out his long neck and begin to grin in pleased surprise.

"Hello, Ol' Mistah Buzzard! Where'd yo'all come from?" shouted Unc' Billy Possum.

"Ah reckon Ah done come straight from the sunny Souf, and Ah reckon this is the lonesomest land Ah ever done see. Ah'm going straight back where Ah come from. What yo'all staying up here fo' anyway, Unc' Billy?" said Ol' Mistah Buzzard.

Unc' Billy grinned. "Ah'm staying because Ah done like here mighty well, and Ah reckon that yo'all is going to like it mighty well, too," replied Unc' Billy.

Ol' Mistah Buzzard shook his head. "All day Ah done try to make friends, and everyone done run away. Ah don' understand it, Unc' Billy. Ah cert'nly don't understand it at all." Ol' Mistah Buzzard shook his head sorrowfully.

Unc' Billy's wits are sharp, and he had guessed right away what the trouble was. So he explained to Ol' Mistah Buzzard how he had been mistaken for a fierce Hawk, and that the reason the Green Meadows had been so lonely was because all the little meadow people had been hiding and shivering with fear as they had watched Ol' Mistah Buzzard sailing round in the sky.

Pretty soon Mistah Buzzard began to see the joke. There he had been sailing round and round in the sky and growing lonesome for someone to talk to, and there down below him had been the very ones he wanted to make friends with, everyone of them frightened most to death because they mistook him for a Hawk. Ol' Mistah Buzzard began to chuckle, and then he began to laugh.

"Ah reckon Ah'll have to stay a day or two just to see if yo'all is right," said he.

"Ah reckon yo'all will," replied Unc' Billy Possum.

And Ol' Mistah Buzzard did.

CHAPTER THREE: OL' MISTAH BUZZARD MAKES FRIENDS

UNC' BILLY POSSUM and Jimmy Skunk tramped through the Green Forest and over the Green Meadows till their feet ached. They had started out to visit the homes of all the little people who live there to tell them that the black stranger who had sailed the skies all the day before and frightened most of them so that they hardly dared put their noses outside of their own doors was as harmless as Peter Rabbit himself.

You see they had all taken him for a fierce Hawk and had been frightened almost to death at the very sight of him. And all the time he wasn't a Hawk at all but just an old friend of Unc' Billy Possum, Ol' Mistah Buzzard, who had come up from way down South.

"My!" exclaimed Unc' Billy, as he stopped to mop his face because it was so warm, "Ah didn't know there were so many little people on the Green Meadows and in the Green Forest."

Just then he spied the Merry Little Breezes of Old Mother West Wind, and a happy thought came to him. He would get them to take his message around. Why hadn't he thought of it before? Of course the Merry Little Breezes were tickled to death, for they are always looking for something to do for others. So off they raced as fast as they could, while Unc' Billy hurried back to have a chat with Ol' Mistah Buzzard.

At first many of the little meadow people were inclined to be very doubtful of the harmlessness of Ol' Mistah Buzzard. "How do you know?" demanded Danny Meadow Mouse of the Merry Little Breezes.

"Because Unc' Billy Possum has known him for a long time, and he says so," replied the Merry Little Breezes.

"I'll believe it when I see Unc' Billy risking his precious old skin where the stranger can reach him," said Danny, stretching his neck to try to see over the grass-tops.

The Merry Little Breezes clapped their hands joyously. "Look right down there by Farmer Brown's old hayrick," they cried.

Danny came out where he could see. Sure enough, there was Ol' Mistah Buzzard, large as life, sitting on the hayrick, and right down below him was sitting Unc' Billy Possum, and the two were talking and laughing fit to kill themselves. More than that, old Mrs. Possum was hurrying up with a broad grin, and behind her scampered all the little Possum children. When Danny saw that, he made up his mind that Ol' Mistah Buzzard really was harmless, and promptly started down to pay his respects.

One by one all day long the little meadow and forest people stole over to pay their respects to Ol' Mistah Buzzard. They found him all ready to make friends and so full of stories that most of them stayed to listen.

Late that afternoon when Ol' Mistah Buzzard sought the dead tree in the Green Forest to roost for the night, Unc' Billy Possum strolled by that way to see if his old friend was comfortable. Ol' Mistah Buzzard looked down at Unc' Billy, and his eyes twinkled.

"Ah reckon," said Ol' Mistah Buzzard, "that yo'all is right, and Ah sho'ly am going to stay here a right smart while. Ah sho'ly am."

CHAPTER FOUR: A FUNNY DISPUTE

"WHEN AH LEFT mah home way down Souf Ah cert'nly did hate to leave Brer Gopher and all the rest of mah friends," said Ol' Mistah Buzzard as he sat on his dead tree in the Green Forest.

"Did I hear you speak of Mr. Gopher?" asked Digger the Badger, who had come up just in time to hear the last words.

"Yo' sho'ly did, Brer Badger, yo' sho'ly did! Ah'm very fond of Brer Gopher," replied Ol' Mistah Buzzard. "Do yo' know him?"

"Do I know him! I should say I do!" exclaimed Digger the Badger, who, you know, came out of the Great West. "Why, when I was a little fellow Mr. Gopher and I used to have digging matches, and he surely can dig! But I didn't know that he had moved down South."

"Do I know him! I should say I do!"
exclaimed Digger the Badger.

"Why, what are you talking about, Brer Badger? He and his family have *always* lived down Souf!" exclaimed Ol' Mistah Buzzard.

Now Digger the Badger is quick-tempered. "You're wrong!" he shouted. "Mr. Gopher and his family have always lived out West!"

To tell anyone that they are untruthful is a dreadful thing. Digger shouldn't have said that, even if he did believe that Ol' Mistah Buzzard was telling an untruth. Ol' Mistah Buzzard was so taken aback that for a few minutes he couldn't find his tongue. When he did he talked very plainly to Digger the Badger. He called him names. The noise of the quarrel brought all the other little meadow and forest people on the run to see what it all meant.

"Ah tell yo' Brer Gopher and his family have always lived in the Souf, and Ah don' believe yo' know Brer Gopher at all!" said Ol' Mistah Buzzard.

Digger the Badger fairly danced up and down, he was so mad. "Not know him!" he shrieked. "Not know him! Why I know every hair in his coat!"

Ol' Mistah Buzzard stared at Digger a full minute. "What was that yo' said?" he asked slowly.

"I said I know every hair in Mr. Gopher's coat," snapped Digger.

Ol' Mistah Buzzard looked around the circle of little meadow and forest people in triumph. "Ah knew he didn't know Brer Gopher," said he. "Brer Gopher's coat isn't made of hair at all; it's of shell."

It was Digger's turn to stare. Then he began to laugh. He laughed and laughed and laughed. "Shell!" he gasped. "Shell!" Then he went off into another fit of laughter, while Ol' Mistah Buzzard grew very red and angry.

"What's all this fuss about?" demanded Old Mother West Wind, who was on her way home to the Purple Hills.

When she had heard all about it she began to laugh. "You are both right and both wrong," said she. "Mr. Gopher who lives way down South does wear a shell coat, and he is cousin to Spotty the Turtle, but lives on the land and digs holes in the ground. Mr. Gopher whom Digger the Badger knows does wear a coat of hair, and he is a distant relative of Striped Chipmunk. And the two Mr. Gophers are not related at all. Now make up."

And Ol' Mistah Buzzard and Digger the Badger did.

CHAPTER FIVE: PETER GROWS CURIOUS ABOUT OL' MISTAH BUZZARD

The more we have the more we want;
At least I find that true,
With almost everyone I know;
Pray, is it so with you?

PETER RABBIT, WHO had been calling at the Smiling Pool, had learned so many curious and interesting things about Spotty the Turtle and Grandfather Frog that his head almost ached as he started for the Green Forest one morning in the spring after Ol' Mistah Buzzard's first appearance. You would think that Peter's curiosity ought to have been satisfied for once, but it wasn't. You see, curiosity is one of those things that is seldom really satisfied.

As Peter hopped along, lipperty-lipperty-lip, he looked up to see that Redtail the Hawk was not near enough to be dangerous. There was no sign of Redtail, but high up in the blue, blue sky, sailing round and round, was Ol' Mistah Buzzard. Now ever since Ol' Mistah Buzzard had come up the first time from way down in Ol' Virginny to make his home in the Green Forest for the summer, Peter had been greatly interested in him.

In the first place no one else could sail and sail and sail without moving his wings as could Ol' Mistah Buzzard. In the second place Ol' Mistah Buzzard was the only one whom Peter was acquainted with who had a bald head. King Eagle is called bald-headed, but isn't bald at all.

On the other hand Ol' Mistah Buzzard, who isn't a Buzzard at all but a Vulture, hasn't a feather on his head. He had told the story of how his family first became bald-headed, and ever since then Peter had taken the liveliest interest in Ol' Mistah Buzzard.

This spring Ol' Mistah Buzzard had brought Mrs. Buzzard up from Ol' Virginny with him, and Peter had spent many hours watching them sail round and round high up in the blue, blue sky, so high sometimes that they were little more than specks.

This morning as he watched Ol' Mistah Buzzard, it suddenly popped into Peter's head that he hadn't seen Mrs. Buzzard for some time. Ol' Mistah Buzzard was alone now, and he had been alone every time Peter had seen him of late, only Peter hadn't happened to think of it before.

Peter paused and gazed up at Ol' Mistah Buzzard thoughtfully. "I wonder," said he, thinking aloud as he sometimes does, "if anything can have happened to Ol' Mrs. Buzzard, or if she has grown tired of the Green Forest and gone back to her old home." He wrinkled his forehead in a way he has when he is puzzled or trying to think. Then as a thought popped into his head his face cleared.

"I know!" he exclaimed. "It must be that Mrs. Buzzard is keeping house. Of course. Why didn't I think of that before? All my feathered friends, and some who are not my friends, have nests now, so why shouldn't Mistah and Mrs. Buzzard have a nest? They have. I feel it in my bones. They've got a nest somewhere, and Mrs. Buzzard is taking care of the eggs, and that is why I haven't seen her lately. Now I wonder where that nest is. I should like to see it. I believe I'll have a look around in the Green Forest. Such big folks as Ol' Mistah and Mrs. Buzzard must have a big nest, and it ought not to be hard to find it."

Fairly bubbling over with curiosity Peter started to run again towards the Green Forest.

CHAPTER SIX: PETER RABBIT'S NECK ACHES

Who blindly seeks will seldom find
The thing he has upon his mind.

IF HE DOES it will be by accident. It will be pure luck. Peter Rabbit should have known this. He had tried it often enough. But Peter is a heedless, happy-go-lucky fellow, and I guess he always will be. So when he made up his mind that he would like to see the nest of Ol' Mistah and Mrs. Buzzard, he promptly started to look for it without having the least idea where to look or what to look for.

He thought he had an idea, but Peter always thinks he has an idea. The trouble is he never thinks enough to know whether or not he has an idea. If Ol' Mistah Buzzard had a nest, of course it must be in the Green Forest, reasoned Peter. And because all the big birds of his acquaintance built big nests high up in the trees, of course Ol' Mistah Buzzard must do the same thing. That was as far as Peter went in his thinking.

"All I need to do is to keep my eyes wide open for a new big nest in a tall tree, and that ought to be easy enough to find," thought Peter, as he scampered into the Green Forest, lipperty-lipperty-lip.

Once in the Green Forest he no longer hurried. It is hard work to hurry with your head tipped back so as to see the tops of the trees. Presently Peter's neck began to ache. He sat down under a friendly little hemlock tree to rest his aching neck. When it felt better he went on again, his head tipped back as before. Whenever he saw a bundle of sticks or leaves high up in a tree he was sure that he had found Ol' Mistah Buzzard's nest. Then he would sit down and stare at it very hard and presently would discover that it was an old nest of Redtail the Hawk or of Blacky the Crow or of Chatterer the Red Squirrel or his cousin, Happy Jack the Gray Squirrel. Then he would work his head back and forth to get the kink out of his neck, sigh, and start on again.

"My goodness! I didn't suppose there were so many old nests in the Green Forest," muttered Peter as for the twentieth time he was disappointed. "And what an everlasting lot of trees! Why the Green Forest is all trees!"

Then Peter looked all around to see if anybody had overheard that foolish remark. Nobody had, and Peter grinned at his own foolishness. He rubbed his neck and started on, head tipped back as before. At last he could stand it no longer.

"I've got to give it up for now, anyway," said he ruefully. "My neck aches so that I can't stand it any longer." Of course he meant the ache, not his neck. "I want awfully to find that nest of Ol' Mistah Buzzard's, but I guess I'll have to wait until another day. I didn't realize that the Green Forest is so big. Why at this rate it will take me all the rest of the summer and more too to look in every tree. If I only had some idea just what part of the Green Forest to look in, it would help some."

Right then and there a sudden idea popped into his funny little head, and he grinned sheepishly. "Why didn't I think of it before?" he said right out loud. "I'll just watch Ol' Mistah Buzzard and see where he goes when he comes down from up in the blue, blue sky. He'll be sure to come down near his nest, and then all I'll have to do is to go right over there and find it. My gracious, goodness me, but my neck certainly does ache! I think I'll rest a bit and try my new plan later."

And Peter did this very thing.

CHAPTER SEVEN: THE RESULT OF PETER'S WATCHING

THE RESULT OF Peter Rabbit's foolish search for the nest of Ol' Mistah Buzzard was a stiff and aching neck from tipping his head back so long in order to look up in the trees. The next day, however, the ache was gone, but his curiosity was not; it was greater than ever. So Peter scampered, lipperty-lipperty-lip, over to the edge of the Green Forest to try his new plan of watching Ol' Mistah Buzzard.

"It can't fail," thought Peter. "No, Sir, it can't fail. All I have to do is to be patient. Ol' Mistah Buzzard is bound to visit his nest, and if I watch him why of course I'll find out where that nest is. Anyway, I'll find the locality, and then it will be easy enough to find the nest because such a great big fellow as Ol' Mistah Buzzard must have a great big nest, and a great big nest cannot very well be hidden."

So Peter made himself comfortable in a little tangle of briars on the edge of the Green Forest where he could look up in the blue, blue sky and watch Ol' Mistah Buzzard sailing round and round. Now as everybody knows, Ol' Mistah Buzzard spends much of his time doing this very thing. He will sail about for hours because for him it is just about as easy as sitting still, and at the same time it gives him a chance to see all that is going on below, for Ol' Mistah Buzzard's eyes are very, very keen. At first it was easy for Peter to sit there and do nothing but watch Ol' Mistah Buzzard, for Peter is very fond of sitting still and doing nothing. Watching Ol' Mistah Buzzard really amounted to doing nothing.

But after a while Peter found that staring up in the sky that way made him sleepy. In spite of all he could do his eyelids would close for a minute or two at a time. Then they would fly open and he would look up hastily to find Ol' Mistah Buzzard still a speck high up in the blue, blue sky. More and more often Peter's eyes closed for tiny naps, and though he didn't know it those naps grew longer and longer. At last his eyes flew open to see nothing but the blue, blue sky and a few fleecy white clouds. Of Ol' Mistah Buzzard there was no sign.

Peter rubbed his eyes and looked again this way and that way, but it was all too evident that Ol' Mistah Buzzard was no longer sailing round and round high up in the blue, blue sky. He had come down while Peter was taking a nap. Peter almost cried with vexation. But there was no one to blame but himself. He knew that. If he had kept his eyes open he would have seen Ol' Mistah Buzzard come down. But he hadn't, and so he was no wiser than before.

Peter called himself names. Yes, Sir, he did just that very thing. He was so provoked with himself that he actually called himself names. "Anyway, it is quite useless to sit here any longer," he concluded. "I'll have to try again later in the day or tomorrow."

So Peter started for home in the dear Old Briar-patch. Half way there he glanced up from force of habit. Up in the blue, blue sky someone was swinging round and round in great circles. Peter stopped short and stared. Then he grinned. It was Ol' Mrs. Buzzard this time. She must have come out of the Green Forest while Peter was on his way home. If he had sat still a little longer he would have seen her rise into the air, and would have known just where she had come from. Peter turned and scurried back to his hiding-place.

"This time I won't go to sleep!" he declared. "I'll keep my eyes on Ol' Mrs. Buzzard if I have to stick brambles into me to keep awake. I have an idea that she won't stay up as long as Ol' Mistah Buzzard, anyway."

CHAPTER EIGHT: PETER RABBIT IS JUBILANT

TO BE JUBILANT is to be filled with joy and gladness. This was exactly Peter Rabbit's condition. He was so jubilant that he had to kick up his heels half a dozen times. You see, Ol' Mrs. Buzzard had stayed up in the air only a very short time. In fact, Peter had been in his hiding-place on the edge of the Green Forest only a very short time when she came down from high up in the blue, blue sky. He hadn't had time to get sleepy this time.

Down, down, down she came and disappeared among the tree-tops. But Peter had seen just where she had disappeared. It was very near a certain tall pine tree. He knew that he could go straight to that certain tall pine tree without any trouble. And once there he had no doubt at all that he would find that nest. A nest big enough for such a big bird as Ol' Mrs. Buzzard surely couldn't be hidden so that he couldn't find it.

So Peter was jubilant and hopped and skipped happily on his way toward that certain tall pine tree. Forgotten was his stiff neck of the day before. Forgotten was his disappointment that very morning when Ol' Mistah Buzzard, whom he had been watching, had come down out of the blue, blue sky while Peter was napping.

His curiosity was about to be satisfied. He was about to find the nest of Ol' Mistah and Mrs. Buzzard. Not a single doubt entered his foolish little head. In fact, he counted that nest as good as found already.

So he hopped and he skipped, and he skipped and he hopped on his way to the certain tall pine tree, and all the way he thought what a smart chap he was.

"Of course," said Peter to himself, "Ol' Mistah and Mrs. Buzzard think their nest is a secret that no one will find out, and yet they give that secret away to anyone as smart as I am. I don't suppose it ever has entered their heads that anyone would watch them. Of course when I have found that nest I won't tell anybody. That wouldn't be fair."

It didn't enter Peter's head that he himself wasn't fair in spying and trying to find that nest.

Of course, it was no business of his. Certainly not. But Peter didn't once think of this. Curiosity had taken possession of him, and when curiosity takes possession of anybody, they are likely to give little heed to right and wrong.

So all in good time Peter came to the certain tall pine tree near which he had seen Ol' Mrs. Buzzard disappear among the tree-tops. First he looked that over carefully, though he didn't expect to find the nest in it because it was such a con-spicuous tree. Con-spic-u-ous means to stand out from surrounding things so as to be easily seen. Peter didn't think that Ol' Mistah and Mrs. Buzzard would build their nest in a tree that would be so easily and quickly picked out from among the other trees, but he looked it over carefully to make sure. While he was doing this a voice startled him.

"Good mo'ning, Brer Rabbit. Yo' seem to be looking fo' something. Can Ah help yo' find it?" said the voice.

Peter whirled about to find Ol' Mistah Buzzard looking down at him from the top of a tall dead tree which is a favorite roost of his, and in his eyes was a twinkle. Peter was confused. Yes, Sir, Peter was very much confused. He didn't know just what to say.

CHAPTER NINE: PETER TELLS THE TRUTH

*Remember this: 'Tis always well
The truth and nothing else to tell.*

PETER RABBIT DIDN'T know what to say when Ol' Mistah Buzzard asked him what he was looking for and if he could help find it. No, Sir, Peter didn't know what to say. He was quite confused. In the first place he had forgotten that Ol' Mistah Buzzard's favorite roost was a tall dead tree close by, and he hadn't seen Ol' Mistah

Buzzard until the latter spoke. This had startled him, but what had confused him still more was the fact that he didn't quite see how he could answer Ol' Mistah Buzzard's questions.

However, Peter is truthful. He has found that not only is it wrong to tell an untruth, but that in the end it never pays. So now he blurted out the truth.

"I—I—I," he stammered and stopped. Ol' Mistah Buzzard's eyes twinkled, but he said nothing, and in a minute Peter began again. "I was just sort of wondering if you and Mrs. Buzzard have a nest up in that tall pine tree," said he.

"Then Ah'll just save yo' the trouble of wondering any mo'," replied Ol' Mistah Buzzard, his eyes twinkling more than ever. "We-uns haven't. What is mo', we-uns wouldn't dream of building a nest in a tree like that—a tree that is so much taller and bigger than the rest that all who come this way are just naturally bound to look at it. May Ah ask, Brer Rabbit, what fo' yo' seem so interested in mah nest?"

Peter hung his head. Of course, there was no reason except idle curiosity, and he was ashamed to admit that. But he did. Yes, Sir, he did. He is too truthful not to admit his own faults.

"I just thought I would like to see it, Mistah Buzzard," he replied. "It just popped into my head the other day that probably you and Mrs. Buzzard have a nest, and I got to wondering what it is like. I've seen the nests of Blacky the Crow and Redtail the Hawk and Hooty the Owl and of a good many others, and I got to wondering if you build a nest anything like those I have seen. So being over this way, I thought I would just call around. Of course I don't mean the least bit of harm by it."

"Ah see," replied Ol' Mistah Buzzard. "May Ah ask yo', Brer Rabbit, how it happened that yo' thought that mah nest might be over here?"

"Why, I saw Ol' Mrs. Buzzard disappear among the tree-tops right near here," said Peter eagerly.

"Which Ah take it means that yo' were watching her to see where she went," returned Ol' Mistah Buzzard dryly.

"Y-e-s," confessed Peter, and looked very much ashamed of himself. You see, he knew then that Ol' Mistah Buzzard knew that he had been spying, and spying is something that nobody likes.

"But yo' didn't see just where she did go, did yo?" continued Ol' Mistah Buzzard.

"No," replied Peter. "I thought that if I knew somewhere near the spot where your nest is I could find it. Such big folks as you and Mrs. Buzzard must have a big nest. You do, don't you, Mr. Buzzard?"

"Hm-m-m, Ah don' see it anywhere," said Ol' Mistah Buzzard, looking this way and that. All the time his eyes twinkled more than ever. "What makes yo' so sure Ah have got a nest, Brer Rabbit?"

CHAPTER TEN: OL' MISTAH BUZZARD TEASES PETER RABBIT

OL' MISTAH BUZZARD looked down at Peter Rabbit and chuckled as he waited for Peter's reply to his question. It was a noiseless chuckle, so of course Peter didn't hear it. Peter scratched his long left ear with his long right hind foot. Then he scratched his long right ear with his long left hind foot. Finally he made reply.

"Of course, I don't know for sure that you have a nest," said he, "but I think you must have. All the birds I know have nests this time of year. Besides, this year you brought Mrs. Buzzard up from the South with you, and I've noticed that lately I haven't seen her very often. She doesn't sail round and round way up in the blue, blue sky with you the way she did when she first arrived. So I think she must be taking care of her eggs. And if you have eggs to be taken care of, why of course you must have a nest. I—I wish you would tell me where it is, Mistah Buzzard. I'd just love to see it, and I will promise not to tell a single living soul where it is." Peter was very much in earnest.

"Not even Mrs. Peter?" asked Ol' Mistah Buzzard.

Peter hesitated. You know he usually tells Mrs. Peter everything. He doesn't believe in keeping secrets from Mrs. Peter. But this was different from most secrets, and he did so want to see that nest. So at last he agreed that he wouldn't tell anybody, not even Mrs. Peter.

Ol' Mistah Buzzard leaned down with a great pretense of secrecy. "Ah'm going to tell yo' something, Brer Rabbit," said he, and Peter's long ears stood straight up expectantly. "Ah haven't any nest. No, Suh, Ah haven't any nest," he concluded.

Peter looked the disappointment he felt. He had been so sure that now he was to find out what he had so wanted to know.

"But—but what is the reason that Mrs. Buzzard keeps out of sight so much?" he asked.

"That," whispered Ol' Mistah Buzzard, as if afraid he might be overheard, "is the real secret. She is so busy with household cares that she hasn't time for anything else."

"But—but—but—why I thought you just said that you haven't any nest?" stammered Peter, looking quite as puzzled as he felt. In fact, he looked so puzzled that Ol' Mistah Buzzard had to turn away his head to hide a grin.

"That is just what Ah did say," replied Ol' Mistah Buzzard. "That is just what Ah did say. We-uns haven't any nest."

"Then how can Mrs. Buzzard be so busy with household cares?" demanded Peter. His voice was just a little sharp. He was beginning to suspect that Ol' Mistah Buzzard was trying to have fun at his expense.

"She is sitting on our two aiggs, and one of these days Ah reckon we-uns are going to have two of the finest babies in the Green Forest," asserted Ol' Mistah Buzzard.

"But you just said you haven't any nest!" exclaimed Peter.

"So Ah did! So Ah did!" replied Ol' Mistah Buzzard. "Cert'nly Ah did. We-uns haven't any nest."

CHAPTER ELEVEN: PETER IS BOTH PUZZLED AND CURIOUS

"MISTAH BUZZARD, YOU are making fun of me! That's what you are doing—making fun of me!" exclaimed Peter Rabbit indignantly.

"Ah'm doing nothing of the kind, Brer Rabbit," declared Ol' Mistah Buzzard. "What fo' do you say that?" He looked very solemn, though if the truth be known he was having hard work to keep a twinkle of mischief from showing in his eyes.

"Because," replied Peter in a tone that showed that he felt hurt and decidedly put out, "you tell me that you and Mrs. Buzzard haven't any nest, and then you tell me that Mrs. Buzzard is so busy with household cares that she hasn't time to fly in the blue, blue sky as she did when she first arrived. You tell me that you haven't any nest, and then you tell me that you have two eggs. Your story doesn't hang together. It doesn't hang together at all. No, Sir, it doesn't hang together at all. If you have two eggs, of course you have a nest. If you haven't a nest, why how can you have two eggs? Tell me that! I can believe one half your story, but only half. Do you know which half I believe?"

"But—but—but—why I thought you just said that you haven't any nest?" stammered Peter.

Ol' Mistah Buzzard turned his head as if to look off over the Green Forest, but really to hide a grin. When he looked down again he appeared to be indignant in his turn.

"Ah'm not used to having mah word doubted, Brer Rabbit," said he with dignity. "Ah always have had a most friendly feeling fo' yo', Brer Rabbit, but Ah reckons Ah don' want anything mo' to do with one who tells me to mah face that he doesn't believe what Ah say. No, Suh, Ah reckon Ah don' want anything mo' to do with any such person as that."

Ol' Mistah Buzzard shifted his position awkwardly and turned his back on Peter Rabbit.

Peter didn't know what to do. He and Ol' Mistah Buzzard had been the best of friends, and he didn't want that friendship to end. He had been quite honest in saying that he didn't believe that story. He didn't believe it because he couldn't believe it. At least, he didn't see how he could. But now that Ol' Mistah Buzzard seemed to be actually offended, a little doubt crept into Peter's head. He had lived long enough to know that there are some things very hard to believe which are true nevertheless.

For some time he sat staring at Ol' Mistah Buzzard's back, and while he stared he did a lot of thinking. Finally he decided that Ol' Mistah Buzzard's friendship was worth a great deal more than satisfying his own idle curiosity.

"Mistah Buzzard," said he in a timid small voice, "of course, if you say on your honor that you are not joking me and that you really have two eggs and no nest I'll believe you. I wouldn't for the world have you think that I doubt your word of honor. I wouldn't think of doing such a thing. You see, I never heard of such a thing as anybody having eggs and no place to put them, and so of course I thought you were joking. I'm sorry if I've offended you. Won't you tell me where those eggs are?"

Ol' Mistah Buzzard kept still so long that Peter feared that after all he was too much offended to make up. But at last he turned around and looked down at Peter.

"Brer Rabbit," said he, "Ah accept your apology. Ah have seen so many things hard to believe mahself that Ah know how yo' feel. What Ah told yo' is true on mah honor. We-uns haven't any nest, but Mrs. Buzzard and Ah done got two as fine aiggs as ever yo' have seen. Where they are is the secret of we-uns. All Ah can tell yo' is that they are here or hereabouts. Ah reckon that now Ah'll stretch my wings a bit."

With this Ol' Mistah Buzzard spread his great wings, flapped them a few times and then sailed up, up, up in the blue, blue sky, leaving Peter more puzzled and curious than ever.

CHAPTER TWELVE: PETER CONSULTS SAMMY JAY

PETER RABBIT STARED up in the blue, blue sky, watching Ol' Mistah Buzzard sail round and round as only Ol' Mistah Buzzard can. Peter sighed. It was clear to him that he had learned all he could learn from Ol' Mistah Buzzard about those eggs which the latter said Ol' Mrs. Buzzard was caring for.

"He said that they are here or hereabouts, and yet not in a nest," said Peter to himself. "What he means by that is too much for me. If they are here, I ought to be able to find them. At least, I ought to be able to find Mrs. Buzzard, and of course if I find her, I will find those eggs. It seems simple enough."

Peter looked this way and looked that way, but mostly up in the trees. Somehow he couldn't, he just couldn't believe that Mrs. Buzzard could be anywhere else. But for all his looking he found nothing, and at last he gave up. The puzzle was too much for him. He was just about to start for his home in the dear Old Briar-patch when he heard the voice of Sammy Jay not far off.

"What I can't find perhaps Sammy can," thought Peter. "There are mighty few things Sammy Jay can't find out if he sets out to. Perhaps he knows all about those eggs of Ol' Mistah Buzzard's now. Anyway, it won't do any harm to ask him."

So off Peter started to look for Sammy Jay. It didn't take him long to find Sammy, for the latter's blue coat is easy to see when he is flying about. "Sammy Jay," began Peter, as soon as he was near enough, "did you ever hear of anybody having eggs and no nest to put them in?"

"Certainly," replied Sammy promptly.

"Who?" demanded Peter eagerly.

"Boomer the Nighthawk, for one," replied Sammy.

"What?" cried Peter as if he hadn't understood, or at least as if he thought he hadn't understood. There was astonishment in the very tone of his voice. "Doesn't Boomer have a nest? If he doesn't, where does Mrs. Boomer lay her eggs?"

"Where would she lay them, Mr. Curiosity?" retorted Sammy. "She lays them on the ground, or on a flat rock. Mrs. Whip-poor-will does the same thing. I supposed everybody knew that. Where have you been—asleep?"

"No," retorted Peter shortly, for it rather upset him to learn that he hadn't known these facts about two of his familiar friends. "But I'm not interested in Boomer and Whip-poor-will just now. It is someone else I want to know about."

"All right," replied Sammy. "What have you got on your mind? The sooner you get it off the better. You are looking too excited, Peter. You know too much excitement is bad for your health."

Sammy Jay was teasing, and Peter knew it. He made up a wry face at Sammy, a good-natured face, you know. Then he laughed as he replied:

"Sammy Jay, tell me, do you know where Mrs. Buzzard lays her eggs?"

Sammy scratched his topknot thoughtfully. "I can't say that I do," he replied. Then, noticing how disappointed Peter looked, he hastened to add:

"But I guess I can find out if I want to. Why do you want to know?"

CHAPTER THIRTEEN: PETER AROUSES SAMMY JAY'S INTEREST

WHEN SAMMY JAY asked Peter Rabbit why he was so anxious to know where Ol' Mrs. Buzzard had laid her eggs, Peter hesitated. Then he blurted out the whole story. He told Sammy how it had popped into his head that he never had seen the nest of Ol' Mistah and Mrs. Buzzard; how he had made up his mind that of course they must have a nest; how he had thought that such big people must have a big nest; how he had looked for it until his neck ached; how he had watched Ol' Mrs. Buzzard, and finally how Ol' Mistah Buzzard had told him that they hadn't a nest but that they had two eggs.

"If they have two eggs, where are they? I ask you that, Sammy Jay," concluded Peter.

Sammy had listened with growing interest. It so happens that he never had given a thought to the affairs of Ol' Mistah and Mrs. Buzzard, which was rather odd, as Sammy is usually interested in the affairs of everybody in his neighborhood. Again he scratched his topknot thoughtfully.

"I shall have to look into this," said he at last, winking at Peter. "If Ol' Mistah Buzzard told you on his word of honor that he hasn't a nest, why, he hasn't, and that is all there is to that. If he hasn't a nest and yet Mrs. Buzzard is sitting on two eggs, why those two eggs must be somewhere."

Peter nodded. "Of course," said he.

"And if others who have no nests lay their eggs on the ground, why shouldn't Mrs. Buzzard?" continued Sammy. "Why shouldn't she do as Mrs. Boomer the Nighthawk and Mrs. Whip-poor-will do?"

"True enough," said Peter gravely. "True enough. Why shouldn't she? I hadn't thought of that because, you see, I didn't know about Mrs. Boomer and Mrs. Whip-poor-will until you told me. Of course, those eggs must be on the ground. The question is, where? I haven't seen Ol' Mrs. Buzzard anywhere on the ground. I wish I had thought of the ground before. If I had it would have saved my neck. Funny, isn't it, that anyone so fond of the air and flying so high should lay eggs on the ground?"

"We don't know yet that they are on the ground," Sammy Jay broke in. "You are jumping at things just as usual, Peter Rabbit. Now I am going to see what I can find out. If my eyes are not sharp enough to find anyone as big as Mrs. Buzzard, I shall think there is something the matter with them." Sammy spread his wings ready to fly.

"If you find out where those eggs are, you'll come back and tell me, won't you, Sammy?" Peter asked anxiously.

"Perhaps," replied Sammy Jay, with a grin.

"Oh, but you must!" cried Peter. "You wouldn't have known anything about them if I hadn't told you."

"I don't know anything about them now," retorted Sammy. "That is why I am going to look for them."

"But please, Sammy, come back and tell me if you find them," begged Peter. "I'll wait right here."

"Perhaps," replied Sammy provokingly, and flew away.

CHAPTER FOURTEEN: SAMMY JAY DISAPPOINTS PETER

When once you've got your mind all set
Upon some special thing
How dreadful disappointing 'tis
To have your hopes take wing.

SOMEHOW PETER RABBIT felt in his bones that Sammy Jay would find out what he himself hadn't been able to find out, for all his trying—Ol' Mistah Buzzard's secret. Perhaps it was because Sammy is a famous hand at finding out the secrets of others. Perhaps it was because Peter has tried in vain to keep secrets of his own from Sammy. Anyway, as he waited there in the Green Forest for Sammy to return, it was with a feeling that when he did come back he surely would have the secret about the eggs of Ol' Mistah and Mrs. Buzzard.

It was a long time before he saw or heard anything of Sammy, but at last he heard his harsh voice in the distance, and presently he caught sight of his blue coat among the trees. Peter fairly danced with impatience. He just couldn't sit still. It seemed to him as if Sammy were taking an unusually long time. He stopped in almost every tree. Finally Peter ran to meet him.

"Well, did you find those eggs?" cried Peter as soon as he was near enough.

Sammy Jay looked very much dejected and disappointed. "No," said he, "I didn't find those eggs."

Peter looked at Sammy Jay sharply to make sure that he was telling the truth, for sometimes, I am sorry to say, Sammy doesn't tell the truth. But this time Sammy looked so honest that Peter didn't doubt him. He tried not to let his disappointment show, but he couldn't help it. "I—I thought surely you'd find them," said he. "I guess if you couldn't nobody can."

That pleased Sammy Jay, and he flew down a little nearer to Peter. "I'm going to tell you something, Peter," said he. "I didn't find those eggs because there aren't any."

"What?" cried Peter, jumping right up in the air.

"It's a fact," replied Sammy. "Ol' Mistah Buzzard and Mrs. Buzzard haven't any eggs. I know it."

"How do you know it?" demanded Peter. "Ol' Mistah Buzzard told me on his honor that they had two."

"And Ol' Mrs. Buzzard told me on her honor that they haven't any," replied Sammy. "What is more, I believe her."

Peter stared at Sammy Jay with such a funny look on his face that Sammy had to turn his head to hide a smile.

"So you found Mrs. Buzzard," said Peter, when he could find his voice. "Did she tell you that they haven't any nest?"

"I didn't ask her," replied

"What?" cried Peter, jumping right up in the air.

Sammy. "All I asked about was the eggs, and as I have already told you they haven't any."

"How do you know that she told the truth?" asked Peter suspiciously.

"I know because I know," retorted Sammy, which wasn't much of an answer.

"Well," said Peter at last, "I think I'll give up and go home to the dear Old Briar-patch. Of course those eggs were no business of mine, anyway. It's funny to me, though, that Ol' Mistah Buzzard should tell me that they have two, and Mrs. Buzzard should tell you that they haven't any. I don't understand it at all."

"By the way, Peter," said Sammy, as Peter started for home, "I saw something which will interest you and perhaps make up for your disappointment."

Peter pricked up his ears hopefully. "What was it?" he demanded.

CHAPTER FIFTEEN: SAMMY JAY GIVES PETER DIRECTIONS

PETER RABBIT WAS all curiosity as he demanded what it was that Sammy Jay had found that would be of interest to him. Of course, Sammy had known that he would be. It doesn't take much to arouse Peter's curiosity. Some people are just that way. A word or two is enough to get them all worked up. Sammy cocked his head to one side and looked at Peter shrewdly.

"Do you think that you can follow my directions exactly?" he asked.

Peter nodded his head vigorously. "Of course," he replied. "Just give them to me and see. But what is it you saw that you think will interest me? It might not, you know."

"I don't know anything of the sort," replied Sammy. "On the contrary, I know that it *will* interest you. It interested me a great deal, and anything that will interest me is bound to interest you. But I'm not going to tell you what it is. I'm going to let you have the fun of finding it. If when you find it you don't say that it is one of the most surprising things you have seen in all your life, my name isn't Sammy Jay."

By this time Peter was all ears, as the saying is. He had forgotten all about his disappointment over his failure to find the secret of Ol' Mistah and Mrs. Buzzard. He was impatient to be off in quest of this mysterious and interesting thing which Sammy Jay had found.

"All right, Sammy; I'll wait to find out for myself what it is," said he. "It is fun sometimes not to know just what it is you are looking for. Where did you say this thing is?"

"I didn't say," replied Sammy, his sharp eyes twinkling with mischief. "First you must promise to do exactly as I say."

"I promise," declared Peter with great promptness.

"Very good," said Sammy. "The first thing to do is to go over to that dead tree where you saw Ol' Mistah Buzzard this morning. You know where that is, don't you?"

"Of course I know where that is," retorted Peter.

"When you get there, turn to your right until you come to a little thicket of young hemlock trees," continued Sammy. "Back of that thicket is a great big hollow log."

"I know all about that log," Peter interrupted. "I've hidden in it more than once. What next?"

"When you reach that log you must be very quiet," replied Sammy. "You must steal along beside it to the open end without making a sound. You mustn't rustle so much as a leaf."

"My, this sounds exciting!" cried Peter. "What then?"

"Poke your head around and look inside. You'll see what it is that I found," replied Sammy.

A sudden suspicion crept into Peter's head. "There isn't anything there that is likely to hurt me, is there?" he demanded. "Reddy Fox isn't asleep in there, or anything like that?"

"No," replied Sammy Jay. "There isn't anybody or anything there to hurt you. But there is something there to interest you."

Sammy looked so earnest that Peter's suspicions left him at once. In fact, he was a little ashamed of having been suspicious.

"All right," said he, "I'm off." And away he went, lipperty-lipperty-lip.

CHAPTER SIXTEEN: PETER JUMPS ALMOST OUT OF HIS SKIN

PETER RABBIT'S CURIOSITY was so aroused by what Sammy Jay had told him that he scampered through the Green Forest as fast as he could make his legs go, and that is very fast indeed. Lipperty-lipperty-lip, lipperty-lipperty-lip, lipperty-lipperty-lip scampered Peter, and didn't once look behind. If he had he might have seen Sammy Jay following, though it is doubtful, for Sammy was taking great care to keep out of sight.

But Peter didn't look behind. His thoughts were all on that mysterious and interesting thing that he was to find in the big hollow log behind the thicket of young hemlock trees. When he reached the tall dead tree on which Ol' Mistah Buzzard delights to sit, he glanced up. Ol' Mistah Buzzard wasn't there, and Peter kept on without a pause. Presently he came to the thicket of young hemlock trees and quickly slipped through this.

Right on the other side lay the great hollow log. As soon as he reached this Peter stopped running. Mindful of what Sammy Jay had said, he crept forward on tiptoe as it were, taking the greatest care not to make a sound. He even held his breath. He put his feet down so as not to snap a single dry twig or rustle a single dry leaf. It was very exciting. It was the most exciting thing Peter had done for a long time. Every step or two he stopped to listen. Not a sound was to be heard, not even the sighing of the pine trees, for there wasn't even one of the Merry Little Breezes about to make them sigh. It was a lonely spot, a very lonely spot. The very silence made the mystery all the greater.

Little by little Peter crept along beside the great hollow log. It was one of the biggest logs in all the Green Forest. On many a stormy winter night it had sheltered him. He knew all about that old log, inside and out. At least, he thought he did. Now as he reached the end of it he stopped. He was eager to peep around and look inside, yet somehow he dreaded to. Just why he didn't know. Probably it was because Sammy Jay had made such a mystery of what was inside. You know how all of us are apt to be a little afraid of things that are mysterious.

Half a dozen times Peter started to peep around, and each time he drew back. At last he mustered up his courage. His curiosity overcame all his fears. Sammy Jay had said that there was nothing in there to harm him, and if that was the case, it was foolish to be so timid. So Peter poked his head around the end of the old log, his eyes very big with wonder and anticipation. Before he could really see what was inside there came a sharp, angry hiss almost in his very face. It was one of the loudest hisses Peter ever had heard.

Poor Peter! He was so frightened that he jumped nearly out of his skin. In fact he turned two back somersaults and then without waiting to see who had frightened him so, away he went, lipperty-lipperty-lip, until he was quite out of breath. Then a sound reached him that made him pause. It was very like the voice of Sammy Jay laughing.

CHAPTER SEVENTEEN: THE MYSTERY IS CLEARED UP

AT THE SOUND of Sammy Jay's voice Peter Rabbit stopped running. In fact, he stopped altogether. He sat up and listened. Yes, there was no doubt about it, that was the voice of Sammy Jay, and it came from right near that great hollow log where Peter had just received such a fright. Moreover, Sammy was chuckling as if at a great joke. Peter looked back, and in his eyes a suspicion grew and grew.

"Sammy Jay knew I was going to get that fright, and he followed me to see what would happen. He played a joke on me, that's what he did," declared Peter indignantly. "But who was it in that old log that could hiss like that? That's what I want to know. Sammy told me that nothing would harm me and somehow I believe him. I suppose I'm foolish to, after such a trick, but just the same I don't believe Sammy would send me into real danger. I don't know anyone who could hiss like that except one of the Snake family, and I'm too big for any of them to hurt me, excepting Buzztail the Rattler or Copperhead, and somehow I don't believe it was either of them. I think I'll go back and find out who it was."

So Peter turned back and very, very carefully he approached the great hollow log. He found a place where he could see the open end of the great hollow log and be unseen himself, for he was hidden in a clump of ferns. At first he couldn't make out anything, for it was dark inside that old log. Then little by little he made out a dim shape inside, but whose shape it was he couldn't for the life of him tell. Presently he discovered Sammy Jay in a tree just above the old log. Sammy was talking to someone. After a little the dim shape in the hollow log moved and then out came—can you guess who? The very last person in the world Peter Rabbit expected to see—Ol' Mrs. Buzzard!

Yes, Sir, it was Ol' Mrs. Buzzard who walked out of the end of that hollow log, and when he saw her Peter was just as much surprised as when that terrible hiss had frightened him. He couldn't possibly have been any more surprised. Of course, he had nothing to fear from Ol' Mrs. Buzzard, so he promptly walked out of his hiding-place.

"Was it you that hissed when I looked in the hollow log a few minutes ago?" he demanded.

"It cert'nly was," replied Mrs. Buzzard. "Yo' startled me so Ah didn't rightly know who you were, so Ah hissed. Mah goodness, but yo' cert'nly can run, Brer Rabbit!"

Peter grinned but he let it pass, for his curiosity was all in what Mrs. Buzzard was doing in that old log. "If you please, Mrs. Buzzard, what were you doing in that old log?" he asked politely.

"That's mah home fo' a while," replied Mrs. Buzzard proudly.

"What?" cried Peter, as if he didn't trust his own ears.

He hopped a few steps nearer and peeped in. Then

Yes, Sir, it was Ol' Mrs. Buzzard who walked out of the end of that hollow log.

his eyes grew wide with astonishment. There was no nest there, but there were two little white downy birds. "Why—why—why—" stammered Peter and then stopped.

Sammy Jay laughed right out. "You see," said Sammy, "Ol' Mistah Buzzard told the truth when he said that they had no nest. Also he told the truth when he said that they had two eggs. That is, he thought he told the truth. He didn't know that they had hatched. And Ol' Mrs. Buzzard told the truth when she told me that they hadn't any eggs. And I told the truth when I said that there was something here to interest you and that wouldn't hurt you. So the great mystery is cleared up, and I hope your curiosity is satisfied, Peter Rabbit."

"It is," declared Peter, drawing a long breath.

CHAPTER EIGHTEEN: OL' MISTAH BUZZARD EXPLAINS THINGS

WHEN PETER RABBIT said that his curiosity was satisfied he really meant it. He had found out what he so wanted to know. He had found out where Mrs. Buzzard had laid her eggs. He had found out that it was true that Ol' Mistah and Mrs. Buzzard do not build a nest. He had found out that in this particular case the eggs had been laid in a great hollow log. So for the time being his curiosity was satisfied.

He promised Ol' Mrs. Buzzard that he would keep her secret. He laughed with her and with Sammy Jay at the way he had been frightened when Ol' Mrs. Buzzard had hissed right in his face, and then he bade them farewell and started for home in the dear Old Briar-patch. Of course he was full of the strange discovery about the ways of Ol' Mistah and Mrs. Buzzard and could think of nothing else.

"It certainly is queer that such big birds shouldn't have a nest," thought Peter, as he sat chewing a leaf of sweet clover. "I never would have thought of looking in a hollow log for their home, never in the world. I wonder what they would do if there wasn't a hollow log big enough. Hollow logs like that one are not to be found everywhere."

This thought was enough to awaken Peter's ever-ready curiosity once more. As he thought it over and wondered, his curiosity grew. So the next day he scampered back to the Green Forest and headed straight for the tall dead tree where Ol' Mistah Buzzard delights to sit. Ol' Mistah Buzzard was there, and his eyes twinkled as he saw Peter coming.

"I know your secret now, Mistah Buzzard," cried Peter, as soon as he reached the foot of the tree.

"Then Ah hopes yo'll keep it," replied Ol' Mistah Buzzard gravely.

"I will," promised Peter. "But Mistah Buzzard, there is one thing more I want to know."

"Only one thing? Yo' surprise me, Brer Rabbit," replied Ol' Mistah Buzzard.

Peter grinned, for he knew that Ol' Mistah Buzzard was joking him about his curiosity. "There is only one thing now," said he, "but there may be more things later."

"Well," replied Ol' Mistah Buzzard, "what is that one thing? Get it off your mind, and perhaps Ah can help yo' out."

"It is this: What do you and Mrs. Buzzard do for a place for your eggs when there isn't a big hollow log handy?" Peter replied promptly.

"Why, that's simple, ve'y simple indeed, Brer Rabbit," said Ol' Mistah Buzzard. "Mrs. Buzzard just naturally lays her aiggs on top of a big stump if there happens to be one handy. If there isn't she just lays her aiggs on the ground. Yo' know, Brer Rabbit, the ground is always handy."

Ol' Mistah Buzzard looked down and grinned, and Peter grinned back. "Do you mean that she doesn't put any grass or sticks or anything under them?" asked Peter.

Ol' Mistah Buzzard nodded. "Of course," said he, "she picks out a place where she reckons she isn't going to be disturbed. Ol' Mrs. Buzzard is a little bit peevish when she done be sitting on her aiggs. She don' like to be disturbed. So she picks out a place where she can be quite by herself, lays her aiggs and then takes care of them until they hatch, and that is all there is to it."

CHAPTER NINETEEN: SAMMY JAY SPEAKS HIS MIND

THE MORE PETER RABBIT thought it over, the stranger it seemed to him that such big people as Ol' Mistah Buzzard and Mrs. Buzzard should be content to have no nest. If he hadn't seen with his own eyes those two Buzzard babies in the great hollow log, and if he hadn't heard with his own ears Ol' Mistah Buzzard say that when there was no big hollow log handy Mrs. Buzzard would lay her eggs on top of a stump, and when there was no stump handy she would lay them on the bare ground, he wouldn't, he was sure, have been able to believe that anything of the kind could be true.

There was no one with whom he could talk the matter over save Sammy Jay. You see Peter had promised not to give the Buzzard secret away, and Sammy was the only one Peter knew of who also knew that secret. So the first chance he got Peter asked Sammy what he thought of the matter, and if he supposed there was any good reason why the Buzzards didn't build a nest.

"Shiftlessness!" replied Sammy scornfully. "Just plain shiftlessness. They are too lazy and shiftless to go to the trouble of building a nest, that's all. Ol' Mistah Buzzard is just naturally lazy, and Mrs. Buzzard is just like him. Have you ever seen Ol' Mistah Buzzard do a stroke of work since you've known him?"

Peter couldn't remember that he had and said so.

"Of course you haven't," asserted Sammy in the same scornful voice as before. "Of course you haven't. Why? Because he hasn't done any work. All he does is just sail round and round in the blue, blue sky or sit in the sun on that old dead tree. When he's sailing round and round he doesn't move his wings any more than he has to. He doesn't even catch his own food."

"I don't hold that against him," declared Peter promptly, thinking how he had always to be on the watch to escape Hooty the Owl and the members of the Hawk family, "but now you mention the matter, I wonder what he does eat. I hadn't thought of it before. Do you know what he does eat?"

"Yes," replied Sammy, "I know." There was both scorn and disgust in his voice this time. "He eats things that no one else would think of eating. He eats dead things, and he don't seem to care how long they have been dead. He is the most shiftless fellow I know of. You are rather shiftless yourself, Peter, but compared with Ol' Mistah Buzzard you are almost industrious. I can't understand how anyone can be so shiftless and lazy. It doesn't surprise me any to find out that he and Mrs.

Buzzard don't build a nest. I guess I would have been more surprised to find that they did. I know a good many shiftless folks, but none equal to Ol' Mistah Buzzard and Mrs. Buzzard. Sometimes I wonder if the reason they have bald heads is because they are too lazy to grow feathers on them."

Sammy grinned at his own joke, and Peter laughed. "You certainly have got a mighty small opinion of the Buzzard family, Sammy," said he.

"I certainly have," retorted Sammy. "I may have faults, but laziness isn't one of them. The idea of great big able-bodied birds like Mistah and Mrs. Buzzard being content to have their eggs on the ground without so much as a stick or a straw under them! I call it a disgrace to the whole feathered tribe."

Sammy Jay flirted his tail, tossed his head, and then flew away, leaving Peter to think things over and, I suspect, with a lot less respect for Ol' Mistah Buzzard than he had had before.

CHAPTER TWENTY: PETER ASKS A PERSONAL QUESTION

To be too personal is impolite,
So watch your tongue and guide it right.

TO ASK PERSONAL questions means to ask questions about things which really concern only those to whom you may happen to put the questions. Personal matters are those which are the business of no one but the ones whom they immediately concern, and there is no greater rudeness or impoliteness than to ask about them out of idle curiosity. Peter Rabbit knows this. Anyway, he should know it. He ought to have learned it by this time. But Peter's curiosity is forever leading him to do things which he shouldn't do.

The more Peter thought over what Sammy Jay had said about the laziness and shiftlessness of Ol' Mistah and Mrs. Buzzard, the more he was inclined to think that Sammy must be right about the matter. It certainly seemed as if no one as big and strong as Ol' Mistah Buzzard would be content to do without a nest of some sort unless he were indeed very lazy and shiftless. Peter himself is not at all fond of work, you know, and right down in his heart he had a little feeling of sympathy for Ol' Mistah Buzzard in avoiding unnecessary work. But even Peter felt that it was quite unpardonable that Ol' Mistah Buzzard's children should have no nest at all. The more he thought about it, the more it seemed impossible that anyone could be quite so shiftless as this. His respect for Ol' Mistah Buzzard had received a great shock. At last he made up his mind that he would find out if what Sammy Jay had said could be true.

So over to the Green Forest scampered Peter, lipperty-lipperty-lip, straight to the tall dead tree where Ol' Mistah Buzzard delighted to sit when he was not sailing round and round high up in the blue, blue sky.

Ol' Mistah Buzzard was there holding his wings half spread for the air to blow through them and the sun to fall on them. His eyes twinkled as he saw Peter.

"Yo' seem to have something on your mind, Brer Rabbit. What is it this time?" said he.

Peter hesitated a minute as if a little ashamed. Then he blurted out what he had on his mind. "Are you really and truly shiftless, Mistah Buzzard?" he asked.

Ol' Mistah Buzzard closed his wings and blinked his eyes very rapidly as if he didn't quite know what to think.

"What's that, Brer Rabbit?" he demanded sharply. "Ah think Ah couldn't have understood yo'. What's that yo' said?"

"I asked if you are really and truly shiftless," repeated Peter.

Ol' Mistah Buzzard ruffled up all his feathers indignantly. "Ah reckons yo' done lost all your manners, Brer Rabbit," said he. "That's a mighty personal question. Who say Ah'm shiftless? Who say that? Ah want to know who say Ah'm shiftless?"

Ol' Mistah Buzzard looked so fierce that Peter began to be afraid of him and wished with all his might that he had held his tongue.

"I—I—" he began, then hesitated. Then he hurried on. "You know, Mistah Buzzard, you haven't any nest and—and I've heard it said that it is because you and Mrs. Buzzard are too lazy and shiftless to build one. I thought there might be some other reason, and so I came to you to find out," he finished lamely.

CHAPTER TWENTY-ONE: OL' MISTAH BUZZARD STARTS A STORY

DO YOU WONDER that Ol' Mistah Buzzard was indignant when Peter Rabbit blurted out such a personal question? At first Ol' Mistah Buzzard was tempted to speak his mind very plainly to Peter and tell him just what he thought of people who gossip about others and their personal affairs, but Peter looked so innocent of any intention to meddle and so truly puzzled that Ol' Mistah Buzzard promptly recovered his good nature.

"Mah affairs are really no business of yours, Brer Rabbit, and Ah reckons yo' know it, but just to set your mind at rest, Ah'm going to tell yo' a story," said he.

At this Peter pricked up his ears and settled himself contentedly. He had heard Ol' Mistah Buzzard tell stories before, and he knew that a story from him was bound to be interesting, whether it was true or not.

"Ah'm not saying that this is the true reason why my family doesn't build nests," began Ol' Mistah Buzzard with a twinkle in his eyes, "but it is a story that has done been handed down to we-uns from way back at the beginning of things when the world was young. It was in the days when Granny and Granddaddy Buzzard, the first of mah family, lived, and eve'ybody was learning or trying to learn how to live. Yo' see, in those days nobody knew just what was best to do. Eve'ybody was trying to work out fo' himself what was best, and learning something every day. Of course, eve'ybody made mistakes, lots of them, Granddaddy and Granny Buzzard just like the rest, and it was because of one of these mistakes that they didn't have a nest like the rest of the birds.

"Yo' see, when the first nesting season came around and Ol' Mother Nature passed the word along fo' all the birds to prepare places fo' their aiggs and young, there were most as many ideas as there were kinds of birds. Each pair had their own idea of what a nest should be made of and where it should be put, and fo' a while there was a right smart lot of confusion. Yes, Suh, there was a right smart lot of confusion.

"Ol' Granddaddy and Granny Buzzard were naturally easy-going. It was powerful warm down there where they lived, and Ah reckons it looked to them plumb foolish to do any mo' work than they had to. Ah know it looks that way to me. Building nests was new to everybody, and nobody knew the best way of going about it.

"We-uns don't know how to build a nest."

"'Ah tell you what,' say Granddaddy Buzzard to Granny Buzzard, 'we-uns don't know how to build a nest. Eve'ybody else has got a different idea, and Ah reckons we-uns haven't any idea at all. Ah don' see any sense in getting all heated up and tired out trying to do something when we-uns don' know what it is we want, so Ah reckons we-uns will just sit tight and watch our neighbors. When they done got their nests built we-uns will just go around and see which one we like best and which is easiest to build, and then we'll build one like it.' This suited Ol' Granny Buzzard and she wasn't a mite slow in saying so.

"Excuse me, Brer Rabbit. Here come Mrs. Buzzard and

Ah reckons she wants to see me about something particular. If yo' will wait here Ah will finish mah story when Ah comes back."

With this off flew Ol' Mistah Buzzard, leaving Peter to wait as patiently as he could for the end of the story.

CHAPTER TWENTY-TWO: OL' MISTAH BUZZARD FINISHES HIS TALE

IT SEEMED TO Peter Rabbit that Ol' Mistah Buzzard was gone a long time. You know how it is when you are waiting for the end of a story when the story-teller has been called away. Really it was only a few minutes that Ol' Mistah Buzzard was gone, but it seemed to Peter ages and ages.

"Let me see, where was Ah?" said Ol' Mistah Buzzard as soon as he had once more seated himself comfortably on the tall dead tree under which Peter sat.

"You had reached the place where Granddaddy and Granny Buzzard decided to wait to see how the other birds built their nests," prompted Peter.

"Just so. Just so," replied Ol' Mistah Buzzard. "Well Granddaddy and Granny Buzzard just sat around and watched the other birds and said nothing, and looked wise. Ah reckons there was a terrible time building those first nests, and when they were all done Ah reckons none of them was much as nests go now. There was a right smart lot of fussing and worrying and quarreling, but Granddaddy and Granny Buzzard kept out of it and when anyone asked them where they were building their nest and what they were making it of, they simply looked wise as befo' and said nothing.

"Of course everybody tried to make a powerful secret of where their nests were, but sitting around just watching, Granddaddy and Granny Buzzard found out where most of them were. They waited until the last of their neighbors had finished their nests and then they just went around looking at each to see how it was made and what it was made of. They found all kinds of nests, some made of sticks and some made of straw, and some made of mud, and some made of moss. Seemed like nary one of them just suited Granddaddy and Granny Buzzard. Anyway, they kept hoping that they would see one that would suit better, and so they kept a-looking and a-looking and a-looking. Granny Buzzard wanted her nest made out of something soft and comfortable, and Granddaddy Buzzard wanted it made of something it wouldn't be much work to find and less work to put together.

"So they couldn't make up their minds, and time went drifting along and drifting along, and first thing they knew eve'y last one of the other birds had a nest and aiggs, and here was Granddaddy and Granny Buzzard without even a place picked to build a nest. When Granddaddy Buzzard realized this he scratched his haid and began to look worried. Granny Buzzard scratched her haid and looked mo' worried.

"'Pears to me like we-uns haven't got time to build a nest,' said Granddaddy Buzzard at last.

"'Ah was thinking that ve'y same thing,' replied Granny Buzzard. 'If we stop to build a nest now, we-uns will be so late the season's gwine to be all over befo' we know it. Ah reckons Ah ought to be sitting on those aiggs right now.'

"'Ah reckons that's right,' replied Granddaddy Buzzard, 'but fo' the life of me, Ah don' see what we-uns gwine to do about it.'

"Two or three days later Granny Buzzard called him aside in a place where nobody is likely to come along and showed him two aiggs right on the ground. 'Ah reckons that is better than any nest,' said she. 'Nobody's gwine to look on the ground fo' aiggs, and if they do there's a powerful lot of ground to look over for two aiggs. The wind can't blow them out of a nest, and when they hatch the babies can't fall and hurt themselves. Ah'm gwine to sit right here until they hatch. Ah reckons this nest building is all plumb foolishness anyway.'

"'Ah reckons it is too,' replied Granddaddy Buzzard with a sigh of relief because he hadn't got to help build a nest. "And ever since then the Buzzard family done get along without nests and have saved theirselves a powerful lot of work," concluded Ol' Mistah Buzzard.

And to this day Peter isn't sure whether the Buzzards are smart or just shiftless.

CHAPTER TWENTY-THREE: REDDY FOX RUNS FOR HIS LIFE

IT WAS ONLY a few days after Peter Rabbit found out the secret of Ol' Mistah and Mrs. Buzzard that Reddy Fox took it into his head to visit that part of the Green Forest where lay the great hollow log in which were the two helpless Buzzard babies. Reddy wasn't looking for them. He had no interest in Ol' Mistah Buzzard or his affairs. Probably if he ever had thought of the matter at all he would have taken it for granted, as Peter had, that Ol' Mistah Buzzard's nest would be in a tall tree.

The fact is he was hunting for the nest of Mrs. Grouse and it had popped into his head that it might be over in that particular part of the Green Forest. He knew all about that big hollow log. There are few such places Reddy doesn't know about. Many a time had he peeped into it, hoping to surprise Peter Rabbit there.

Just as Peter did Reddy stole softly alongside the old log and poked his head around the end to look inside. Just imagine how surprised he was when two funny little heads were suddenly raised and two funny mouths opened wide. The baby Buzzards had heard him and thought it was their mother coming to feed them.

Reddy jumped in front of the opening and sat down to stare, for he never had seen any babies at all like these and he didn't know what to make of them. "Now whose babies are these?" he muttered. "Not that it makes any real difference, for they will make just as good a dinner as if I knew all about them," he added and grinned as only Reddy can. Then he started to crawl in after them.

Right that very instant things began to happen. With an angry hiss such as Reddy never had heard before something struck him and knocked him over and over. Before he could get his breath or even look to see what or who had hit him he received such a shower of blows that it seemed to him there wasn't a spot on his whole body that wasn't hit. The air seemed to be filled with great claws and beaks which tore his red coat and made him yell. He had just one thought and that was to get away from that place, to get as far away from it as he could.

At last he managed to get to his feet and then how Reddy did run! He didn't even look behind to see who it was who had pounded and scratched and pecked him so. He simply ran and ran and ran, whimpering with every breath. He was running for his life. At least he thought he was. Every instant he expected to be knocked over again.

Of course you know what had happened. Mrs. Buzzard had been standing just back of a little tree only a few steps from the great hollow log. She had seen Reddy just as he started to crawl in after her precious babies and she hadn't wasted any time. She had rushed at him like a fury. With her great wings she had pounded him and with claws and beak she had pulled his hair out and torn his coat. And all the time she had kept up a hissing quite frightful to hear.

When Reddy at last got away from her she had not tried to follow him, but had rushed back to her precious babies to make sure that they were safe. Reddy didn't know this. He was too badly scared to know much of anything save that he wanted to get home as quickly as his legs could take him. He was sure this terrible creature was right at his heels all the way there, and to this day he doesn't know whose babies he found, for it was a long, long time before he dared visit that part of the Green Forest again and by that time the baby Buzzards were big enough to sail round and round high up in the blue, blue sky like their father, Ol' Mistah Buzzard.

CHAPTER TWENTY-FOUR: PETER RABBIT AND WINSOME BLUEBIRD GOSSIP

TO GOSSIP IS to talk about other people and what they are doing, or what they have done, or what they are going to do. Peter Rabbit and Winsome Bluebird were gossiping in the dear Old Briar-patch. Winsome sat in a little cherry tree, and right under him sat Peter. Winsome had just arrived from way down South to spread the glad news that Mistress Spring was on her way and would soon reach the Green

Meadows, the Green Forest and the Smiling Pool. You see, Winsome is the herald of Mistress Spring and keeps just a little way ahead of her. When the little meadow and forest people first see his beautiful blue coat, or hear his soft sweet whistle, they know that Mistress Spring is surely on the way and not very far behind, and then great joy fills their hearts. First comes gentle Sister South Wind to prepare the way, then Winsome Bluebird, and after him beautiful Mistress Spring.

Peter Rabbit was brimful of curiosity, just as he always is. You see, it was a long time since he had last seen Winsome Bluebird and all the other birds who had gone to the far-away South when the leaves began to drop in the fall, and of course he wanted to know all about his old friends and neighbors, how they were, what they had been doing, and when they were coming back.

And Winsome wanted to know all about how Peter and Reddy Fox and all the other little people who hadn't gone to the beautiful South had spent the long winter. So there was a great deal to talk about. Yes, indeed, there was a very great deal to talk about. Winsome felt that he ought to be flying about over the Green Meadows and the Green Forest where other little people could see him and hear him and so know that he had arrived, but he had traveled a very, very great distance and he was tired, and so he sat and rested, and while he rested he gossiped with Peter Rabbit.

"Is Ol' Mistah Buzzard on his way here?" asked Peter eagerly.

"Not yet," replied Winsome. "He won't start until after he is sure that Mistress Spring has got here," replied Winsome.

Peter looked a little disappointed, for there is nothing that he enjoys more than to watch Ol' Mistah Buzzard sail round and round, way, way up in the blue, blue sky. He is rather fond of Ol' Mistah Buzzard, is Peter, for big as he is Mistah Buzzard never offers to hurt any of the very little people, not even little Danny Meadow Mouse. "Why isn't he starting right away?" he asked.

"Well, you see," replied Winsome, "Mistah Buzzard doesn't like the cold."

"But it isn't cold now!" interrupted Peter. "Why, this isn't cold at all. You ought to have been here when it really was cold—when the Smiling Pool and the Laughing Brook were covered with ice, and the Green Meadows and the Green Forest were all white with snow, and poor Mrs. Grouse was a prisoner under the hard icy crust. Then it was cold! Why, this isn't cold at all."

Winsome Bluebird ruffled up his feathers just a little. It was almost like a shiver. "This is cold enough for me!" said he. "Tell me about poor Mrs. Grouse, Peter. Did she get out?"

"You tell me about Ol' Mistah Buzzard first, and how he spends the winter, and then I'll tell you about poor Mrs. Grouse," replied Peter.

"All right," said Winsome. "There isn't a great deal to tell, but I'll do the best I can. I'll tell you how he warms his toes."

CHAPTER TWENTY-FIVE: HOW
OL' MISTAH BUZZARD WARMS HIS TOES

OFTEN AND OFTEN had Peter wondered how Ol' Mistah Buzzard and all his other feathered friends who had flown away to the far-away South at the first hint that Jack Frost was on his way to the Green Meadows spent the long winter. It seemed to Peter that the South must be a very wonderful and very strange place. He was not at all sure that he would like it. It must be very nice not to have to worry about finding enough to eat, and yet—well, Peter did have lots of fun in the snow. It seemed to him that all those little people who went away certainly missed a great deal. Now Winsome Bluebird had returned from that far-away South with the good news that Mistress Spring was not far behind, and Winsome had promised to tell him all the news of Ol' Mistah Buzzard and the other friends, and how Ol' Mistah Buzzard keeps his toes warm.

"You see," began Winsome, "Ol' Mistah Buzzard was born and brought up in the South where it is always warm, and he just can't stand cold weather. No, Sir, he can't stand cold weather. Why, weather that you and I would call comfortable will make him shiver and shake. That is why he wasn't ready to come up with me. Now I come ahead of Mistress Spring, but Ol' Mistah Buzzard won't start until he is sure that Mistress Spring has been here some time and he will be sure not to have cold feet."

"Cold feet!" cried Peter. "Who ever heard of such a thing! Why I run around on the snow and ice all winter long, and I never have cold feet."

"Well, Ol' Mistah Buzzard has them," replied Winsome Bluebird. "Yes, Sir, he is always complaining about cold feet. You know he hasn't any shoes or stockings like you, Peter, so between his bare feet and his bald head he has, or thinks he has, a great deal to worry about every time there is a cool day, and they sometimes have cool days even way down South. Then you will always find Ol' Mistah Buzzard warming his toes."

Peter scratched his head in a funny way. "If you please, Winsome, how does he warm his toes?" asked Peter. "I never see him warming his toes when he is up here. He's always sailing round and round way up in the blue, blue sky or else sitting on a dead tree in the Green Forest. I've never heard him complaining of cold feet or seen him try to warm his toes."

"Of course you haven't!" replied Winsome. "He doesn't have cold feet then because it's summer time. It's just as you say, if you don't see him up in the blue,

blue sky you are sure to find him on that old dead tree. But down South it is different. If you want to see him there and he isn't way up in the blue, blue sky trying to get nearer to Mr. Sun so as to warm his bald head, why you just look for him on a toe-warmer."

Peter's eyes seemed to fairly pop out with curiosity. "What's a toe-warmer?" he demanded. "I never heard of such a thing. What does it look like?"

Winsome Bluebird chuckled softly. "Have you ever been up by Farmer Brown's house?" he asked.

Peter nodded.

"Then you've seen that thing on the roof out of which smoke sometimes comes," continued Winsome.

Again Peter nodded.

"Well," continued Winsome, "if Farmer Brown's house was down South, that thing out of which the smoke comes would be one of Ol' Mistah Buzzard's toe-warmers."

Peter looked sharply at Winsome to see if he really meant what he said. "Doesn't anybody live in those houses down South?" he asked suspiciously.

"Of course," replied Winsome. "If they didn't how could Mistah Buzzard warm his toes?"

"And he isn't afraid?" persisted Peter, as if it was very hard to believe.

"Afraid!" cried Winsome. "Why, he hasn't anything to be afraid of. Mr. Buzzard is thought a great deal of, a very great deal of, in the South, and no one would hurt him for the world. So every house has a toe-warmer for him, which is very nice for him. And you won't see him back here until it is so warm that he forgets all about cold feet," concluded Winsome Bluebird.

And so we will leave Peter Rabbit watching for the return of Ol' Mistah Buzzard, and we will leave Ol' Mistah Buzzard warming his toes on a chimney-top, for this is the end of this little book.

Other Wholesome Children's Titles

The National Review Treasury of Classic Children's Literature, **Original Volume**
Selected by William F. Buckley Jr. 528 pages/hardcover. Lavishly illustrated. $29.95.
Over 40 stories, tales, fables, and adventures—most originally published in *St. Nicholas Magazine,* the most revered children's publication in American history—written by the literary giants of the time, including Lewis Carroll, Mark Twain, Jack London, Louisa May Alcott, L. Frank Baum, Rudyard Kipling, Frances Hodgson Burnett, and many more. Includes Buckley's own story, "The Temptation of Wilfred Malachey." Ideal for middle school-aged children and early teens.

The National Review Treasury of Classic Children's Literature, **Volume Two**
Selected by William F. Buckley Jr. 528 pages/hardcover. Lavishly illustrated. $29.95.
Over three dozen stories, tales, fables, and adventures—many of them originally published in *St. Nicholas Magazine* and *Harper's Young People*—written by Mark Twain, Jack London, Louisa May Alcott, L. Frank Baum, Rudyard Kipling, Frances Hodgson Burnett, Joel Chandler Harris, Ellis Parker Butler, and many more literary giants. Ideal for middle school-aged children and early teens.

The National Review Treasury of Classic Bedtime Stories, **Original Volume**
By Thornton Burgess. 360 pages/hardcover. Lavishly illustrated by Harrison Cady. $29.95.
The faithful reproduction of the first ten of Burgess's revered "Bedtime Story Books"—written from 1913 to 1920—which delighted millions of American children, with 60 exquisite drawings by Harrison Cady. Children will love Burgess's colorful characters—Reddy Fox, Johnny Chuck, Unc' Billy Possum, Mistah Mocker, Jerry Muskrat, Danny Meadow Mouse, Grandfather Frog, Chatterer the Red Squirrel, Sammy Jay, and countless others—who populate the Green Forest, the Green Meadow, the Smiling Brook, and the Briar Patch. Ideal for beginning readers, and exactly the kind of little dramas you can read to your wee ones as a prelude to sweet dreams.

The National Review Treasury of Classic Bedtime Stories, **Volume Two**
By Thornton Burgess. 352 pages/hardcover. Lavishly illustrated by Harrison Cady. $30.00.
This handsome work—providing the next ten of Burgess's revered "Bedtime Story Books"—completes the collection of this beloved series, and, like the original volume, brims with 60 exquisite drawings by Harrison Cady of Buster Bear, Old Mr. Toad, Prickly Porky, Old Man Coyote, Paddy the Beaver, Poor Mrs. Quack, Bobby Coon, Jimmy Skunk, Bob White, Ol' Mistah Buzzard, and countless other denizens and charming creatures living in Burgess's special world. Great for little readers.

The Wonder Clock, or Four and Twenty Marvelous Tales
By Howard Pyle. Embellished by Katharine Pyle. 272 pages/hardcover. Lavishly illustrated. $22.50.
This beautifully written and illustrated collection of fables, tales, poems, and fantasies will enthrall children. First published in 1888, *The Wonder Clock* contains a delightful and instructive tale for each hour of the day, each one accompanied by numerous glorious line-art drawings of Pyle (1853-1911), one of America's greatest and most influential illustrators, and the poems of his sister Katharine. Ideal for middle school-aged children and early teens.

Pepper & Salt, or Seasoning for Young Folk
By Howard Pyle. 128 pages/hardcover. Lavishly illustrated. $22.50.
From within these covers come the sweet and powerful fragrances of an entire spice shop. This wonderful and delicate tome was not so much written by Howard Pyle as it was *designed* by him. *Pepper & Salt* is so special and so distinct that it will capture the attention and the imagination of all, from children to adults. Two dozen beautiful and enchanting full-page fable-poems—mischievous, humorous, and instructive lessons adorned by Pyle's delightful line art and enhanced by his unique lettering—embrace *Pepper & Salt's* eight finely told tales. A remarkable book, it is ideal for middle school-aged children and early teens.

About National Review Books

National Review Books is a division of National Review, Inc., which publishes America's foremost opinion journal, and which also operates National Review Online, where all our children's titles can be purchased directly. The web address is www.nationalreview.com. There you can find appropriate links to our book store. National Review Books titles may also be purchased by writing us at

National Review Books
215 Lexington Avenue
New York, NY 10016

Please include payment (check payable to "National Review"). New York State residents must add sales tax.

About ISI Books

ISI Books is the imprint of the Intercollegiate Studies Institute (ISI), a national educational foundation. ISI Books publishes interdisciplinary titles that strike at the heart of the prevailing orthodoxies of contemporary scholarship and debate. Its list, which includes original titles, classic reprints, and collections of writings by leading authorities in the humanities and social sciences, explores the philosophical first principles underlying the urgent political, cultural, and social issues of the day. Each title sheds new light on a topic of perennial interest. ISI Books seeks to conserve a tradition of scholarship and public conversation largely abandoned by many of today's university and commercial presses. Enduring in substance and quality, our titles are meant to persist in their importance and to serve successive generations of readers. For more information visit www.isibooks.org, call (800) 526-7022, or write

Intercollegiate Studies Institute
3901 Centerville Road
P.O. Box 4431
Wilmington, DE 19807-0431